Napoleon's Gold -
The Wages Of Sin

Alex E. Robertson

NAPOLEON'S GOLD: THE WAGES OF SIN

Published by:

ALPHA Education Press
9010 93 Street NW
Edmonton, Alberta, Canada, T6C 3T4

Background and cameo image on cover created by Ana María Espiñeira Luksić (Viña del Mar, Chile)
Cover layout and colour shading by Hilary Strickland (Bath, UK)
Illustrations and maps by Hilary Strickland (Bath, UK)
The image on the front cover is of a French lithograph c.1830 by Paul Gavarni (1804-66)

Library and Archives Canada Cataloguing in Publication

Robertson, Alex E., author
    Napoleon's gold : the wages of sin / Alex E. Robertson.

Issued in print and electronic formats.
ISBN 978-0-9938764-3-1 (softcover).--ISBN 978-0-9938764-9-3 (hardcover).--ISBN 978-0-9938764-8-6 (PDF)

    I. Title.

PS8635.O228335N37 2017   C813'.6   C2017-902725-5
                                             C2017-902726-3

Printed and bound by CPI Group (UK) Ltd, Croydon, CR0 4YY

Contents

Cast of principal characters

Agents and officials of the British government

Nathaniel Parry	gentleman, employed as government agent
John Drake	Foreign Office employee
Lord Palmerston	Foreign Secretary
Lord Melbourne	Home Secretary
Richard Percy	Home Office administrator

Agents of the Imperial Chinese government

Cornelius Fu Lee	undercover agent
Fong and Chen	his retainers

The Parry household

Emma Parry	Nathaniel's wife
Caradoc	his dog, a Welsh terrier
Frances Price	Emma's maid
Tobias Caudle	manservant
Mrs Rollinson	housekeeper
Harriet Pullen	kitchen maid

The Peterson household

Captain Oliver Peterson	retired sea captain
Lydia	his wife
Maddie and Ginette	his twin teenage daughters
Céline Junot	their governess

The Vere household

Mathilda Vere	lady, resident of Lansdown Crescent
Howard Dill	her gentleman friend
Mrs Danby	her mother

The Spence household

Martha Spence	landlady, resident of Walcot
Thomas	her father-in-law
Matthew	her son
Mary	her daughter-in-law
Johnty	her grandson
Benjamin Prestwick	tenant and comrade of her late husband
Declan O'Dowd	tenant
Finn O'Malley	tenant
Jimmy Congo	Matthew's African parrot

The Shadwell household

Joshua Shadwell	owner of the Green Park brothel
Rosie	his wife
Jabez and Billy	his bodyguards and enforcers
Clarissa Marchant	prostitute, known as Clari
Letty Watson	prostitute

Bath characters

Dr Charles Parry	physician, related to Nathaniel
Mrs Parry	his wife
Diarmuid Casey	Member of Parliament
Colette Montrachet	courtesan, known as Coco
Robert Turner	printer
Arthur Jamieson	printer

The Ravenswood household in Bristol and contacts

Edwin Ravenswood	ship owner and merchant
Amanda	his wife
Eli Trevellis	captain of the *Blue Dragon*, Ravenswood's clipper
Mr Kizhe	Ravenswood's Russian-Mongolian business associate, (pronounced: Kee-jay)

v

| Mr Qiang | Kizhe's servant, (pronounced: Chahng) |
| Jerry Tiler | Kizhe's associate and "shadow" |

The Drake household in London

| Charlotte Drake | wife of John Drake, known as Lottie |
| Elizabeth | his daughter, known as Lizzie |

The Mortimer-Buckley household in London

Sir Giles Mortimer-Buckley	baronet and Member of Parliament
Lady Leonora	his wife
Prudence Battersby	his daughter
Lulu Battersby	his granddaughter
Maisie Trickett	Lulu's nanny

The Montrachet household in the Medoc, France

Jules Delgarde-Montrachet	Coco's brother
Claudette	his wife
Marc and Simone	his children
Pierre Valdez	his foreman
Antoine Lacaze	his labourer

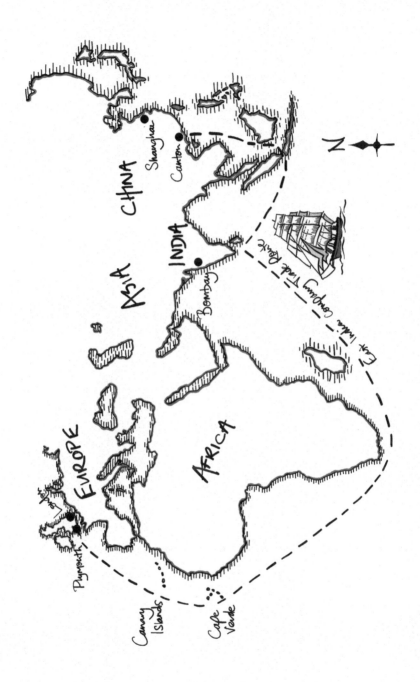

The Trade Route to China

Prologue

Twenty-five years before the events related in this book.

Evening: 20th December, 1808.

Beñat's *Posada*, the Spanish Basque country.

They sat motionless before the fire, intent on the flames and the seething mixture in the pot. At first you would not notice them; they were so still, one on each side of the hearth, like caryatids, the stone maidens of Karyai. Then on an instant their heads lifted and they looked into each other's eyes, the one a mirror image of the other, both flesh and blood, with the same sharp beauty. Izar's bracelets rang and flashed as she reached for more of the gritty powder in her pack and sprinkled it into the broth. She smiled to her other self with satisfaction as she stirred the mixture and it smoothed and cleared. Her sister took up the bellows, gently squeezed a rush of air under the logs to make the sparks fly and then reached for a handful of seeds. Her hand circling, she murmured a low chant and cast the dry husks into the flames. Aromatic smoke wreathed up to fill the ingle-nook of the rough stone fireplace and crept out into the room, flowing round the wooden tables and rising in clouds, crowding the blackened ceiling. The girls crouched lower, mesmerised by their

1

task, absent-mindedly hitching up their skirts as the heat built, running their hands over their legs as they felt the fire burn.

The tall fair man at the bar had eyes only for them. He took another slug of the local spirit, searing his throat with the heat, and let his eyes roam over their bodies. They had arrived an hour before and set to work. As the fire had beaten hotter, they had shed their fur-lined cloaks and woollen shawls; shaken out long manes of black hair which snaked down to their waists. They had lithe brown arms, high sculpted breasts showing above tight-laced bodices and they moved like wild cats. He felt more than equal to taking the both of them that very night and sniggered to himself at the thought of it. But even as his mind played with the idea, savouring it, a cloud of denser smoke billowed out into the room and for a moment he thought he saw in its depths the shade of a third woman, a white sister, turning cavernous eye sockets on him and a gash of a smile. Alarmed and confused he turned away, fingers fumbling for the silver medallion at his throat. Rattled out of his lust, he fixed his eyes instead on the capacious rump of the innkeeper's wife, which wobbled busily as she hacked up cold meat for the supper.

Izar spoke softly as she rose from the hearth.

"The wagon has left the valley. It is time."

Without a word, the silent sister wrapped her shawl round the pot handle, lifted it from the fire and followed Izar round the side of the bar and down the dark corridor to the kitchen, out of sight of prying eyes.

Owen Parry had paid off the innkeeper and brought the twins down from the mountain to play their part. They needed little persuasion to join in any plan designed to torment the French invaders, as he had discovered earlier that year. Shot and beaten, he had been retrieved from the mountain by the pair of them and patched up in their hut. His wounds had healed quickly and neatly, so he had proof they had the touch to cure, but he also knew they could wreak destruction. There was no need to worry about their part in the night's work. Most of his experiences in

Spain had been in these mountains and he was used to their discomforts, which was fortunate. He sat perched on top of the stable roof, braced against the side of its stone chimney, his eyes locked on to a distant peak of the Montes Vascos, scouring it for the tell-tale glimmer of a lantern. He had not slept for two days and his eyes burned as he peered into the gloom, willing himself to stay awake. It was dark and murky, and as usual, ruthlessly cold, with a hard frost petrifying every surface and piercing through his cloak to his bones. An iron silence gripped the mountain and the grey shred of road that hung on its slopes like a cadaver's tattered bandage, marking the way to the isolated inn. Not one peasant, beast or bird had ventured abroad, not even one creature of the night, not a fox, not one hunting owl. It was unfortunate that he could not trust the jovial Captain, or either of his raw assistants, to take the watch. But that was probably as it should be. Life, in his experience, never offered good fortune without a balancing dose of bad. It was in the nature of things. Owen grimaced as the inn door swung open, shedding a spear of light and snatches of talk across the courtyard. A powerfully-built man, over-tall for his role as a Basque shepherd, strode towards the stable.

"Fancy a mug of brandy and water? Hot as hell and kicks like a donkey!"

Waving a full mug, Captain Giles Mortimer-Buckley grinned up at Owen, carelessly slopping some of the hell brew over his boots as he did so. He appeared bland and affable, but Owen was not convinced. Captain Buckley's antics over the last week had suggested he had the potential for much more than his face offered and most of it would be unwelcome. Conventionally handsome, but with early signs of dissipation blurring his features, Buckley had an eye to the main chance. His war was being waged to fill his pockets, rather than for personal or national glory. He was not a typical recruit for the intelligence corps, in which Owen had served throughout his career, but these days his masters were in no position to be particular. Most of the best agents were either dead or imprisoned and pickings were scanty. An effective swordsman, quick with his fists, Giles Buckley had hastily volunteered himself and two of his more biddable men for this mission, this desperate little show of defiance. Madrid had fallen over two weeks previously, victim to Napoleon's "avalanche of fire and steel" and the Emperor's brother Joseph was safely installed as King of Spain in the *Palacio Real* for his Christmas celebrations. It was not a bad time for Buckley to absent himself from his regiment. Bar the consolation of besting the French in a skirmish here or there all that waited for them was a retreat to the coast, likely to be followed by an inglorious sail home.

Owen did not feel like a drink. "No thanks. Go back in, Buckley. They can't be much longer." Seeing the slack smile spread further on the Captain's face, he added: "And remember, now you've had a few drinks, don't try to talk to the innkeeper in Castilian Spanish. Don't put his back up. Do you understand?"

Captain Buckley bowed briefly, not lowering his eyes, turned on his heel and made for the comfort of the bar, but even before he had crossed the yard Owen caught sight of the warning from the peak a mile away. One after another, five unmistakeable twinkles of light shone out. The prey had passed his man and was heading for the trap. Owen slid down the roof and the wastewater chain, sprinted lightly over the frozen yard and caught up with Buckley as he reached the door.

By the time the sound of hooves, the faint clinking of horses' harnesses and the grinding of wheels had reached the approach to the inn, Owen, Buckley and their two men were waiting in the dark corners of the stable to dispatch any guards who might be left to watch the wagon. Their breathing had slowed, taking in the stale scent of old hay, mules and horses. Their hearing strained above the muted rustles from the beasts, and they watched the cracks in the door, picked out in stark white by the moonlight and the guttering flicker of the yard lantern. Owen held his Basque shepherd's stick, the makila, double-handed and at a slant, its brutally solid handle raised whilst the others tightened their grips on makeshift cudgels from Beñat's store.

Following the receipt of an intelligence report warning of a British attack, the French soldiers had been detailed to drive the covered wagon out of the valley and away from the armed column. They had started their detour a couple of kilometres before the rest of the baggage train reached the site of the expected ambush, a pinch-point where the river wound in a blind bend and the valley sides steepened. They were to proceed up the mountain track and complete a circuit of fifteen kilometres before rejoining the armoured division as it made its way to Madrid, laden with the royal supplies for Christmas and the next campaigning season. They were to halt at the only inn along the track, which they could now see, bulky but indistinct, in the gloom ahead.

"I'm so starving hungered, I could probably eat your nag," grumbled one of the rearguard, loud enough for the ears of the man who rode in frozen silence alongside, but low enough to avoid the notice of the officer leading the detail.

"And I could probably eat you as well you fat bastard. And drink this stinking apology for a *posada* dry as a bone."

The stocky cavalryman pursed his lips then countered.

"Could you now? I could eat my horse and yours, and you, you worm-eaten skeleton. Not that you're worth the eating! Did you see the vultures circling when we left the column, François? One sight of your stringy carcass and they took off!" His shoulders rose in a wheezy chuckle.

"Dismount!"

They reined in with relief, eager for a more comfortable roost for the banter or at least for some foetid warmth and whatever else the inn could offer, but their hopes were not high. It was uninviting, a squat, dark huddle by the wayside, which became further obscured by a fresh belch of smoke from its chimney as they prepared to dismount. It could never have sustained the column, but it did not need to. They would not have to fight for their rations, as there were just six of them: the

5

officer and the sergeant at the front, two regulars in the wagon and the two bringing up the rear. The officer barked out his orders and the words loitered out of his mouth in freezing clouds.

"François, Alphonse! Take the wagon into the stables, see to the horses yourselves if there's no help, then come and eat. You two stay inside the wagon, we'll relieve you in two hours."

The French masters were not suspicious. They did not expect the Basques to love them. They did not seem to love anyone, certainly not their old masters the Spaniards, or any other alien power seeking to interfere with their race or their land. The officer and his men closed the door on the night and made for the settles round the fire. He called for food and drink in passable Gascon, which he had been assured the locals would recognise, but expected no more in the way of cheer than he got. The massive figure behind the bar nodded sourly and growled an order to a bundle of a woman, swaddled in shawls. The couple looked like a pair of Pyrenean bears in their brown homespun, he with his rough pelt of chestnut hair and irritable, reddened eyes, she waddling and submissive. The two soldiers watched her progress as she padded out towards the kitchen, cracked jokes in French at her expense, and then lapsed into silence with the others, thawing out, eyes adjusting to the leaping firelight and the smoke which gusted from the hearth with every swing of a door.

Within minutes, their piled plates, wide-bowled glasses and jugs of drink appeared, but they were not brought in by the bear-woman of the inn, but by the sisters. In they came, all bold smiles and swaying hips, laughing now, trailing their hands over the men's shoulders and leaning close as they poured each one a generous drink. The tired men's faces lit up, then fell slack with desire, drunk already as the crafty smoke fumes worked on their exhaustion, unravelling their defences as their bodies relaxed in the warmth.

6

"Sup your fill, gentlemen," teased Izar, her Gascon was rusty and halting but her smile seemed to ring true. "Long life to the Emperor!"

"Amen to that," replied the officer, lifting his glass and reluctantly taking his eyes from her. "Well men, you probably caught the gist. To the Emperor, then, and a quiet night followed by a successful day!"

The four raised their glasses to each other, drank deeply and in seconds gasped their last. Clawing at their throats, shuddering to their knees, their choking cries lasted only moments before the four bodies were still, bent in tormented death throes amongst the straw and the filth of the floor, whilst from behind the bar bounded two huge white shapes, rough-coated mountain dogs with fangs bared, pushing past the women, bearing down on the bodies, growling and snarling.

"Leave them!" ordered the innkeeper. "I'll not have you poisoned!" As the dogs backed away he rolled out from behind the bar, lifted the platters of meat and flung the food onto the floor. "It was going to be your supper anyway, my beauties. All comes, in time, to those who wait."

"I hope that is also true for all your people in *Euskal Herria*," said Owen, in perfect Basque and with a smile, as he led his men into the inn and motioned for them to haul the bodies away.

"*Ongi etorri!* Welcome again, my friend. I thought you might have frozen to the roof before now," growled Beñat, but his bushy moustaches and eyebrows rose to show he smiled as he reached for the bottle of Txakoli. "A glass for you all before you clear this vermin?"

The sparkling white-green wine lent an air of celebration and their spirits rose. Giles Buckley looked round the bar expectantly.

"Where are the sisters?" he asked.

Owen smiled. "Gone. You will not see them again tonight."

"I liked the look of them," said Buckley, reluctant to let it go. "What was Izar's sister called?"

7

"Her name is Amaia," said Owen. "In Basque it means: The End". You would do well to leave them for your next life, Buckley, whatever that might be. For now, all of you set to work and take these corpses out. Leave the other two in the stable as they are, strip and bury these four. Bring all their belongings back here." He bowed briefly to the innkeeper. "Beñat, we have left the two corpses clothed, armed and under sacks and guarantee they have no knife or gunshot wounds. They are ready to be planted in the ravine. Remember, leave them partly in the river but trap them with boulders. The French should believe the wagon and the rest of them were swept away. My friend, *eskerrik asko*, we are truly grateful for your help tonight."

"It was a pleasure," rumbled Beñat, as he carefully lifted the used glasses and the jugs with their lethal charges. "Don't worry about the French, it will be done. But don't imagine we wouldn't deal the same hand to every last Englishman who plans to overstay his welcome!"

"The entire British army will probably quit Spain before the spring," said Owen, running one hand through his unruly black hair, concentrating his thoughts. "But we will return. Napoleon will be kept out of Portugal and driven from Spain before we're done. We have sworn it."

Beñat shrugged as he made his way to the kitchen. "Good luck with that oath, Englishman." He paused, looking back slyly. "*Eskerrik asko etortzeagatik!* We'll look out for your return. You're good for business. You paid well for help to kidnap a supply wagon and give it a lick of paint to change its loyalty, if that in truth is all you've done tonight."

"We always do fair deals," said Owen, easily, "and you are welcome to your wages. We'll be off smartly, as planned, when we've finished the burial and we'll take the rest of the paint and the brushes, if you don't mind. We might need them again before we make the coast. You are welcome to the rifles, and the uniforms. The clothes will do for fuel if nothing else. But hide them well for now. The attack on the main column will be a token gesture. It will only hold up the French briefly, but you

8

should still have at least a day before the search parties arrive. And Beñat," said Owen pausing as he made his way to the door, "I'm not English. I'm Welsh. As a Basque, you should make it your business to understand the difference."

"*Agur*, Welshman," said Beñat, his eyes crinkling into a smile. "Until the next time."

The descent from the Montes Vascos was uneventful. They drove the wagon in its new muddy-green livery in the opposite direction from that taken by the column and pushed on north to the coast. They snatched sleep in rotas and disturbed nothing more challenging than a few herds of mountain goats. Above them the blue sky was studded and seamed with the black shapes of hunting birds. Vultures soared over the peaks and closer to hand an inquisitive raven flew down alongside them as they reached the coastal plain. Avoiding the walled port of San Sebastian, they made their way towards a sheltered harbour where Owen had a rendezvous with a Royal Navy frigate, the *Renowned*. On their last night together, sitting by the campfire, Owen told them how they would divide the night's watches and a companionable silence fell.

"So d'ye think the rest of the Frenchies will 'ave given up waitin' for the wagon by now?" asked Benjamin Prestwick suddenly.

"For sure," said Captain Buckley. "Don't fret Prestwick. They will have swallowed the tale of the accident in the mountains and be trailing down the Madrid road by now, mourning their losses and polishing their excuses. They will need them to ring true when they fetch up at the court of Joseph I, *Jose el Primero,*" he paused to add heft to his newly acquired Spanish. "It will take some nerve to admit they've lost his Christmas boxes. Mind you, as the claret is going to make it he will be pleased enough. *Pepe Botella* likes his drink."

"He is probably no more of a drunkard than the next man," said Owen, as he lifted the fire with his boot, letting a rush of air feed the flames. "No one said a bad word about him when he ruled in Naples."

They sat in silence, staring into the fire, until Captain Buckley's self-interest surfaced.

"So we're to be cut loose to make our own way back to the regiment?"

"Yes you are, Captain Buckley," said Owen, "but not empty handed. In the best tradition of the British forces, prize money will be awarded."

Buckley remained guarded but his eyes gleamed in the firelight, and the two soldiers stole a quick glance to each other. Benjamin Prestwick's hands slowly commenced to rub in anticipation.

"We need to check the goods anyway. I don't want to debouche at Plymouth and get a nasty surprise when I reveal the loot to my superiors," Owen laughed.

"Sir, what if it be just regular stores, or ammunition?" said Prestwick fearfully.

Owen rose and flung back the tarpaulin on the back of the wagon.

"I have it on the best information that British gold can buy, that we have a haul of coin here to make Croesus himself flush up and his eyes water. Fouche's spies are not above double-dealing and apparently Napoleon does not even trust the spymaster himself. My contact is one of them. He infiltrated the armed column, convinced the officers that they were going to be attacked and lined up the detour. He gave me his personal guarantee that this is the most important consignment of the Emperor's Christmas bounty to his beloved brother Joseph. There was enough for *Pepe Botella* and the aristocracy of Madrid in exchange for their unconditional love and loyalty, or so Boney thought. Enough to convince Jo he is better off struggling in Spain, where he is despised, than lolling back in comfort in Naples. It is also enough to provide finance for whatever the new campaigning season might bring. My contact will already be on the *Renowned*, and he returns to England with me. Now, help me get these down!"

The men hurried over, clumsy with excitement. A dozen strongboxes were dragged out and lined up. Owen drew out hammers and chisels and the work began. The first was forced open and proved, as billed, to be full to the brim with canvas moneybags. Buckley lifted one, grunting with the effort, and set it down between the four of them. Owen loosened the ties and folded down the sides to reveal a shimmering cache of gold napoleons. His men stared at it dumbfounded for a moment, then fell on their knees before the mound. Gibbering in wide-eyed delight they plunged their hands into it, lifting waterfalls of forty-franc pieces, which slithered and winked like a thousand suns in the dancing firelight. As their cries died, Owen took charge.

"Close it," he ordered. "Let's get on. We must check them all."

And they did, methodically forcing open each chest in turn to reveal its hoard of gold. But the penultimate box yielded even more than gold napoleons. In this they found a king's ransom of jewels. Boxes of brilliants flashed in the starlight, necklaces of sapphires and diamonds, rubies and emeralds, every woman's gaud they had ever imagined and bags of other duller, but even more useful rocks, anonymous and austere. Pack after pack of uncut stones, nestling like withered seeds which, when cut and faceted, would bloom to sire a forest of wealth. And beneath them all, stranger still, a hoard of ancient talismans set in gold and dark stones: birds, beasts and staring eyes, exotic loot from Napoleon's Egyptian campaign.

"God's teeth!" breathed Buckley. "We've found the Crown Jewels!"

"Oiy never did see the loike," muttered the normally silent Philip Spence. "In all me born days! No, Oiy never did so, nor ever thought to." He was ashamed to discover that he had tears in his eyes and dashed them away roughly. "Ben, what say you?"

Benjamin Prestwick, thunderstruck, could only nod.

11

"As senior officer I authorise the division of spoils," said Owen briskly. "Fifty napoleons each, same for all ranks, and one item of jewellery. Take your pick."

Prestwick and Spence hung back to allow Buckley first choice and then reached out with trembling hands to lift their own prizes. Owen left the coins, but when they had finished he made his choice from the jewels, a necklace of blue stones, in a curious antique gold setting. Each man's booty was tied into his handkerchief and packed into his knapsack before they began the task of securing the boxes.

Owen and Spence took first watch, each with a pair of pistols and a Baker rifled carbine primed and ready, whilst Buckley and Prestwick bedded down by the fire. The hours slipped by quietly and now they had descended to the coastal plain it was not so numbingly cold. They also had their thoughts to keep them warm. Owen pulled his cloak tighter. He kept his eyes sharp, but his thoughts drifted to London and Sarah, his wife. He pictured her laughing with delight, and their son, Nathaniel, holding her hands and standing uncertainly on her lap. In his mind's eye the grave toddler let go of his mother and held out his arms, and as Owen reached for him he looked into a mirror of his younger self, the same blue eyes and dark looks. They did not need the money. They had all they needed. But would she like the sapphires? She was a wealthy woman in her own right, it would be a welcome bauble, but his return would be the jewel.

Sitting by him, but a world away, Philip Spence's heart still beat with a joy it had never known. The money and the jewels would transform his life. How much would he get for the foreign money? It was a windfall of years of wages at one go! How many years? Four? More? And the precious stones! Nothing would ever be the same, and he prayed as he had never done before.

"God 'elp me make it back to Martha! No more soldiering, Lord. I'll get a steady job and buy a place of our own. Back to

Bath for me for good, and plenty victuals every day for all of us. God bless Mr Parry. God bless Martha!"

He conjured up a vision of his ramrod straight wife. The windfall should put him in her good books for life, let it be long! He grinned widely, then suddenly remembered the child, the bawling red-faced bundle he had kissed goodbye.

"And God bless little Matthew, and Father. Amen, amen!"

Captain Buckley and Benjamin Prestwick took over in the middle of their short night. They would complete the journey to the coast before dawn, at which point the three soldiers would be released to strike out west and return to their regiment to face whatever hell awaited them in the next battle with Emperor Napoleon and his *Grande Armée*. Buckley had slipped one of his napoleons into his pocket, and felt it now with his cold fingers. He could feel the heavily embossed head of the Emperor and the wreath on the reverse. As he turned it over speculatively, he made a decision.

The following day marked the parting of their ways. Equipped with new horses, rations and directions for the return to the base at Corunna, the three soldiers bade farewell to Owen Parry and their brief careers with intelligence, saddled up and made their way west. After nightfall, when they had made camp and Captain Buckley dozed by the fire, Benjamin Prestwick had the opportunity to acquaint his friend with the events of the previous night.

"So 'ow much did you take Ben?" whispered Philip, warily. He felt a sinking sickness in his stomach at the thought of the betrayal of Mr Parry. They had been given a handsome pay-off; more seemed like theft from their own.

"Captain Buckley said as 'e ought to have more than us as 'e is an officer. Oiy wasn't going to argue. Then 'e upped and said Oiy deserved more too. Oiy said Oiy would share mine with you. 'E was not so pleased, said Oiy was not to tell a soul, but that didn't seem fair to you, moiy old mate." Ben eyed Philip cautiously, weighing his responses. "Any'ow, 'e loaded up with napoleons and jewels. Oiy filled moiy knapsack too, Phil, but 'alf 's yours Oiy swear. It's going to be alroight for the both of us." His brow darkened and he shot a glance over to the fireside as Buckley moaned in his sleep. "It'll be fine and dandy," he said, gripping Philip's arm and shaking it to stifle his doubts. "There'll be no trouble. There's plenty left and we closed the sacks up perfect. Nobody will know."

Benjamin Prestwick was right in many ways. They heard no more of the wagon and its fate. Neither Owen nor his superiors reported any problem with the sacks. The government registered only pleasant surprise, and welcomed the haul as a bonus for effort after a poor year. Benjamin himself escaped with his share, but there his prophesies fell short, as Philip Spence did not. The fate of the rifle regiment turned out to be a cruel one and he was one casualty in the deluge. As Owen had foretold, in company with the whole British Peninsular Army they were in full retreat through Northern Spain by Christmas Day, heading for Corunna and escape on Royal Navy transports. By January they had reached their destination but thousands had already perished. Constantly harried by Napoleon's army they had also suffered a chaos of vile weather, alternately sodden in rainstorms then frozen in blizzards. Time and again discipline had collapsed and the British soldiers had avenged their despair on the miserable villages they passed through. Before Napoleon lost interest in the pursuit and left Marshal Soult to finish off, he noted gleefully that the cruelty of the British soldiers had made them hated by everybody in Spain and he could think of no better way to neutralise resistance to French control. To compound the misery, most of the promised ships had not arrived in port. The British fought like madmen as they waited, making time to bury their commander, Sir John Moore, who perished amongst the thousands of men from the ranks. During the retreat Philip had been made up to Sergeant for conspicuous bravery, but there was no time to bury him with respect. His body was left, broken and bloody, on the road into Corunna. As shot had whistled past them and the thunderous French cannon roared, Benjamin had

14

held Philip's head and sworn on his knees to take his share to Martha. It had salved his conscience to promise this and made it easier to take his leave of the pitiful body on the road. It seemed to make what they had done fitting. It was repayment for loss. Making this last promise to a friend proved to be a stroke of luck for Benjamin Prestwick, though at the time it seemed to bring nothing but bitter misfortune. As he knelt on the frozen road, intent on his last words to Philip, he caught a blast from exploding ordnance and fell, unconscious, by the body of his friend. It was another day before he entered the city, without his boots, battered and deafened, but cradling his bulging knapsack like a sick child, far behind his unit and with men unknown to him.

"Captain Buckley. Report on the roll call, if you please!"

The few remaining officers in the rifle regiment had gathered in the Captain's cabin on board their transport vessel for a final review of losses. The broad-based decanters stood their ground on the table as the ship rolled in the heavy January seas and there was no desire to postpone dinner any longer than necessary. Captain Giles Mortimer-Buckley scanned the regimental roster very closely, efficiently suppressing his delight. Spence and Prestwick had not survived to embark. He had seen them both felled on the road, and the others in their platoon were accounted for. It had not been necessary to help them on their way, but it had been unfortunate that their share of the loot had to be left for the Frenchies. Magnanimously, he accepted this small set-back.

"Fortunes of war," he said to himself, as he arranged his face for the delivery of his valedictory on the virtues of all the missing men.

Five years before the events related in this book.

Evening: 20th December, 1828.

The Restaurant Le Grand Véfour, Palais Royal, Paris.

Colette Montrachet gathered the folds of her furred cloak over her arm, reached out for the gloved hand of the footman and stepped daintily out of the carriage, exactly as she was expected to. The Marquis was waiting to put a protective arm around her, steer her past the Louvre and through the pavement crowds to their rendezvous at the Palais Royal. The old palace reared up before them, massive and sparkling in the darkness, alive with lights and flares. The noise of the revellers hit them like a wave as they hurried forward to be enveloped in the swirling cream of Parisian high society. Richelieu's old lair had been built close to the royal residence so he could serve Louis XIII whilst keeping a close eye on the deceits of his queen, Anne of Austria, and the Palais had been a centre for intrigue ever since. The Dukes of Orleans had commercialised the place, capitalising on the secluded gardens and profusion of charming arcades, which now housed the theatre, cafes and restaurants, billiard parlours, perfumers, jewellers and stores of every type. You could buy food, furniture, toys, truffles, every toy and trifle under the sun, or so it seemed.

Two of the arcades were dedicated to the provision of prostitutes for gentlemen clients, and as Colette and her Marquis sauntered by, she spared a glance for them as they flaunted their louche gaiety, painted faces and trilling laughs. She thanked God she was not with them, plying her trade. Securing the Marquis de la Blanquefort had been surprisingly easy. Her Marseilles Count had brought her to the capital, and when business had called him away she had quickly transferred herself to a new patron. Most nights had been satisfactory, but tonight promised more than the usual round of dining and cards followed by the enthusiastic attentions of the Marquis. She nodded absent-mindedly as he pointed out his favourite eyeglass shop, his favourite snuff merchant and, in his view, the most distinguished purveyor of

16

cologne, but as she did so, she felt beneath the shawl collar of her cloak to run her fingers round a hard gold edge. Lying blind beneath the fur was a miniature, and apart from some scattered tales and memories, it was her only link with her family's past. She often found herself touching it, as a talisman, a guarantee of good fortune.

The brooch held a tiny painting of a young woman in a high white wig and low-necked ball gown. She wore a heavily-wrought gold necklace, studded with diamonds. This was just one set, so she had been told, of the famous suite of Montrachet jewels commissioned by her grandfather from Maison Bapst, court jewellers to Louis XV and his doomed grandson Louis XVI. Like her grandmother, whose likeness it was, the jewels had all been lost, as had her grandfather and all their people, their lands and chattels. The enduring family myth was that the collection of jewels had been acquired by Napoleon himself, though the rest of the estate had been broken up into hundreds of lots and sold separately: a commonplace fate for the aristocratic families of the *Ancien Régime* and their fortunes. The Revolution had claimed many heads and ruined many lives. It had been unfortunate for the Montrachets that they had failed to catch the tide of compensation which had flowed after the defeat of Napoleon and Louis XVIII's coronation. By the time Charles X had taken the throne it was too late. France was in no shape to compensate more of the old aristocracy; on the contrary, another revolution was more likely than not.

In her current career as a courtesan, Colette was used to playing for high stakes and she had felt that she lived a reasonable life, as far as it went. But only the previous week she had glimpsed the hope of something much more. At the *salon* of Laure, Duchesse d'Abrantès, she had caught sight of an English woman wearing a rope of gold and gems that was unmistakeable. Not her grandmother's diamonds, but emeralds, set in the same heavy tell-tale links, each shaped as a capital M. Over the intervening days the idea of recovering them had grown to an obsession and, against his better judgement, she had manoeuvred

17

the Marquis into accepting a dinner invitation to a party which would include the Duchess. Colette had no plan as yet, apart from finding out more about the woman, but she knew she would stop at nothing to reclaim what was rightfully hers. The necklace represented more than money, it was a link with all that she lacked, and all that her family had lost before. There had been three of them left after her mother followed her father to the grave. One brother had picked up the strands of a new life in the south, the other lay two years dead in an American grave. She felt that she had found a new direction for her life and saw it as a quest. It was going to be a religion, a purpose. The Marquis glanced at her and mistook the gleam in her eyes.

"Don't expect too much, Coco my darling," he said, tucking her arm through his and pressing her hand to his lips. "The Duchess was on good form last week but can often be far from engaging. Some of her followers are dull dogs and her latest beau, young Balzac, is an opinionated puppy, who monopolises the conversation abominably. She dotes on him as he is working through a Napoleon fixation at present. He is capable of spending all evening teasing tales out of her about the imperial glory days and he is coaxing her through scrawling endless volumes of her memoirs. He is set on publishing them himself and making a killing. I strongly advise you to avoid any mention of Bonaparte. Once her tales start there will be no stopping the flow until the carriages arrive!"

"Oh Émile," said Coco, fluttering her eyelashes and turning her exquisite heart-shaped face to his, "that is exactly what I am hoping for. I am so much looking forward to hearing more of Madame the Duchess's adventures with the Emperor! How clever of you to arrange this evening. I am so grateful." She reached up to plant a kiss just below his ear. More than grateful: the promise of infinitely more. Émile promptly banished the threat of a dull interval in the evening with the prospect of an excellent night ahead and strode on with a spring in his step.

18

The brilliance of the interior of Le Grand Véfour was overwhelming. For the eye it was a vision in gold and white, its exquisite pastel frescoes set off and echoed by the profusion of gilt-edged neo-classical mirrors lining the walls. Likewise every other sense was swept off its feet. The air rang with excited noise and clatter and was heavy with a confusion of smells and smoke as customers sank into the plush upholstery and competed in lavishing extravagant praise on the divine food. By some tables Turkish tobacco overlaid the luscious aromas of meats, fish and wines, and as they passed the women, clouds of competing perfumes rose in the air. King of all: *Les Parfums de Lubin*, favoured since the fall of Napoleon by the returning aristocracy of the old regime. Despite the Marquis's regular gifts from this house, Coco had resisted it, wearing only a light floral from the new Guerlain shop, which she had trained him to buy for her. She had learned that it was unwise to be too easily pleased.

The restaurant was packed and the Marquis followed the waiter's lead in searching out their party.

"The Duchess does not have a regular seat these days," he said, leaning close to Coco and raising his voice above the hubbub. "She could be anywhere!" He smiled, excited to show off his contacts and pointing to a corner table. "There are government men in tonight. Look!"

Coco looked over and quickly scrutinised the serious men in dark frock coats. She immediately recognised the Comte de la Ferronnays, Minister of Foreign Affairs, and Louis de Caux, Minister of War, the one dark-headed, the other white and distinguished, both leaning towards their guests in rapt attention. Two men, seemingly foreigners from the cut of their coats, though oddly similar, with piercing blue eyes and dark hair, were similarly intent. The older one was speaking in faultless French, the younger listened.

"Oh really!" she said. "How exciting, Émile. Is one of them the Prime Minister? Is it that naughty Monsieur Martignac you were so cross about yesterday?"

"No darling, not Martignac," he said fondly, "just some of

19

his Ministers. Now look over there, literary lions my dear! You should recognise Monsieur Victor Hugo. I have his work in my library. See he bows to us!"

Coco nodded briefly over the heads of the diners to a young man sporting a broad velvet collar, he seemed little older than herself, romantic, not quite foppish but with his hair brushed theatrically to the side. She spent no time on comment and hurried the Marquis forward, for there, at the next table, numbering about a dozen and in the midst of their dinner, was the party of the Duchesse d'Abrantès.

"Madame la Duchesse!" said the Marquis, kissing his hostess's hand and taking the empty seat by her. "A thousand pardons for our unconscionably late appearance!"

"My dear Marquis," said Laure, her mouth smiling, her eyes suspicious beneath her intricate piles of curls and girlish floral head-piece. "I knew you would be here as soon as you were able. But all is not lost! You have arrived in time for the *poulet marengo*."

The Marquis blenched slightly at the prospect, never having been a fan of crayfish, but he smiled gamely whilst serving dishes as big as shields and loaded with the restaurant's iconic dish approached their table, carried shoulder high by a line of waiters.

"A treat indeed. But Madame la Duchesse, before we begin, may I present again Mademoiselle Colette Montrachet? I believe you two ladies had no opportunity to speak at your *soirée* last week."

"Coco, the Duchesse d'Abrantès."

"Madame," said Coco, "I could hardly wait to have the pleasure of speaking with you since I heard that you have been tempted to write about your remarkable adventures with the Emperor."

Laure was at a late stage in her life and a particularly dire period in her finances, so any flattery was welcome, particularly when coming from a guest of the Marquis. He was known to be a generous man and had a substantial fortune founded on

Caribbean sugar interests, so the girl's friendship might prove useful. He was obviously enthralled by her, and her choice of opening gambit allowed Laure to bring dear Honoré into the conversation.

Honoré de Balzac was a fleshy, ruddy young dandy. Wildly ambitious, and like Laure herself, willing to utilise any contact in his relentless drive for self-advancement. He had secured his *entrée* into society *via* the Duchess, who was old enough to be his mother, but nevertheless kept herself smart and was a cheerful and adequate bed-mate. She matched him in spite, and her work not only fascinated him because of her youthful closeness to his current idol, the Emperor, but also might very well provide a much needed cash boost for his fledgling career as a publisher. He set about showing off to the Marquis's new doxy by enlarging on his successes and plans, but before the *poulet marengo* had been dispatched, his conversation had turned to dalliance and he had decided he had fallen, just a little, in love with her, as he was meant to.

As the conversation drifted, as it inevitably did, to the weighty matters of the Duchess's doings with Napoleon, the Marquis made his excuses and moved off to join the table with the two ministers and the foreign visitors. At the same time, Balzac was suddenly monopolised by Madame de Girardin on his left, leaving Coco a clear field. She slid over into the seat abandoned by the Marquis and wasted no time.

"Duchess, did you eat a *poulet marengo* in the company of the Emperor? Please say you did!"

Laure relaxed into her seat and raised a languid hand to her chin. "Oh my dear, so many times. On innumerable occasions, some grand, some," she paused for further effect, "some intimate."

Coco managed a squeak of delight, which encouraged Laure to embark on a version of her recitation that would fit neatly into the pause before the arrival of the meringues and fruit. It ranged over Napoleon's youthful appearances at her mother's *salon* and his great affection for them both, her husband's affair with the

Emperor's sister Caroline, the effort it had taken herself to escape the clutches of the great Prince Metternich and the abiding love the Emperor cherished for her dear departed husband. Coco had already acquainted herself with the realities of Napoleon's despair over the mental degeneration of the Duke, his *aide de camp*, with the mad extravagances of both Duke and Duchess resulting in her being packed off home to France from Spain, then expelled from Paris by Napoleon for disloyalty. The Duke's suicide seemed to be an event in some doubt. He had certainly disappeared. After spending longer with Laure, Coco could see the value to the old boy of a swift exit.

As the meringues and fruit began to make an appearance, Laure eventually touched on an issue which gave Coco the break she needed.

"And now you see," she said, her eyes tragic, heavy with kohl and brimming with unshed tears, "after such a life, after such privilege, it is my duty to commit my memoirs to the page for the benefit of others. I have four children, Mademoiselle Montrachet. They must be provided for, and my expenses, even in my modest *hermitage* far from the centre of the city, are considerable."

"How well I understand your predicament," Coco replied, returning Laure's gaze, her own liquid gold-brown eyes obediently welling up in sympathy. "I too need an independent income. I do not wish to depend on dear Émile, but need to harness my own resources. I am from an ancient lineage Madam, but all was lost in the Revolution. My family did not obtain compensation in 1815, and though I could never be a talented writer in your league, I aspire to writing a history of my family and a treatise on the design of our family jewels, which were famous in their day."

Coco watched Laure very carefully at this point, it was vital not to threaten her self-satisfaction or appear as a rival, yet she must give a plausible excuse for pursuing the gems. "Your closeness to the Emperor during the Iberian Campaign might have enabled you to hear of them or even to see them, as I gather

22

that the Emperor himself acquired them all as a *suite entière.*"

"The Emperor acquired many gifts, bought many things," said Laure evasively, "but from what I heard when I was back in Paris, a very large cache was lost just before our great victory at Corunna. Let me think, the winter of 1808 it must have been. A quantity of baggage was on its way overland to the Emperor's brother in Madrid. Maybe it was lost in the mountain snows, or maybe the English had it." She seemed to tire of the subject, "Who knows? It was wartime."

"But, Madame," persisted Coco, "at your *salon* last week I saw an English woman wearing one of the set and I would dearly love to meet her so that I may ask about the origin of her jewels."

Coco reached for her cloak and showed Laure the miniature.

"Yes," said the Duchess, peering closely then letting the cloak fall through her fingers onto Coco's lap. "The same unusual setting, but hers were emeralds, yes? I cannot remember her name, she came with other guests, but I do know they were bound for Ireland and then on to the port of Bristol in England."

"Ladies, ladies," boomed Balzac, leaning in to join their conversation and resting his head on Laure's shoulder. "Why so secretive? What was being shown? Do tell!"

It suited Coco very well to see the Marquis threading his way back to their table.

"Émile, darling," she called, as she rose to close her conversation with Laure, "what a wonderful time we have had, despite the fact that the Ministers robbed us of your company!"

"Ah ladies, here I am, here I am," he said, well-suited with himself as he reclaimed his seat beside the Duchess. "I needed a word with them, I'm afraid, times being as they are." He looked over to where the older foreigner, pale now and somewhat haggard, was making his way out with the Ministers. "Talks will be continuing into the night for some I'm afraid, though not for all."

They followed his gaze to see the younger foreigner make his way to the clutch of writers carousing at a side table. "Whilst

23

the British father attends to duty, the son makes his way over to young Hugo and his friends, to crown the evening with poetry no doubt!" Émile smiled broadly, slipping his hand round Coco's waist. "Now, have I missed all the meringues?"

Concerned by his father's ill health, but reassured that he would make his way to the hotel after a final session with the Count; Nathaniel Parry had decided to stay at Le Véfour and give himself up to pleasure for the rest of the evening. The two bottles of claret he had already had would now be followed by numerous noggins of cognac in the entrancing company he had ear-marked earlier in the evening. He waved his swordstick as he negotiated his way through the crowded tables and called a greeting.

"Victor, *mon ami! Ça va?* "

"*Salut, Nathaniel! Je vais bien, merci, merci!*" replied Monsieur Hugo, leaping to his feet and greeting him with his customary bear hug. "Now meet another friend of mine." He propelled Nathaniel round the table to meet a lounging young man with a shock of dark hair, thin sensitive face and a goatee beard. "This is Alexandre Dumas. At present clerk to the Duc d'Orléans but threatening to outshine me as a literary luminary as soon as he possibly can. Is that right! Alex, here is Nathaniel Parry of his Britannic Majesty's staff."

"Pleased to make your acquaintance, sir," said Dumas, shaking Nathaniel's hand readily. "As for you Victor, as you say, sharpened pens at dawn. Despite your name, it remains to be seen who shall triumph!"

Nathaniel took a seat, shutting out the uncertainties of the day and the dire warnings of the Ministers. He wanted to abandon himself to a night of drink and talk, in the magical company of Victor, doyen of French Romantics, and the new man Dumas, who looked interesting. But as he sat back and glanced round the table it was obvious that both of them had expensive women in tow. Dumas was examining his prize through an eyeglass he kept round his neck on a ribbon and

Hugo, despite his wedding band, was exchanging smiles with a showy young woman in red. Nathaniel suddenly felt bereft, and thought of his widowed father returning to the hotel alone. He ran his fingers round the silver pommel of his stick, extravagantly engraved with Owen's initials and presented to him on his twenty-first birthday. Their work and the constant travel abroad in the service of their country had sacrificed family life, such as it was. He could not remember exactly when they had last been to their home in Wales. For years they had lived in a series of rented rooms and hotel suites without even regular servants to call their own. The sight of complacently happy matrons with white-haired spouses at nearby tables did nothing to lift his mood, but reminded him that he could barely remember his own mother's face. He drank his cognac, sombrely watching his reflection in the giant mirror before him, a still dark figure against a restless backdrop of talk and music, glaring light and colour.

Chapter 1

The early hours: 26th January, 1833.
The York House Hotel, George Street, Bath.

Sir Giles Mortimer-Buckley Bt MP did not particularly like hotels, especially provincial ones. His body ached after being jolted down from London in the mail coach and he had heartburn after overindulging at dinner. Cursing briefly for leaving his valet behind, he dropped his evening clothes onto the floor, struggled into his nightshirt and threw himself into the unfamiliar bed. Most surprisingly, it proved to be comfortable and within minutes he had descended into a deep pit of tangled dreams.

The first vision started well. He was tumbling the most willing of the servants, a cheeky, hefty piece called Maisie Trickett who was officially employed as his granddaughter's nanny, but had also become his regular choice for bed-sport. Considering his age he had been going well, a veritable steam engine, when without warning Maisie reared up and flicked him over, her great red mouth roaring with laughter as she landed her fleshy bulk on top of him, her vast rolling bosom crushing his face, suffocating him as he lay helpless. He struggled to move but was powerless.

Groaning, he woke and turned over, but the image was stubborn, as the reality of Maisie was even more disturbing than the dream. He sat up, rubbing his hands over his face but he could see her still. Unlike the compliant servants who had been treated to his attentions over the years, she did not play to the rules of the game. The others had meekly accepted economical settlements when his enthusiasm waned, or when his wife, the Lady Leonora, had objected to them, or when they were vulgar enough to advertise a pregnancy. Maisie had announced she was breeding, demanded to keep her position, and the baby, and to be set up for life. She was adored by his wife, daughter and granddaughter, and was offensively confident that she could dig in for the long term. Her attitude reminded him unpleasantly of Johnathan Swift's: *Directions to Servants*, where employed females were reminded to be pert, rude and saucy and to charge for every accommodation they allowed their employer, from a friendly squeeze all the way to what he delicately referred to as "the last favour", which should net them a one hundred guinea prize, or twenty pounds a year for life. Maisie had refused to see the reliable doctor he had used before, and when he had tried to get her to drink a draught of pennyroyal to "return her system to normal", she had refused outright and accused him of trying to do away with her.

He thrust himself under the covers again and closed his eyes, but unwelcome thoughts of the trollop would not disperse. She was the primary reason for him being in the West Country. His predicament had encouraged him to accompany a parliamentary colleague and his wife to a house party at Mr Edwin Ravenswood's mansion on the outskirts of Bristol, where he hoped to solicit a solution to his problem. The Ravenswoods were old family friends, and though he had not visited them for a number of years, he had kept up a connection through the current Mr Ravenswood's infrequent visits to London. Edwin's father had been a legitimate and successful Bristol slave trader before the 1807 ban and the family sugar plantations in the West Indies still ran at a profit. But Edwin had diversified into other

27

businesses, some more legal than others, and by all accounts was more astute and ruthless than his father had ever been. His advice and spider's web of contacts should help to curtail Maisie Trickett's career with minimum fuss.

But every benefit has a price.

He slid again into a troubled sleep, this time haunted by a kaleidoscope of nightmares from the past, of war service in Spain, of bayonets and burning bodies and of a man swinging on the end of a rope, screaming his innocence. Mercifully, the last scene acted as a grand finale and yanked him awake again, soaked with sweat and panting for breath.

Thinking of the Ravenswoods had reminded him of the war. His father's friendship with Ravenswood Senior had first tied him to them when, as a young man returning from Spain laden with loot, it had been the Ravenswood connections which enabled him to make the most of it. Not that he normally dwelt on that. Buckley encouraged his thoughts to wander down less problematic byways. His elder brother's fortuitous riding accident had allowed him to inherit the family pile in Gloucestershire and a canny marriage to the dull but moneyed Leonora had set him up in a life of ease, culminating in him landing a county seat in the 1832 election. He liked to describe himself as a self-made man.

He rolled over to the other side of the bed to see if a fresh pillow would help him nod off to sleep, but instead found himself thinking of his travelling companions. Mr John Drake from the Foreign Office, and his wife Charlotte, had caused him to be quartered in the hotel for the night rather than the new Ravenswood mansion, as they needed to break their journey in Bath to attend a wedding. It had suited him to remain with them. Officially he and Drake were on a diplomatic mission to consolidate links with Ravenswood concerning his involvement with the China trade so it was wise to arrive together, but also Mrs Drake, or Lottie, as she preferred to be called, had proved to be a desirable piece in her own right. She had sat next to him in the coach from London and whiled away the miles by flirting and pressing herself against him most agreeably. He had managed a little squeeze of her waist as the coach rocked and just one casual brush of his hand over the side of her breast. Drake had not seemed disturbed by her performance and it probably would not have mattered to her if he had been. Lottie was obviously the one with the power in the relationship, as well as the status and the money. It had been annoying when Leonora announced that she was too unwell to accompany him on the trip, but perhaps it was a happy coincidence which would provide him with the leeway to get to know Lottie rather better. Buckley cheered up at the thought and sank into a few hours of uninterrupted sleep.

A modest tapping at the door brought him round, and once fully conscious he perked up even more at the prospect of the arrival of a chambermaid.

"Come," he called.

For a moment, a jaded twinkle lit his eye, but it was soon extinguished by the sight of a matronly rear reversing into the room.

"Good mornin' to ye, sir. 'Tis Dorcas 'ere. Oiy 'ave yer breakfast for ye," she said, redundantly, as she landed the laden tray on his bedside table. "Would you loike me to open yer drapes whilst Tabby sees to the fire?"

A juvenile of about ten years of age had struggled in behind her with a jug of hot water, which she clattered to its rest in the washstand bowl.

Buckley glowered, but accepted that it was for the best. "Yes," he snapped, as he hoisted himself higher against the pillows to inspect the provisions on the tray. "Get on with it."

As Tabby rattled the fire into life, the velvet drapes were twitched back to reveal a sullen sky and a sparkling white layer of frost riming the roof of the building across the street.

"Will that be all, sir?" enquired Dorcas, who on closer inspection bore a remarkable resemblance to a bulldog. He glanced at the juvenile answering to the name of Tabby, who turned her pasty, sullen face and one eye towards him, the other

29

being wayward had rolled to the wall.

"That will most definitely be all," he said impatiently, waving them both away.

He gazed, unseeing, at the rolls, butter, jams and coffee, the nodding ferns and flower buds in the crystal vase, but then remembered that he had a day to play with in the old spa. Being a resort city, foul-tasting warm water should not be the only diversion on offer. Feeling marginally more optimistic, he set to work on the rolls.

Later that morning, another meal was served at the York House, a more convivial one. It was a wedding breakfast to celebrate the marriage of Mr Nathaniel Parry, from Llanddaniel on the Isle of Anglesey and Carlisle Lane, Lambeth, to Miss Emma Peterson of Marlborough Buildings, Bath, daughter of Captain Oliver and Mrs Lydia Peterson. They had been driven to the hotel in Captain Peterson's carriage after a service in Bath Abbey. The bells had rung out behind them and a vocal knot of well-wishers had scattered rice and blessings as they had been borne away up Broad Street. Drink had been taken and food eaten; it only remained for the formalities to be concluded. Nathaniel was looking over the assembled guests before making his groom's speech in response to the efforts of his new father-in-law, waiting for the guests to resume their seats and the rattle of applause to wear itself out. Captain Peterson had managed to bark out a gruffly emotional welcome and propose a toast before taking everyone by surprise and abruptly dropping back into his seat as if shot. A tear stood in the Captain's eye though he beamed still on Emma, his second and favourite daughter. Oliver Peterson was embarrassed to find himself overwhelmed by the occasion, a state of affairs he put down to advancing age and more happiness than was probably good for him.

"Too much fuss, damn it!" he blustered to himself.

He blew his nose volcanically and reflected on his good fortune. The ship of family relations was holding a steady course, a welcome relief for which he gave silent thanks. His son

30

remained at sea with his vessel, which he now commanded, and his eldest girl was busy producing another child in Cirencester. His wife Lydia was in a state of unconfined delight, having seen Emma safely married off to the dashing young Parry, who had seemed frustratingly elusive in the early days of their acquaintance. Four girls had seemed a daunting responsibility in those lean days after the war, when far too many young women had buzzed around the reduced cohort of eligible young men.

"Two down and two to go," he reflected thankfully. "Half-time as it were."

The twins, in a high state of excitement, had giggled and flounced about all morning in their bridesmaid's gowns, unregulated by their mama, who had been occupied in overseeing the bridal preparations, entertaining honoured guests from London and greeting aged aunts and uncles, cousins, and a profusion of nephews and nieces. Oliver had seen the twins knock back at least two glasses of champagne each, but had chosen to ignore it.

Nathaniel winked at his father-in-law as he surveyed the tables of guests. He had been able to muster only one local relative and his family for the bridegroom's side in church, one Dr Charles Parry a cousin of his late father, a few times removed, so he had extended the invitation to new friends and a colleague, John Drake. This last gesture had shown how far their toleration of each other had grown since they had first met in the autumn of 1831, though Nathaniel trusted Drake little more than on first viewing. Captain Peterson had also wanted to invite Drake, as he knew him through connections with Lord Melbourne, and Nathaniel had been interested to see them conversing earlier, obviously on very familiar terms. It was still a matter of some surprise to Nathaniel that Oliver had neglected to take him into his confidence in the early days of their friendship, or even to drop a hint of warning about his continuing role with the Office. But he really should have guessed the truth of it, as he had known of Oliver's work with his own father, Owen,

31

which had been clandestine and undertaken during the dangerous days of the war. Captain Peterson, though bluff and honest, was a man adept at keeping secrets, which could only be to his credit. He had also been charming to Lottie Drake, who had reciprocated and even succeeded in suppressing her metropolitan boredom and been pleasant in turn to Mrs Peterson. This attention had driven the mother of the bride into transports of delight. London connections were as gold dust in Bath society, especially when associated with the government.

Nathaniel was more pleased to see that his fencing club friends had taken the time to attend, Captain Charles Wilkins of the Yeomanry doing him the honour of serving as his best man. Half a dozen of Charles's officers from the Bath volunteers were there in uniform, giving the occasion a dash of martial grandeur. Fairfield and Cruttwell were there with their wives, in the company of Howard Dill, who was, as usual, escorting Tilly Vere. All six were in a jovial huddle raising their glasses again for some additional private toast. Nathaniel noticed this with great relief, as until this day he had always had an uncomfortable feeling that at some distant point in the future he might wake up and find himself married to Tilly, a victim to misplaced sympathy, or guilt, or maybe even lust. Tilly was still luminously beautiful, though after the mysterious disappearance of her husband she had an odd position in society, hovering on the edges of widowhood but not quite qualifying. Luckily, she seemed to get about town and lived high without attracting too much comment by attaching herself to Howard and his friends.

It was with more mixed emotions that he caught sight of Coco Montrachet and Diarmuid Casey. He had not seen them in the Abbey, but that was no surprise, as once there he had been preoccupied with the ceremony. He looked again at his new wife. She looked pretty, but strained in her finery, the tightly fitting wedding gown of gold embroidered ivory muslin and foaming blond lace, the net of sparkling diamante flowers taming her chestnut hair. Despite his successes as an agent for the government, his years abroad, his easy popularity with women, his had not been a charmed life. He had made a decision to join the Peterson clan to acquire a wife and a family to fill the void where the centre of his life should have been. It had been a calculated choice and there was a price to pay. He now had others to consider, a wife and household he had to protect in an unpredictable world. He glanced back at the officers in full dress uniform, sabres at their sides. Involuntarily he shrugged his shoulders. He was surprised to be enjoying the day as much as he was. It had been quickly planned to coincide with a pause in his business affairs after a meandering year-long engagement and was proving to be a strangely unreal experience, an insubstantial bubble quite separate from normal life. On her wedding band he had commissioned an engraving: *For Emma, my Bright Star*. It had seemed right at the time, in homage to their shared love for Keats, and she had been pleased. But perhaps it should have been something from Shelley. Keats always brought with him a sense of impending doom.

"Our man's gathering himself up to speak," said Diarmuid, on top rakish form as he returned to a table by the door to join his companion. His green eyes glinted with mischief as he sank the rest of his champagne.

"So I see," said Coco, smiling fondly at Nathaniel, who was as usual running a hand through his thick black hair to tame it and focus his thoughts before he spoke.

She enjoyed looking at him as much as she had enjoyed exploring his body. His eyes were arctic blue, his winter skin a bleached Celtic white, but he smelled always of warm summer. Emma should have the first of many enjoyable evenings once they made their escape from the reception. She rather liked Emma and wished her no harm, but that did not affect her views on Nathaniel in the slightest. She had enjoyed getting to know him, and making herself useful to him in a number of ways. And he in turn was not without his usefulness.

Her mission in Bath had almost stalled before the tasty little episode generated during his first investigations in the city at the time of the Reform Riots. Thanks to him and the events of 1831, Ravenswood and his wife had been tempted to come to Bath and she had caught sight of her very own El Dorado in the shape of Mrs Ravenswood waltzing round the Guildhall wearing the same Montrachet gold-mounted emeralds that she had spotted round her scrawny neck at the Duchesse d'Abrantès' *salon* in Paris three years before. It had taken time to determine the best way to close in on her quarry, but it had been worth the wait. Her relationship with Diarmuid was still casual in terms of commitment, but it had prospered modestly, as had he, and news from her surviving brother in France was encouraging. She had the makings of a plan, which had reasonable hopes of success.

"I bumped into Sir Giles Mortimer-Buckley in the foyer," continued Diarmuid, lowering his voice as Nathaniel began his thanks. "You know who I mean, sweetheart? The county member who's coming to the dinner with us tomorrow: entering the lion's den! But he reckons he's known Ravenswood man and boy, so he should realise what he's getting into."

"Do you still mix with him in the House, Diarmuid?" asked Coco, leaning closer to whisper in his ear. "Any information I can get on the Ravenswoods before tomorrow will be welcome."

"Sure, and it's a conniving hussy you are, my darling," said Diarmuid. As his arm encircled her waist, he planted a kiss on her cheek and squeezed her tight. There was always an element of danger in being close to Mademoiselle Montrachet, which he enjoyed. They continued to rent the same suites of rooms in Queen Square, a floor apart, close enough for dalliance but still separate. When they had first met in Bath and wanted to step out together in respectable society they had put about the tale that he was an old family friend chaperoning her on behalf of her brother. Surprisingly it still seemed to pass muster. He sometimes gave her money, but only as a casual present as he knew she had other men and was not short of funds. It suited Diarmuid not to ask for details as he loved her mysteries and found her tantalising.

They both found it amusing that they had managed to infiltrate most circles of society despite the irregularity of their relationship, but Diarmuid was clearly more welcome to attend alone at some events, and the cold wind of moral disapproval was blowing more fiercely as the century progressed. He had also noticed that its increase had a proportional effect on the numbers and repellent qualities of undergarments favoured by women. There might come a day when his career demanded the banishing of the delectable Coco from public view, but it was not yet. He craned his neck to make eye contact with a serving maid and motioned her over to re-charge their glasses.

Dairmuid Casey had entered parliament at the same time as Sir Giles Mortimer-Buckley after the 1832 elections, and the new reforming members had spent useful time together, forming alliances in the bars and tearooms, making themselves known to the Ministers. Diarmuid knew exactly what kind of man Mortimer-Buckley was: a ladies' man and a wastrel with irregular appetites. He seemed wealthy, and would need to remain so. He lived fast, whereas Diarmuid gave the impression of being a man about town without sacrificing his hard won resources to pleasure. Diarmuid had worked his way up, acting for Daniel O'Connell throughout the late 1820s, and he had achieved a great victory in winning a seat previously known for its Tory loyalties. Buckley had come in unopposed after extensive bribery had rendered the staging of an election unnecessary. The Great Reform Act might have given the vote to more men, but voters were still few enough in number to allow wealthy candidates to buy their way into many constituencies. Corruption had simply been tidied up round the edges rather than removed.

"He's said nothing to me about Ravenswood. But really, Coco my love, what more do we need to know? He'll trade in anything and anybody to turn a profit; he's a dangerous bastard and I vowed I would never get within striking distance of him. He would probably have done away with the both of us if he ever knew we had lifted a finger against him. I suggest you are simply grateful that I've wangled us an invitation to his dinner and try to behave whilst you are there in my company. He is rather beloved of Lord Palmerston. So remember that, and no monkey tricks or you might damage my brilliant career."

"We did not exactly raise a finger against him personally," said Coco pouting, as she knew he liked it.

"We got close enough and I would rather you wanted to pick anyone else's pocket rather than his! You had better be sure his wife's still got your family trinkets."

Coco patted his knee consolingly. "That is rather the point of the visit. Now, shush. Listen to the groom."

On board the *Zhen Tian Lei* , London Docks, Wapping.

Two figures stood together, deep in conversation on the foredeck of the junk as it prepared to sail down the Thames on the receding tide. The Dutch crew handling the unfamiliar sails made sure they stayed at a respectful distance from the two men, well out of earshot and far enough away not to attract attention. One of them was known to them, a Mr Kizhe, the emissary of their employer, the Count. Kizhe had become a regular passenger on their own merchant ship over the last few months and had ordered them to sail his vessel to Amsterdam. Few were willing volunteers and some still bore the scars of his attentions. He was not a man to cross or one to be close to when displeased and the word was that the interview with the Londoner would not go well.

"So, Tiler," said Kizhe, turning his massive head from his scrutiny of the quay and fixing the other man with a searing, reptilian glare. "The problem stemmed from my scouts taking girls for the trade as part payment for gambling debts."

"Yes, sir," said Tiler, his eyes darting over Kizhe's rectangular frame, the bludgeon of a hand at rest on the weapon in his belt, his trademark "helmet breaker". He was new to Kizhe's employ and needed to be wary, but his master was unreadable, his closed face frozen long before in the wastes of the Russian-Mongolian borderlands. Tiler plastered an approximation to honesty onto his rat-like face and continued. "The man who calls himself Smith directed them, he's waiting below. They would've failed to meet your quota if they hadn't used more versatile methods. There weren't enough people ready to sell unwanted kids." He swallowed nervously. "The problem came as the men didn't explain the situation to their wives. Next minute the women are runnin' to the London police bawlin' that their girls are kidnapped and attractin' too much attention from the authorities. The papers are reportin' a wave of kidnappin' and the police are stickin' their noses in everyone's business round the docks. An' there's plenty to find out if they sniff for it. Quite a tidy few of the last consignment were taken off the streets, mudlarks and the like. Some of 'em had families or friends and they went to the police as well."

Kizhe nodded briefly. "The scouts must be more selective or my men will pay them a visit. I will make sure Smith understands this. And we need better quality stock. I know we have taken women and harlots from debtors before as part payment for debts, but they are not valuable prizes, Tiler. They are second hand goods." He paused to think, cracking his knuckles and flexing his massive shoulders. "Now, on another matter, I will return shortly to see a Mr Ravenswood of Bristol, he has two vessels at dock here. Watch them, discreetly. Be my shadow. Look out for a Chinese man called Lee, Cornelius Lee. He was working for me but left a job unfinished some time ago. Others have tried to locate him but failed and I have some new intelligence that he has left China and sailed for Europe. My man Qiang will be your contact until I return."

"Yes, sir," said Tiler. "See it as done."

They fell silent as Captain van der Linde strode up to them.

"Excuse me, sir. The cabins are ready for you to inspect."

The Captain led the way below decks but once there left Tiler and Kizhe to their own devices. So it was Tiler who led the way past the locked doors, sliding each inspection hatch open as they negotiated the narrow passageway. The atmosphere was cloying; heavy with the stench of perfume and drugs. The rooms were occupied by children and young women, all ominously silent, slumped semi-conscious on the bunks or asleep, ready to be transported to their fates at the hands of the highest bidders.

Kizhe nodded his head as they progressed, well-satisfied. After they left the cargo hold they made their way to the Captain's cabin, where Kizhe's men waited for their master to interview the second visitor. Kizhe settled in with his back to the porthole and ordered the Englishman to be summoned, but he was not the most urgent matter for consideration. A letter from China rested in his pocket with news from Canton. His operatives had sent word that the Emperor was tightening his grip on the criminal underworld at home and that the Count was now a person of interest. Kizhe's mouth set in an iron line. His patience with the scout would be short.

The Englishman ushered through the door was a slick, over-dressed rake of thirty years or so, puffed up with self-importance and heading for a fall.

"Mr Kizhe, you know my worth. Your quotas have been met in every particular and well within the time limit." He leered round the room, thumbs in his waistcoat pockets, his head cocked at an angle. "Double my pay or you lose my services!" He flung the ultimatum grandly, but had addressed it to Qiang who sat in the Captain's chair close to the door. It was his second mistake and an easy one to make, but it was a costly one, given the inaccuracy of the first.

"Mr Kizhe is seated at the head of the table," said Qiang, gesturing to his master. "You'd be well advised to make your pitch to him."

"Come closer," said Kizhe. "Sit by me." He patted the chair by him, and the Englishman, disconcerted and with a sudden sweat beading his brow, worked his way round the table to take the seat. "So you feel you deserve more rewards, Mr Smith? It is as Mr Smith you prefer to be known, I gather?" said Kizhe.

"Yes, Smith," said the man, reviving as he spotted Tiler in the shadows to Kizhe's right. "That is as I'm known, ain't it

Tiler!"

But Tiler was wise enough not to say one word.

"I think you deserve more than you have," said Kizhe, placing a line of sovereigns on the table between them. "Do you think you deserve these as a start?"

Smith's face relaxed and his lips drew back in a grin, but even as he made a move to claim his prize, Kizhe drew a dagger with lightning speed and impaled the grasping hand before it closed.

Unmoved by the agonised howls, Kizhe said quietly. "This is only the beginning of what you deserve, Smith." He gestured to the quaking man's pocket watch chain and its dangling crucifix, "Do you read your Bible? Though not to my taste it is instructive. The wages of sin should be death. You have been spared today for your sins against the Count. Your stupidity in stimulating the rash of kidnappings has alerted the authorities and attracted unwanted attention to our business. Any future experimentation will be done only with my explicit permission. Do you understand?"

Ignoring the rambling assurances of his victim, he tore the dagger from Smith's hand and its anchorage in the table beneath. He signalled to Qiang. "Get him out of my sight. And Tiler, before you go back on shore, bring the woman from cabin number two to my quarters. The creature will have little retail value and I have some time to kill."

As Smith was dragged away, and Tiler disappeared to do his bidding, Kizhe surveyed the line of coins and the pool of blood. The prospect of meeting with Ravenswood again was a welcome one and would be lucrative. He hoped that the meeting with Lee would be equally rewarding but in a very different sense. As the ship pitched in the wash of a passing vessel, he watched the blood spread its gore further and his seamed face crinkled involuntarily into the harshest of smiles.

Afternoon: Saint James's Square, Bath.

Captain Peterson's carriage, heavily loaded with the new Mrs Parry's trunks and boxes, had first laboured up the hill earlier that day. It had made the short journey from her family home in Marlborough Buildings to her new married quarters in Saint James's Square whilst the marriage ceremony took place in the Abbey. Nathaniel had bought the house well before Christmas and had had time to prepare. The most tired parts of the paintwork had been given a fresh coat, basic furniture had been acquired and, since the previous week, staff had been put in place. This was the first time he had assembled a cohort of retainers, as the rent for his rooms in Lambeth included domestic service and the family home he had inherited on Anglesey had a farm attached, which provided servants in the shape of the farmer, his wife and numerous off-spring.

The Bath contingent had been assembled at speed, but the boot *cum* knife boy, Tobias, he had known for some time and had originally employed as an informer. Nathaniel now planned to train him as manservant and general *factotum*. Em knew the boy and liked him, so that was good. Similarly she was kindly disposed towards Frances, a newly-promoted parlour maid whom she wanted to train as her lady's maid. Nathaniel had rescued this particular waif from criminal clutches some time ago and had been pleased to see her placed in the Peterson's kitchen. Em had resolved to bring Frances with her when she left home and saw her as a project in progress, which was also good. The aspect that might not be so good resided in the unknown quantity of the lynchpin of the staff. Since their household was small, he had hired a woman to be cook and housekeeper combined, the formidable Mrs Rollinson, whose expression in repose resembled that of a hippopotamus disturbed at dinner. She would have to oversee the comings and goings of the daily and weekly staff: the cleaners, the laundresses and the gardeners, and deal with any problems they generated. Her references were impeccable but unless Em could manage her there might be trouble on the home front. Mrs Rollinson had been issued with a scullery maid, one Harriet Pullen, and the whole troupe was out on the pavement, ready and waiting to greet the new master and mistress, as the carriage made its second appearance of the day in the square and the new owners were handed out onto the pavement.

Emma Parry stepped out in her wedding finery, still holding a spray of greenery and white roses but with the addition of a white velvet cloak around her shoulders, which flapped wide and billowed away from her in the bitter January wind. Her eyes shone with an unnatural brightness and she did not feel the cold. Being practical she put this down to the champagne, but it was also because of a delirious dose of happiness, which was for her very unusual and proving to be uncomfortable. During the speeches at the reception she had had too much time to reflect. To be realistic, and she was nothing if not brutally honest with herself, Nathaniel Parry was an extraordinarily good catch who attracted women wherever he went. She had seen his effect on them; some of them she readily admitted had the edge on her in looks, though she gave place to none in devotion. She had been even more relieved than Nathaniel to see Tilly Vere so securely latched on to Howard Dill. It seemed a lifetime ago that she had entertained a real anxiety about Tilly's designs on Nathaniel. Fortunately he had not been wealthy enough for her to make a determined play for him. Coco, however, was an entirely different matter and she really did not want to know the full details of his relationship with her.

But despite the current reality of her happiness, she had wasted time constructing mantras of insurance to protect herself against future disaster. She had repeated to herself foolishness such as: "Even if everything goes wrong tomorrow, this morning has happened. It's real. It can't be taken away." And a treacherous tear would roll down her face in sympathy with the foolishness. If she were unlucky someone would see it. Her mother had spotted one and said she should not be frightened and that marriage was normal. She must follow her husband's instructions and all would be well. Her father had seen one whilst Nathaniel was making his speech and asked if she was all right and she had told him they were tears of happiness, which in part they were, for she was happier than she had ever thought possible. It was a strangely ominous feeling.

So she stood, hesitating in the rising wind, trying to shake off her thoughts and return to reality by greeting the servants, when Nathaniel suddenly bent down and swept her off her feet, lifting her in his arms and striding forward to the open door.

"You shall be carried across the threshold, Mrs Parry," he declared. "Welcome to your new home! And look, here's Caradoc waiting for us! Here, sir! The new mistress is moving in, come and say hello."

"Oh Mr Parry, watch 'im!" yelled Tobias from the path, losing all the carefully tutored aitches he had built up painstakingly over the last year. "'E 'as bin in the old quarry and is all over mud!"

It was, of course, too late. Caradoc, Nathaniel's black and tan Welsh terrier, had at first resented being left behind by his master, who had looked unusually well-groomed that morning and was wearing new clothes trailing foreign scents; the strongest being tailor's shop and cologne water. Magnanimously, Caradoc had not complained but had abandoned the servants and spent the morning excavating a fox hole in a nearby park. He was now in a better mood and ready to pay his respects. With one enterprising leap he managed to land on top of Emma and her bouquet, whilst both were still bundled in Nathaniel's arms, in order to set about licking a ferocious welcome. It was not so much the additional weight but the velocity which toppled the lot of them onto the hall floor in a confusion of gold muslin, feminine squeaks, manly bellows, yaps and mud.

Emma wriggled free of Nathaniel, gasping with laughter, and attempted to struggle to her knees whilst fending off Caradoc. She did not mind the fall and was surprised to realise she did not care that there had been an audience.

"Good to see you too," she said, rubbing the dog's head before letting her new husband and staff rescue her and set her on her feet.

"Are you all right, my dear?" said Nathaniel, guiltily brushing her soiled sleeve. "Sorry about Caradoc, he was excited."

"Me too," said Emma. "It doesn't matter about the dress. I rather liked the welcome, but it was a baptism of mud! I need to change. Frances, could you lead me to my dressing room?"

Nathaniel kissed her before she went, which stimulated a ragged burst of applause from the domestic staff; a phenomenon brought on by the excitement of the wedding day and never again repeated. He then bent down, scooped up the wriggling and grimy Caradoc and bore him off to the outhouse.

Frances had helped her mistress out of the frothy gown, which was now additionally decorated with blotched paw prints, and laid it on the chaise longue.

"And the corset, if you please, Frances. I can't wait to get rid of it. You will soon discover in your new role as my maid that I am not a regular wearer of stays. I am no fashion plate I'm afraid. Now the head-dress, that's better, and brush my hair."

Emma sat before her dressing mirror in her petticoats and chemise, scrutinising her reflection. She felt back to normal and much calmer, as if the fall had shaken some sense into her.

"How are you getting on with Mrs Rollinson?"

"Well, Miss. Sorry, Madam, I should say," said Frances, pausing in her vigorous brushing of Emma's mass of glinting chestnut hair. Newly released from the netting, it fell over the back of the chair to her waist. "She's a powerful woman and no mistake. I'm right glad I'm parlour and bedrooms and not scullery no more. That little Harriet will have to jump to it."

"Well, since you are sharing a room with Harriet, keep an eye on her and let me know how she fares. What is your room like? I've not seen it myself yet."

"It's on the back, nice view of the garden, Madam. Mr Parry chose everything in it. It's unusual. It's good though," she said hurriedly.

Emma resolved to put on a plain gown and explore the house. They had just two days' grace in their new home and then they would pack and drive to the manor farm on the Isle of Anglesey for their honeymoon. It was a journey she had never made before, up the Wye Valley, by the mountains of North Wales, a great distance of over two hundred and fifty miles, so Nathaniel said. Her spirits soared at the prospect of a month of dallying there, Nathaniel free from work and she free of everything and everybody except him.

Whilst Emma was setting about her new role as mistress of the household, Nathaniel had summoned Tobias to receive his instructions for the rest of the afternoon. He was to go to the York House to collect and distribute a consignment of wedding cake.

"Take it to Mrs Spence's family," said Nathaniel, struggling to hold down a reluctant Caradoc in the tin dog bath. "Send them all my best wishes and spend some time with them, they will want to hear all about the wedding."

Tobias left willingly enough. A walk through town and a cup of tea at his old lodgings was a pleasant way to spend the rest of the afternoon. He made his way by the mews behind Royal Crescent, along Rivers Street and then turned down Lansdown Hill and made for the London Road. The York House was a large coaching inn on a corner site, dominating the crossroads and much of the coaching trade from the capital. Half a dozen servants were busy outside the front entrance dealing with two coaches full of travellers and their luggage, lately arrived from London. A third coach was turning into Broad Street, making for the stables' entrance at the rear and Tobias followed on behind it, weaving his way through the waiting ostlers and teams of fresh horses to make his way to the kitchen entrance. Nothing seemed to have changed since his brief stint there as a boot boy and it gave him a thrill to swagger in sporting his frock coat and striped waistcoat, playing the man, giving his instructions to the potboy like a regular gent. He took delivery of the cake box and within the quarter hour presented himself at Martha Spence's house in the trim Georgian terrace in Walcot, only just remembering to run the soles of his shoes over the boot scraper before she opened the door.

"Master Tobias Caudle," she said, rubbing her hands on her apron and stepping back theatrically to survey him. "Look at you in your finery! What have you got there?"

"Wedding cake for us all, Mrs Spence, from Mr Parry!"

He followed her down the dark hallway to the kitchen and was surprised to find it thronged with people in full flow. As expected Old Tom was in his place by the fire with the Johnty close by him, no longer a babe creeping round Tom's feet but a sturdy toddler, jumping, clapping and babbling his way through a high-pitched tale at his great-grandfather's knee. He was accompanied by coos, whistles and squawks from Jimmy Congo, Matthew's grey and red African parrot, who was shackled by the foot to his corner perch. Johnty's parents, Mary and Matthew, were also there, both on a shift off work and sitting at the table deep in talk with a weather-beaten old soldier. Tobias had never seen him before and stared, taking in the Waterloo medal hanging awry on his worn coat, his bowed back and the scanty grizzled beard, not thick enough to disguise a burn scar, livid white on the left side of his face.

"Mr Prestwick is our new lodger, Tobias," said Martha, with surprising warmth and stilling all other talk in the room as she did so. "He was an old friend of Mr Spence, my dear late husband." Smiling fondly at him as she placed the kettle on the fire, the severe lines of her face softened. "He came to us this week after too many years away. Sit you down. We'll all take tea shortly and eat this fine cake to celebrate Mr Parry's marriage!"

"Afternoon to all," said Tobias, taking a seat. "Pleased to make your acquaintance, Mr Prestwick."

"And Oiy yours, young man," replied the visitor, rising to attention and shaking Tobias by the hand.

"Hello, hello! Sit down, sit down damn you!" squawked the parrot, his greyish-yellow eyes glinting evilly.

"'Ee do be a caution to be sure, do old Jimmy," declared Old Tom, delighted by the bird and breaking into a cackling laugh.

"Ignore him, Father," ordered Martha, setting out the tea cups and fixing them both with her customary glare. "He's showing off and we want no more of it."

"Foine bird 'e do be!" grinned the old soldier. "Matthew 'ere told me 'e brought 'im back from the voyage when 'e lost 'is fingers! Oiy seen some things at sea 'twould make yer 'air curl," he added confidentially, eyeing Tobias to gauge which tale to offer next. "Once on the India run we 'ad a man overboard and 'e was eaten by a shark before our very eyes."

"What do sharks look like, sir?" said Tobias, thrilled.

"Like monstrous fish with jaws the size o' this table!" declared Ben. "Ripped into 'im they did and left just one boot complete with foot a-floatin' to mark the spot!"

Mary's squeak of alarm caused him to try a change of tack.

"And on land 'twas stranger still, as if the cursed heat weren't enough, widows threw 'emselves alive on their men's funeral pyres, wailin' and howlin'."

"Never! Don't say it!" said Mary, clapping her hands to her cheeks.

"Piece of cake, Mr Prestwick?" said Martha briskly. "We need to talk of happier events."

Reluctant to displace the old soldier, Tobias had to be coaxed to tell some tales of the wedding. Most were vague and at second hand as he had not attended but he gained enthusiasm and authority when he started on Caradoc's reception for the bride.

"So over they went, but she didn't turn a hair, not she! Proper good sport is Missis." The visitor had sat in silence as he listened to Tobias, but his brow furrowed as a slow realisation dawned on him.

"You say yer employer is a Mr Parry and a government man? Welsh you say?"

"I do say so."

"Would 'e by any chance have a father by the name of Owen?"

"I believe so, sir."

"Martha, bless me if 'e ain't likely to be the son of the self-same officer as Phil and me served before Phil's untimely death. Fine man was Owen Parry. He bein' the one who gave us leave to take our prize money in Spain, as Oiy told you all they years ago."

"So you knew my master's father," said Tobias, leaning forward, keen to learn more.

"Oh Ben, you must meet young Mr Parry," exclaimed Martha. "Fine young man he is and a model tenant here a while back. He would welcome a kind word regarding his father as I reckon he was devoted to that gentleman."

"He surely was," added Mary. "His father's death struck him to the heart. About four years past, wasn't it Mother? Tell us about the prizes, Mr Prestwick, and the part Mr Parry played, for I know Mother had great cause to be grateful. Why," she said, smiling round the room, "we do owe this house to the Spanish prize!"

Ben's eyes clouded as other memories surfaced.

"Well, well, terrible toimes, better left lie," he muttered, but immediately sensed the disappointment in the party, and Mary's embarrassment. He had to give more. "But Oiy must say that Mr Parry brought us all three a great stroke o' luck. Without 'im we'd 'ave 'ad no sniff of Napoleon's treasure. For such it was, from the Emperor 'imself bound for King Joseph in Madrid. Sacks of gold and jewels we seen, mounds of 'em! Napoleon's gold we called it! But before we redirected it to Old England, Mr Parry saw to it that we all 'ad our due share, dear old Phil, me and the Captain. 'Tis sad though that my fortunes have now fallen lower than they were. Cheated out of moiy business Oiy was and all Oiy 'ave now is what Oiy stands up in!"

"Napoley's gold!" squawked Jimmy Congo. "Napoley's gold!" flapping his wings wildly and following up with a piercing whistle to draw attention away from the newcomer and back to him where it belonged. As the company clapped and petted Jimmy Congo, Old Tom shot a suspicious glance in the direction of the new tenant. His eyesight was very poor and his legs were letting him down, but over ninety years of living had made him wise.

"As long as ye pays the rent at the month's end ye will be given the respect of a king, Ben Prestwick," he said. Memories of Prestwick as a youth were surfacing. He had led Philip into plenty of scrapes not of his choosing. Perhaps the leopard had not changed its spots.

"More cake?" asked Martha warningly.

"Aye, Mother," said Matthew. "And now, Mr Prestwick, more tales of my father, if you please!"

"And of my master's sire," said Tobias, pushing the cake plate nearer to the shabby man and drawing his chair closer.

Evening: The Parry Residence, Saint James's Square, Bath.

Free at last from the relatives, the guests and the staff, the newly-weds had gone up to their bedroom and stood before the open fire, which was locked in an unequal struggle to keep the chill of the room at bay. Nathaniel put his hands round Emma's waist and kissed her, running his hands over her hips and her breasts as he started to unhook her gown. Putting her arms around his neck she felt unsteady, her body answering his touch with a dizzying surge of pleasure.

"Shall I help?" she whispered shyly in his ear.

He smiled and stepped back as she took off her day gown.

"And the rest," he said, slipping off his jacket, waistcoat and stock, pulling his shirt over his head.

Emma stood uncertainly. "All of it? Do I put on my nightgown?"

"No, my darling Em, you do not," said Nathaniel. "And take

48

off your chemise, and your stockings, every last stitch!"

He watched as she dropped the layers of silk to her feet to stand naked and vulnerable before him. It was his first sight of her body and it was a relief to see it was as comely as her face. He dropped the rest of his wedding finery to the floor and took her in his arms, pressing close to her, feeling her tremble, he hoped with desire rather than fear and the creeping cold.

"Come on Em, it's freezing," he laughed, "Let's get warm."

Under the mounds of sheets and blankets they could relax and explore. Her skin felt smooth and firm, like the silk of her gown to his touch and as he buried his head in her, she smelled of roses. Nathaniel was in no hurry as he had known many women. He could afford to be gentle and he knew the ways to make their first love last, which he did, hour on hour, and far into the night.

They woke early, locked in each others' arms and Emma ran her fingers gently over his chest, finding again the scars she had felt in the darkness. The exhausted anxieties of the wedding day had receded and she felt a profound peace, her body pleasantly a-fire and triumphant, as if she had passed a test, which in part she had. From eavesdropping on women's conversations since she had been a child she had some idea that the marriage bed might bring not just joy, but also pain and abject humiliation. Young ladies were not meant to have the slightest idea of what a husband might do, with what, and where, but her sister had been useful on that score. It had made up for the hours of boredom she had inflicted by boasting of her Cirencester farmer before Emma had a man of her own. A little knowledge was power indeed, but her sister had been wrong about never taking off your chemise.

Reluctant to go down for breakfast, they decided to look through the neglected wedding correspondence they had brought up with them the night before. Nathaniel sat up, wrapped himself in his Damascus dressing gown and started to work through the mound of cards and letters. Most were brief good wishes, quickly read, and the pile was almost finished when he stopped abruptly.

"Change of plan required, Em," he said frowning. "We need to go to a dinner with the Ravenswoods tonight. There's a command from the Office and apparently an official invitation from the host will follow. We have a day in hand so our honeymoon in Wales will not be delayed."

"So be it," said Emma, snuggling closer under his arm, "I've never been to Arno's Tower, but I met Mr Ravenswood and his wife at a few events in the Assembly Rooms when I attended with my parents. The Ravenswoods started to come to the Reform Balls here after the Bristol Riots and we occasionally sat in their company. I know that Father, Mr Dill and Dr Parry have invested in Mr Ravenswood's shipping ventures, but I don't remember my parents ever dining with him before."

She paused, wondering if she should mention the unease she always felt in Mr Ravenswood's company. As Nathaniel remained silent she hurried on.

"The mansion is rumoured to be very grand. What exactly does the letter say?"

"Apparently Ravenswood has been informed that we are coming. No doubt an invitation is lurking somewhere in this pile of mail, or it will arrive at some point today. I am not sure how thrilled he will be about having to issue it. Apart from seeing him in the Rooms, I only met him once to speak to privately and I would not say that that either of us was particularly keen to repeat the experience."

Nathaniel leaned over to kiss Emma, who looked troubled.

"It seems that your father will be there with all of Ravenswood's other principal investors from Bath with their guests, which means Howard Dill and Tilly and my cousin Parry and Mrs P. But Drake will be there as well, so there's government business to keep warm. There will be some MPs, a county MP called Mortimer-Buckley and Diarmuid Casey, definitely. General Palmer isn't available. Melbourne wants me there, which now means us. He likes me to be his eyes and ears when business includes Ravenswood and the Office. So my dear, now that you are in my confidence, make sure you also watch our host carefully, he's a dangerous customer. Your father is aware of this now through his links with Lord Melbourne, but please don't discuss it with him."

He looked down at her and was immediately distracted. He ran his hands over her and kissed her again. "Are you content about this?"

"Very," she breathed, her mouth opening to his.

Nathaniel pulled back. "And about limiting what you say to your father?"

She smiled back into his eyes. "Of course. I wouldn't share our confidences. As for the evening, it should not be too much of a chore. I like Diarmuid, and Coco of course, no doubt she will be there as well," she risked a glance at Nathaniel, but he seemed unmoved to hear her name. "But I must say I am not eager to spend long in the company of the host."

"So you still like Diarmuid, do you, Mrs Parry. Then he's one I shall be keeping a particularly close eye on."

"Well there's no need," she smiled again and pulled him back to her for another kiss.

But neither of them joked about Coco.

Pleased to change the subject, Emma sat up and began to collect the discarded envelopes.

"Oh look here, we missed this."

She rescued a sealed letter which had been re-directed.

"It has been sent from the Office in London," said Nathaniel, scrutinising the scrawled script, "but it looks like it started off in Paris." He smoothed out the single sheet and read aloud.

My dear friend,

I hope you received my letter which I sent last spring informing you of the successful conclusion of the trip I undertook in late 1831. I am in France in order to attend to some further business connected with that trip and discovered through contacts in Paris that you were still in England and had plans to

51

marry.

Congratulations to you and your bride whenever your wedding may be! I wish you good luck and hope to see you both in the near future. This will be sooner than I thought, as I have business in the Port of Liverpool where I can be contacted at the Golden Fleece Inn. I am sorry to say that the enterprise we were able to inconvenience after our last meeting has flourished despite our attentions, especially in Liverpool and London.

Perhaps we may discuss these matters together.

I remain, your faithful servant,
C.L.

"Who is C.L. Nathaniel?" asked Emma, but instantly thought better of it. "No, sorry, I should not have asked. I do understand that parts of your job are not to be discussed."

"Well said, Em," said Nathaniel thoughtfully. "But it looks as if you might meet this particular part so you need to know a few things. His name is Cornelius Lee and his permanent home, if he still has one, is in China. I regard him very highly and I know him to be a good man. I would not have been able to rescue Frances without him. However, having said that, it is important to know that he is connected with the Chinese government so his loyalties cannot lie with Britain. Will that do?"

As Emma nodded and sat up to gather together the rest of the scattered envelopes and packaging, Nathaniel put his hands behind his head and stretched out on the bed. The sight of his old friend's name had reawakened the sense of kinship and respect he had felt during their first meetings. He resolved to ensure that he would meet with his Chinese friend. At seventy odd miles from Liverpool to Anglesey it was only a matter of a day's travel on the mail coach. He grinned at the prospect and determined to write to Mr Cornelius Lee, care of the Golden Fleece.

The previous evening:
The Saracen's Head, Broad Street, Bath.

Sir Giles Mortimer-Buckley had had a strenuous and satisfying evening after a congenial day and was ensconced for a final drinking session in the smoke room of the Saracen's Head. He had started with an early session in the Pump Room where he had taken the waters, a full pint of it from the spring. It had been steamily hot and, in line with its reputation, was far from moreish, having an odd, metallic taste. He had quickly overlaid it with hot chocolate and Bath Buns. To follow there had been some gentle walking on the parades fuelled by regular meals in various restaurants, before he moved on to some successful play at a couple of gaming establishments. From the last of these, and following the advice of a fellow backgammon player, he had allowed himself to be led to a rather superior brothel. Though it was in the lower town, Madam Shadwell's was located in a terrace of substantial houses in Green Park and offered an imaginative array of services. It had been something of a slow evening in the house, and he had been able to choose from a bevy of assorted prostitutes, which paraded before him as he lounged on a striped sofa in the first floor drawing room.

To the tinkling accompaniment of the grand piano, he listened to the Madam offer an explanation of the catalogue of talents available and, waving aside some frankly alarming offers from a dominatrix in a leather carnival mask and another sadistic piece wielding a whip, he settled for a more conventional option. His companion for the evening, a statuesque hussy called Clari, had proved to be totally exhilarating and he had resolved to be back for more of the same before the end of the week and his return journey to London. The combination of her yokel's accent, her overflowing, bounteous bosom and the sway of her rolling hips transported him into a rural fantasy of peasant girls and hayricks. She was a far more glorious version of Maisie Trickett and with no strings attached. He toyed with asking her to wear a frilled cap next week. Innocent pleasures!

He had strolled back to the upper town with Babcock, his comrade from the backgammon club, and they had made their way to the Saracen's Head, a small gable-fronted hostelry in the centre of town. Settled in the smoke room and well attended by the waiters, they had attracted more of their own kind. By late evening they had formed a loud company, their booming conversation dominating the room and, depending on their tastes, entertaining or irritating the rest of the customers.

As ill luck would have it, it was to the Saracen's that Matthew Spence brought his mother's new lodger, Benjamin Prestwick. This was the venue for Matthew's usual Saturday night entertainment: an hour or two in the company of his employer, a barge owner by the name of Declan O'Dowd. This night they would have the novelty of Ben to vary the usual desultory talk of horses, barges, steam engines and the merits of competing local ciders. Matthew looked forward to a few more stories of Philip Spence, the father he could not remember, and his famous adventures in Spain. These had been provided by Ben throughout the day, suitably embroidered to please his old friend's son and calculated to make him well-disposed towards the visitor. Ben was unlikely to be able to pay more than one month's rent, despite his assurances to Old Tom, and Martha's good nature was going to be imposed upon for as long as she would stand it. The last years had not been kind to Benjamin Prestwick. As he had admitted to the company in Walcot Street earlier that day, his business ventures, financed by his share of Napoleon's gold, had failed, as had his marriage. He found himself alone in his old age, his only prospects being parish relief followed by a pauper's grave. As his miserable wanderings brought him back to the West Country he had started to think again about Martha and view her as something of a last hope.

They jawed until they had finished their third mugs of cider, all of Ben's having been at Matthew's expense, and then, reluctantly, they made a move to leave. Their path led them past the voluble group of swells by the smoke room door.

"So your people are still in Gloucestershire!" brayed one.

"Name again, Sir Giles! Must know 'em!"

"Mortimer-Buckley, old chap," drawled a voice.

It was unmistakable. Perhaps Ben was more attuned to his old life than he usually was after telling the tales of Spain all day. Perhaps it was also the freak coincidence of hearing again the name of Parry when the boy brought the cake from the wedding. Whatever it was, he stopped in his tracks and turned to that voice. It was him: there was the Captain, older and plumper, his features coarser, but still handsome. Stunned by the sight and sound from the past, Ben seized Matthew's arm.

"By God, there's moiy old Captain!" he gasped, causing Matthew and Declan to hold up and turn to gape at the gentlemen seated round the side table.

"Sir," said Ben, advancing to the group. "Captain Buckley, sir! Oiy last saw ye on the retreat to Corunna. The start of 1809 'twas! Moiy respects to ye, sir!"

Buckley surveyed the bent and bedraggled figure with horrified astonishment and quickly rose from his seat. He blundered round the chairs in his haste, excusing himself as he went, swiftly isolating his new chums from any exchanges he might have to make.

"Upon my soul," he said. "Private Prestwick. I did not know you survived the retreat."

More words were impossible.

Fortunately Benjamin Prestwick filled the void. He introduced Matthew, son of his old comrade Philip Spence, who he was certain Captain Buckley would remember from those old days. He introduced Mr Declan O'Dowd, Matthew's employer and proprietor of barges on the Bath run to Parker's Wharf in Bristol. He also, and in retrospect most unwisely, advertised his current status as tenant in the Walcot home of Matthew and the Widow Spence and expressed a firm desire that he should have the honour of speaking with the Captain at greater length some time in the very near future.

As their eyes locked, Buckley and Prestwick experienced the same vision, but took from it conclusions which were diametrically opposed. They were back on that westerly road to Corunna, night had fallen and a wicked wind blew. Cold and hungry, their small platoon of men had chanced on a village as yet unspoiled by the retreating army. At once and without leave they had fed on whatever could be found, to the bitter fury of the inhabitants, and followed up by draining the wine and spirit stores of every cottage. The night had disintegrated into carnage. Opposition was met by slaughter and the women suffered cruelly at the hands of the British soldiers amongst whom none had conducted themselves more despicably than Captain Giles Mortimer–Buckley. As dawn had broken, Ben had been in a shack with Buckley and another private, the family lying dead at Buckley's hands after his clumsy assault on the daughter and their desperate attempts at revenge, the other private reduced to a comatose bundle on the floor, sodden with drink. They had been discovered by a troop of redcoats sent by Sir John Moore to scour the rearguard for acts of villainy and summarily execute the perpetrators. Ben could see the drunken private now in his mind's eye, swinging on the end of a rope, accused and convicted on Buckley's word, and taking his place on the scaffold.

"Terrible toimes, Captain!" said Ben, slyly.

He saw before him a far better meal ticket than Martha could ever be. Concerning the sacking of the village, his silence had saved Buckley's life. Concerning the sustained looting of the gold and jewels, it had saved his reputation. Mr Parry would not have looked kindly on Buckley's appropriation of the additional shares.

"Terrible indeed," agreed Buckley, reading in Ben's survival and poverty as severe and present a threat as had ever menaced his wellbeing since the end of the wars. He would have made it his business to ensure Prestwick had never survived the retreat if he had known that he had lived. He managed a smile.

"We must indeed meet again my good fellow. I will pass through Bath again in a few days. Shall we say next Wednesday evening? Here at eight o'clock?"

"Oiy look forward to it, sir," said Ben, shaking Buckley's hand energetically, hardly able to believe his good fortune.

Buckley's reactions were not so sanguine. He made his excuses and toiled up Broad Street to his hotel, head bowed, suddenly exhausted by the prospect of what he now had to arrange. The difference between this ignominious return and his sprightly swagger into town that morning was profoundly depressing. On turning the corner he arrived at the front entrance of the York House, chilled to the bone and shivering, he passed the hall porter, ignored the servant's respectful greeting and retired to his room for the night. He tore off his clothes and threw them onto the carpet, fumbled into his flannel nightgown and jammed his nightcap onto his head.

"A drink," he muttered. "Need to warm up."

He poured himself a generous slug of whisky from the decanter he had wisely requested for his room that morning and sank into his armchair. Resolving that another one could not hurt, he drank another three glasses swiftly and, beginning to feel slightly better, he abandoned the glass and crept into bed. Warm at last beneath the blankets and an eiderdown, he dozed off fretfully into a disturbed sleep, crowded by dreams of dark nights on frozen mountains, the rattle of gunfire, blood and the sickly stench of bodies. He passed again through burning villages and saw the ravaged dead. Crying aloud he awoke briefly then sank again into sleep. As a blessed relief, instead of horror his dreams conjured up a vision of the buxom Clari, kneeling up above him in the bed on the second floor at Madam Shadwell's. He saw again her red lips and dark hair, heard her throaty chuckle as she rolled back her head, but instead of her strong arms reaching for him, well-muscled and supple, there came a creeping white cloud, sinuous and wreathing into the shape of other arms and of another face, the skeletal arms of a white sister with black cavernous eyes and a gash of a smile. He screamed in his sleep and woke lathered in sweat, reaching convulsively for his talisman, his Saint Christopher medal which had seen him safe through worse toils than this. But even as his grasping fingers closed on it, he sank again into the morass of nightmare. He saw a twitching figure on the gallows, and by its side the next condemned man, it was himself, and in the front row of the crowd were Izar and Amaia, crowing in victory, reaching out across the years.

"No, no!" he cried in anguish, and opening his eyes to look up he saw a woman and a child. "No, Maisie, damn you, I told you that you could not have a child! This cannot be!"

As his focus sharpened he became aware of the cold morning light, which allowed him to recognise the matronly chambermaid and her assistant, both wearing the conventional uniform of the York House.

"Oiy be Dorcas, sir, with Tabby," said the maid, peering at him with interest.

So great was his relief and shame he knew not whether to laugh or cry.

Chapter 2

Six o'clock in the evening: 27th January, 1833. The carriage drive to Arno's Tower, Arno's Vale, near Bristol.

The wheels crackled over the frozen gravel of Ravenswood's drive as Captain Peterson's *Berlin* rounded the last bend before they reached the house. All four horses in the team were blowing hard after the run from Bath; their breath flying behind them in steaming clouds and their coats glistening with sweat in defiance of the piercing cold. Gas flares illuminated the dark road at intervals, flooding it with pools of light which caught the heaving flanks of the horses as they passed and lit the faces of the passengers with a fleeting pallor. The four inside passengers were tightly packed, sitting two by two on the bench seats facing each other, knees carefully positioned to the side to avoid collisions. The Captain and his wife had their backs to the horse and driver, favouring the newly-weds with the best view.

"It is bitterly cold in here, Oliver," complained Lydia Peterson to her husband, as she retreated still further into her fur-lined cloak and pulled the lap robe higher. "You ought to have had the foresight to order warmed bricks for our feet."

"Yes my dear, that would have been a damned good idea," agreed her husband. "It's even colder now that we've left the city. Dashed isolated, what! Good duck shooting though, I believe."

"Look! There is the house," said Emma, pointing ahead excitedly. "What are those huge stone figures? They look quite sinister."

"Surely not! Whatever do you mean?" snapped her mother, determined to quash any negativity which might mar the evening. She had warned her husband repeatedly over the preceding week about the doubtful look he had taken to assuming at the mere mention of Edwin Ravenswood's name. She had been looking forward to the dinner enormously and it had been too bad of Oliver to entertain any reservations concerning their host. He and Mr Ravenswood had been such friends until quite recently. The praise for the shooting was a very good sign and she would not have Emma casting aspersions which might fuel the estrangement. "I am sure that they will look quite splendid in the daylight, my dear. Now, remind me again Oliver, where are the other Ravenswood properties?"

Captain Peterson and his wife exchanged polite celebratory gossip about their hosts until the coachman reined in the team at the main entrance to Arno's Tower and all four visitors were handed out by footmen in the Ravenswood livery. Nathaniel glanced away from the flunkeys, and as he expected, he could just make out the shapes of more men guarding the wings of the house, their dark coats hardly distinguishable from the shadows. He looked back to the black mass looming above them, the door framed by stone griffin sentinels. Lit from below by gas flares, they seemed to leap up before him: gothic colossi, black in tooth and claw, investing the pillared doorway with a macabre grandeur. Emma had been quite right. Designed to alarm, they were part of a stage-set for Ravenswood's own *Divine Comedy*.

"Abandon hope all ye who enter here!" muttered Nathaniel to himself, taking advantage of the covering chatter provided by Mrs Peterson.

"What's that?" whispered Emma.

"Dante. We are passing through the vestibule to the underworld, or at least that's what he seems to be hinting at. Don't be intimidated, sweetheart."

"I'm not. Which particular circle of hell do you think would best suit our host?"

"He is greedy and adept at violence, fraud and treachery, which are the fourth, seventh, eighth and ninth circles."

Emma smiled thinly and followed her parents up the steps.

Whilst the Petersons and the Parrys were being shown to the drawing room, three more carriages were approaching Arno's Tower for the dinner appointment. The first was a private coach belonging to Dr Parry and housed not only that genial medical man, but also his wife, and their friends Howard Dill and Tilly Vere. The mood in the coach was buoyant as Dr Parry's anecdotes were flowing well and their guests were not only making all of the right noises, but also topping some of his tales with outrageous ones of their own and generally earning their seats. They were followed by a hired vehicle conveying John and Lottie Drake and Sir Giles Mortimer-Buckley where the mood had turned sombre after John Drake had admitted that they might be joined by the colleague whose wedding he had attended the previous day.

"You say his name is Parry," said Buckley querulously. "Are you sure? The son of Owen Parry who served under Castlereagh in the wars?"

"The very same," said Drake bitterly. "Not my choice old boy, nor Ravenswood's I might add. Melbourne particularly wanted him to attend as he and I worked together down here in '31. Melbourne valued his contributions, which were in fact damned undiplomatic in view of some business developments I was negotiating with Ravenswood. However, he will likely have left already for his honeymoon. He didn't mention the dinner when I spoke to him yesterday." Seeking to make the best of it, he added, "And even if he does dine, we four are definitely the only guests who have been invited to stay."

"I would have thought that your presence would have been sufficient as far as the Office was concerned," persisted Buckley. "We have important trading issues to discuss. He isn't a shareholder in Ravenswood's business is he?"

"I doubt it."

There seemed nothing more to be said, and Sir Giles Mortimer-Buckley turned his face resolutely to the rushing black void outside the window.

Rocketing along half a mile behind the London visitors and pulled by a sleek black cob, was Diarmuid Casey's brand new *Tilbury* gig. It was small, fast, sporty and dangerous and as such appealed to both Diarmuid and his guest, Mademoiselle Colette Montrachet, who were both set up on the single seat under the hood, cocooned in blankets and taking turns to drive. This allowed Diarmuid to show off his talent and his possessions, and helped Coco to relax and work off nervous energy.

"So you have never been here before?" she said, as she passed the reins to Diarmuid for the final stretch down the drive.

"I have not," said Diarmuid, taking in the extravagant gas flares, broad greenswards and deep woods. "'Tis a grand estate. It surely is. Crime pays, Coco. But I don't have to tell you that do I?"

Coco smiled. "I haven't the slightest idea what you mean. All my transactions are transparently virtuous. I cater for important needs and am given rewards for my efforts. As for tonight?" she shrugged her shoulders. "I am on a mission to view my family's property. Nothing criminal there, darling."

Diarmuid planted a gentle kiss on her cheek as he reined in at the entrance. "Here we are. And remember, discretion is the better part."

Coco looked at him and kissed him back hard on the mouth. Her strange amber eyes, gold flecked and brilliant, were alight with mischief. "It may be so, but it is not the only part I intend to play."

After a welcome interlude of warmth and drinking in the drawing room, Amanda Ravenswood had acted the grand hostess to perfection and transferred her guests smoothly to the dining room. She allowed her footman to slide her seat forward and she settled into it. As planned, Sir Giles had led her out and seated her at the table, exchanging amiable pleasantries, pressing her arm confidentially, and flattering her. He was handsome enough, early fifties she supposed; he had ten years on Edwin and lacked the sculpted rigour of his body, but he had kept a debonair swagger, still quite the "dasher". It had amused her that Lady Mortimer-Buckley had cried off. Perhaps the West Country had no appeal when one lived in Mayfair? It certainly would not have had any for Amanda. She had only been to London a handful of times, Paris twice and Dublin once. It was a matter of continuing annoyance that Edwin had resisted all of her attempts to arrange more trips. But she dared not ask again.

The absence of Sir Giles's wife, without notice, had caused a gap to open at the bottom of the table and Edwin had brought up the rear of the dining party alone as they processed from the drawing room. He now sat opposite Amanda at the far end of the table with a space to his right, where a footman was busily clearing the place setting. Edwin was talking animatedly to Captain Peterson, who she knew socially as a principal investor in the Ravenswood shipping interests. Her husband looked stunningly handsome as he worked on the Captain, a bluff, ruddy customer who had been unaccountably distant of late and needed softening up. She liked to look at her husband, especially from a distance. Living with Edwin was rather like dancing on the edge of the abyss.

She glanced round the rest of the table and felt very satisfied with her arrangements. The dining room was at its magnificent best: richly warm and heavy with the scent of flowers and fruits. Golden candlelight flickered from the wall sconces and the table candelabra, showing everyone to best advantage. Behind every seat was a footman: silent, white-wigged and extravagantly liveried. Fortunately Edwin had been too preoccupied with other matters and she had been allowed to arrange the formalities of the evening. It had given her great delight to construct her table, based not purely on social convention and business interests but

63

also her own needs. Some rules had to apply. She had to be led in by Sir Giles, as the principal guest. Apart from his title and existing family connections, from well before her time as a Ravenswood, Edwin was particularly keen to tap him over the next couple of days for investment in the company, so his position was not negotiable. She still regarded Lottie Drake as a friend of sorts, or at any rate a good contact, but the relationship had soured in the face of Lottie's persistent play for Edwin. She had been shameless in her pursuit and Amanda was in the midst of a campaign to bring her down. When Amanda had written the cards pairing the couples for dining she had taken particular delight in joining Lottie with the rotund and jolly Howard Dill, whose besotted attachment to Tilly Vere made him invulnerable, even if Lottie were bored enough to set about him.

John Drake recognised Lottie's enthusiasm for Edwin and had become something of a partner in misery for Amanda. He deserved some pleasurable distraction, so she had paired him with Tilly Vere. This choice had just a little touch of malice to spice it, as she had gathered that Tilly and John had known each when young and attended the same Assemblies in Frome. If John were to be particularly gallant to Tilly, Lottie might be jealous and taste a little of her own medicine. Amanda homed in on Tilly's fluting little voice whilst still smiling at Sir Giles and nodding approval of his story about a triumphant grouse shoot in Scotland. Tilly was pretty, frothy and superficial, attributes which were clearly appealing to John Drake.

"But you were by far the handsomest young man in Frome, Mr Drake!" Tilly said in conclusion, after a particularly extravagant run of compliments, whilst continuing to pat his arm affectionately. "We all missed you frightfully when you left for London. You say you worked in France, how exciting! Do tell me what you enjoyed most."

Amanda could not bear to hear any more of the same, and looked further down the table to John's handsome subordinate, foisted on them by an official letter from the office of Lord Melbourne himself. She understood that his marriage had taken place only the previous day, and it had amused her to link the new couple with tempting partners. The dashing Nathaniel Parry had been paired with the French harlot that the Irish MP Casey paraded around with, whilst Casey himself entertained the little wife. There had been gossip about Nathaniel Parry and Coco Montrachet and they seemed to be getting on well. Emma in her turn seemed to be listening, entranced, to Diarmuid, yet Amanda was piqued to note that the newly-weds still took the opportunity to exchange glances, full of love and deep joy: quite tiresome for an observer. She also noticed with some bitterness that Emma Parry was no ordinary "little wife". Apart from being statuesque, a good head higher than Amanda herself, Emma had presence, a ready laugh and plenty to say. This was rather a shame, as Nathaniel Parry had appealed to Amanda from first sighting. The rest of the table had afforded less opportunity for amusement. Dr Parry and Mrs Peterson were old friends, as were Captain Peterson and Mrs Parry, and they partnered each other with pleasure. The only comfort gleaned was to punish Edwin by corralling him at the end of the table with that respectable quartet, well away from the sexual allure of the predatory Lottie and the pretty faces of the rest of the young women.

Amanda sat up poised and elegant in her chair as she surveyed her guests and waited for the white soup and sherry. Despite trivial set-backs, she felt oddly victorious, a rare feeling over the last few years after those first few months of marriage. If she squinted down at her chest she could just see the pendant of her heavy gold necklace, the emeralds flashing in the candlelight, and on her brow was the light touch of her new diamond tiara. No jewels rivalled hers around her table. Not even The Honourable Mrs Lottie Drake was wearing anything remarkable. She was pleased that Edwin had reminded her to wear the emeralds; as Sir Giles had originally presented them to her mother-in-law. That would create a pleasant talking point. Things really could not be better. She felt perfect, though at a cost, as her corset was laced viciously tight to show off the sleek lines of her new white satin gown and serve up maximum breast cleavage to be admired. Dairmuid's gaze had certainly lingered and Sir Giles had barely been able to keep his eyes off her chest. She had even caught a flash of envy in the eyes of Mademoiselle Montrachet. As the soup made its way round the table she reminded herself severely that one spoonful was her limit. It was a pity; as she loved almond soup, so exquisite and wildly fashionable, she could have made a whole meal of it, but there were other courses to consider. The tighter the corset, the more soup was left in the bowl. It was instructive to see that she, Lottie, Tilly, Mrs Peterson and Sir Giles left the most.

By the time the turbot had been finished Edwin Ravenswood was certain that Captain Peterson had discovered something unpalatable about his business but realised he was too closely tied through his investments to sever connections. It was also plain that Peterson still had government links and must know that Lord Palmerston supported his swashbuckling narcotics trade with China, would encourage more of it when the East India Company's monopoly lapsed and would keep a blind eye turned to any of his other endeavours, provided that they were not brought to his attention. The most discreet of these, the trafficking of women to the east, had suffered a set back over a year ago and Edwin suspected that the Captain had had wind of it. Despite this, the host felt more relaxed. Peterson was in check, virtually checkmate, and Ravenswood Enterprises was in no danger of losing that particular source of investment.

Whilst Edwin and the Captain had talked, Lydia Peterson and the senior Parrys had enjoyed their food and drink, blissfully unaware of the tensions at the end of the table. Diarmuid Casey, as Amanda had hoped, had made himself most agreeable to Emma Parry, as had John to Tilly Vere. He had been totally won over by her blue eyes, wide as saucers, and her drifts of blonde corkscrew curls: she had the happy knack of making any man feel that he was the most eligible creature in the world and John Drake was basking in the attention like a bull seal. However, Amanda had not foreseen that Lottie too would have an enjoyable evening. She had underestimated Howard Dill, who was as charming a man as one could wish to meet, and had overestimated Lottie. Once she realised the extent of Howard's wealth and linked it to his good nature, being attended by him was nothing short of delightful. At any lull in that attention, Lottie happily transferred her gracious appreciation to Sir Giles.

Another reaction, which would have surprised Amanda if she had known of it, was the agitation she caused for her principal guest. She could not miss the fact that Sir Giles seemed mightily impressed by her. They talked a great deal and he clearly admired her as a woman. What she was ignorant of was the consternation caused by her necklace. As he stole regular furtive glances at the display on her bosom she decided to open the batting on that topic.

"I see you recognise my emeralds, Sir Giles! I was so delighted when my husband presented them to me after his mother's death and I know their history!"

Sir Giles's stomach turned over at the thought of what was to follow. Quickly, he glanced over the table, hoping that Nathaniel Parry was engaged elsewhere to give him a chance to close the subject down, but it was too late. His heart lurched as his eyes met Parry's; the blighter had heard every word.

"Mrs Ravenswood," said Nathaniel smoothly. "I could not help but overhear your remark about the emeralds. I must confess that they had caught my eye earlier as they are in precisely the same setting as my mother's sapphires! Those curious links and the double chain are unmistakeable!"

Emma had looked up, smiling, as she heard his voice rise to reach Amanda at the top of the table. He drew her in.

"My dear! You see Mrs Ravenswood's emeralds? It was to be a surprise but I must tell you now. When we arrive in Wales I am going to retrieve my mother's necklace from the bank and present it to you as a wedding gift! You have a preview of the setting. It is an exact match and Mrs Ravenswood tells us that she knows some details of their provenance."

He looked encouragingly at Amanda, who was happy to oblige and, unlike Nathaniel, entirely missed the collapse of Sir Giles Mortimer-Buckley's features. They had crumpled like a rag as he foresaw what might develop into a third torment to add to his other two.

"Yes, indeed," said Amanda, smiling coyly. "Sir Giles brought them back from Spain during the wars. He was in the retreat to Corunna, weren't you Sir Giles? After most distinguished service. These emeralds are French and were part of his reward. He was a close family friend and gave them to my late mother-in-law as a gift. In fact," she added, looking up to see a procession of footmen arriving with the next course, "we have introduced two courses this evening to celebrate Sir Giles's war career. Here is the *poulet à la portugaise*, and later we shall have *aubergines à l'espagnole*. Two dishes from the Iberian Peninsula, specially created in your honour by our French chef!"

Sir Giles mustered a faint smile as the chicken arrived in its lurid red bell pepper sauce. It reminded him of blood. He felt nauseous and looked away from the table, beyond the food and his hostess, to the burning fire and the rising smoke which bloomed and curled as it lifted. And in it he saw the dark shapes of his nightmares: the cavernous eyes, and beneath, a gash of a smile. The room seemed to swirl away and in his throat he tasted again the raw Basque spirit. Horrified, he turned his head back to the table and fixed his eyes on Drake who sat opposite him, busily sniggering into the ear of the little blonde. He must not let his mind wander; must not let his imagination run away with him. But as he marshalled his wits, a hoarse voice whispered in his head.

"Keep sharp, Giles. You can do it."

It was not his voice, not his thought. He felt a twinge of fear but dismissed it. The advice was sound. There was no need for Parry to make any unfavourable links. Buckley shook his head clear and turned to look past Drake and Tilly to Nathaniel Parry, who was innocently occupied with the chicken.

"For God's sake, Buckley!" He rebuked himself sternly. "Parry was a mere child at the time. His father would never have shared intelligence information then, or later, he was a man of integrity. And he knew nothing of the second division of the spoils. We parted south of San Sebastian. He knew nothing of the road to Corunna." He had said it slowly, willing himself to believe it and accept that the damage could be limited. He rallied, permitted himself to smile again, complimented his hostess on her impeccable taste and began a lengthy monologue on Iberian cuisine.

But Nathaniel was not the only diner to have heard Amanda's announcement. Coco's eyes were glinting as she assessed the new situation. Perhaps Nathaniel also needed to be relieved of his ill-gotten gains. She had had a pleasant evening thus far, being entertained by Nathaniel on her right and Dr Parry on her left. There had been plenty of time, as she turned politely from one to the other, to inspect the Ravenswood assets. The dining room was vast and stately, the walls hung with expensive last century oils, mainly portraits and pastoral scenes, many of which were clearly European, a room stressing wealth and possession. The whole mansion was designed to inspire, and not just feelings of envy, but also of awe, and the discomfort of foreboding. Coco saw in Edwin Ravenswood's bleak good looks all the warning signs which would make her reject his attentions. She did not envy Amanda, but rather pitied her. Before she had felt jealousy and had scorned her starved looks and her harshness. Now she had some idea of the hell of her private life, but it would not alter her purpose. The emeralds were from the Montrachet collection and Amanda would be relieved of them.

A champagne sorbet cleansed their palates and was followed by a rich duck course, which allowed free rein for the French chef's national loyalties. Ravenswood had concluded his assessment of Captain Peterson and Coco had attracted him.

"Mademoiselle Montrachet," he said, catching her eye. "You might find this dish more to your taste. It's French, *canard à la rouennaise*. I can vouch for the meat, I shot it myself."

"Do you like shooting birds, Mr Ravenswood," said Coco, meeting his glance.

"Of course. I am a hunter, Mademoiselle. Now tell me about yourself, are you familiar with Rouen?"

The bottom of the table fell quiet, not just out of respect for the host but also in curiosity.

"I'm afraid not. I have lived in Paris most recently and know the south quite well."

"Do you have family there, Mademoiselle?" enquired Mrs Peterson, unable to stop herself, despite her usual reluctance to converse with Coco. If her host deigned to speak with her so freely, it was only good manners to do likewise.

"I have a brother in the Medoc, Madam," said Coco, but regretted it instantly. The desire to show she was not alone in the world had clouded her judgement. For reasons of her own, Jules and all his doings should have remained unknown.

"And this is a *bordelaise* sauce, if I am not mistaken, but with the addition of duck liver. Both variations will be popular in the Medoc, I would imagine," said Mrs Parry.

"You are absolutely right, Madam," said Amanda. "Our chef is from the south-west of France."

"And is your brother connected with the Bordeaux wine trade, Mademoiselle Montrachet?" enquired Dr Parry, beaming down at Coco.

"Ah well, Doctor," she said evasively, "few who live in the Medoc are not."

"You must know that one of our Bath MPs owns a number of vineyards in that area," said Dr Parry, warming to his theme. "General Palmer I mean of course, not Mr Roebuck. Ha! Ha! What a thought, "Tear 'em" Roebuck concerning himself with the cultivation of vines! Not quite his style, what! I'd be surprised if there were a rural side to that gentleman. Too busy haranguing the House! However, as I was saying, the General has had property there since the end of the wars. Palmer's Claret is still a famous drink and it was quite the toast of London at one point! Should have been here tonight, shouldn't he Ravenswood?

But he's too busy in Town. The General owns vineyards next to Margaux and also on the right bank of the Garonne. Do you know them, Mademoiselle?"

Surprisingly, Ravenswood himself rescued Coco, first as he introduced the distinguished 1814 Chateau Palmer, which had been provided in the expectation of Charles Palmer's attendance, and then at greater length as he launched into a spirited description of his wine collection. This side-tracked Dr Parry and attracted the attention of all the guests. This was a favourite topic of Ravenswood's and it saw them through to the serving of the *aubergines à l'espagnole*, when Buckley had another difficult phase as the conversation turned inexorably to the war in Spain.

"My father also served in the Iberian campaign, Sir Giles," said Nathaniel amiably. "Isn't it remarkable that you both had trophies from the same collection! Did you ever meet? His name was Owen Parry. He served the Office in Constantinople and had travelled in the Far East."

Buckley pretended to think deeply. "You know, Mr Parry, I do think his name strikes a chord. But it is such a long time ago! Forgive me, I cannot say more."

John Drake shot him a glance, doubting he could carry off the bluff, but incredibly, he seemed to have done just that. Buckley dared to relax and started to believe that he was off the hook, unaware that Nathaniel continued to observe him, watching the man struggle with a wave of relief and the growing heat in the room, watching his face turn as red as the wine and his fingers tug surreptitiously at his collar for more air. Nathaniel was convinced that neither the high-banked fire nor the excessive feeding and drinking explained all of Sir Giles's discomfort and continued to observe him as general conversations broke out and moved the focus of attention away from 1809.

The evening wore on without further indiscretion and dinner continued successfully past the Spanish style aubergines to the desserts, the finale being the *iced bombe*, 1820 style, with maraschino flavouring. Immediately after the barrage of praise died, Amanda rose to lead the ladies out to the drawing room.

"Gentlemen," she smiled, "if you will excuse us."

"Now, gentlemen," said Ravenswood, as the footmen closed the double doors and the men resumed their seats, "first to our port. Again, an offering selected in honour of Sir Giles and his adventures against the French." He allowed himself a satisfied smile of self-congratulation as a decanter was borne in on a silver tray by one of the footmen. "May I present the 1815 Porto Ferreira, Waterloo vintage."

In the respectful silence which fell at the mention of a treat so sublime, Buckley winced and Drake ran his tongue over his lips in greedy expectation.

Ravenswood continued. "You may also smoke and, forgive me, but as you know we must also now turn to business."

The gentlemen moved to Ravenswood's end of the table as another footman removed the cloth and others brought an additional array of *digestifs*: madeira, various brandies and *eaux de vie*, offerings provided merely to reinforce the image of the generous host rather than with any thought that they might be of interest after the majestic port. Ravenswood dismissed the servants, as tradition demanded, and filled Dr Parry's glass, then his own, before passing the decanter to Captain Peterson. Its progress past Dairmuid and Howard was swift, but when it reached Buckley it became marooned. Ravenswood's steely glare bored into him impatiently.

"The port stands by you, Sir Giles."

"Indeed, indeed. Thank you, Ravenswood," blustered Buckley, rapidly filling his glass and allowing the decanter to renew its progress. Once John Drake and Nathaniel had provided themselves with full glasses the host was able to proceed.

"Your good health, gentlemen!" he said, re-assuming the role of genial host and raising his glass. "And also, if I may, a toast to our mutual enterprises." The glasses landed back on the table, spills were held to the candle flames, cigars were lit, and all eyes turned again to Edwin Ravenswood. He raked the company with a penetrating glance and made a snap decision to dispatch the business very quickly indeed. Apart from treating his principal investors to dinner, assuring himself of government support *via* Drake and wooing the MPs, his biggest concern had been to assess Peterson's attitude, which had caused him some concern. He was a major investor who had also been shaping up as an enemy. In theory, they should have been even closer allies as Lord Melbourne the Home Secretary had encouraged the Lord Lieutenant to secure both their appointments as magistrates, but he knew that it had been Lord Palmerston's insistence that had secured his position in the first place. His shipping activities and successful opium trade with China had impressed the Foreign Secretary, but by some means, Melbourne had been apprised of his other activities and the business had been seriously damaged. He was satisfied now that Peterson was not going to be obstructive, but the attitude of Peterson's new son-in-law was more difficult to gauge. Young Parry had not been on the original guest list and Edwin had no intention of discussing more business than was necessary in his hearing. It had been disappointing that the only Members available for the dinner had been Sir Giles and Casey, but he would make the most of a bad job.

"It is a pleasure to welcome Mr John Drake and Mr Nathaniel Parry, who represent the views of the noble Lords. Please assure them that my businesses will be delighted to take up some of the slack when open season is declared on the Chinese tea trade. In conjunction with that new business, my opium runs from India are poised to expand in the very near future. As you will know, I've profited substantially since the Company monopoly expired there in 1813." He smiled without mirth, his eyes implacable. "My new vessel, like the rest, custom built in America, is in the final stage of commissioning for her first voyage to the East and I am actively pursuing additional investment. As most of you will be aware, extensive repairs are still being carried out on the *Mathilda* which was burnt out by rioters in '31. Honourable Members, Sir Giles, Mr Casey, perhaps you would like to join our syndicate at some point?"

Nathaniel felt the familiar flood of relief that his part in the destruction of the *Mathilda* remained undetected. This house was not a place for discoveries or confessions. The men he had seen outside would not be the only ones in Ravenswood's entourage and he sensed that retribution would be illegal, unpleasant and swift. He watched the responses narrowly. Sir Giles seemed to have regained his *sang froid,* and become effusive, promising much, which he looked forward to discussing in detail before he returned to London. Diarmuid blustered about his capital being tied up in extensive investment in French vineyards after a few long evenings with the persuasive General Palmer. Nathaniel had to suppress a smile and wondered if Diarmuid was drunk and simply hung his excuse on the last bit of table conversation he could remember, or if there really was any truth in it. Knowing the turbulent state of Diarmuid's finances he doubted it.

"Couldn't recommend you putting much his way, old chap!" said Howard, his glasses flashing at Diarmuid in the candlelight. "You know Charles Palmer has sunk thousands into his new vines, with no pay-off to date. It's not going as well as it was. I urge you to consider Mr Ravenswood's suggestion. My family has had money in Bristol shipping for generations and never looked back. Sugar's down and the western run's had its day, but for an up and coming young man you cannot better the Far East trade and we are on the crest of that wave, wouldn't you say, Ravenswood!"

"Certainly: and will remain so."

John Drake knew that Ravenswood needed to shield any further discussion from Nathaniel Parry and moved in swiftly.

"So, Mr Ravenswood, on behalf of His Majesty's Government I can assure you and your investors that you will be given every assistance in the pursuance of your trade. The next phase in the development of the eastern market and the anticipated opportunities in tea trading are ideal for your business, as you say, in line with your current enterprises, and all your endeavours will be supported. Gentlemen, may I propose a toast to the future!"

The rest of the hour spent apart from the ladies was measured out in port for the majority, though Buckley, Drake and Diarmuid Casey were tempted to diversify and moved on to brandy, after which Drake coaxed Buckley into a boisterous mood. Soon he and Casey were taking turns to tell increasingly audacious tales. These stimulated ready guffaws from John Drake, Howard Dill and Dr Parry, coaxed reluctant chuckles from the Captain and Nathaniel but attracted only stony indifference from their host.

The ladies first withdrew to the white and gold drawing room where the guests had been received and Amanda served coffee with the help of a footman. The two matrons and Tilly set the pace, admiring the *décor* and giving Amanda opportunities to show off, whilst Lottie entertained herself by examining her hostess, Coco and Emma. She was pleased that there would be no embroidery session that night, she knew Amanda well enough to be able to rely on that. The tyranny of the needle ruined many an evening and the absence of such annoyance at Arno's Tower was one of its many attractions. It had been unfortunate that Amanda had taken exception to her little game with Edwin. Her master plan was for Amanda to entertain herself with John until she tired of Edwin, but it had not been working out well. Perhaps they were too alike. She looked again at Amanda; avaricious, jealous, anxiously thin, yet also ruthless with those strange pointed eyeteeth. So like John, who was foxy yet also insecure. He was good for the long term as his ambitions were paying off, but she needed variation, a little danger and excitement. She smiled to herself, reflecting on what the night might yet bring.

Emma Parry, the new bride, was of less interest, as were her connections. Lottie always saw Nathaniel Parry as a rather worthy subordinate of John's, upright and depressingly strong on moral rectitude, though she knew Amanda was taken by his looks. By all accounts he should not have been invited and was here on sufferance because of some ruling from Melbourne. However, Coco Montrachet was altogether more interesting.

Lottie had spent time in Paris in the 1820s and recognised in Coco the same effortless elegance which had fascinated her there. It was rumoured that she had been a high-class courtesan. Perhaps she could learn a few things from Mademoiselle. Amanda obviously had the same idea, tiring of the subject of drapes she had turned to Coco for some light relief.

"So, Mademoiselle Montrachet, you know Paris well?"

"Oh yes," said Coco. "I believe we attended the same *soirée* in the winter of 1828. The Duchesse d'Abrantès was the hostess and I was in the party of the Marquis de la Blanquefort."

Amanda and Lottie drew visibly closer, leaning in towards Coco as she spoke.

"How fascinating!" said Amanda, smiling, eyebrow raised at Lottie, to signal revenge for the hours of torment she had previously endured. Amanda's failure to penetrate high society on her trips to Paris had entertained Lottie hugely and encouraged her to annoy the provincial Mrs Ravenswood with tales of aristocratic revelry at Versailles. If only Amanda had known that the Marquis was at the Duchess's gathering, she could have scored that particular point much earlier.

"Yes, quite diverting," said Coco, radiating charm, "but I am having a marvellous time in England. And this is the most wonderful house I have visited since I arrived! I gather it has been constructed recently and I have also heard that the design is exceptional. I have spent much time in older buildings in France but am longing to see innovative architecture, especially that which re-imagines the Gothic so splendidly. The Marquis himself was able to reclaim a number of his properties when Louis XVIII returned to the throne so at present he has to concentrate wholly on restoration." As the men were missing and it was a time to exchange confidences she risked another reference to her family. "My dear brother is renovating and extending a *château* in the Medoc. He sees it very much as a family project and often asks for my views on design. Mrs Ravenswood, would it be too much to ask to be allowed to see the upper floors here?"

"By all means, it would be a pleasure," said Amanda. "Would anyone else care to join us for ten minutes?"

"I'm happy here, thank you," said Lottie quickly. As a house guest she had plenty of time for snooping.

Coco, Tilly, Emma and Lydia Peterson had already risen to their feet but the senior Mrs Parry declined.

"I noticed your impressive staircases, Mrs Ravenswood," she said gravely. "I will remain with Mrs Drake, if I may."

Coco could not believe her luck. A brief idea of the lay-out of the house, the design of its shutters and the extent of its security was all she needed and it was to be handed to her on a plate. "Altogether," she reflected to herself, whilst smiling amiably at her hostess, "quite remarkable progress." It was the icing on the cake, as it had already been a very satisfactory evening. The matrons had been forced to be gracious to her, Amanda Ravenswood had proved astonishingly amenable and she even sensed some fellow feeling in the haughty Lottie. Emma had been on sparkling form and good company. Coco exchanged a glance with the new Mrs Parry as they moved to the door.

"Marriage suits you, Emma," she said.

"Thank you," said Emma warily, but liked the twinkle in Coco's eye and added smiling, "Does it show?"

Amanda led the way from the brilliant drawing room to the wide hall with its sweeping staircase circling round in a great arc to the grand first-floor landing. As the visitors followed Amanda up the marble stairs, Lydia Peterson looked about her in such a state of reverential awe that she missed her footing and would have slipped if Coco's arm had not darted out to save her before she went down.

"The music room, ballroom, library and art gallery are all on this floor," Amanda was saying. "They all have beautiful views. Let's start with the music room."

"What a superb collection of instruments, Mrs Ravenswood!" exclaimed Coco, relinquishing her grip on Lydia and flitting from harp to piano, to the instruments mounted on stands and then to the windows, inspecting the balcony and shutters as she did so. "Do you lock any of these violins away in safes to protect them?"

"No need," said Amanda with a short laugh. "My husband's men patrol the grounds at night, we have no security worries!"

"Do you play?" said Coco. "I confess I would want to be in this room all the day!"

"I do, but have little time to devote to music," said Amanda, leading them back to the landing. "As you see, the bedroom and dressing room floors above all look down on the hall from the circular balconies."

"And do the upper floor rooms all have the wonderful balcony views that the music room has?" inquired Coco innocently. "I would want the room in the very centre of the second floor I think. It seems larger than the others."

"That is mine," said Amanda triumphantly. "And yes, the balcony is marvellous. You can see right over to the wood. Come into the gallery now with the lights out and the shutters open."

They trooped into the darkened room and made for the French windows which could be opened onto the stone balcony. Standing close and quietly, looking into the night, they saw a sloping green and in the distance, the tree line, misty and indistinct.

Suddenly Emma caught her breath. "Oh look!" she gasped. "Someone is running by the edge of the trees! He's carrying a heavy bag."

"Where?"

Amanda pressed closer to the window, and the rest peered out in the direction of Emma's pointing finger.

"I can't see anyone," said Coco.

"Just mist my dear, do not cause consternation," cautioned Lydia.

Emma dropped her hand. "He's gone," she said, puzzled. "Just there towards the sundial, he disappeared."

"It must have been one of the men," said Amanda dismissively. "Now come with me." They followed her, but not before Emma looked out once more across the cold garden, and saw four of Ravenswood's men talking in a group, well away from the trees and the gathering mist.

"If you look up you might see a feature with which my husband is particularly pleased, but our view rather depends on the moon."

The moon was obliging, for when the women looked up towards the skylight at the top of the central tower they saw its stained glass brightly illuminated by a ghostly white lunar glare, which spilled down icy splinters of coloured light.

"Oh!" squeaked Tilly. "It's a dragon! Is there a Saint George?"

"No," said Amanda. "It's part of my husband's homage to the East. He has a suite of rooms dedicated to his collection on the ground floor of the west wing, but this keeps its eye on the whole house."

The women surveyed the green and silver scales, the licking flames gushing from its mouth, the leathery wings. Despite the beauty of the work, the malevolence was palpable.

"I see now," continued Tilly, quite unaware of any threat. "It has blue eyes like the *Blue Dragon* itself, Mr Ravenswood's ship!"

"Yes," said Amanda. "Mr Ravenswood tells me that this isn't like the dragon Saint George kills. That is a monster, but this one is the eastern dragon, it symbolises health and banishes evil spirits. Rather like the Welsh dragon."

"He still looks," Emma struggled for the polite word, "formidable. He is a force of nature."

Amanda laughed shortly. "Yes, he is, rather like my husband."

Shortly after they returned to the drawing room, the gentlemen joined them. Amanda played the piano and Lottie was persuaded to sing, which exhausted the matrons in the audience, and within another hour carriages were called. The two Bath bound vehicles were quieter on the return. In one, Nathaniel and Emma saved their deconstructions of the evening until they had privacy, and allowed Lydia Peterson to enlarge on the excellence of the event. Tucked into the *Tilbury,* Coco drove and kept her discoveries to herself, allowing the drunken Diarmuid to entertain her. Meanwhile, as the night wore on and the hostess and the guests turned in for the night, silence fell in Arno's Tower. The host remained in the drawing room in solitary state, stoking up the dying embers of the fire. But he did not remain alone for long, as a steady snore sounded from the second floor rooms allocated to the Drakes, Lottie slipped out onto the landing. Barefoot and wrapped in a silk dressing gown, she closed the door considerately on her sleeping husband and made her way to her rendezvous by the drawing room fire.

Morning: 28th January, 1833.
The Parry Residence, Saint James's Square, Bath.

Nathaniel and Emma had left the drapes open so they would wake early. Emma had looked pale and exhausted after the coach ride home with her parents, so Nathaniel had postponed any discussion of the evening at Arno's Tower to the morning. He had chosen to lie awake for an hour or two to review the intelligence gained and decide how much he wanted to discuss with her. He had no intention of burdening her with the full details of Ravenswood's Asiatic contacts and his lucrative line in kidnapped women and girls for the overseas flesh trades, but he was sure that her growing attachment to Frances would lead to her finding out eventually. Sadly, it seemed that Ravenswood was still prospering and poised to expand in all directions. The *Mathilda* was to be refurbished despite his best efforts and the new vessel would soon be afloat. He had no doubt that he was not yet trusted by Drake and Ravenswood as he had been pointedly excluded from the appeal for additional investment in Ravenswood Enterprises.

What would he need to convey to the Office? Officially all was well. The small sector of the opium trade run by Ravenswood would continue to prosper in common with the rest of the industry, ensuring a steady stream of silver out of China into British hands, which would then be exchanged back again for the purchase of tea; which was all very convenient for the British balance of payments. He still found it difficult to condemn the opium trade, despite his friend Cornelius Lee's sober warnings about addiction levels in China. Drake had not committed any glaring indiscretions in public, apart from the over solicitous pawing of Tilly when they rose from the table and recklessly encouraging Sir Giles to ever cruder reminiscences over the fourth round of *digestifs*. Both were not reportable offences. Drake's oblique assurance that all of Ravenswood's businesses would receive government support meant that a blind eye was still being turned to the unsavoury side of Ravenswood's trade, but there was no fresh evidence.

He awoke to find that the same thoughts were still circling in his mind, but was soon disturbed by a sustained yelping and scratching on the door.

"All right, Caradoc," said Nathaniel, yawning. "I'll let you out, but don't go far, we will be off for the wild north by mid-morning and you'll lose your seat in the coach if you're late!"

Caradoc shot him a withering look before bolting down the stairs to find the garden.

"Good morning," said Emma, rubbing her eyes and looking through the window. "No snow, that's good for us! How far will we get today?"

"Let's see how ambitious we feel once we are on the road," said Nathaniel, leaping back into bed. "But first, you have five minutes maximum to give your post mortem on yesterday evening, Mrs Parry!"

Emma folded her arms behind her head and considered. "The Parrys, Senior Branch, and my parents all seemed to have had a good time except I didn't like the look on Father's face when Mr Ravenswood interrogated him at the start of dinner.

Something is not right there. Mr Dill still loves Tilly Vere, which is good and she seemed to have a fine time. Neither of them minded Mr Drake's zealous attention to her which everyone must have noticed, though Mrs Drake didn't seem to care! Diarmuid was fun, as usual, but Coco was a little different I thought. She asked to be shown around the house when we ladies went out to the drawing room. I wouldn't have thought she would be interested. Also, I had not realised how nimble she was or how strong. Mama slipped on the stairs and Coco saved her. She was so quick that Mama did not even touch the floor!" Emma fell silent for a moment.

"Go on," said Nathaniel. "I sense there is more."

"One really odd thing happened. I saw a figure, a man with a bag running through the grounds. He seemed to be trying to escape from something, or someone, but it was misty and no one else caught sight of him. Mrs Ravenswood said it must have been a guard, but I'm sure it wasn't. I saw a group of them talking together quite a way off. No one else was running." She looked perplexed.

"Never mind, darling, there must be a simple explanation. What about Mortimer-Buckley?"

"I have to say Sir Giles made rather familiar remarks, but it was later in the evening and I think he had had too much wine. At the table I thought he might say more about the emeralds he gave to Mr Ravenswood's mother, as he seemed to like talking about himself." She paused, "It was odd that he didn't, especially as Mrs Ravenswood had gone to so much trouble to celebrate his war experiences with ... the Iberian selection at dinner."

Emma offered the last phrase in a spot-on perfect imitation of Amanda Ravenswood's pinched accents and Nathaniel hooted with laughter.

"You are right, dear one: on all counts. Interesting observations of Coco: she has hidden depths, and she bites, metaphorically speaking. I agree about Mortimer-Buckley, he seems a shady cove. Now for the finale: what about our hosts? Be frank."

"I think we would do well to spend as little time in their company as possible," said Emma gravely. "Mr Ravenswood has a chill about him. You were right, he seems dangerous, and Mrs Ravenswood does not seem to bear anyone goodwill, except for herself. But in a way, I felt sorry for her. I wouldn't like to be stranded out there in that forbidding place with him."

"Impressive analysis," said Nathaniel.

"And what was your verdict?" she laughed, pleased at the praise.

"Oh, I agree with you," said Nathaniel, pulling her close to plant a lingering kiss on her lips. And with the first thrill of desire she lost all interest in his verdict on last night's dinner.

After breakfast, they returned to their room to prepare for the journey. Nathaniel always packed his own trunk, one habit from his bachelor days he intended to keep. He checked his medicaments, home remedies for everything from cuts and bruises to fevers, put in some more clothing, though he knew he had a heavy coat and scarf waiting in the Welsh house, provided the moths had not got to them first. Most importantly, he needed to check the secret compartment. There were his silver-handled swordstick, pistols, ammunition, and his makila, the Basque walking stick with the concealed knife; indispensable for rural use. He selected the swordstick for the journey, hesitated and then took the pistols as well. Handling the weapons reminded him of another duty. He reached into the compartment again and took the makila.

"Em, I'm just going to have a word with Tobias. How long will you be? We need to catch the mail coach to Cheltenham."

Emma looked up from the mound of garments she had spread on the bed.

"How cold will it be in Wales?"

"Very," replied Nathaniel as he made his way downstairs.

"Send Frances up, darling," she called after him. "I'm ready for her help now, and I need to leave her instructions about unpacking the rest of the boxes whilst we are gone."

Nathaniel loped off down the stairs to the basement, sent Frances to wait on Emma, avoided Mrs Rollinson and caught Tobias shining boots in the garden.

"Mornin', sir," said Tobias, standing to greet Nathaniel.

"Good morning. Excellent job, Tobias! I'll take those riding boots with me, don't let me forget them."

"You leavin' soon, sir?"

Tobias looked forlorn at the prospect and it occurred to Nathaniel that the boy might have hoped to be included in the trip. "We'll be back by the start of March at the latest. Meanwhile, you will be the man of the house. Help out where you can but remember you must set aside time each day for training. I'll make sure Mrs Rollinson knows you will be out running and you must make time for some practice with your stick. Go and get it now."

"Yes, sir!"

Tobias needed no second telling. Nathaniel had taken it upon himself to train Tobias and work up his slight frame into something more substantial. Regular meals, warm clothes and a comfortable bed were not enough and Nathaniel had enjoyed working out a training schedule for the boy. He had presented him with a walking cane and taught him a few basic self-defence moves which had to be practised and perfected before he returned from Wales. They went to the bottom of the garden where there was a small paved area hidden behind the shed and vegetable plot and sheltered by the high stone walls.

"Right," said Nathaniel, "let's see what you remember. Take your stick in your left hand."

"I'm right-handed, sir," said Tobias, alarmed.

"That's the point. If you injured your right hand would you ask an enemy to wait for it to heal! I am also right-handed, but I will attack you holding my stick in the left."

Tobias blushed, uneasy, and took his stick in his left hand.

"Now keep still, trust that I won't split your pate."

Before the blush had faded Nathaniel had shifted his weight to his right foot, swung his stick in a swingeing arc, slid the right hand to support his hold and brought the weapon down to within a fist's height of Tobias's head. The boy yelped in shock, feeling the rush of air and a shiver of fear and excitement down his back.

"Your turn, but I'll use my replacement head!"

Nathaniel disappeared briefly into the shed and emerged with a post, on the top of which he had impaled a small pumpkin.

"Don't hit the pumpkin, Tobias. Swing and stop. You need control."

Tobias gloried in the attention. He started slowly, the technique slowly flowing to perfection. They tired his left hand and then moved on to the right, then back to the left, but faster.

"Well done. Now one more variation," said Nathaniel, his eyes shining like a boy's. "Body blows. Remember, left, then right. Let's start with the left."

After both sides were tried to the limit, and the pumpkin had shed more pulp than was good for it, Nathaniel called a halt.

"Excellent. You are allowed one new head a week so tell Mrs R I said so. See if you can perfect the moves by the time I return. Put these things away now. The next important task is to locate Caradoc. Has he gone to the park?"

"Not he," said Tobias, as he returned from the shed. "He be under the table in the kitchen catchin' scraps. Mrs R's bakin'."

"Flush him out," said Nathaniel firmly. "Then I would like you to be on call to help Captain Peterson's coachman with our trunks. He's driving us to the posthouse and he'll be here soon, so look lively."

Early Evening:
The George and Dragon, Walcot Street, Bath.

After an early supper with Mrs Rollinson, Frances and Harriet, Tobias wrapped a scarf round his neck and set off for Walcot Street. He had his walking cane with him and showed off his new moves, beating down imaginary foes whenever he had a clear stretch of pavement. He laughed to himself as he swaggered along, remembering Frances's jokes at the table; they had been funny and she had been put in her place by Mrs Rollinson. Harriet was a little rabbit but Frances was sharp as a pin and always made him laugh, though she was younger than he was. He wondered if he shouldn't have encouraged her, for after all he was fifteen next birthday. He shrugged his shoulders and moved on. Life was good, and he was looking forward to the evening's meeting in the George and Dragon. Matthew Spence and his new lodger would be there and maybe Matthew's grandfather, Old Tom. Matthew had fixed wheels on a chair so he could push the old man down the road to the Dragon to give him a change.

The sky was clear and glittering with cold starlight; under his feet, ice had made the pavements treacherous. Already, he had slipped once, so he slowed down as he neared the pub, not wanting to be seen on his backside. The door was tightly shut against the night and he put his shoulder to it to make sure it closed behind him after he entered, spluttering and coughing, his breath taken by the fug of heat. The meeting was in the front parlour as usual and he pushed in, craning his neck to see his friends. There by the fire was Tom on his throne, with Ben sticking close to him as a limpet, sat in a wooden captain's chair and leaning over to shout into the old man's ear above the roar in the room. Matthew was on the settle next to them and beckoned for Tobias to come over.

"Ale, young 'un?" said Matthew, as he poured Tobias a full mug. "Arthur's gone for another jug. He's been reading powerfully with no break for an hour. We've news of Mr Hetherington from *The Poor Man's Guardian* and also a lot on Cooperative Living and Unionism from Mr Owen's *Crisis* paper."

Matthew said the words slowly, he had listened but he not really understood all that he had heard. "Mr Hetherington's still in Clerkenwell Gaol, but spreading his good words from his cell. John Doherty, the spinners' union man from Manchester, is working with Mr Owen."

"Anythin' more on the Labour Bazaars and them using their own notes for money?" said Tobias, agog for more.

"London branch is in sore trouble," said Matthew, shaking his head. "I must say that using notes of labour hours for money sounds very rum. Their hearts are in the right place but I can't see it catching on. But Mr Owen keeps on preaching that if we only follow his way we'll leave error and misery behind and swap it for truth and happiness. God bless him!"

"Robert Owen 'ee lives in a fairytale land!" cackled a reedy voice. "Gave up on Old England and went to Amerikey 'ee did. Set up a co-operatin' community for Yankees! Crept back with 'is tail between 'is legs! Now 'ee's thinkin' 'ee can get printers loike old Arthur and Robert to unite with every other workin' man from carpenters to plasterers. 'Tain't natural! Young Doherty tried up north and failed good and proper."

"O' course, you 'ave seen all this afore, Mr Spence," said Ben encouragingly. He was keen to increase his stock with Old Tom, who of all the inhabitants in the Spence household would probably be the first to throw him out on his ear if he defaulted on the rent.

"That Oiy 'ave, young Benjamin Prestwick," said Tom.

"Grandfather," said Matthew, "we are in new times. You cannot deny that parliament was reformed last summer. We've a new-broom of a government under Lord Grey and they are set to pass some grand new laws."

Old Tom wheezed in delight. "Aye, young Matthew. Mighty impressive. 'Ave 'ee got the vote then? 'Ave Oiy? 'As any bugger round this 'ere table? No they ain't! And mark my words, this 'ere Factory Law for to protect little 'uns will be as weak as maid's water no matter what Mr Sadler says."

"We don't know yet what it will do, Mr Spence. And the slavery law is going through," said Tobias, unwilling to lose his good cheer. "There's no two ways about that one. If it wins the vote there will be no more slavery in the British Empire! Full stop!"

"Just loike there's no more slave trade in the Atlantic!"

mocked Old Tom triumphantly.

"Aye," said Ben. "We barred that back in 1807 and it flourishes to this day when 'Is Majesty's West Africa squadron don't catch 'em at it."

"Look Grandfather, here's Arthur and Robert," said Matthew, tiring of Ben playing up to the old man.

Arthur Jamieson collapsed into his seat with a fresh jug, breathing hard, closely followed by Robert Turner, red in the face and frowning.

"Arthur, ye be the oracle of this 'ere pub," chuckled Tom. "Ye be a champion reader and ye keeps the peace!"

"Hello, young 'un," said Arthur to Tobias. "Oiy wondered where you was!"

"Wouldn't miss the meeting, Mr Jamieson," said Tobias eagerly. "Sorry I was late for the reading. Evening, Mr Turner."

"Nothing joyful to report as such," said Arthur. "More snippets from Mr Sadler's enquiry into children's work in factories. What's good is that what 'e found is so shockin' bad that government's bound to cut the little 'uns day to ten hours, what with the beatin' and the cruel wheels turning relentless, and no natural breaks as God intended."

"Aye," said Robert Turner, breaking his gloomy silence. "It's not the hours that's wrong, it's the unnatural state of being in a factory. That's what needs attention. Children away from their parents, worked too 'ard or running wild and getting thrashed by strangers. Any farmin' child will toil just as many hours, and do 'arder work, and no 'arm done. But when they're tired, they takes a nap, then up and off again scaring the birds away for Father! White slaves they do be in factories. Unnatural work can rightly be called slavery."

"Nobody's forcin' 'em to stay, Robert Turner," yapped Old Tom, revived by another slug of ale. "Slaves be damned, ye don't know the meanin' of the word! Their parents clamour for the chance to get 'em into the factories. Lining up for the jobs they be! Oiy think no black man's keen to be a slave."

Dyed in the wool reformer as he was, he liked to play devil's advocate and give young Bobbie Turner a run for his money. There was too much slack ale-talk as the night wore on. It was not often he had the chance to chaff the young lads these days and he relished it. He hadn't felt as well in years.

Brooks's Club, Saint James's Street, London.

The gaming rooms upstairs were crowded and raucous. Some members were betting on card games at the tables, mainly faro; some were carousing in corners; some were crowded round an aspiring conductor who was lashing out the time with his walking cane as they roared their way through an obscene version of "William and Dinah". A couple of younger members, drunk as boiled owls, were slumped on a sofa, one offering noisy, slurred challenges to the other who was laboriously trying, but failing, to write up the wager in the betting book.

All of this was a mere distant buzz of irritation for Lord Melbourne as he sat alone in the comfortable Members' Room downstairs. He felt melancholy. Naughty Caro Norton, his lovely young companion, was pregnant, and entertaining herself far away from London on endless house party jaunts. On some of these she was accompanied by her boorish husband, and on some she was not. The last letter had suggested that she was alone and had sought to be amusing by taunting him with her casual flirtations. One of these had blossomed and caused her to bolt her bedroom door at nights to keep the bounder out. George Norton could not have been there or fist-fights would have ensued, bloodily.

Melbourne was owed a letter by his ex-mistress, Lady Brandon, and yearned for it to raise his spirits, but a more prosaic distraction materialised by his side in the shape of a club servant checking to see if he needed anything.

"Yes, Chis-lett, I do," drawled Lord Melbourne. "Another bottle. Taylor's 1811. There are a few cases left, I trust?"

"Yes, mi'lord," said Chislett with a slight bow.

"And bring a glass for Lord Palmerston. He will be here presently."

Despite the warm fire, he was feeling the cold. He wondered if it might be fatigue. Deuced chilly of course, being January, but it was not just the season, he had too much to do and it was sapping his strength.

It became even colder as the door opened to admit his fellow Minister and Club Member, the Foreign Secretary, Lord Palmerston.

"What-ho, Melbourne!"

"What-ho, old chap."

"Russell wants to play faro tonight. We arrived together. Coming up to the tables?"

"Presently, but I've just ordered another bottle of 1811. Fancy sharing a glass or two before we go?"

Palmerston strode over to the fire and turned his rear to it, flicking up the skirts of his frock coat.

"That's better! Damned cold out there, Melbourne."

Chislett returned with the port. At a signal from Melbourne he poured it and then retreated noiselessly from whence he came.

Palmerston was tempted back to the armchairs and lifted his glass. "To us! To the Whigs. Long may we reign!"

"Amen to that," said Melbourne, washing the port round his teeth. "We are going well. Tories dead in the water! Who would have thought it?" After considering the unlikely situation he continued. "Thank the Lord that Wellington's leadership remains decidedly dull for the young fellows, and what with their Evangelicals setting the pace for all this damned reform, we are sitting pretty to be credited for doing rather little!"

"Strange world."

"And getting damnably stranger. Sadler's report on the factories is poor stuff. Don't know if you've read any of it yet. Ghastly overwrought "penny blood" style horrors. Years out of date most of it. He seems to have dragged out a collection of human derelicts to wail over their ill treatment donkeys' years ago. Damned lucky to have had any jobs at all I would have thought. Also he's leading them by the nose. You know the form: "So my poor sad creature, tell me of your childhood, tell me about the beatings. How often were you beaten? How much did it hurt? Are you crippled? Oh dear, so you are." He never lets the wretches just talk. Always makes them sing to the same tune."

"Damned bore and you are obviously tired of it! I suppose you wish you were Foreign Secretary now?"

"Not at all, you seem to be filling the role most capaciously. And actually," said Melbourne, a slow, cynical smile lighting his face. "Sadler has played into our hands. The report is so exaggerated, we are obliged to follow up with a Royal Commission to check it, and I know just the man to steer that, taking a back seat of course, but hand firmly on the tiller."

"Would that be the *sehr effizient* Edwin Chadwick by any chance? I gather that he is referred to as *The Prussian* for his ferocious statistical efforts."

"Yes, the very same, my sober bureaucrat! He will, quite rightly, be brisk and businesslike, allowing the factory owners their right of reply, which Sadler of the bleeding heart did not. He will quietly, perhaps over dinner, ascertain the working conditions from the proprietors. He will repeat the interviews of the workers in a fairer manner, allowing each witness free rein."

Palmerston grinned broadly. "Enough rope to hang themselves by any chance?"

"I have no idea what you are talking about, my dear fellow."

The port flowed again, lusciously.

"I am more concerned about the slavery bill," said Palmerston, frowning suddenly as his thoughts returned to an angry exchange in the Lords with a plantation owner.

"Our friends in the West Indies will need generous compensation if we interfere with their business." He poured another large port. "Generous compensation Melbourne, and to a fault, depend upon it."

"Any thoughts on the scale?"

"Well, clearly, it will need to be a goodwill gesture," said Palmerston, "which is acceptable to all."

"And an overall figure? I've done some preliminary calculations. Well over ten million pounds will be needed."

"Absolutely. Double that perhaps."

"It would not do to inconvenience the West Indian lobby."

"Certainly not," agreed Palmerston, shaking his jowls vehemently.

"Nor," continued Melbourne, "can we afford to alienate the owners of our cotton factories. They are the men of the future. They dominate our export market don't forget. Cotton has been king for over thirty years and every year the trade grows. Confound it, sometimes you are so immersed in the regulation of foreign imports it seems to have slipped your mind!"

"Don't let my kindly exterior fool you, dear boy. Nothing gets past Pam!"

Melbourne sank the rest of his port and rose to his feet. "Is that so? Well let's see if you can get a few cards past Johnny Russell tonight."

"No problem even on a bad day."

Palmerston paused before entering the hall. "Speaking of domestic matters, can't you accelerate the enquiry into the Poor Law? It costs too damned much."

"All in good time," said Melbourne, now thoroughly warm and restored. "Chadwick has some ambitious ideas for the development of workhouses. He wants them in every town, city and county. Believe me, they will not be comfortable, no one will be keen to move in and Chadwick believes there should be no poor relief for the able-bodied unless the paupers live in a workhouse. That will make the claiming of relief an unattractive prospect. You can see that I don't want him rushed. He will pilot the factory enquiry through before summer and complete the work on the Poor Law next year. Then there will be a fine uproar no doubt. Let sleeping dogs lie for now, Pam: sufficient unto the day is the evil thereof."

Morning: 29th January, 1833. The Ravenswood Residence, Arno's Tower, Arno's Vale, near Bristol.

Edwin Ravenswood had been down for an early breakfast, as he did every morning. Small talk over the rolls and coffee was not to his taste. He had eaten sparingly and in silence and then gone straight to his suite of rooms in the west wing. He knew that Sir Giles was anxious to have a word with him in private and he expected him shortly. It might have been better to deal with him earlier in the visit, but yesterday had been busy with the house party and it had not been possible. In the morning they had walked over the estate and after lunch had been on a shoot. Before dinner, as planned, they had driven down to the wharf at Redcliffe to see his ships, but there he had been obliged to stay to speak with Captain Trevellis to finalise contracts for the next sailing. The rest of the party had been sent back for dinner without him, so it was on the final morning of his visit that Sir Giles managed to share his miseries.

The west wing was a place for confidences. They would not be disturbed in the Oriental Salon which served Ravenswood as an office and den, isolated from the main house by a separate corridor which was lined with wooden mannequins wearing suits from his extensive collection of armour. It was an eclectic mix, ranging from fourteenth-century European chain mail and the full brutality of sixteenth-century plate armour, to the elaborate equipage of a Japanese samurai warrior. In his suite of rooms there were other costumes, eastern confections of painted wood, feathered wings and gaping masks, shelves and cabinets of exotic weaponry, assorted treasures and macabre curiosities. Amanda rarely ventured into the west wing unless she was invited.

He glanced up from his papers to look through the French windows and saw her at a distance with Lottie and John Drake, strolling across the park towards the wood. She was still attractive, elegant and fastidious, still diverting, but there again, they had only been married for four years. The gloss should not

93

have worn off quite yet. She suited him in many ways so why had he let Lottie into his life? It had surprised him when he had done so, as he was not a man who needed a variety of women. Lust was a weakness which he knew he did not have, but he was acquisitive. He bared his teeth as he smiled, without mirth. The Honourable Mrs Drake was a hunting trophy like the mounted animal heads on the wall, though he was quite well aware that she viewed him in exactly the same light.

A quiet knock was followed by the entrance of his butler.

"Sir Giles to see you, Mr Ravenswood."

Buckley walked in hurriedly and took a seat by Ravenswood at his table. He was anxious and had skipped breakfast, his eyes bulged, watery and sore after an unwise late night drinking session with Drake, and his heart beat unpleasantly hard. Though superficially handsome and urbane, he had let his body go to seed. An indulged life had taken its toll and he was now unable, as well as unwilling, to fight his own battles. He clasped his hands on the table top and laid himself on the mercy of his host; pouring out the details of his two torments: the London problem, the blowsy Maisie Trickett who could turn into a very expensive embarrassment, and the Bath problem, the unwelcome re-appearance of Ben Prestwick, whose indiscretions could lead him to the gallows.

Ravenswood listened in silence, toying with a jewelled paper knife as he did so. He had three options: the first, and easiest, being to close the issue down by disposing of Buckley for bringing the possibility of prosecution to his door. The Ravenswood family had helped launder money and jewels which were rightly the property of the Crown. Secondly, he could refuse to help, which left a desperate and incompetent Buckley floundering and it was clear to Ravenswood that Prestwick was likely to turn to blackmail, which could last a lifetime. Thirdly, he could resolve the problems of this long standing family ally, who was now not only a Member of Parliament, but also in possession of a fortune, some of which he was willing to invest in the business. Self interest would be best served by option three.

By the time Buckley had finished Edwin Ravenswood had devised two plans.

"Sir Giles, I have known you all my life and our families have been close for much longer than that. I can solve your problems but my methods will bring about final solutions."

"Edwin, my dear man," said Buckley, trembling under Ravenswood's penetrating gaze. "I understand what I have asked of you and I am entirely at your disposal in these matters. I will follow your suggestions to the letter."

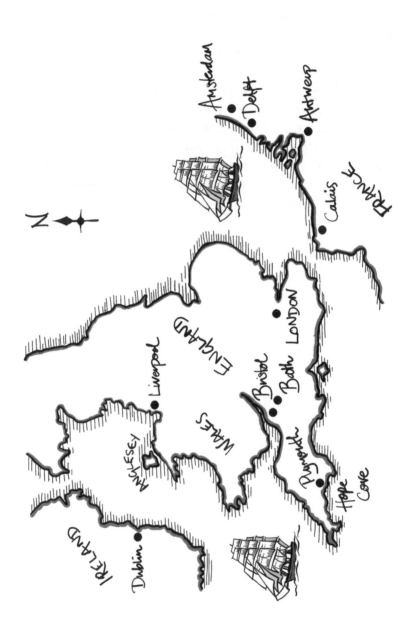

Great Britian: the location of the Isle of Anglesey

Chapter 3

Late afternoon: 1st February, 1833.
Beaumaris Castle, the Isle of Anglesey.

They stood side-by-side, arms linked against the wind, as they looked out over the ruined battlements. Beyond the white-capped rushing water of the Menai Straits the wild mountains of Snowdonia reared up before them, etched against the darkening sky, their peaks iced and scattered with a light snow. The air was clear, but buffeting, searching and bitter. A feeling of otherness grew upon them as they stood together; separating them from the world they had left. It was not the otherness of alienation, but the addition of another dimension of themselves. The low, rolling fields of Anglesey spread out behind them in the gloom of the gathering dusk and they were a part of it, cut off from their other lives by the swirling air and water, and the curtain wall of mountains.

The harsh croak of a raven drew her eyes down to the ivy grown wall of the tower. There he was, folding his wings as he settled on his stone perch, hunched up against the cold, glaring and baleful. He seemed to have called to her and Emma felt a threat shivering up her spine at the sight of him. The bird appeared to consider, inspected her more closely, and then made a decision. He put his head to one side and changed his tune to a high interrogatory: "Toc, toc, toc!" She smiled at him, her alarm melting away. Even in the failing light his plumage was captivating, sleekly blue-black, steely and iridescent. He preened his thick neck feathers and nodded his head.

"I think he wanted to know why we are here," she said. "When I looked at him he seemed to know that we belong here too."

"You feel part of it then, Em?" said Nathaniel.

"Oh, yes."

To her surprise and relief, she did. She had not wanted to play the part of an outsider. The language, the customs and the hostile climate: she had looked forward to all of these, but as challenges, not as gifts or punishments. She would not take them for granted.

"I'm glad," said Nathaniel.

He had not worried about bringing her to Anglesey as it was not in his nature to do so. But in his dreams of the mountains and the island she had not been there. He had hoped she would like it, but if she had not, he would have continued to come alone. As they looked at each other, still learning, a crazed barking broke out from below them, over towards the beach, and a flock of seabirds scattered into the sky. Nathaniel smiled broadly. He would not have been alone.

"Caradoc seems to be in his element. Do you think he remembers it? He probably does as he was full-grown when I took him from Llanddaniel."

"He knew where he was as we crossed the bridge," said Emma. "Remember, he was up at the window and yapped his way across. Maybe he could smell the sea air. Perhaps he recognised the scent of the land. Do you think it's possible?"

The other passengers had left the coach as they had entered Wales and she had spent their last day on the road encouraging

Nathaniel to tell her more stories of the island. Her head was full of them; partially woven threads of magic and tales of holy wells, druid groves and standing stones. The stories had matched the lonely road in strangeness and now they had arrived she felt a flood of relief to be at one with it. It had been important to her, and important for them, though he might not know it.

"I am glad that you like the raven," he said, pulling her closer. "Some say they are birds of ill omen but I don't feel that."

"I know the superstitions," said Emma. "But the old wives' tales say the same about seeing just one magpie instead of two. It must be to do with their dark looks."

Nathaniel smiled at her, pleased. "Maybe it's because they are scavengers, they prey on dead meat."

She looked at the raven closely. "He looks stern but he is curious and lively, unlike his namesake!"

"What do you mean?"

"Edwin Ravenswood! The thought of him makes me uneasy, Nathaniel," she said, suddenly serious. "There's something dark as Hades about him."

Nathaniel changed the subject. "Well, this feathered friend here is linked to the gods above not below. In Welsh his name is Bran. In the old days there was a god called Bran the Blessed and there is also a tale of an Irish Celtic goddess who takes the form of a raven. She is Morrighan. And did you know that in the myths the ravens were messengers to other worlds?"

Emma smiled encouragement so he pressed on, happy to steer the conversation away from all thoughts of the mainland and the troubles of their ordinary lives. "Odin had two ravens called Huginn and Muninn: thought and memory. They travelled the world for him and told him of men's deeds."

She looked at the raven, who suddenly flapped his wings and whistled. They laughed and whistled back, then turned together to make their way down the broken steps.

"Do carriages ever blow off Mr Telford's bridge? I swear I felt it sway as we drove over," she said, moving carefully, feeling for the edges of the stone treads as they descended into the black hole of the spiral stair.

"There is movement," said Nathaniel, leading her down, out of the closeness of the stairwell and onto the cobbled path. "But no one has been blown away to my knowledge. The biggest injury it has done is to the ferrymen. They are ruined."

They crossed the empty moat and walked by the courthouse to the beach where Nathaniel whistled up Caradoc. He soon bounded into view, lugging a stick heavy with a sodden garland of kelp, and followed them as they turned to make their way back through the deserted town to the warmth of the Old Bull's Head. It was a cold walk, their feet ringing on the iron hard road, Caradoc labouring behind with his prize. They had almost made it to the door when the wind rose to a sudden howl behind them, tearing down the Strait and funnelling the length of Castle Street.

"Leave it, Caradoc," shouted Nathaniel above the shriek of the blast, as the terrier rammed the stick broadsides across the entrance. "Put it round the corner for tomorrow."

Caradoc was not pleased but could barely keep on his paws in the mounting gale and saw the sense in it. He disappeared round the side of the inn towards the dark archway leading to the stable yard, and returned, tail up.

They opened the parlour door at the Old Bull's Head to be met by a wall of sweltering heat and noise, so they made instead for the calmer dark of the dining room and a meal before an early night. On Nathaniel's recommendation, they ate well on *cawl eildwyn*, twice heated leek broth, and melting slabs of honeyed lamb. Afterwards, warmed through, they made their way up the creaking stairs. The maid had stoked up the fire in their room and piled the blankets high on the ancient four-poster. All other assistance had been refused. They undressed hurriedly, each helping the other, laughing at their haste, struggling into nightgowns. As Emma moved away and slid under the covers, watching him, Nathaniel drew the curtains round the bedposts, leaving just one candle burning on the ledge by the bed, and followed her in.

Always drawn to the comfort of a fire, Caradoc had made a bee-line for the hearth and flung himself down before it. He had learned that any early attempt to move onto the bed for the night would be hopelessly premature and doomed to failure. Stifled giggles and the creak of the bed ropes from behind the curtain confirmed his decision. He would bide his time.

Presently, the pair fell quiet. Warm and content, with Emma in his arms, Nathaniel began to plan: "Bank first tomorrow, sweetheart. I will collect my father's remaining boxes, including mother's jewellery for you. And I'll check the accounts. The manager is an old family friend and will want us both for luncheon. We'll meet the solicitor too. You'll be all right on your own after that for a while? As you see the shore is five minutes away, there is much more of the castle behind the barbican entrance. Apart from being blasted in the Civil War, it was Edward I's last castle and never finished in the first place, but there is still plenty to see. I can arrange for a short drive for you if you want it. Penmon Priory is worth a visit, there's a holy well, a church and some romantic ruins. It's about three miles down the coast. I will ride to the house at Llanddaniel in the afternoon; it's only about ten miles and I'll be quicker on horseback than in a gig. I'll see Jones and get Mrs Jones to make everything ready for us. All being well, we will have Sunday here then travel to the house together on Monday."

Emma pulled away in alarm.

"Nathaniel, please let me ride with you," she felt a sinking in the pit of her stomach and knew she needed to make a successful strategic move, not just for now but also for the future.

He looked uncertain. "Sweetheart, it will likely be raining, definitely cold. That's twenty miles in the open air, plus lengthy talks with the Joneses, who speak not one word of English. And," he added, frowning, "the house will not look as I wished for you. It is over a year since I visited and I intended to instruct them in how to prepare it for us, which rooms to clean ...," he hesitated as he also realised he had been looking forward to a fast hack over the fields with Caradoc and a long talk with Dafydd Jones over a pot of ale, probably ankle-deep in mud, whilst they inspected the beasts' stalls.

Emma took a gamble and reached for his face so that she could hold it in her hands, pushing back his trademark mane of hair to look him full in the eyes. She had not long had the right to do this and despite their other intimacies, it still felt bold, presumptuous. She swallowed down a stab of anxiety and steadied her voice.

"Nathaniel, darling, because of your work I know there'll be many times you will have to leave me behind. I know you will travel abroad and go to London when I won't be able to be with you. Whenever we can, I want to be by your side. I so much want to go tomorrow and have that first sight of Llanddaniel with you. It doesn't matter what it looks like. I can listen to the Joneses or take a walk on the farm whilst you talk business if you prefer. I want to help you; talk to you on the road, especially if it's miserable travelling weather. I want us to walk to Penmon together on Sunday. Especially if it is romantic!" She was relieved to see his frown lift and be replaced by amusement. "I've brought my riding habit with me and I am competent," she said. "And it is our honeymoon."

"Right then," said Nathaniel, taking both her hands and planting a kiss on each. It was novel to remember that he did not need to be alone again, there were different pleasures now. "So be it, my dear, *fy nghariad*, as we are in Wales. We ride together."

Emma kissed him in relief and gratitude. She had a fleeting vision of Edwin Ravenswood and Amanda's deference to him. No, it was more than that; she had sensed Amanda's fear of that grim man and thanked God she did not have to suffer the same.

"Tell me again about the stones," she said as she relaxed, exhaustion flooding through her body, which she now admitted to herself, ached in every inch after the five days on the road and would be immeasurably worse after the ride tomorrow. She moved closer, enfolding him in her arms, rested her head on his chest and closed her eyes.

Absent-mindedly he breathed in the scent of her and stroked her shoulder, but saw again the long low manor house he had inherited but never lived in: a few nights now and then, business and burials. It was stone built and strong, butting up against the elements, and beyond the house, enduring, was Bryn Celhi Ddu, the Mound in the Dark Grove. Beneath, he was sure; other bodies remained, not those of family who were laid to rest in the trim little churchyard but the pagan remains of the ancients. To his knowledge no one had dug it out to see what was hidden inside. It slumbered still. Boulders from the stone circle survived and guarded a ritual enclosure. A passage grave led into the hillock that for eons of time had survived as witness to the lost days. The Roman Army had destroyed the oak groves of the Druids, but some trees grew again by the stones, a small copse bordered the fields, which were now filled with his beasts and Jones's sheep and cattle. In his misery and loneliness after his father's death he had stretched out on the mound and drunk himself free of thought, only to be plunged in his dreams into a chaos of violence, poetry and songs howled to the moon.

"They are old, Em," he whispered, feeling the regular rise and fall of her breast against his, "as old as man."

He quietly disentangled one arm, reached over and snuffed out the candle.

By the fire, the terrier heard the sheet rustle and raised his head. Now, even for him uncomfortably hot, Caradoc took the darkness as a signal, padded silently over to the bed, nosed under the curtains and crept soundlessly under the eiderdown for the night.

The Ravenswood Townhouse, Redcliffe Parade, Bristol.

Eli Trevellis stood uncomfortably before his employer, eyes focused away from Ravenswood's relentless gaze and fixing instead on the lines of masts swaying against the dying light above the moorings on Redcliffe Back. It was better not to catch

103

Ravenswood's eye unless absolutely necessary, it could be seen as an impertinence, a challenge. No one in their right mind would upset Mr Ravenswood, and Eli was sane enough to know it. He had bided his time with his news as instructed, checked and double-checked the men and their stories, read the news story on the coroner's report. All ship-shape and Bristol fashion. He smiled cynically to himself to keep up his spirits, which narrowed his eyes unpleasantly to crafty slits. He smoothed his shock of brindled hair and shifted uneasily.

Then a good sign: Ravenswood gestured to him to be seated at the central table which served for dining and board meetings. To be taken to his master's desk at the window and made to stand would have been a poor start. Ravenswood had clearly had a successful couple of days in London. Eli noticed he was wearing a new waistcoat, canary coloured silk, cream striped with a leaf pattern on the stripe: an unusual choice for the master.

"So, Captain Trevellis," said Ravenswood, "let me hear your report on the events of Wednesday night."

"It's done, sir, the soldier's dead. Burial Monday. No trouble," said Trevellis: business-like, curt, as his master preferred and looking at him straight now, level to the eyes.

Ravenswood nodded, but he had not finished. "Good. Now the details."

Trevellis shifted in his seat and brought his fists onto the table, clenching and unclenching them to help order his thoughts as he recounted the events.

"That morning I went to Joshua Shadwell's brothel in Green Park and picked up his two men, Billy and Jabez. Paid 'em 'alf in advance and slipped a royalty to Shadwell. By the way, Sir Giles was 'avin' an hour with the whore called Clari when I got there. 'E 'ad not gone straight to London as planned."

Ravenswood nodded, noted the discrepancy.

"I went to the York House and paid one of the footmen to come to the Saracen's after eight with the message that Sir Giles was ill and had gone back to London. I planted myself in the

Saracen's away from Billy and Jabez and watched for our men. In comes the footman, regular as clockwork and asks for Prestwick, which picked 'im out for me. Soon as I eyeballed 'im I was over and stood 'im some drinks. The old cove was downcast and ready to be cheered up. We jawed for an hour, swapped stories about the war and Spain, so 'e was 'appier. Then I left, barman saw me leave. I waited by the wall of Saint Michael's next to Saracen's. Billy slipped out the back through the stable yard and Jabez come out the front, walked up the street and waited in Gracious Court, up from Saracen's. Prestwick come out the front and set off up Broad Street so I went through Michael's churchyard and round the back of Saracen's to tip off Billy to go and wait on the passage steps between Bladud's Buildings and the Paragon."

Trevellis allowed himself a self-satisfied nod as he detailed the pincer movement: he was particularly proud of it.

"Then I cut back and caught up with Prestwick as 'e rounded Broad Street. Jabez was trailing 'im close. Just passed Bladud's Buildings, comin' up to the steps, Jabez stoved 'is skull in. 'E 'ad a crowbar. 'E then shoved Prestwick and he went down the steps like a ninepin. Billy was 'alf way down in the dark and finished the job, then rolled 'im down to Walcot Street."

Trevellis paused. "I didn't need to pretend to chase Jabez off as it were deserted on the road. Billy came up the steps and we all made our way separately to Shadwell's. I paid 'em off. Prestwick was laid out in the George and Dragon by Thursday morn and the coroner ruled death by misadventure in the *Chronicle* that night. Like I said, funeral's on Monday."

Ravenswood reflected on the tale. It seemed secure: an improvement on the shambles which would have ensued if he had instructed Shadwell to deal with it. A few years ago he would not have had to send Trevellis on such a mission. He glowered at the memory. Shadwell was a spent force. He had noticed that Shadwell's wife, Rosie, seemed to be taking charge of the Green Park brothel and the Avon Street businesses. Joshua Shadwell had never been the same after the stabbing. Some mad

105

whore and a gang of men taking revenge had ambushed him in his own yard. Shadwell had been reluctant to speak of it. Fortunately Ravenswood's business interests in human cargo had shifted focus to London, and Shadwell was no longer needed for the supply chain. This had been fortuitous in many respects. Ravenswood's days in London had been very well spent. Lottie's property portfolio was impressive and included a secluded suite of rooms in Mayfair that they had made very good use of. He suddenly felt expansive, took out his purse, and slid five sovereigns over the table.

"You have done well," he said with a rare smile of satisfaction. "Progress is being made. My new vessel in London dock is almost ready. You are still on target to leave next week, I take it?"

"Yes, sir," said Trevellis. "We'll quit Bristol by Wednesday."

"Drink, Captain?"

"Yes please, sir," said Trevellis, trying to sound unmoved and stifling his alarm. Ravenswood's rare shows of generosity were always unsettling and he cursed inwardly to see that his hand shook as he reached out for the coins.

Fortunately for him, Ravenswood missed the sign of weakness. After ringing for the footman he strode over to the window and stood, arms folded, watching the pale moon shine on the waters of the Floating Harbour. Buckley's first problem had been eliminated, and after the instructions he had given in London, the second was poised to go the same way. Sir Giles would be extremely grateful, in perpetuity. Ravenswood's fleet was growing. He had berths in London, vessels on the high seas and his various trades were rising exponentially. Normally, he had no time for poetry but something Drake had said came back to him.

"Look on my Works, ye Mighty, and despair!"

He liked it.

Morning: 4th February, 1833.
Saint Mary's Burial Ground, Bathwick, Bath.

The small group attending Benjamin Prestwick's funeral stood hunched against the intermittent gusts of wind like gaunt black birds, resigned and silent round the empty grave. They stood in the lee of the little mortuary chapel, so had a modicum of shelter as they listened to the curate gallop his way through the service. He knew nothing of Benjamin Prestwick but had some sympathetic feeling for old soldiers and, generally speaking, Martha said to herself, had made a brave show. As, she reflected with tight lips, had she. The fees had been paid out of her own pocket and she had made arrangements with a church she had always viewed with the greatest suspicion. Saint Mary the Virgin indeed: little better than Papists they were, to keep such a name. The worship of saints she deplored as particularly sinful. To add to the annoyance, the fees were higher than they should have been, being as they were not regular parishioners. She had made sure there was no profligacy, no adding of insult to injury. With parish fees, burial service, clerk and sexton, who also tolled the bell, she had been charged two pounds and three shillings. Ben was buried with no stone or wall, his resting place was unmarked and shallow dug, near the freshly turned line of paupers' graves, but she would be providing refreshments when the time came.

She stole a glance around the unfamiliar churchyard. The chapel had only stood for fifteen years and she remembered it being built from the stones of the old Saint Mary's church itself, a squat, crumbling place left over from the old dark days before the blessed light of the Reformation had dawned. The march of progress, she thought to herself, satisfied. But then a sour thought, it had been demolished in an outbreak of road widening and new building encouraged by the Lord of the Manor, the Earl of Darlington. Martha's frown deepened at the thought of him. Only last month he had been made up to be His Grace the Duke of Cleveland. Everyone knew he chose the title in memory of his ancestor and notorious trollop, the first Duchess of Cleveland. Some duchess! Martha felt her blood boil. More of a doxy: that's what she was, one of bad old King Charles's harlots.

She tossed her head and glared at the unfortunate curate, who mistakenly assumed his address had missed the mark and gabbled all the faster. Martha forced her mind back to the business in hand. It was a duty to her late husband Philip to bury his friend decently, which meant in the ways of his family, and the old Prestwicks had been Anglicans. It was also a duty for her class of family to attend the service. Old Tom had stayed by the fireside with the Johnty, who had developed into a noisy and ebullient child, unsuitable for a funeral congregation, but her son Matthew and his wife Mary were there. She nodded her head in approval as she caught sight of Tobias Caudle slip through the iron gate to join the mourners. He had met Ben many times whilst the old soldier had been in Bath, it was right that he attended. It was a duty for him. She inspected him critically: he looked clean, well-clothed and was broadening out. He even had a gentleman's walking cane; that was new. Not so much of an urchin these days but a young man, though she knew his mother had spent plenty of her days in the poor house and on the wrong side of the law. No ornament to the city that one. She sniffed disapprovingly but caught Tobias's eye and beckoned him to join the family. He smiled nervously and made his way round the clutch of habitual funeral attendees who had turned up and swollen the numbers to a dozen: the obligatory scattering of dames and spinsters of the parish, two skeletal old men in greasy coats and battered hats. They would all expect a glass or two and a bite to eat afterwards.

Martha totted up the cost again, carefully, but only from habit. She did not mind it, though Ben had died owing a week's rent and would probably have sunk deeper into her debt if he had lived. She would have tolerated that too, for a while. What irked her still was the manner of his passing. She fixed her eyes back on the curate, who smiled. It was a brave grin, rather disarming, but she did not see it or hear him. Benjamin Prestwick had not fallen down the Paragon steps to Walcot in a drunken stupor, she was sure of it. He had not been out long enough for one thing, for, according to the watch, he had been found before ten that evening. She had seen him drink over the weeks of his stay as her lodger and knew his capacity.

Might he have been merry? Oh yes, and talkative too, even before taking a drop, but drunk before midnight? Never!

He was an old soldier and a good sailor, steady on his feet and tough as old rope. The suggestion that he might have been struck by a thief was possible, but he did not look a good prospect for a footpad. Apart from these nagging doubts, there was more. She recalled his last night and his mood. He was cock-a-hoop. Shaved and washed, his shabby coat with his Waterloo medal brushed almost clean, his eyes alight; he had taken her hands and danced her round the kitchen before he left.

"Martha," he said, "tonight's the night. Oiy be off to meet moiy salvation!"

"Salvation!" she'd said. "What salvation!"

"Moiy crock o' gold at the end of the rainbow! Yer rent will be paid and Benjamin will be in clover."

"Who are you seeing?" she'd said, "a magician?"

"A gentleman," he'd said. "An old officer of mine 'e was, from the Spanish wars. 'E'll see me roight."

And with that he had pranced out of the door and she had never seen him alive again. For her next sighting of him he was stretched out on the table in the parlour of the George and Dragon, with the watch and the coroner in attendance asking her to identify the body. He had been carried in there dead and the landlord remembered that he had seen him with Matthew and Old Tom at the reform meetings. The knock had come to her door before she had locked up for the night.

A sad end.

She had seen Ben's old eyes regain some of their youthful sparkle as he had taken her hands and they had vamped round her kitchen and she had thought of her husband Philip, long dead. She had been powerless then, but she was not now.

109

Who had Ben seen that night? An officer he'd said. Perhaps Philip would have known him too. Would such a man have done away with Ben? Ben's optimism now became ominous, grotesquely misplaced. It had ill-wished him.

They made their way out down the short gravel path to congregate on Henrietta Road, waiting for the gate to clank shut behind the curate and the rest of the party. Matthew and Mary linked arms with her for the walk home and Tobias trotted along at Matthew's side, keeping in step and beating time as he did with his cane. He felt a release in quitting the churchyard. Though many stones had recorded the deaths of old people, some even in their eightieth year and over, he had seen some sad records of dead children. He was just pleased he had not seen anyone his own age, or with his name, even part of his name, it would have been a bad omen.

"There's something not right about this death," said Martha. "I know I've said it before but I'll say it again. We need to find out who he was to meet in the Saracen's Head last Wednesday night. Someone did him a mischief!"

Matthew gestured to Mary to keep silent as they exchanged glances over Martha's grey head. They thought they had exhausted this subject over interminable discussions together, and with Martha, over the weekend. It seemed more than likely to them that an old man would fall down a steep run of dark steps after a skin-full of drink and break his head on the way. Furthermore, they had already agreed, privately, that the removal of the garrulous and poverty stricken Benjamin from the house was not a wholly bad thing. In fact, Matthew had already persuaded his mother to replace the impecunious Benjamin with a new lodger in the shape of a Mr Finn O'Malley, a friend of Matthew's employer, Declan. She had vetted him on the Saturday, decided he was not a drunk and could afford the rent, and had agreed he should move in at the start of next week, thus allowing a "decent interval".

"I'll look into it, Mother," said Matthew smoothly. "I'll talk to the landlord next time I'm in the Saracen's Head and find out who he met: see if there was any trouble. Though I'm sure he would have told the watch if there had been."

Martha looked up sharply. "Tonight, Matthew. Ask tonight."

"I can ask for you, Mrs Spence," piped up Tobias earnestly, keen to help. He had liked Benjamin, and his tales. "I can go tonight if Matthew cannot."

"Good," said Martha, glaring at Matthew for his hesitation, she did not like her son to be slow in showing obedience to his mother.

They had tramped along for a while, letting the offer rest, crossed the river and turned down Walcot Street, before Martha had another and even better thought. She stopped in her tracks.

"Tobias, when are Mr and Mrs Parry returning from their honeymoon?"

"By the start of March at the latest," said Tobias, well pleased with himself, his tone giving them to know of his importance in knowing his master's movements.

"Too late for my needs," said Martha dismissively.

"I know why you ask, Missis," said Tobias, suddenly excited. "Mr Prestwick said he knew my master's father from the days of soldiering in Spain. Mr Parry is a righteous man and he'll want to help you find out the truth. I know it! I've not had the right opportunity to tell him what Mr Prestwick said, but he'll hang on every word when I do. His father's memory is that precious to him, y'see. And I've another idea," Tobias paused for effect. "Do you remember Mr Prestwick's tales? He said that my master's father sailed away from Spain on the *Renowned* when he and the other soldiers went on to Corunna." He shot an anxious glance at Martha. "Sorry to mention the place, Missis, as I know it was fateful for Mr Spence, but I also know that the *Renowned* was Captain Peterson's ship!"

"Captain Peterson!" exclaimed Martha. "Well I never!"

"I used to visit Frances when she was a kitchen maid at the Captain's. Just now and then." He flushed and hurried on. "There's pictures of all the Captain's ships along the below-stairs corridor. I sat and looked at 'em a few times." He also remembered the gruesome discomfort that had accompanied the looking, as he struggled to read the captions, but he managed to keep that thought to himself. Time after time he had stared at those letters as he waited for a few words with Frances, eating his way through the raw pastry parings that he had begged from Cook in the kitchen after she had run her knife round the pie plate. He had sat, chewed, and raked his memory through the gleanings that remained from his weekly reading lessons. Then one day, he had read the names straight off.

"And apart from that, I've heard Mr Parry mention that his father knew the Captain. And he is himself firm friends with him, as his new father-in-law. Captain Peterson will help I'm sure. And he is not just connected with Mr Parry's family; he is also a magistrate," added Tobias grandly. There was a stunned silence, so he added, "Of the court."

"Yes, Tobias Caudle, we know what a magistrate does," said Martha briskly. "I shall see him. Tomorrow."

Matthew shot a dark and meaningful look at Tobias, who weathered it and basked in Martha's gratitude. She fairly beamed at him.

Now the Captain really was a gentleman and no mistake. He would listen. Feeling more positive and a touch victorious, she smiled tartly at the glum faces of her son and daughter-in-law, drew their arms more tightly under hers and stepped out with a will. She was now more than equal to providing the cold collation of funeral meats, the expected cordials and even, perhaps, the glasses of sherry that the guests would have despaired of, hers being a Methodist home.

Afternoon: 5th February, 1833.
The Peterson Residence, Marlborough Buildings.

Martha Spence was not feeling quite so combative by the time she had dressed herself the next morning, carefully buttoning herself into the unfamiliar mourning gown. She had bought it second hand from a Walcot Street clothes trader and the bombazine was a touch rusty, even moth-eaten in some well disguised parts of the skirt, but it had to be worn. The hat likewise with its trailing veil was not the most flattering. She had excused the rest of the family from mourning dress, apart from some decent black ribbons. Anyway, Matthew's best coat was black, so it served well and Mary's cloak was dark. Ben had not been family, any more would have been a needless expense, but she felt she had to show willing, for a month at least, as you might for a cousin, and especially on the mission she had given herself for that day.

She had seen Tobias in the morning when he had brought some news from the Saracen's Head, most of it discouraging. The barman who had worked the previous Wednesday had been there again and he had remembered Ben, as he had seen him a few times before; he especially remembered the Waterloo medal, just like his own father's. It had been only moderately busy in the smoke room early that evening and Ben had taken a seat by the door. He remembered that there had been some locals and a few strangers. It seemed that a footman from the York House had come looking for Ben, the barman had pointed him out and heard that a gentleman who was to come was taken ill and so was not coming after all, but had returned to London. That had been a blow. The "officer" and "gentleman" had never been there at all. Ben's tryst with him had not taken place. One other thing had transpired though. One of the strangers had bought Ben some drinks, more than a stranger normally would. The barman had heard snatches of the talk and some of it had touched on Spain and the wars. Before nine o'clock a few men had left, including the stranger, and Ben had made his way out, sober, that was telling, some little time afterwards. All the barman could say about the stranger was that he was a Somerset man to be sure, likely Bristol, but not a native of that city. Not: "Bris'le born and bred", said he.

She presented herself at the Peterson's door in Marlborough Buildings, late enough for even a tardy luncheon to have been

113

concluded, and pulled on the bell. She allowed herself one glance up at the gracious facade towering above her and stretching out in a mighty terrace down the length of Marlborough Lane, facing the open parkland. She also turned, just once, to survey the magnificent vista of the Royal Crescent behind her and to her right, which arched perfectly round its private green, separated from the common grass of the park by the stone wall of the ha-ha. No beast would be permitted to stray onto the hallowed turf. And, she reflected uneasily, not one person wandered along the pavement. All was still. How unlike the crowds on Walcot Street! Tom could sit at the gate and greet dozens in a morning, especially on market days. She felt suddenly awkward and steeled herself. Indistinctly, a maid's steps sounded on the marble tiles of the hall and the white door opened.

It proved easier than she had hoped. Mrs Peterson was evidently entertaining a group of ladies. She could hear their refined voices drifting down the stairs from the drawing room, restrained laughter, the chinking of tea-cups. From higher still she could hear the distant sounds of music practice, which suggested that the young twin daughters were gainfully employed and unlikely to distract. Surprisingly, Captain Peterson agreed to see her promptly and had her brought up to his study which overlooked the rear of the property. She felt relieved. The Captain had paid a visit to her home in Walcot Street when Mr Parry had lodged with her. That might have helped. It had certainly given her the courage to arrive uninvited, unannounced. She felt she could speak with him on a more professional footing without his wife there. He was, after all, a magistrate, who dealt with crime and injustice and there was a family link, of sorts, through the Parry connection.

The Captain smiled encouragingly at the shabby woman seated facing him at his desk. The low afternoon sun caught her face cruelly and he leapt up to twitch the drape over. Ever the gallant, it offered some shade for her eyes, and a kinder twilight for her care-lined face. He struck at his old tinderbox and lit the candelabra.

"Well, Mrs Spence, how might I be of assistance?"

Carefully, missing nothing, she told her tale. He would have welcomed her as a witness in court, so precise was she.

"So although the coroner declared it was a case of misadventure I fear someone did away with Benjamin Prestwick and I don't rightly know what to do next." She was horrified to feel a blush creeping up her neck. "I am sorry, sir, that I did not write to you to request this meeting. I would not have bothered you in person, but for the connection with Mr Parry's father and the mention of your ship. I feel there is need for haste."

Aspects of her tale intrigued him, especially as he had been running out of excuses for staying in his study and avoiding a tea session in the drawing room. Beautiful as the audacious Tilly Vere was, and charming as he knew the respectable Mrs Charles Parry to be, an hour of them and his dear wife Lydia dissecting the events of Emma and Nathaniel's recent wedding was more than he was willing to bear. He had been biding his time, in hiding, until forcibly winkled out.

He smiled again, expansively, letting his mind roll back to the events of the winter of 1808-9.

"I was indeed the Captain of the *Renowned* Mrs Spence, and conveyed Mr Parry's late father home to England, with a quantity of gold and gems. Now then, how shall we say he came by them?" His eyes twinkled conspiratorially, "Perhaps we can say, which he had liberated from the clutches of the Emperor Napoleon Bonaparte. All fair in love and war, what!"

Martha Spence was staring at him intently; she was not smiling, so the Captain smothered his usual bark of a laugh.

"I remember Mr Owen Parry and myself discussing the booty, as it were, and that three soldiers, a Captain, Mr Prestwick and your husband, had been recompensed for their efforts. They had been awarded prize money. Common enough in the army, and not set amounts, unlike the navy you know."

Martha Spence clearly did not know and continued to peer at Oliver Peterson, hoping for a solution. She struggled again for clarity.

"Benjamin Prestwick was going to meet an officer who he thought was going to give him so much money he would be set up for life, but the meeting did not take place and now he is dead. I smell a rat, Captain Peterson. It seems to me when poor folk think they are going to get possession of a money tree from rich folk they are usually mistaken or up to no good, sometimes both. Ben needed money, I know it. He was behind with his rent. So tell me, who was that officer in the Spanish war? The man who was to meet Ben has gone back to London according to the footman of the York House. This man had not been seen by Ben in Bath before so he must be a stranger."

Captain Peterson raked his memory and selected his next words carefully.

"I do seem to recall some adverse comments from Mr Parry's father about the officer in question. Nothing certain, just a general dissatisfaction I believe. I'm sorry, Mrs Spence, I am short of a name here, but I do remember the incident."

Martha Spence's reference to smelling a rat had the unfortunate result of tuning Captain Peterson's nose in to the stench of camphor emanating from her mourning dress. This was not too bad on its own, but more sinister aromas under-laid it and were drifting towards him in the heat of the room. The fire was extremely well banked up.

"What I propose," he said rising to draw the interview to a close, "is that I contact Mr Parry, who is at the family home on the island of Anglesey, acquaint him with your concerns and see if we can discover any further intelligence on the financial connections between Mr Prestwick and the anonymous Captain. I am sure that when Mr Parry returns he will speak with you on the matter."

He could see Martha's face fall.

"Mr Parry is a successful investigator you know," he said kindly. "Remember the part he played in bringing young Frances to Bath, and the other girls. Though, of course," he said guardedly, watching her closely and approving her brisk nod, "some aspects of that matter should still not be discussed."

A gush of renewed laughter from the drawing room reminded him of another mystery, not quite so well solved. Tilly Vere's husband was still missing, though presumed dead by most. According to Nathaniel, Vere had not been entirely blameless in an unpleasant case of murder and had been up to his neck in other unsavoury activities, so he was no great loss, though Tilly's anticipated marriage to Howard Dill was waiting on a solution to the conundrum of his disappearance. However, he reflected, she did not seem unduly distressed by the delay, judging from the silvery peals of glee she was busily venting next door.

Martha had risen to her feet and was finishing pushing the chair ruthlessly into place under the desk.

"So you will contact Mr Parry then, Captain? I am that grateful to you, sir."

"I shall do it this very afternoon, Mrs Spence," said Captain Peterson with a slight bow.

"It really is unlike the Captain not to join us, at least briefly," complained Lydia Peterson, perplexed. "His visitor left some time ago."

The women smiled, bonnet feathers nodding agreement that the ways of men, in particular husbands, were often unfathomable.

"The dear Captain must be longing for some company," said Tilly, sighing prettily at the prospect of the deprivation he suffered, cruel business having denied him a comfortable seat by her and the benefit of her charms. She was well aware that he found her rather beautiful and spent a pleasing amount of time admiring her physical assets, particularly when displayed by a low-necked ball gown. Mrs Charles Parry was also very fond of Oliver Peterson but was quite a different type of friend, in that she fully understood his reluctance to join them. She had the capacity to enjoy gossip, as long as it was not too regular and the personalities were varied, but she preferred to ration herself strictly to one dose of Lydia Peterson per month. Anymore was unnecessarily fatiguing.

Lydia had pulled the bell for the maid and sent her to chase Oliver out of his fastness in the study, but all this achieved was the briefest appearance from her husband, a flurry of hand shaking and bonhomie, after which he disappeared once more, pleading urgent and unavoidable business. Once back in his lair, he lit a cigar, smoothed out his headed writing paper, sharpened his pen nib and prepared to draft two letters, one a leisurely communication to his son-in-law and favourite daughter in the depths of rural Wales, the other, brief and much more formal, would be addressed to Lord Melbourne, Home Secretary, with reference to his noble colleague Lord Palmerston, Foreign Secretary. The second letter would be a duty, the conveyance of a nugget of intelligence.

Early afternoon: 20th February, 1833. The Mortimer-Buckley Residence, Park Street, Mayfair, London.

The Honourable Charlotte Drake was not pleased with the progress of her call on Lady Mortimer-Buckley and her daughter. It had been convenient to visit, as the family lived across the road from her *pied-à-terre* in Park Street; her suite of rooms in her father's Mayfair mansion. But convenience was not everything: the Mortimer-Buckleys were not proving to be convivial. In fact, they were as dull as ditch-water. Lottie had only recently taken to exploiting her holdings in this corner of Mayfair and this call was her first one. Her affair with Edwin Ravenswood had prospered in Park Street, under the guise of Edwin being a visitor to her brother, an elusive rakehell who occasionally occupied the lower floors, either personally or by throwing it open to noisy groups of his fellow young bucks. She had spent more afternoons at the house of late and a friendship with Lady Mortimer-Buckley had seemed to be a shrewd move on two fronts. Firstly, it provided an excellent official reason for visiting Mayfair, apart from the necessary need to limit her

118

brother's designs on her share of their father's house, and secondly it might provide entertainment in the shape of the louche Sir Giles. She had obviously entranced him at the Ravenswood dinner, and after spending a half hour in the company of his wife and daughter she could see why.

The female Mortimer-Buckleys had been pleased to entertain her, but only as a captive audience for the matron's rehearsal of the latest family drama. It really had been a waste of her new outfit. Lottie was resplendent in a dark green gown, viciously belted to twenty inches at the waist, with a row of bows down the front as big as chrysanthemums, billowing leg o' mutton sleeves, a white starched ruff and collar, and, the *pièce-de-résistance*, a green bonnet with iridescent peacock plumes. Really: quite sensational. Lady Mortimer-Buckley had not even had the grace to notice, though she herself was turned out, offensively, in enough ill-fitting burgundy satin to provide sails for a ship of the line. Of course she had heard the gossip about the nanny's scandalous disappearance, but had hardly expected it to dominate every moment of her visit.

Leonora Mortimer-Buckley's plump face was puckered with suppressed rage and disappointment as she continued to deliver her tale. This had had an unfortunate effect on the layers of powder adhering to it, particularly around the mouth, where they had cracked under the strain of her displeasure.

"My own granddaughter, left alone in the park! Unattended! And Nanny gone, vanished! She took nothing with her! Nothing! Is that not telling?"

Lottie managed a half-hearted smile of encouragement, though this was not the first time her hostess had drawn these facts to her attention.

"Nannies which match a child's needs precisely are not easily found, as you must know. You have a daughter, do you not? Miss Trickett, though in some ways a strident young woman, dealt with my granddaughter beautifully. She doted on the child and likewise the dear little one was devoted to her. Miss Trickett was a jewel! Though Sir Giles, unaccountably, felt she was becoming increasingly unsuitable, I will not have a word said about her! And neither will you, will you Prudence?" At this she shot a self-satisfied glance at her daughter and drew out a damp handkerchief with which she dabbed haphazardly at her watering eyes. "Oh dear, forgive me. But I really do not know what we shall do. Dear little Lulu, my granddaughter, is crying night and day for Nanny. My daughter is a shadow of her former self!"

Lottie rather hoped she was. Surely Prudence must have looked better at some point? The young woman drooped unattractively, her heavy white brocade dress, patterned with light brown, was insipid against her drained skin. Its heavy weave, scaly and gill-like, gave the appearance of desiccated fish skin. The limp black ribbon round her neck was also no ornament. Presumably it was a nod to the uncomfortable possibility that the absent nanny could by now be dead. If she had absconded, she would at any rate be dead to them. Lottie smiled again at that thought, but was now totally bored and glanced at the clock on the mantle-piece. She could reasonably conclude the conversation and leave within ten minutes. Her scrutiny took in the both of them: one last show of interest before the fond farewell.

"You said the child was found on a park bench. What did she say when the servants found her?"

Lady Mortimer-Buckley cut through her daughter's stammering effort to respond. "Shush Prudence, calm yourself. She simply said that men had come and Nanny had gone away with them. Maisie Trickett would never have done such a thing willingly. Who knows what pressure was applied! And as I said, her room is as she left it that morning. All her clothes are here, her trunk is full and her purse is left behind. Mrs Drake, she was kidnapped! What sort of world do we live in?"

Overcome by the possibilities, she let out a low, animal wail, bringing Lottie to her feet rather more quickly than she had intended. Fortunately action was not required, as Prudence relinquished her mother's hands and moved in to apply a full and tight embrace.

"There, there, Mother dear," she muttered, patting her mother's ample back.

"Well," said Lottie, capitalising on the break, "I must go and leave you to comfort your mother. I do hope that you have better news of your nanny."

The women reluctantly allowed her to stay on her feet and a servant was summoned to see her out. Lottie trotted downstairs from the drawing room with a spring in her step, as renewed sobs were muffled behind the closing door. Close to the foot of the stairs, her optimism was rewarded by a sighting of the man of the house. The front door was being hauled open by a footman to admit Sir Giles into the hall.

"Well met, Sir Giles," she said archly, posing on the bottom step. "I have just paid a call on your wife and daughter, but how lovely to catch you before I leave!"

In truth, Buckley was not looking good. Though spruce and clearly pleased to see her, he had a haggard look about him. His spirits rose marginally, as the company of Lottie would put off the unpleasant prospect of resuming relations with his family.

"Mrs Drake," he said, marching over to her swiftly, bowing and lifting her right hand for a lingering kiss, "how utterly delightful to see you. Do step into the library for a few minutes if you can spare the time."

Things were looking up. Within two minutes Lottie was in a comfortable leather chair, cherry brandy in hand, basking in the warmth of Buckley's appreciative gaze.

"May I say, Mrs Drake, that, as ever, you look wonderful," he purred, almost his old self, as he drank in the full effect of the dazzling green gown, framing the voluptuous curves beneath. The day had looked up for him too. "It is a treat to see you again, my dear lady. I realized that your father had a residence here, but did not know that you are now visiting in the neighbourhood."

A strangled yelp broke loose from above as a door opened, followed by the caterwauling of prolonged sobbing, then the sounds of footfalls and timorous servants bustling the ladies upstairs to the bedchambers.

"Oh dear," said Lottie, her eyes darting with mischief, "the ladies seem to have retired. The news of your nanny's disappearance is weighing heavily upon them."

Sir Giles's newly regained bonhomie seemed to deflate like a balloon, she noticed his hand shake and tighten on the glass.

"Yes," he said, faintly, "most distressing. She has probably run off, what?"

Lottie suddenly had a vision of her husband's face, urgent concern overlaying his usual expression which typically varied between cynical, greedy and facetious. "John has warned me that kidnapping is increasing. Mainly of unaccompanied women, lower class women, also children, apparently. Such perversion in the world isn't there!" She pulled a face. Their class and possible fates were both subjects which could not be discussed in mixed company. "Not that a lady would be out alone of course. Frightful bad luck if your nanny really was taken; she was clearly out with a child of rank, which should have served as a warning. Of course, it would have been so much worse if little Lulu had gone, wouldn't it? They might take children of rank, mightn't they, if they are planning to extort a ransom? John has warned our servants that they are not to take our daughter Lizzie out alone, but must be in twos, and one must be a footman carrying a pistol."

Sir Giles moved to pour her another cherry brandy. She noticed that he took a cognac for himself, a large one. His face was ashen.

"Are you feeling quite all right, Sir Giles?"

"Yes, yes, of course. Just not sleeping too well, to tell the truth. A little tired." He struggled to steer the conversation into safer waters but she kept him in danger of drowning.

"The last time we met was when we travelled to Bristol, wasn't it Sir Giles? Have you seen Mr Ravenswood since?"

At the mention of his name Buckley felt he was suffocating and gulped down a deep breath before the next strengthening draught of brandy.

"Yes, I have," he said. "He was in town last week."

How could he forget? Eating out with Ravenswood in the Strand he had been briefly elated to learn that his two problems had indeed been eliminated by the interventions of his host, but his food had turned to ashes in his mouth when he realized the scope of recompense to be exacted by Ravenswood. He now had fellow feeling with Doctor Faustus, as his soul was wrung in the cruel hands of his new tormentor. The first payment had already been made. He was now a principal investor in Ravenswood's new vessel, which was installed in a London dock. An intense weariness coursed through him, sapping his remaining energy.

She knew that it had been a risk to ask about Edwin, but really, the afternoon had been so tedious. And now she knew that Edwin had not been spotted in Park Street, though she would have been surprised if he had, they had been so careful. Sir Giles would presumably pull himself together, another nanny would be engaged and he would regain his *savoir-faire*.

"And you met did you? With Mr Ravenswood?"

The voice sounded in his head, hoarse yet insistent. "Giles! Pull yourself together. You can do it."

"Yes, Madam, we did meet," said Sir Giles. With a supreme effort he managed the ghost of his old smile. "Now, when might we have the pleasure of entertaining you and your husband?"

Lord Melbourne's Office: Downing Street, London.

Lord Melbourne looked up from his dispatches and frowned at the sulky fire in the grate. "Percy, for Gawd's sake man," he drawled, "can't you see mi'fire's dwindlin' damn it?"

Percy could not see, as he was in the adjacent office, scribbling energetically to finish the last task issued by the noble lord. "On my way, mi'lord," he called, scraping the chair back as he leapt to his feet and bounded through the communicating door. He knelt before the smoking fire and set about it with poker, fuel, and shortly thereafter, bellows. Satisfied, he rocked back on his heels, waiting for judgement.

"Excellent, mi'dear fellow," said Melbourne, returning to his papers. "Excellent. Dashed long winter, what!"

He rustled through the documents most insistently drawn to his attention by Percy's coloured notation, until his gaze fixed on the report from the docks which had been eluding him.

"Bad business, Percy," he said, his customary cynical smirk briefly eclipsed by a shadow of genuine concern. "That spate of kidnappings in the parishes near the docks seems to be turning into something more serious. Damn it! Have you heard? A nanny on the staff of one of the Members has been snatched in Hyde Park!"

Percy stood to attention, pushing his round-rimmed gold glasses further up his nose. "Yes, mi'lord, the story's all over Westminster. The child was found in the park and the nanny was seen being hurried off by two men."

"Not that kidnapping is a rare occurrence, mark you," said Melbourne expansively, "but the current outbreak seems dashed sustained. I mention it to you as you will recall some paper work from the year before last. That business in Bristol at the time of the reform riots? You remember our man Parry, don't you Percy? He was onto some white slave trade out of the port. We dampened it down, if you remember. Lord Palmerston was keeping a weather eye on the personnel if you recall."

Percy did recall. He had personally retrieved the report from Nathaniel Parry which Lord Palmerston had discarded and drawn its battered contents to Lord Melbourne's attention. Pam had insisted on staying tight with his Bristol merchant, a Mr Edwin Ravenswood, who seemed to be up to his neck in the traffic. He was also a very useful informant and operator in the essential, and illegal, opium trade to China, which Pam was doing everything in his power to develop. Without that drain on their silver, the balance of trade with China would have been crushingly negative and Chinese tea, porcelain and silk had to be bought. The economic scales had to be tipped.

Melbourne fell silent for a moment, dredging up his memories of the affair. Not only had the merchant not been prosecuted, as Parry had advised, but he had been rewarded by an invitation to join the bench: Justice of the Peace forsooth!

"Contact Parry, would you," he rapped out at length. "Bring him in. Drake needs to be contacted as well. Lord Palmerston regards him as his principal agent for reporting on trade out of the West Country."

"Yes, mi'lord," said Percy, rubbing his hands on the sides of his trousers as he made for the door.

"Oh and Percy," called Melbourne, bringing him up short. "Speaking of the West Country, find me the recent letter from Captain Peterson, our man in Bath."

On a much lighter note and a rather fascinating one, he had been alerted by that particular contact that enquiries had been made touching on an old and beguiling mystery. Raising the name of Parry had brought it back to his notice.

"And have a rummage in the foreign archives. I am interested in the details of a consignment of treasure brought back from Spain in the winter of 1808-9. Owen Parry would have written the report on it and it was sailed back to Britain in the *Renowned* captained by Peterson. There was a question mark over the whereabouts of some of the consignment. One of the persons involved surfaced recently and very briefly as a matter of fact. He declared he was meeting an old army acquaintance and was about to become wealthy, then promptly got himself killed! It is a long shot, but there might be some connection with the missing goods."

Percy brought the Captain's letter, wrote the notes to Drake in London and Parry in Anglesey, then made his way to the archive vault. It was early evening before he emerged, looking the worse for his tussle with the dust and cobwebs, but triumphantly bearing a box of papers. Melbourne ordered veal pie and claret, cleared his desk and set about levering open the tin lid which gave way with a sharp crack. Blowing dust and grit off the bundle, he took it out and untied the string which held it. Smoothing out the roll of papers over the desk, he leaned closer to inspect the faded writing. The report confirmed that the

125

mission to relieve Napoleon of a wagon of gold and assorted treasures bound for his brother Joseph in Madrid had been entirely successful. With just three soldiers to assist, and the useful offices of a French traitor, Parry had captured the goods and brought them to Britain. However, a question mark remained over the fate of one specific item. Parry reported that the soldiers had been awarded prize money in kind from the haul, but that he had noticed, once returned to Britain, that an artefact of particular significance was missing. He was sure he had seen it and it had definitely not been granted as a prize, though Parry had ensured he had not attracted attention to the piece by forbidding it or making any comment on its provenance. It could have been stolen on the ship, but more likely had been taken by one of the soldiers accompanying him on the raid.

Melbourne, the Honourable Member for Portarlington at the time, remembered something of the story concerning that artefact which, fortunately, had never reached the press. This particular treasure was more than the sum of its gold chain and jewelled inlays, as it was an antique pendant dating from the Middle Kingdom of Ancient Egypt. It had originally been stolen by marauding French troops early in 1799 during Napoleon's Egyptian campaign, only to be confiscated from them by the victorious British army in 1801. Along with countless other items, it had been taken to London and placed in the British Museum for the edification of the British public. What made this piece so very controversial was that Napoleon himself had been taken by it, and before he quit the country in the face of impending military defeat at the hands of the British, had ordered it be fitted with a new fastener in the shape of a gold and jewelled clasp bearing his initials: NB.

This adornment had sealed its fate. Within weeks of its arrival at the British Museum it had disappeared from view. Melbourne remembered the fanciful tales of occult power operating in connection with the disappearance, of dark mysteries and the displeasure of the pharaohs. Such stories were suppressed immediately, as was all mention of the piece, which

126

he remembered had been stolen yet again, in an act of audacious larceny, presumably by a French agent. News of the theft had gone no further than Westminster but Parry would have known of it, and no doubt his eyes had lit up when he caught sight of it nestling in the miscellaneous bounty of Napoleon's gold! A special gift for his brother Joseph, calculated to inspire and strengthen him, it was more than a trinket; it was an ancient sign of power. The pendant, a full six inches in breadth, was a golden falcon inlaid with dark glimmering stones; blue lapis lazuli, green feldspar and red cornelian. The bird signified the god Horus, god of the sky, the sun and the moon, god of kingship, majesty, power and war. In its talons it gripped the Shen rings, the twined ropes of eternal protection, and above each claw, linking it to a mighty wing; there was a loop-tipped cross, the Ankh, the breath of life.

Melbourne sat back, deep in thought. To track down Napoleon's falcon and display it at the British Museum would be a triumphant piece of news, just the thing for these pedestrian days of endless drafting and redrafting of new pieces of unnecessary legislation. He sighed, windily. Surely to God, he declared to himself, we have enough laws already! Walpole had been right, bless him: let sleeping dogs lie. But, he reflected morosely, the dogs were no longer asleep and their order papers were as long as your arm. It really seemed that the public expected a government to be responsible for the welfare of every damned individual. Preposterous!

"Percy!"

"Yes, mi'lord?" The eager face, framed by lank overlong hair, shot round the door, the nose twitching up the glasses inquisitively, like a short-sighted squirrel.

"Jump to it. Write to Captain Peterson. Inform him that I am indeed most interested to hear that one of the party involved in … well, just say, involved in the mission in question … has been brought to his notice. The individual's unfortunate demise might just provide something of a lead on a very cold trail. Keep me posted. Yours, etc."

Percy jumped as required, but ensured that it was in His Lordship's direction before he headed for his own room.

"Shall I replace the documents, mi'lord?"

Melbourne had already transferred his attention to the veal pie, but managed to nod in assent and waved him away. Percy swept up the box and papers and made himself scarce, hauling his chair over to a side desk, out of his master's line of sight. Before he drafted the letter he read through the crucial documents left on top of the pile by his employer, and could barely believe his eyes. A tingle flashed up his spine and the back hairs of his neck lifted as he read of the strange adventures of the golden falcon. The office seemed to fade from view and he was transported to the sands of the desert, he felt the sweltering heat and saw in his mind's eye the waving palms and stone triangles of the mighty pyramids. All things Egyptian had been a grand European passion since Napoleon's soldiers and scholars had invaded a generation ago. Egyptology was all the rage and Percy was a demon for it. As if by an oasis he drank in the mysteries of the Nile, and as he daydreamed he suddenly had a rather good thought.

He had always liked Nathaniel Parry, saw him as, *sympatico*, a fellow Romantic who was shipwrecked on the same raft, adrift in the shark-infested waters of government service. He, Richard Percy, fixer *extraordinaire* of the Home Office, would make sure it was his friend and ally Nathaniel and not the detestable John Drake who was on the inside track if there was any treasure hunting to be done. There was probably nothing in it, but the thought of it scattered a little magical dust and enlivened a dull day. Invigorated, he rifled through the correspondence he had prepared that afternoon, located the note to Anglesey, and, dipping his pen in the inkpot, set to work on a postscript.

128

Chapter 4

Late afternoon: 25th February, 1833.
The road to Llanddaniel, the Isle of Anglesey.

The commercial traveller leaned round the door of the Old Bull's Head and shouted a last instruction to him as he rode away from the inn.

"You cannot miss Llanddaniel, Mr Lee! Keep to the coast road until you see the sign, then down the track to the village. Parry's farm is near an old burial mound by a copse. It's an ancient site with great stones at its mouth, guarding the bodies of the first men! You can't miss it!"

Cornelius Fu Lee rode out of Beaumaris and left behind the bustle of the town, the roaming dogs and the barefoot children, the cries of the fishwives and the shopkeepers touting for the last customers before closing time. In the cold twilight he covered a mile along the deserted coast road before he had more company. A harsh call sounded across the darkening fields and he looked up to see a raven sweep over the hedge and pause to wheel above his head. After catching his attention, the bird lit out towards the coast, patterning the fading sky with his soaring climbs and swoops before setting a straight course over the enamelled waves of the Strait to the mountains of Snowdonia. It was an auspicious sign to see such a bird at close quarters, a creature of wisdom and prophesy, and Cornelius paused to consider it. The raven was both a divine messenger of good news, and an omen of death. But though dark was falling, it was not yet late evening, so his call was lucky. Like the crow, the raven was a creature of harmony, embodying the light and the dark. He felt himself transported across time and space to the China of his youth and listened again to the strains of the *Wu Ye Ti*, "The evening call of the raven", a melody hundreds of years old, passed from teacher to pupil, and played for guests by shy girls in the small music room of his father's house.

He had already been lucky to arrive on the island of Anglesey in the company of an English speaker. The talkative commercial traveller from Liverpool had shared a bench seat with him in the mail coach and on arrival at the Beaumaris inn had insisted on negotiating his lodging and the hire of a horse. It became apparent that the traveller was an enthusiastic Evangelical Christian and leading light of his local anti-slavery society, so Cornelius was not surprised that the sight of a foreigner had intrigued him. The traveller was determined that the journey would be used for improving discussion, but he had not noticed that he was doing most of the talking and that the theme had shifted from him coaxing views from the stranger and preaching the ways of the just, to delivering his own life story. Cornelius was philosophical by nature, and on his travels in Europe enjoyed reading western literature on that subject. He often turned to Goethe's *Reflections,* which were instructive on the subject of conversation and the art of listening. Cornelius was a skilled practitioner of that art.

As they had left the straggling border towns and night had fallen, he had been obliged to demonstrate some of his other skills, which had cemented the bond between himself and the traveller. The horses had struggled to keep upright on a lonely stretch of icy road, pitch black and dense with evergreens on the verges. The passengers had been ordered out to ease the burden at the start of a sharp incline and, predictably, a couple of thieves had materialised from the shadows to confront them as the coach pulled on ahead. One faced Cornelius, waving two flintlock pistols erratically and demanding silence with an oath, whilst the other started to make a move towards the commercial traveller, an older, plumper target. They were both far too slow and standing together was their downfall. Before the oath was fully out of the snarling mouth or the other man had covered any ground, Cornelius had sprung forward, side-stepped the armed man and delivered a crashing left-arm block to sweep aside his outstretched arms. The shock caused both guns to discharge wildly, and the sharp retorts, smoke and sparks screened Cornelius's second blow, a lethal right-hander, which collapsed the gunman's throat, and his third, a side-kick to his left which dropped the other thief before he took a step. The commercial traveller had not even time to cry out before Cornelius had turned from one slumped body to the other. But it was another corpse. Amateurs to the last, one of the pistol balls shot in error had found a mark. The guard had rushed back on hearing the guns, bawling his intention to fire, but was only too glad to find his duties restricted to shovelling the bodies off the road and shepherding his passengers back to the coach. In fact, he decided to shepherd just the one plump passenger, as a glance at the bodies had persuaded him that the other one should be left to his own devices.

"God save us!" the traveller had stuttered, as they settled back into their seats. "Thank you, sir. I owe you my life!"

"You are welcome," Cornelius had said, with a slight bow of his head. He had decided not to add that it was "nothing". Would it have offended the man's self-worth? English manners were interesting, but labyrinthine to fathom. He left the challenge for another day and instead reflected briefly on the two footpads lying dead by the roadside. The loss of life was always regrettable and he had borne the men no particular ill-will, but the choice had been a simple one, their lives or his. And the application of a few basic techniques had not been without another advantage. He had had little time for training in Liverpool where he had rented an anonymous room, with, as the English said, barely the space to swing a cat. Also, despite his preference for discretion, he had personal reasons for defusing the situation. He had no intention of allowing his bag to be rifled.

It had made the long journey from Paris unmolested and he was a visitor bearing gifts. He was determined that they would reach their destination.

Cornelius was used to surviving in strange lands and outwitting both assailants and the idly curious. It would not have been difficult for him to get what he needed from the innkeeper, Welsh speaker or not. But to have the deals done, and more than that, for him to arrive at this remote place, looking as outlandish as he did, with a sponsor and "friend" had been useful. Ports were cosmopolitan places, and in Liverpool the thin sprinkling of foreigners had allowed him a degree of freedom and anonymity. Once he had travelled into the countryside and crossed the border into Wales, he had become more conspicuous, much more than he cared to be.

The black horse hired at the Old Bull's Head was a powerful and stoical beast, not swift, but intelligent. It seemed to know its way along the deserted coast road, which gave Cornelius time for reflection. So far the mission had been moderately lucky. The journey from Paris to Liverpool had been easy, a horse-drawn diligence to the coast, then a steamer to the City of Liverpool. The port had been a rare sight, its vast wet dock filled with vessels. Fully one hundred were held at anchor and the quays were thronged with sailors and dock workers, travellers leaving and arriving, thieves and dealers all jostling together and moving like a tide round mounds of bales and barrels. The port rivalled London and put Bristol in the shade, though he knew it had not always been so. Cotton spinning and weaving had bankrolled the flowering of the North and one day, on a whim, he had taken himself off to Manchester to see its famous factories. These had proved to be vast brick-built blocks, their walls studded with blank windows. From each roof rose one tall blackened chimney, which together formed a forest of spires, piercing the gloom above and belching out more poisonous black clouds to fuel it. It had been a bright day by the coast, but the Manchester sun glowed only as a grey disc, masked by the inky smoke. Beneath this Stygian canopy the air rang with the insistent metallic clatter of machines and the periodic shrieks of boiler steam which played counterpoint to the low incessant rumble of carts on the crowded roads. He could hear Manchester and taste it still in his throat when he was ten miles out on the return trip to Liverpool.

The journey to the cotton city had been remarkable as he had travelled on one of the new steam locomotives which ran independently on iron rails all the way from Liverpool to Manchester, a full thirty miles to the northeast. Never tired and rolling at a steady seventeen miles per hour, fuelled by the roaring furnace, the iron horses ploughed up and down the tracks, moving goods and people in ever growing numbers. It was the future, he knew it to be so, and imagined a world where all towns were linked, across hills and through forests, deserts and swamps. A vast endeavour of huge cost, but with profits to be made: the world would change.

Apart from the useful reconnoitring, and uncovering a lead which he would pursue in London, the trip to Liverpool had been productive mainly in a negative sense as it ruled out possibilities. He had hoped to track down his quarry, a savagely successful criminal, and also to forge links within the port for future work. He had failed to locate his man, and had been disappointed to see only half a dozen Chinese faces, none of which provided useful material for his purpose. At such a great port he had thought there might be more but he had drawn a blank. On his last visit to London he had found a few gangs of Chinese lascars working on the ships in the docks by Limehouse causeway, and two of his men were already placed in Ravenswood's crew, preparing another new American-built vessel for its first voyage to the East. Entrepreneurs in London and Liverpool were hungry for a share of the growing Chinese market and it was easy to guess which goods the merchants would favour. He frowned at the thought of the cursed opium run from India to China which beckoned to the English like a Satanic Grail. It was a trade he was sworn to destroy, under sacred oath to his Emperor.

His journeys in Europe had filled him with dismay. During

his last stay in Paris the well-informed talk was all of entrepreneurs and their rights, of liberalism and free trade. The homespun philosophers traded the words of their hero Jean-Baptiste Say and of that grim Scot who had inspired him, the economist Adam Smith. Cornelius had come to know them both through the enthusiasm of their disciples, and it seemed to him that all they preached was the selfish pursuit of wealth. Wealth and profit: the twin towers of their faith were to him false gods, both entirely alien to his country, his faith and the dictates of his soul.

The horse shied suddenly and shook him from his thoughts as a growling roll of thunder sounded across the Strait from the mountains. Cornelius quietened him, checked the skies, and as he did so the rain started to fall. As he had been warned at the inn, it soon commenced to tear across the island in horizontal rods, drenching him, his pack and his stolid horse as they laboured on, down the narrow track towards Llanddaniel. A cloudy mist dropped, swathing the landscape and blotting out the sight of the sea. Wind and rain bit into him and, pulling his hat over his eyes, he turned to pleasanter thoughts to sustain him over the last few miles. He was looking forward to seeing Nathaniel Parry again. It was rare in his line of work to have any warm feelings for an acquaintance: rare and usually unwise. Nathaniel and he had been helpful to each other in the past and Nathaniel's steadfastness had surprised him. But more than that, he felt a bond with Parry, who seemed to be a westernised version of himself: not so much a brother, but a second self, an alter ego. Both worked for their own governments, had similar moral codes, were of an age and build and, bizarrely, both were born of American mothers. This discovery was also a sign. It had been a welcome one, in the solitary and precarious life of Cornelius Lee. But the match was not exact as the opium question separated them. It was the principal cause of distrust between their countries as the British ignored all pleas from his Emperor's government to cease their illegal trade in China, and the problem grew as the years passed. But that was for the future.

134

For today, on this cold February day, Nathaniel's house beckoned to him as a haven. He looked forward to presenting his gifts to the newly-weds. These were the greatest of human pleasures: the giving and the taking, and as his study of Goethe had taught him, for contentment of the soul, nothing should be more highly prized than this day.

As he listened to the rhythmic, muddy squelch of his horse's hooves as it plodded on, snatches of the commercial traveller's tales returned to him. "Be warned, it always rains heavy in these parts in February. Do you know English sayings? February brings the rain, thaws the frozen lakes again! But sometimes it still snows. February is also called "fill dyke", black or white! This is a strange spot you've fetched up in. Oh yes: my, my. 'Twas the last stronghold of the Druids before the Roman army killed the lot of them: burned all their oak groves they did. It's always been a wild, pagan place and there are traces of the old days still." Then he had glanced furtively at Cornelius, "No offence," he had said, suddenly uncomfortable. "You are a good Christian I take it from your attire, sir?" Cornelius's smile had reassured him and he had rushed on. "No English spoken on Anglesey as a rule: be ready for that. I'm not a native of the place. Born on the mainland I was, Welsh borders. Welsh mother. Most folk in the borders speak English and Welsh."

Cornelius spotted a faded sign by the wayside and turned his horse towards the village. As the traveller had said, he soon came to a hillock ringed with stones. Some stood sentinel, grey and lichen covered, some were toppled, and others framed the entrance to the ancient burial mound. Through that low portal, a stone-lined passageway could be seen; reaching into profound darkness. He felt the presence of the ancestors and of the earth as it once was: it was a place of power. He had not advertised the Taoism of his childhood to his Evangelical acquaintance as it served no purpose. Not that he was in any way a zealous pagan. His beliefs had been battered along the way, but he retained his spirituality: an unshakeable belief in harmony and a profound empathy for the natural world, times past and to come. He felt it

135

overwhelmingly as he approached the stones, and reined in the unwilling horse.

And it was there that they found him.

Nathaniel and Emma had been sitting in the farm parlour when Caradoc first raised his head. Sensing the approach of a stranger the terrier bolted to the door and set up a ferocious barking. Nathaniel pulled on a cloak, picked up the old hunting rifle which always stood, primed and ready by the door, and let Caradoc loose. He smiled to Emma who had looked up, startled, from her reading. She was huddled into the corner, making the best of the pool of light shed by the oil lamp.

"What do you think it is?" she said. She had a town girl's fears of the swirling dark outside and her heart thumped unpleasantly.

"Probably foxes," he said.

Striding out into the yard, he saw no disturbance in the hen house, but heard a strange horse neigh to his mare in its stall and as he ran out to the fence overlooking the copse and the burial mound of Bryn Celli Ddu, he saw a gaunt figure clothed entirely in black, standing motionless in the driving rain. Nathaniel's face broke into a smile as he vaulted the fence to welcome the man he had not seen for well over a year, and once thought he might never see again, in this life.

Later, introductions done, pleasantries exchanged, and seated together in the farm dining room with their backs to the fire, there was a place and time for more than small talk. They had dined well on Mrs Jones's seaweed soup, the formidable *cawl lafwr*, followed by a substantial rack of mutton and a rice pudding. Emma had fretted about the pudding, which appeared Welsh style, sugarless, and flavoured with nutmeg and bay leaf. She had withdrawn from the table with a promise to have Aberffraw cakes brought out with coffee after the men had finished with their brandy, but there were still three at the table.

Caradoc had recognised Cornelius immediately, he smelled the same, though he was thinner and his black hair had grown longer. The terrier had settled down, proprietorially, with his head on the visitor's feet. It was good to welcome an ally. The last weeks had been full of strangers and a revelation for Caradoc in many ways. He had met dogs exactly like himself for the first time since he was a pup and it had not been altogether pleasant. One in particular had arrived with a cowman and had swaggered about the farm as if he owned it. Caradoc had given him notice to quit, and still bore a few scars from delivering that message, but it had been heeded. The interloper had visited again, but under the cowman's orders. The dog was humbled, tail down, and stayed skulking at the entrance to the yard. Also on the plus side, the farm was a sound billet for food. The Joneses were as useful for rations, if not better, than Mrs Rollinson and the air was good, familiar, as was the soil. But he had to watch himself with the sheep. The temptation was sometimes too great. And there was the sheepdog to consider, a lean and intolerant collie by the name of Idris who lived in Jones's cottage. Idris was a force to be reckoned with, but they had an understanding. Caradoc lolled at ease as the voices of his master and the visitor continued, low, sometimes urgent, but comforting nonetheless. He was off duty and lost himself in dreams.

"The Welsh air suits you, Nathaniel," said Cornelius, "or perhaps it is your married state?"

"I am happy in both, I must confess," said Nathaniel, refilling Cornelius's brandy glass. "Though I doubted once I would ever marry."

Silence fell comfortably between them as they sat, their chairs close together, each retreating into their own thoughts as the fire cracked and settled in the grate.

When the grandfather clock in the hall struck nine, Cornelius took it as a cue to return to business. In a low voice, he took up the threads of their earlier talk. "So, I gather that you are not to play the contented Welsh squire for ever. Your news from

137

London suggests we still have a mutual interest in the doings of Mr Kizhe and his English contacts. Their white slave trade continues to flourish and the recent disappearance of a servant connected with a politician has attracted the attention of your superiors. This is fortuitous, as my mission in England is to conclude Kizhe's activities." He looked steadily at Nathaniel, weighing again his worth, choosing his words with care. "I would welcome your help. I know that you and your masters are unconcerned by his involvement in the China opium trade where he is a powerful trafficker, but my masters view it as a grave matter, as does the Emperor himself."

Cornelius's face clouded with memory, and, uncharacteristically, he chose to speak freely. "Remember, Nathaniel, my own brother died an addict. The man I seek: Kizhe," he pronounced the word again, slowly, "Kee-jay: remember, it is just an alias for him, it means, "the others". He has many guises, and there are many such as he. He works for the Count, whose business interests in trading women outrage you. We too deplore this, but we also concern ourselves with the Count's other affairs, which extend beyond importing opium to robbery and extortion. His powers also allow him to influence the Triads, to stir up conspiracies which mask his trade and occupy the authorities. Only last year the Yao highlanders of Hunan rose up, led by Zhao Jinlong, their Golden Dragon King. They are simple mountain people, devout Taoists, but their ways of peace had been shattered by the local Triad society, descendent of the so-called Three Harmonies Society of heaven, earth and man, yet who know nothing of harmony. Once these societies were revolutionaries but are now simply criminals. They stole cattle from the Yao, whose vengeance has laid waste to the province. The Emperor's troops were so weakened by opium that the only way they could bring peace was by paying off the Yao, bribing them to go back to their homes. The Triads and the Count continue to wreak their evil on the land." Cornelius paused and looked directly at Nathaniel, his eyes like twin black pools. "In the words of the philosopher Lao Tzu, a

138

journey of a thousand miles begins with a single step. So, my friend, with our first step, we tread on the Count's man, Kizhe."

Nathaniel raised his glass to Cornelius. "So be it," he said, and bowed his head briefly, confirming their understanding before he continued: "Emma and I return to Bath shortly, at the end of this month, and then I will leave for London directly. Shall we meet there? I have rooms in Lambeth."

Cornelius nodded. "We will meet, preferably close to the docks where our business will be. I will leave a note at your Office with details by mid-March."

They fell silent again, but looked up at the sound of feet approaching across the hall. The door creaked open to reveal a maid carrying the coffee tray, with a plate of tiny cakes like sugared scallop shells just maintaining a trembling balance on top of the milk jug. The youngest Jones girl was a novice at waiting-on and edged forward uncertainly, her eyes wide and fearful as she approached the master and the stranger. With relief, her shaking hands landed the rattling tray and she managed to scuttle out unnoticed, fleeing down the lobby to tell her tale in the kitchen, for Emma Parry had followed her into the room.

Cornelius had already been struck by the natural beauty of Nathaniel's bride. Her bright auburn hair was tied up in a sky-blue band, the same fabric as her gown, sprigged all in white flowers with green leaves. She was tall and straight, graceful, with a pleasing voice and a smile in her eyes. But there was more, he sensed it in her. She had a quietness of spirit which allowed her an acute perception if she cared to heed it. And tonight she was dressed for dinner in his honour. Though the gown was in character, restrained and gentle on the eye, for the occasion she had also chosen to wear a heavy necklace of curiously wrought golden links and great sapphires which flashed about her neck and white breast with a cold and alien brilliance.

"Are you ready for coffee, gentlemen? And perhaps you might like to try these cakes. They will taste sweeter than the pudding. Also, I think you might prefer to remain here, the drawing room is colder and the fire is smoking. You will be more comfortable out of it. I can leave you in peace if you have more to discuss."

The men rose to their feet, Cornelius dislodging Caradoc, who slouched away, half asleep, and flung himself down closer to the fire.

"Nathaniel," said Cornelius. "May I request that Mrs Parry does me the honour of remaining with us, if it pleases you both?"

It pleased them all and as they sat down together Emma set about pouring the coffee. The aroma revealed it to be overly pungent and slightly burned. She pulled a wry face as she passed the first cup to their guest. "Try this, if you would care to Mr Lee. We do not have many visitors here and our cook prefers to make tea."

"I hope to have the privilege of sampling it," said Cornelius smiling.

"You must. Do not let this be your only visit, Cornelius," said Nathaniel impulsively. "You will always find a welcome here." He glanced again at Emma and his eyes were drawn to his mother's sapphires. "What do you think of our family jewels? We have reclaimed this necklace from the bank vault for Emma."

"Spectacular," said Cornelius guardedly, "though not Welsh. European I would say. French, before the Revolution."

Emma unclasped the rope of gems and passed them to him. "On the back of each jewel setting there are tiny letters. One is a B," she said.

Cornelius examined one of the settings closely. "Yes. This is one of the marks used by Maison Bapst, the once and present court jeweller. They are survivors and they marry well. They are still trading on the Quai de l'École. Though Nathaniel will know that."

Nathaniel did know of the Parisian *atelier* but had never examined the stones closely. They had been locked away after his mother's early death and, apart from a brief viewing at the reading of this father's will, had remained undisturbed in the dark of the Beaumaris bank vault for over twenty years, too poignant to be disturbed without good reason. He smiled ruefully and hurried on.

"There is a tale connected with them, which is related to our earlier talk. My father brought them back from Spain during the wars and there are more in the set. Edwin Ravenswood owns one rope of emeralds. You probably saw them worn by his wife when you stayed in their house. They were given to the family by a man now known as Sir Giles Mortimer-Buckley. And," he said, his eyes now sparkling as hard and blue as the sapphires, "there is more. We dined with the Ravenswoods after our marriage and Sir Giles also attended as a guest. He deliberately misled me about the gems, disclaiming any knowledge of my father's presence on the expedition. I now have evidence from Percy at the Office that my father undertook the mission with a Captain and two men from the ranks. I have no doubt he will soon confirm that Sir Giles was that Captain. I have many volumes of my father's papers to check, which may shed more light on the incident. But apart from that, other matters have emerged which make the business of interest. I will not trouble you with the details, Cornelius, suffice to say there has been a death in Bath which seems linked to the mission, and according to Percy a mystery remains about another piece in that collection of jewels, which the government would dearly like to recover. When I return from London I intend to stay in Bath until the links there are clear."

Emma handed round the cakes as Nathaniel narrated the tangled tale of the gems, and as she did so the necklace seemed to weigh more heavily on her breast, warm now in the heat of the fire, suddenly oppressive. She took a deep breath and felt for the lowest stone, lifting it away from her body, and distracted herself by considering their unusual guest. She had enjoyed exchanging a few words with him, all quite polite but very measured, with nothing given away. Yet his restraint had encouraged rather than inhibited conversation. Cornelius was an impeccable dinner guest, but apart from his contributions to the talk, his presence also fascinated her. He had remarkable economy of movement and his body had the sleek power of the panther. She had seen drawings of them, shadowy creatures with a calm grace, watchful in deep green jungles. He was mesmerising. It was easy to understand why Nathaniel had taken to him, why anyone would. She cast her mind back to what she had read about the theories of Franz Mesmer, that a magnetic force exerted by an individual can be so attractive that you are as if spellbound by them. In truth she was hypnotised by his looks alone. She could not remember ever seeing a person from the East before, at least not at such close range, and had to be careful not to stare. But when she let her eyes slide back to glance at him he was already looking at her, and smiled.

"Did you see the burial mound as you rode here?" she asked before she could stop herself. "I have had such dreams after I walked into the heart of it, down the stone passage."

"Do the dreams alarm you?" asked Cornelius.

"No," said Emma, thoughtfully. "But they are vivid, rushing dreams of strange people and snatches of songs. They are confused, hard to explain."

"I have had dreams when I slept out on the mound," laughed Nathaniel. "But it was the brandy and maybe Mrs Jones's forest mushrooms to blame!" He did not add that the worst dreams were fired by utter misery and desolation after the death of his father. He spoke only from gallantry, from good manners, to disguise his discomfort.

"In your case, it is so," said Cornelius gravely. "But I think Mrs Parry is very open to hearing echoes of the past," he turned to her. "Madam, have you ever seen things in your waking hours which others have not?"

"I think I might have done. It was only once, last month, just after Nathaniel and I married," said Emma, suddenly realising how pleased she was to speak of it and allow the words to release a recurring worry about that night. Cornelius was skilled in asking, as well as in listening. "It was at Arno's Tower. Mrs

142

Ravenswood was showing the ladies the upper rooms. It was evening, but the moon was bright. Over the lawn I saw a man running by the trees, he seemed to be dodging, evading something. I felt his fear. Then he disappeared. But the others didn't see!"

"Did he carry a bag?"

"Yes."

"Did he cross from left to right."

"Yes! How could you know this?" asked Emma

"It is just a suggestion," said Cornelius. "The figure could easily have been an intruder; the shadows could have given you a vantage point the others did not have. But it might be that what you saw was a shade of another kind: that of a poacher I saw die there two years ago." He neglected to add that Kizhe's shot had shattered the man's face, but it had been his own knife which had released his soul. "If I was there again," he continued, "it is possible that I too would see him."

"Remind me to stay with both of you to improve my vision," said Nathaniel, amused and also unsettled, looking from one to the other.

"Now," said Cornelius, rising quickly. "Please allow me to present you both with my wedding gifts! Too late for the wedding, but brought within the first month to bless your honeymoon."

He bowed and left the room.

Nathaniel looked quizzically at Emma. "Do you like him, Em?"

"Oh yes," she said. "I understand why he is important to you. Why he has become important."

"I wouldn't say important," began Nathaniel, but then realised she had seen far more than he had, and nodded.

Cornelius returned with a parcel and moved the tray aside to place it on the table between them. He pulled away the brown paper and tissue layers to reveal a bolt of midnight blue Chinese silk, embroidered with pink and russet blooms.

"For you, Madam: the new Mrs Parry."

"How beautiful," exclaimed Emma, her fingers tracing the swirling embroidery. "I thank you. These hues match my colouring perfectly!"

"They were chosen to do so." Cornelius laughed suddenly at their awestruck looks. "My contact in Paris described you to me. He had met you both in London," said Cornelius. "But I did not know then that the silk would match your family jewels so well."

Under the roll of fabric was a black box. "This is for you, Nathaniel," said Cornelius, presenting it with a bow. "Like your sapphires, it dates from before the Revolution."

The box was opened to reveal a gold pocket watch on a chain.

"Cornelius," said Nathaniel," you honour me indeed! A Breguet, by God!"

Cornelius knew of Nathaniel's attachment to Paris, the place where his parents first met, as well as his misery there when his father had died. It was a gift to acknowledge both extremes of experience and mark a new phase of life.

"Tell me about it!" said Emma, leaning forward to see the prize.

"Breguet's *atelier* in Paris has been open since the 1770s," said Nathaniel, opening the case reverently. "They made watches for the cream of French society, including the royal family, and still do. Breguet was rumoured to have spent over forty years making the greatest watch in the world for Marie-Antoinette. I don't suppose she got it in time to enjoy it."

He examined the treasure lovingly. "Look, Em! The Breguet trademark, blue hands and phases of the moon. Exquisite!"

He ran his fingers to the chain's end where there was something else; a golden medallion with a Chinese symbol picked out and fretted.

"What does it say?" asked Emma.

Nathaniel put down the gift and extended his hand to Cornelius. "It says friendship. Thank you, my good friend."

The handshake and the sudden silence were both sensed by the dozing Caradoc who snapped awake, shot over yapping and wormed between them to investigate the mound of paper on the table. Nathaniel grabbed him as he attempted to leap on it and hauled him away laughing.

"Down, sir! Nothing for you here!"

Cornelius remained standing as the others sat, Nathaniel pushing back his chair to accommodate Caradoc who now sprawled on his lap.

"Thank you for an excellent dinner," said Cornelius. "And your kind offer of a bed for the night. I will retire now, and leave in the morning, if that is convenient."

His face was closed, distant. It was important for him not to stay longer, not to give in to the temptation to sit down with them at the family table by the fire; to move out of reach of the creeping cold which seeped through the gaps in the shutters and stole round the edges of the room. Outside he could hear the wild winds and squalls of rain buffeting the house, tearing over the mound and rattling the bare boughs of the trees in the copse, raw reminders of that other, brutal world, which waited for them all across the narrow straits. He could not afford to lose touch with it.

Late morning: 8th March, 1833.
Nathaniel's rented rooms, Carlisle Lane, Lambeth, London.

Cross-legged on the floor, naked but for his favourite Damascus robe and surrounded by his personal arsenal, blackened rags and polishers, bottles of oil and unguents, Nathaniel selected a particularly soft cloth for the final polish of his percussion pistols. After a boisterous session of exercises which had brought the landlady rushing upstairs to investigate, he had whiled away the morning cleaning them, checking the mechanisms and stowing his ammunition. The ruinous cost of converting them from flintlocks had been worth every penny. His eyes shone with delight as he held up first one, then the other, admiring each at arm's length and then placing them down, precisely. Though only in the ranks briefly whilst on a mission, he took a soldier's pleasure in his weapons, never allowing a servant to clean or carry them. His life was his own responsibility and he took it seriously. He reached next for his makila, his Basque walking stick, checked the handle and then pulled it hard to draw its concealed blade from the shaft and rubbed it until it shone. Like the pistols, it would not be needed today. Westminster did not call for guns or a mountain stick, but he had the very thing. He leaned over and pulled his slim walking cane towards him. Perfect. He polished the silver handle and the ebony shaft and then drew the glinting steel, no ordinary sword in this stick, but a blade from the East. He held it up to catch the light and the watermark seemed to swirl along the edge with a life of its own, sinuous and deadly.

There had been a real pleasure in being in his Lambeth rooms again, returning to reality and taking up the reins of his previous life after the joyous but bizarrely over-heated experience of getting married, and the strange, magical limbo of the month on Anglesey. Earlier that week they had arrived back in Bath, where he had left Em, Caradoc, and all the luggage bar his small travelling bag before catching the next mail coach to London. His landlady had been forewarned and all was in order when he arrived. But it was quiet without Caradoc and after the first couple of nights of unconsciousness he had been restless in his empty bed. He had been mildly surprised that he had not wanted to find alternative company, as there was plenty to be had with little effort. Marriage seemed to be working out as it should. He pushed his hair from his eyes and shook his head, clearing his thoughts. To business: first, lunch in the nearest chop house, then to the Office for the afternoon meeting, and later, a rendezvous in Wapping at a tavern called the Prospect of Whitby. A letter from Cornelius had been waiting for him at the Office, in the safekeeping of Richard Percy. He would be in the Prospect at nine o'clock every evening this week, and it looked like tonight the coast was clear. Drake had been keen to let him know that he was occupied for the evening, so there was no possibility of a duty call Chez Drake to detain him. Nathaniel sprang to his feet and packed away the pistols and the Basque stick in his travelling bag. The walking cane he placed on the bed, quickly found linen, trousers, frock coat, top hat and put his mind to choosing a suitable waistcoat and cravat for the meeting in Downing Street.

By early afternoon he was making his way over Westminster Bridge, holding on to his hat as he glanced over the parapet to the teeming waterway below. The river was crowded with craft, mostly small and pushy; bustling about their city business, but the water by the bank was sluggish and putrid, the March wind lifting poisonous fumes from its slimy surface. An eddy from a passing boat rolled the paw of a bloated dead cat in a ghastly salute. He turned away, suddenly nauseous, pulled his scarf round his mouth and pressed on to Downing Street. Threading his way past the sight-seers who loitered by the Prime Minister's residence, he made his way to the buildings which housed the Offices of State. Once there, he reported to Richard Percy, whom he found at his usual post, scribbling away in the anteroom to Lord Melbourne's office.

"I appreciated your letter, Percy," he said quietly, as the secretary nodded an enthusiastic welcome, stowed his pen and gathered his papers together for the meeting.

"My pleasure, Parry," he answered, pushing his gold spectacles further up his nose. "And I made it my business to save your report which gave chapter and verse on the nefarious doings of a certain Bristol trader." He smiled primly and then suddenly a flash of excitement lit his earnest features and reduced his age by ten years. "On a lighter note," he said, grinning broadly, "dashed fascinating news about the Egyptian falcon! Do you think you will get it back?"

"Unlikely," said Nathaniel. "But possible. Tell me, does Captain Peterson, Lord Melbourne's man in Bath, keep close contact with the Office these days?"

"Just the odd report, but regular I would say, maybe once a quarter."

Regular enough: Nathaniel noted he would need to bear this

in mind in his conversations with the Captain.

"Speaking of Bath," said Percy. "Congratulations! I hear that you are married and have a home there now." He paused delicately. "In terms of my records for financial arrangements, will your account also be in Bath?"

"Thanks for the good wishes," said Nathaniel, breaking into a wry smile. "For your information, my new father-in-law is none other than Captain Oliver Peterson. So you will understand why his activities are of interest to me. As to my whereabouts, I do have a house in Bath, but I shall keep my London rooms, so there is no need for any change. Your records can stand easy as I will continue to do my banking in London."

"But of course," said Percy, grinning. "The case of Vere the disappearing Bath banker remains unsolved doesn't it?"

"In so far as that no body has ever been found."

Percy made a move to the communicating door. "We had better go through. Mr Drake is already in with Lord Melbourne."

"Of course he is," said Nathaniel, as he followed Percy into Melbourne's lair.

John Drake was looking confident, usually a sign that he had effectively promoted his own interests and skewered everyone else's.

"Sit down, Parry," said Melbourne, gesturing languidly to a corner seat. "This shouldn't take long, thank God. Not a great deal to occupy us here at the Home Office I am delighted to say. Drake and I have just reviewed the state of play. Am I correctly informed that you have been getting married and holidaying in North Wales for a month?"

"I have been on the island of Anglesey, my lord," said Nathaniel. He could see exactly how Drake had utilised his private session with Melbourne, took the opportunity to flash a stony glare in his direction as Melbourne glanced down at his papers, and resigned himself to enduring a lordly homily on the satisfactory state of current affairs.

"Quite so, dashed isolated. Out of touch, what! Oh,

congratulations by the way Parry, I wish you well of your changed marital status. Now, briefly, in your absence Drake and I have pronounced ourselves a nation at peace; only the most extreme liberals and republicans are agitating for a further extension of the vote. That issue has been well and truly solved for all right thinking people and, since the disappearance of the cholera, public hysteria has ebbed. I envisage a few months of calm as voters await the imminent passage of the factory bill into law. Chadwick's work has ensured that most owners are sanguine about the loss of the under nine year old workers, and there will be flexibility elsewhere. Speaking of compensation, very acceptable terms will be offered to the West Indian sugar lobby after the impending abolition of slavery. Looking a little ahead, Chadwick's other current enquiry into the ludicrously high level of poor rate will return a verdict most advantageous to rate payers, probably by early next year. I suspect that, come the day, come the new Poor Law, there will be restlessness amongst the pauper classes who will find it far less attractive to apply for poor relief. Therefore, all in all, it is not a bad time for us to encounter an increase in unexplained disappearances, which as you know, has now impinged on the family of a baronet, Sir Giles Mortimer-Buckley. Drake will question Sir Giles on the matter, as well as another item which concerns us today, his close involvement with a valuable cache of loot."

He allowed a smile to crinkle his lips, but as usual it failed to reach his hooded eyes.

"As you will have gathered, it would be most advantageous if we could locate an item of missing treasure trove intended for the Crown, to whit, an Egyptian piece acquired when Napoleon was ousted from that land, and which was stolen from the British Museum shortly after it arrived. Egyptian pieces capture the public imagination, it would lift the mood. Now Parry, I gather you are to investigate a death in Bath which might link to that treasure trove. The connection with Sir Giles is crucial as it appears he was the officer involved with the mission to locate the treasure during the Peninsular War, under the command of your father." Detecting no change from Nathaniel Parry in response to this; Melbourne rolled his eyes over to his secretary who was busy taking minutes. "Well done for verifying that, Percy."

"Thank you, mi'lord."

As Percy was busy flushing with pride, Drake and Nathaniel for once shared an identical thought, a vivid memory of the dinner at Ravenswood's and Buckley's unconvincing denial of ever coming into contact with Owen Parry.

"Drake, you will discuss the matter with Sir Giles presently?"

"Tonight, mi'lord," said Drake.

"Parry, I also have your correspondence from a couple of years ago," said Melbourne. "It refers to your contact, Drake, a Mr Ravenswood, a merchant who remains most active in the China trade, and according to Parry has contacts with traffickers of," he paused, "shall we call them, white slaves? Some people do, don't they? Though one might perhaps see them as servants of a particularly intimate type. Laundresses, I am informed, often operate a side-line as common prostitutes. Some are keen to sell themselves abroad I gather. You might take the opportunity to question Mr Ravenswood, who might shed some light on who might be behind the current rash of disappearances. Of course, Mr Ravenswood himself, as a close ally of Lord Palmerston, will continue in his businesses unmolested."

"By great good fortune," said Drake, looking straight at Melbourne but horribly aware of Nathaniel's piercing scrutiny, ran his fingers round his collar as though he were short of space to breathe, "I dine not only with Sir Giles this evening but also with Mr Ravenswood." He risked an uneasy glance at Nathaniel. Drake had never been sure if Ravenswood had informed Parry of his involvement in the various activities of Ravenswood Enterprises. Cornelius he knew only as the sinister ally of Kizhe and Nathaniel was in no hurry to put him right.

"I will use the occasion to question them both."

Drake had been dreading the evening ahead even before he was lumbered with additional duties which might turn unpleasant. He did not like to see his wife in the company of her lover, Ravenswood. Not that he was a passionately jealous husband to the Honourable Charlotte, as she functioned for him mainly as a stepping stone into the highest ranks of society, but in matters of adultery, out of sight and thus out of mind was always the more comfortable option. Paraded in front of his face, and without Amanda Ravenswood to share his pain, it was a grim prospect. However, it would give him an opportunity to see Sir Giles and Ravenswood without Parry. That had to be a plus. The situation needed to be dampened down, and quickly, for everyone's sake, particularly his own.

Melbourne nodded lazily and turned to Nathaniel. "You will wait to see if Drake requires your assistance after his meeting tonight and profit from anything pertinent he might discover. Then return to Bath to enquire into the untimely death. It is highly unlikely, but if Sir Giles can shed any light on the victim, you might uncover a lead concerning the disappearing Napoleonic bauble."

He chuckled to himself and then barked out a short, brutish laugh. "Damned nonsense!" he muttered, before subsiding into a motionless reverie. When he looked up the three younger men were still sitting, waiting. Oh the joy of power! Melbourne waved them away. "It really doesn't matter one way or another but it is an interesting stratagem. Do your best." But then the clock on the mantelpiece chimed insistently and he was reinvigorated. "Good God," he exclaimed, standing abruptly to attention. "Brooks's calls! I'm due at my club! Away with you immediately my three wise men! I expect a full report by the end of the month. Percy, my coat and gloves there's a good fellow."

Nathaniel and Drake were soon stood out on the street together.

"I'll drop you a note, Parry," said Drake, dismissively. "Do you still have the rooms in Lambeth?"

"Yes," said Nathaniel, holding out his hand to Drake. "Good day to you then. I will delay my journey to Bath until tomorrow afternoon in case you need to discuss anything from tonight's meeting."

Drake shook his hand, reluctantly, and winced under the pressure: another reason to dislike Parry. "Hardly think it will be necessary. This whole affair is most likely a colossal waste of our time. But, as you like." Shoulders hunched and his mouth set in a hard line, he turned on his heel and marched away quickly, down the street and sharp left, to lose himself in the crowds of Whitehall.

Early evening:
The Mortimer-Buckley Residence, Park Street, Mayfair.

In John Drake's view, it could have turned out a lot worse. The dinner party proved to be a small one and easily managed in terms of business. He was lucky to arrive at the same time as Ravenswood and before they had even crossed the threshold had given him a discreet warning about official interest in his oriental connections, as well as the proximity of Nathaniel Parry who would be following up links between Buckley and a recent death in Bath. He had been impressed to see that Ravenswood's footman had been dispatched to the docks immediately to put interested parties on alert.

Once indoors he found there were only half a dozen of them round the table: just the hosts, himself and Lottie, Ravenswood and Sir Giles's nondescript daughter, drafted in to make up the numbers as her husband was out of town. Drake had lost no time in looking her over but it had been a disappointing exercise. In the husband's place he too would have had urgent business out of town, and on a very frequent basis. Lottie was decked out in yet another new evening gown and topped off by some of her costlier diamonds but was corralled between himself and Sir Giles, whilst Ravenswood had Lady Leonora on one side and her daughter on the other. The contrast between the two Buckley women could not have been greater. Lottie had given him a spiteful and accurate description of the matron after an afternoon call so he was ready for the excess of flesh, the ill-chosen gown, and the twittering monologues. All of these were acceptable tariffs that Sir Giles had to pay for her wealth, but the daughter was a disappointment. Sir Giles had been a handsome man, and was attractive still, but their heiress was not, lacking even the ample proportions of her mother, she fluttered and simpered in Ravenswood's shadow like an etiolated weed. Perhaps it was for the best, taking petty revenge on Lottie for her misdemeanours was not a good choice. She would eventually tire of Ravenswood, he was sure of it. And she brushed up well. He reminded himself that he was in for the long game.

After the cloth was removed and the ladies left it was time for brandy and cigars, and for him to move into the second phase of his campaign.

"Excellent brandy, Sir Giles," he began affably. "It is good to get a chance to talk over such a superb Armagnac. I did not want to allude to the subject earlier, as your lady wife and daughter do now seem to be putting the incident behind them, but do you have any news on the mysterious disappearance of your daughter's nanny?"

Ravenswood's staff would have seen the warning signs, the tightening of their employer's jaw and the hardening of his eyes, but Drake ploughed on, ignorant and oblivious.

"As you know there were a number of kidnappings reported last month in the lower class tenements of the East End. All victims were female. Closer investigations by the police revealed that there had been even more, previously unreported incidents, and the disappearance of your servant has been linked to these cases."

"Haven't heard a word," said Sir Giles, his stomach somersaulting, his eyes fixed on Drake, studiously avoiding the brooding presence of Ravenswood.

"We have employed another nanny who seems quite acceptable. Time moves on. I suppose the young woman was lured away by men. It happens."

"But her belongings are all still here?"

"Yes," said Buckley, making a mental note that they must be called for in the not too distant future. Perhaps Ravenswood could make it happen.

Drake took a measured slug of his brandy and ran a nervous finger round his collar: the second subject would be trickier.

"Just one more question, in an official capacity I'm afraid," he glanced towards Ravenswood, then away again even more rapidly. "I recall our last meeting at Arno's Tower. We all talked of Mrs Ravenswood's emeralds which you presented to the family during the last war, and mention was made of a certain Owen Parry's role in the mission." No one was offering any help, so he soldiered on. "It has transpired that this man did in fact lead the operation and that there was a discrepancy in the contents of the haul when it returned to England. Parry recorded the presence of an Egyptian trinket, lately stolen from the British Museum, but when the haul was unloaded," he attempted a facetious grin. "Poof! It had disappeared like magic. And here is another interesting factor, apparently a man died in Bath recently who was very likely one of your men from that operation in Spain. His death was at first seen as misadventure, but new evidence has suggested a link to the mission. Isn't that interesting, Sir Giles! I wonder now, could you shed any light on this mystery? I might add that Lord Melbourne would very much like to retrieve any of His Majesty's treasure trove which has wandered. The Egyptology section at the British Museum is one of the most popular and the curators are already rubbing their hands in anticipation of its return."

Drake knew that Buckley had committed some misdemeanour on that mission. He knew it in his water, he knew as he would probably have done the same. But he was not prepared for the effect of his words on his host. Buckley seemed to diminish before his eyes, his hand shook and he drained of colour.

"You know, Drake," he said faintly, "after the dinner at Ravenswood's, I thought again about those old days in Spain, and I did just recall Parry. Yes, I believe I did. So long ago, he had slipped my mind."

He took a steadying breath as the voice, low and grating, sounded insistently in his ear. "Steady now. You are amongst friends, Giles. Be bold!"

He felt Ravenswood's eyes boring into him. He would say little but he would look the man in the eye. "As to the trinket. I cannot remember seeing it. No, I am afraid not." He smiled and reached for his glass.

"Good man," said the voice, steadying his hand, helping him grip the glass as though his life depended on it.

"And it had better stay forgotten," reflected Edwin Ravenswood.

Both he and Buckley were well aware that the Ravenswood family had benefited in many ways from their connections with him in his previous existence as Captain Mortimer-Buckley. It had not just been the receipt of a solitary rope of emeralds. There had been a purse of napoleons, there had been works of art from other sources, and from the robbery in the hills of Spain there had been, amongst other items, the falcon necklace. Edwin's father had requested it as a gift for his dear son, to add to his growing collection of artefacts from the Far East and the Middle East. And there it had remained, in a display case amongst the weapons, suits of armour and statuettes which adorned his Oriental Salon, one of the less sinister pieces, one which Amanda had often looked at, but was not permitted to touch.

"As I thought," said Drake, relieved to hear the denial. But even as his ears rejoiced, he remembered his visit to Arno's Tower, the guided tour of Ravenswood's collection. Thank God, that his host's enthusiasm for his swords had steered them away from the Egyptian cases. His new watchwords must be: out of sight, out of mind. He saw nothing, and neither did they. He looked from one to the other, confirming their stories. "I will inform Nathaniel Parry that you have never seen the item in question. I feel I should warn you, however, that he will be investigating the death in Bath and might want to speak with you about related incidents."

The voice tried to get him to tell Drake to go to hell, but Buckley did not trust himself to say more. He nodded and attempted a smile but had not succeeded in thoroughly launching it before a footman entered and announced that coffee awaited them, with the ladies, in the drawing room.

Late evening: Wapping Wall, London.

Nathaniel had taken the precaution of packing his reversible frock coat, collapsible top hat and soft cap, as he had no intention of quitting his lodgings in Lambeth looking the same type of cove as he would appear in Wapping. He put both pistols in his belt and took the makila for good measure. He took a ferry down the river and made his way to the vicinity of the riverside tavern where Cornelius was waiting before he dodged into an alley, turned his coat inside out, stuffed the hat in his pocket and swapped it for the cap. Hunching his shoulders and digging his hands into his pockets, he sidled out and made for the Prospect. At eye level the streets were alive with drinkers, sailors swaggering and singing, women screeching, boys still trying to sell the final editions of the papers, and posses of children careering between them all, their bony fingers sliding into unwary pockets to relieve them of their silk handkerchiefs, purses and watches. As his glance dropped, he saw the detritus of the dock population, limbless beggars, many with tarnished campaign medals hanging forlornly on their chests, felled drunks, feral cats and stray dogs, all mired in the filth of the streets.

He passed ranks of warehouses and lodgings until he came to the ink-black passage of the Pelican Steps, where he looked up to inspect the tavern sign swinging above him. It showed a coal ship at anchor and the name painted on the bow was *The Prospect*, registered in Whitby. He glanced quickly down the steps, made out the glint of water and the dark shape of a ferry passing, and then entered the front bar, a foetid cauldron of heat and noise. Above him the ceiling shook with the stamps and jeers of the prize fight fanciers supporting a match and all around him crammed a press of drinkers, dogs and hoydens looking for business. But he knew where to look for Cornelius. He would be sitting in a shadowy corner, his back to the wall with an eye on the entrance, and one down-at-heel Chinese sailor fitted the bill. Sitting behind a couple of glasses and a jug was an unkempt lascar with matted hair and a tattered coat. But through the straggling fringe glinted two familiar dark eyes, sharp as razors.

"Porter?" offered Cornelius as Nathaniel took a seat next to him. "It is the usual drink in here."

"Then, yes, thank you," said Nathaniel, helping himself to a glass of the treacle-dark ale.

Cornelius dropped his voice but kept his eyes on the door.

"We will go down to Ravenswood's mooring in the dock, his new vessel lies there and it will be ready to sail in a day or two. It is being loaded, so the crew have been ordered to quit their lodgings and move into their quarters on board. I have not been able to locate my contacts."

"Are these contacts the men who helped me in '31?" asked Nathaniel, a vivid memory of two assassins flashing through his brain, masked men, responsible for torching Ravenswood's precious ship, *Mathilda*, reducing it to an inferno whilst puncturing his watchmen's throats with arrows. He remembered the steep climb up from Bristol's floating harbour with the four wretched prisoners, bundling them into the waiting coach and leaving those two grim men to the chaos as he drove away.

"No, not them," said Cornelius. "It was wiser for them to vanish, but the contacts I speak of have served Ravenswood for over three years with their heads down, biding their time and gathering information. They will remain so until I give them specific orders to act. I found out from some lascars on the dockside that another of Kizhe's vessels sailed last month, but only to the Hook of Holland, and will return shortly. No one mentioned Kizhe, but he might be on Ravenswood's vessel with

157

the crew, or could be lodging locally. Whether he is or not, I need to find a way to get on board. I will give you directions to the berth and when the time comes, we will leave separately."

Cornelius poured himself another drink, and as he passed the jug to Nathaniel he pressed a sketch map of the location of the ship's berth into his hand.

Shortly before midnight they liaised near Ravenswood's elegant new clipper, keeping to the shadows by a stack of barrels with a good view of the vessel. Nathaniel noticed it was named the *Leonora,* no doubt as a sop to that lady's pride, and to acknowledge the extensive new role of the Mortimer-Buckley family in financing Ravenswood's activities. There was still a mountain of crates and tubs to be taken on board, an idle hoist, some ropes were hanging over the deck and a mass of fishing nets pooled on the dockside, but there was no sign of any sailors.

"I thought I might slip on board with the men if my contacts were working, but there is no chance of that," whispered Cornelius. "Stay here, I will see if there is another possibility of getting aboard."

Without waiting for an answer he slid away into the dark, avoiding the light from the lanterns strung along the quay, and visible only as a darker shadow moving over the nets towards the looming hull of the clipper. The stench on the dockside was foul and Nathaniel's eyes were stinging. It was hard to focus and he rubbed them with the back of his hand. In that one second, there was uproar, in a loud sliding rush of noise the idle hoist sprang to life and the ropes and nets snaked upwards, sweeping Cornelius off his feet and swinging him, a ball of struggling limbs, over the bow and onto the deck of the *Leonora.*

Chapter 5

Midnight: 8th March, 1833.
On the deck of the clipper, *Leonora*, London docks.

At a signal from the mate the swinging net, with Cornelius trapped and struggling inside, was dropped nine feet from the hoist to crash, suddenly motionless, onto the deck. It was immediately surrounded by a clutch of jabbering sailors, who had been lying in wait, cold and mutinous, since the message arrived from the owner. They had been put on alert to waylay any strangers attempting to board the vessel, particularly an English gentleman, tall, pale skinned and black headed. The mate turned on his heel and went below with the good news. With one in the bag as evidence of effort, the extra crew he had detailed for the night watch could get some sleep.

"'E's dead," said the cook, disappointed after kicking speculatively at the curled body in the roll of netting. "We'll get nought out of 'im."

"'Course 'e ain't," said another, an ox-headed midshipman, more used to brawls. "'E's out cold. Must 'ave taken a rap on the 'ead."

"And 'e ain't no English gent a-spyin' neither," said the cabin boy. "It's just one o' the lascars, poor devil. And I dunno why the mate wanted 'im bagged. It's a bit more than waylayin' if you ask me."

"Stow it," said ox-head. "Matey's comin' with Captain Vance."

The sailors fell back to allow their superiors to approach and inspect the prisoner. For his part, Cornelius had decided to continue playing dead. At the moment he was first swung up into the air, making a mental note never, ever, to fall for the jungle trap ploy again, he could not resist the fleeting thought that at least he had managed to get on board. But as Goethe observed, be careful what you wish for. His means of arrival had created plenty of challenges, but the situation had deteriorated further when the net was dropped from the hoist. Tangled in the mesh and unable to break his fall effectively, he had landed badly on his left side and his ribs were on fire with pain. Moving was excruciating and would remain so, at least until he had bound his chest, and even breathing was proving difficult, so he cut both to a minimum.

"Frisk him," demanded an authoritative voice. "And check he's alive."

He sensed bodies surging around him again. Hands tore away the net, rolled him over, felt his neck for a pulse and his heart for a beat, swarmed over and into his ragged coat and checked his legs, his ankles, his wrists.

"No weapons, Captain. In fact, nothin' at all, but he is breathin'." It was the voice of the kicker. Cornelius would not forget it.

"Well done, lads. Take him below and lock him in the grain store. Bar the regular watch, the rest of you can stand down. We've a busy day tomorrow."

Fortunately for Cornelius they did not take him by the arms and stretch his battered chest. One set of arms picked him up, hoisted him over a shoulder and carried him away.

Cornelius flicked his eyes open for a second as he was carried down a hatchway to the lower deck. He needed to get his bearings and prepare himself for a second unwelcome landing: but in the event it never came. A door opened onto a small, airless store room, which was to be his cell, but he was placed rather than dropped onto the floor. Another flicker of his eyelids explained why. The man who had picked him up was Fong, one of his own, last seen over a year ago in a meeting snatched on the dockside. At the sight of him, even the cracked ribs seemed more bearable.

"Tie him," ordered the Captain briskly. "We'll see if he sings when he comes round."

A length of rope was thrown to Fong, who knelt and leaned over Cornelius, his back turned to the others and their lantern light. Ankles tied, the rope looped up to secure his wrists, and trying to nurse his ribs, Cornelius managed to breathe a word of thanks, as a cold blade slid up his sleeve and the smooth knife handle slipped into his palm. As Fong rose from the floor, Cornelius risked another glimpse around the room. The sailors had been sent away and the Captain was about to leave with the lantern, when a massive figure appeared in the doorway: a rectangular, heavily-muscled man, with no discernable neck, and arms like tree boles. He pushed the Captain aside and moved towards Cornelius, eclipsing the light. It was a grotesquely familiar silhouette.

"Bring the light over," he rasped, amused, in his habitually harsh voice, ground down in the years of his youth by the desert winds of Mongolia. "Let me inspect your catch."

The man's silk coat fell open as he clasped his hands behind his back like an admiral and the light flashed on a brutal blade, the hooked hachiwari. Cornelius knew of only one man who carried such a weapon.

"Mr Kizhe, sir," said the Captain. "We caught this man stepping up to the ship, right under the bow. We were instructed to apprehend intruders."

161

Kizhe peered down at the figure, the matted hair and the filthy clothes. He gave a harsh snort of laughter.

"Your men have caught a stray lascar, Captain Vance. What's in his pockets?"

"Nothing, sir," said the Captain.

"Bring him round," demanded Kizhe. "Fetch a bucket of water."

Cornelius decided to risk consciousness. As the bucket of river water spewed over him he flicked his head forward so his hair stuck to his face, proceeded to roll feebly on the floor and set up a wailing cry.

"Where am I? Oh save me! Where am I? Never meant harm, my lords! I come in on a Company ship out of Calcutta and lost my billet. I was only after a place to sleep lords, but I got pulled up into the air and landed on your deck! I mean no harm!"

Kizhe lost interest. "Enough! You were trespassing and will stay here tonight and be dealt with in the morning. The men will jog your memory for you and you can tell them your life story." In an aside to the Captain he added, "I'm leaving now, we have no more to discuss. Mr Ravenswood will be here in the morning." His eyes gleamed with malice at the prospect of Ravenswood's fury. "You can display your sprat to him."

Cornelius let his head fall to the floor and moaned, which took little in the way of acting. The men withdrew, the door slammed shut and the lock turned. The leaping shadows of the store room, and his disguise, had saved him from discovery by Kizhe, but the light of day and interrogation by the crew would make him immediately recognisable to Ravenswood. He had once been a resident at Arno's Tower for months on end, and Ravenswood never forgot a face. It was imperative that he left before dawn. He knew that Fong would be back to slide the lock, and when he had torn his shirt and bound his chest, he would compose himself and make ready to do the rest. In the utter blackness of the store, he slid the knife down his sleeve and began to saw at the rope.

Meanwhile, Nathaniel had continued to watch from his vantage point behind the barrels until the commotion on deck had ceased and Cornelius had been taken below. He cursed to himself, barely able to believe what he had seen. There was no need for such preparations in the normal run of taking on provisions for a voyage. It was obvious that the crew had been tipped off to expect visitors and he had a shrewd idea as to whom the culprit might be. But that score could be settled later. Cornelius was in a dangerous place and he needed to get him out of it. It was unlikely that they would kill him before extracting information, but that would definitely be unpleasant and could start soon. Balanced against that, his disguise was good and his story would match it. Nathaniel thought quickly. Cornelius looked disreputable enough to be guilty of anything, so it should be child's play to set the dock police on him. Cheering himself up with that thought, he stole away from the harbour, turned his coat, swapped his cap for his top hat and donned an ostentatious white scarf for his visit to the office of the Marine Police Force in Wapping High Street.

It took longer than he had hoped, and a bone-white dawn was seeping up the slate-grey of the sky before he returned with a posse of dock police and a warrant coaxed out of a tetchy, yawning magistrate. The Captain ordered the dropping of the gangplank and they followed him to his cabin, passing two morose sailors with recent and impressive head wounds. Nathaniel allowed himself a degree of grim satisfaction, even if events had gone badly for Cornelius, the punishment had not all been one way.

"Captain," said the officer self-importantly, "this gent here, who is attached to the government," this last was added with due reverence, and followed by a pause. "Was robbed last night by a Chinese malefactor who legged it to your boat and was drawn on board sharpish by your men. I have reason to believe therefore that he is either one of your crew, or at the least is being

163

harboured by them. I have a warrant to search your ship forthwith."

"You are too late, Officer," said Captain Vance wearily. "I was awoken not an hour ago by my first mate. We just passed him on deck; you cannot fail to have noticed that he has barely escaped with his life! The man you speak of was not of our crew but had been detained by them to be questioned for trespassing. In the night he escaped from the room where I had ordered him to be confined and fought his way off the ship. Two of my men are missing, presumed overboard and dead, five others are wounded. Four of these we had to retrieve from the water. You can charge him with murder as well as robbery when you catch him."

The dock police made a cursory search of the vessel whilst Nathaniel started to enjoy himself and extract intelligence. He chatted amiably with the Captain, commiserating and accepting a drink, brought by a cook with an open shirt and heavily bandaged chest. It was only as a carriage was heard drawing to a halt at the harbour side that a terrible realisation began to dawn on the Captain. An English gentleman, tall, white skinned and black headed? Oh God! And even worse, was it a conspiracy? Had a posse of bludgeon men come aboard last night for the lascar? And some "stray lascar" he had turned out to be!

His inward cursing of Kizhe was interrupted by the sound of Mr Ravenswood giving some terse instructions to his coachman. His guest, who had already risen, bowed and took his leave. Shouting words of encouragement to the police officers, he made his way across the gangplank and into the awakening hubbub on the quay.

After lunch: 14th March, 1833.
The Parry Residence, Saint James's Square, Bath.

Emma sat at her dressing table watching her maid's face in the mirror as she worked on the tangle of chestnut hair which still flowed down her back, defying the struggle to tame it into a bunch of seemly curls for the afternoon's bout of visiting. The girl was pre-occupied. Her usual stream of chatter had dried up and she was surprisingly clumsy. Emma's scalp was still burning after a rough raking from the comb and a reckless stab or two from the hair-pins.

"What is the matter, Frances?" said Emma, looking directly at the troubled blue eyes in the reflection, noting the flush as it ran up the thin white neck to the ears.

"Sorry, Madam," said Frances, smiling only with her mouth. "Nothing is the matter."

She had no intention of telling the Missis what had upset her, and cursed herself for letting her feelings show, declaring with a silent and bloody oath that she had gone soft in the head with too much good living. The last couple of years in service had been the best of her short life. She had food, shelter, clean clothes, some of them stylish, and for the first time, as well as the pity and care offered by the Parrys, she had the true affection of another human being. The love of another. As a slow tear rolled down her cheek she knew that the game was up, she had to give something and it had to give a nod to the truth in order to convince.

Emma turned round to face the girl, took the pins and comb from her hands and patted the seat by her. "Sit down and tell me, Frances. The hair can wait."

"I'm just a bit low about Toby, I mean Tobias, Madam," she started, watching Emma's face, gauging how much to say. She took a breath and started. "You know he likes to go to the George in Walcot with the men and listen to the reformers in the bar, well he goes pretty often now. And when we talk it's all of big affairs. I don't rightly understand the meaning of them. He seems that carried away with it, he's no time for the talk we used to have."

That would do, with no mention of the scene that morning when she had walked in on a shouting match between Tobias and the woman who came in to do the cleaning. Sweeping under his bed she had chanced on a package all done up with string and had dragged it out, just as he had nipped back to his room for his coat. Tobias had gone wild. As he tore the pack from her, cursing her for a nosey drab, it had opened and showered its contents over the floor. Frances had almost cannoned into the woman as she fled and found him gathering up the scattered papers from the floor in a panic. They were all the same, scores of copies of the new paper *The Destructive and Poor Man's Conservative*. Frances knew what it was, she had heard him quoting from it often enough, when he wasn't on about *The Poor Man's Guardian*, both Hetherington's rags, and this new one firmly linked to the trade unions: every copy unstamped and every copy illegal.

"Tobias, what the hell are you doin' with this lot?" she had asked, terror struck. "You're not fixin' to sell them are you? You'll be arrested! You'll lose your place. God Almighty, Toby, what were you thinkin' of!"

"No! I'm not, Fran," he had said, a cold sweat sheening his brow, "not sellin', just keeping hold of 'em 'til tonight, for Robert Turner."

But she did not believe him.

Emma watched the girl's face closely. She had joked with Nathaniel often enough about Tobias's dog-like devotion to Frances and his burgeoning interest in politics, both traits they had approved. She knew there was more, but it was enough for now.

"Well, Frances," she said, taking the girl's hands. "My best advice to you is to improve your reading, ask him about the things he is learning and show some interest. I happen to know that Tobias regards you most highly so I will help you myself. I too have an interest in politics. I've been to many meetings with my father."

"Thank you, Madam," said Frances, pleased to move away, re-plaster a compliant smile and renew her battle with Emma's *coiffure*. Frances was a survivor, the smile became more confident. If Madam was that interested in politics she might have an ally yet to help her keep Toby Caudle on the right side of the law.

For her part, Emma was pleased to see that no more tears dripped down. She had never known Frances to cry before; despite all her previous miseries and misfortunes. As the girl commenced to work on the rest of her hair Emma relaxed and allowed her thoughts to drift. The days of Nathaniel's absence in London had been busy ones as it was the first time she had ruled alone as mistress of the house. She had managed to diffuse the trial of strength between herself and Mrs Rollinson, who actually did know better on matters of household finance, ordering provisions, laundry, in fact almost everything. Emma felt quietly pleased with her progress. She had thanked and congratulated Mrs Rollinson on running the house so well in her absence and the gifts from Wales had been successful. Both the Welsh clover honey and the length of intricately checked woollen cloth had brought, if not a smile, at least a relaxation in the obstinate lines of Mr Rollinson's face. If she could keep her formidable housekeeper from bullying her, and harness her talents to run the house in the family's best interests, rather than in her own, it would be a victory indeed.

Emma had been busy with other matters since her return, visiting her parents, her friend Anna and her new baby, and mid-week, a most unexpected caller. The delivery of Mademoiselle Colette Montrachet's card had been followed by a visitation from the lady herself. Coco had provided entrancing company, especially in comparison with Anna who had provided an afternoon of surpassing dullness, tediously occupied by the exhibition of her offspring. But Emma could not meet with Coco without a tremor of anxiety. Coco's long-standing friendship with Nathaniel had caused her many sleepless nights before her marriage, and though she could love her as a friend and had almost convinced herself that Coco was setting her cap at Dairmuid as a husband, she was unsettled by her dangerous allure. Devastatingly charming and probably as duplicitous as the courtesan she was supposed to have been, Coco seemed capable of anything.

But the flawless oval face had been all smiles. She had been avid for tales of Anglesey and the sea, wishing Emma and Nathaniel well. She had been full of her forthcoming trip to France with Dairmuid, who had been spending more time with Charles Palmer, Bath's MP, and had become convinced that he needed to see the Medoc and its wondrous vines for himself. He had Irish friends there who were keen to host him and they would leave within the week. Delighted to learn of Emma's proficiency in French, Coco had prattled happily in her native language, allowing Emma the chance to practise and show off.

"*Formidable*, by dear," she had said. "You have quite the Parisian accent!"

Just before she had left she had recalled their evening together at the Ravenswood mansion, and in particular Nathaniel's announcement that Emma would be presented with his mother's gems when they arrived in Anglesey. How she would like to see them! And she had seen the sapphires. She had remarked politely on their beauty, and kissed Emma a fond goodbye.

How very lucky if one can transform rivals in love into friends, she thought. There was a time when she had also feared that Nathaniel might marry Tilly and now she was about to visit her for tea. She looked down to the ring on her hand and thought about the power of love, the elemental force which could bring even the toughest, like Frances, to their knees and stir up the most unruly emotions in everyone from ladies to drabs. The days might have been busy, but being separated from Nathaniel for all those nights after the passionate month in Wales had been purgatory. Her body had ached for him and his return from London had been a sweet relief. Before she had married she never had any real idea of what "wedded bliss" might actually feel like. To think of it sent a heady rush of desire coursing through her, a sensation completely unknown and unimagined during those lonely, empty nights in Marlborough Buildings.

The comparison of her position then, as a girl at home, and now, was as water unto wine. But her whole happiness was totally dependent on Nathaniel staying in her life. Without him it would be over. One error on his part, one enemy too many and she could lose him and all would fall into ruin. Her heart bumped unpleasantly at the thought of such a loss, of life's fragile thread. His story about Cornelius Lee, though carefully edited she was sure, still conveyed that Cornelius had been in danger in London and had escaped. Beside the possible threat to Nathaniel himself, she had also felt a measure of alarm for Cornelius Lee. He was a fascinating man and she was drawn to him, and more than to a friend, like Dairmuid Casey. She glanced at her needlework on the seat by the window. She was making a small reticule to match the blue silk evening gown made from the wedding gift Cornelius had brought to her. She hoped he might see her wear it someday.

She shot an encouraging smile to Frances and decided to share her plans. "The reason that I'm expected at my parent's before three o'clock is that my mother and I are going to Mrs Vere's. So we had better get on and make me fit to face Bath society! By the way, did Mr Parry take Caradoc to Walcot Street?"

"There was no stopping him, Madam," said Frances, deftly twirling a long curl and draping it over Emma's shoulder. "He was waiting over the road by the Crescent so he couldn't be shut in. And Mr Parry said they might not be back for dinner."

Caradoc had spent his time wisely during Nathaniel's absence. He had reacquainted himself with the garden and the park and been on the town in the company of Tobias. They often went to Walcot, either to meet the men, an excellent option, as the fire at the George was always well stoked and prowling under the tables provided more food than he could manage, or to visit the Spence household, which had been decidedly less pleasurable of late. He had many happy memories of the kitchen at the Spence's, the old woman, the ancient man, the fat baby and always a few other people, especially Mary, who treated him most befittingly, in fact, like a god. But there was an addition that had soured the experience, a squawking bird, coloured like a flag and flapping on a perch, high up out of reach. He knew birds and their noises, or he thought he did. But the creature was like no other. It had called his name and had him running round the kitchen. When he was wise to that it had whistled for him, and not like the shepherd when he had called for Idris, but in the self same whistle of his master.

On the subject of his master, this was their first walk out since his return. They had skirted round the back of the Crescent and crossed the steep slope of Lansdown Road, so it could have been an exceptional expedition, perhaps a left turn and up the hill to see the blonde woman in the big house, or even further, to the very top, with its tearing winds and sporting opportunities in the rabbit warrens. But they had not climbed the hill. They had crossed it, dodged the carriages on the London road and taken the dark steps to Walcot Street, a closed passage between dank and blackened stone walls where there was always a riot of smells, markers of threats and warnings. He kept his wits about him as he trotted behind Nathaniel. He knew where they were going, and he was ready.

When they arrived at the small Georgian terrace which housed the Spence family, Martha settled Nathaniel into the best armchair in the front parlour, Caradoc sat at his feet whilst his master waded through the essential tea drinking, cake eating and exchange of social niceties; the health of the Spence and the Parry families, the thanks for the cake, the wonders of the Parry trip to Wales and the happiness of the new bride, before getting down to business.

Martha still felt uncomfortably ashamed of her decision to visit Captain Peterson. "I felt I had no choice, Mr Parry," she said bluntly. "Ben's death was suspicious to me but no one else seemed to see it. I was that relieved when the Captain said he would ask you to help!" Her eyes glinted with determination. "He was no drunkard, though he liked a drink and if someone did away with him I want them to pay for it."

170

Nathaniel listened to the story again, jotting down the facts in his pocket book.

"So the man he was to meet was definitely a stranger staying in Bath. I have some ideas Mrs Spence and I intend to check the hotel registers, but first I need to go to the Saracen's Head to speak with the barman. You are sure of the date? The 30th January?"

"It is not something I would lightly forget," said Martha tartly.

Nathaniel rose to leave. "Indeed not, forgive me. I will get on then, Mrs Spence, thank you for your hospitality." He suddenly bethought himself of the Bristol connection. "Tell me, is Matthew still working on the Bristol barge?"

"That he is, Mr Parry," said Martha gratefully. "Having him at home has changed our lives. Mary works less now and she can see to the Johnty, who is a young rip I might add. And we have another tenant in your old rooms. He's a friend of Matthew's employer, a Mr O'Malley." She folded her arms defensively. "He is Irish Mr Parry, but not of the Avon Street stamp."

"I would never have imagined he would be if you allowed him under your roof," smiled Nathaniel.

"And I have some more good news, sir," said Martha, suddenly and oddly coy. "As well as Mr O'Malley I have the prospects of more lodgers with regular incomes. Other friends of Mr O'Dowd. So what with the prospects of more business, and with Matthew here now regular, I am going to move us all to a bigger house." She rushed on, "It seems everything has come together, just as one of my investments paid out, I've had enquiries for this place. So we're off. Not far though. Just across the way to Chatham Row."

"Congratulations, Mrs Spence," said Nathaniel. "And good luck. I am pleased you won't be leaving the city. It has been a pleasure to see you as always. Perhaps I could have a word with Mr Spence before I leave?"

Martha looked doubtful but led the way into the kitchen where Old Tom was seated in a chair by the fire, coddled in his blanket and slowly peeling turnips for the stew. Nathaniel took a chair and placed it within Tom's uncertain range of vision.

"Hello, Mr Spence," he said, cutting to the chase before Tom began a meandering tale. "I have come to see if we can find out more about the death of Benjamin Prestwick."

Tom's glazed eyes roamed uncertainly over the figure beside him, a powerfully built young man, with a familiar voice, and smell, he seemed to have brought a breath of fresh air in with him. "Oiy know ye, Mr Parry. Welcome. Oiy see ye're faring well. Now 'ere it is, Ben Prestwick was a fool, led our Philip into all sorts of scrapes as a lad. And 'ee squandered 'is treasure ye know." A claw-like hand dropped the knife and shot out to grip Nathaniel's arm. "Lost 'is gold and came 'ere to get a sniff of some of ours!"

"Napoley's gold! Napoley's gold!" squawked the parrot.

"Quiet Jimmy Congo, ye pert pest!" shouted Tom, but fondly and with a toothless smile. It crossed Nathaniel's mind that the bird might know more than Old Tom but forced himself to focus on the tale.

"Martha's a canny damsel, Mr Parry," he said confidentially. "Always was. Invested 'er winnin's from that partic'lar little adventure and saved enough to buy this dwellin', and now it's to be a flit to a grander one. Oiy 'eard 'er a-tellin' you the tale! Well, where was Oiy?" He recovered his knife and tapped it on the edge of the turnip basin to help him re-orientate his memory. It seemed to do the trick. He let out a wheezy cackle and pressed on. "Now, Ben met with 'is old Captain one night and 'ee reckoned 'ee was bound to be in clover ever after. Captain must 'ave taken a lion's share I'm thinkin' and Ben knew somethin' to encourage another sharin' out."

"I know that, Mr Spence," said Nathaniel as he rose to leave. "And I will make it my business to discover more. Good day to you, sir."

He made his way to the hall, followed by Caradoc, and as they were bidding farewell to Martha on the front step, Jimmy Congo delivered his final insult. The bird let out a torrent of

172

barks, yaps and growls behind them, driving Caradoc to fury. He shot back to the kitchen and launched himself at the perch which over-toppled onto the back of Tom's chair and deposited Jimmy Congo, in a flurry of beating wings and ear-splitting caws onto the old man's back. It was lucky for them all that within minutes Matthew returned from a shift on the barge, calmed the bird and re-settled him on his perch. It gave Nathaniel space to pounce on Caradoc and haul him out as Martha ministered to Old Tom, shushing him in vain to stem the stream of raucous and fluent cursing he had set up as an accompaniment to the parrot, who had retrieved enough breath to damn everybody to hell. Matthew left them to it and caught up with Nathaniel at the gate.

"I don't know there's much to the story of Ben Prestwick's death, Mr Parry," he said doubtfully. "Mother is set on it, I know, and it's good of you to see about it."

"I'll do what I can," said Nathaniel, watching the man closely. He knew Matthew's job at the quay suited him and it was better for the family to have him home from the sea, especially for Matthew's gentle wife, Mary. But he knew that Matthew kept unsavoury company. The owner of the barge was one Declan O'Dowd. The man was previously employed by Joshua Shadwell, who not only owned a collection of brothels, but was also responsible for the attempted sale of Frances, amongst others, and was a Bath contact of Edwin Ravenswood's, this last being the one reason that Shadwell was still at liberty. That one of O'Dowd's friends was a tenant at the Spence's was not good news, and that others were set to follow was worse. Martha would be reliant on their money to help her with the new house and the damage was already done if Matthew was pouring cold water on his mother's fears at O'Dowd's bidding.

Uneasy about the news from the Spence family, Nathaniel made a mental inventory of the current state of affairs as he turned left up Walcot Street and walked towards the London road. On the plus side, always a good one to start with, Matthew Spence seemed a sound man and might even be useful through his connections with Declan O'Dowd; he had a good lead and a plan, of sorts; no news about Cornelius Lee was probably good news, he could very well be on Kizhe's tail by now and homing in; Tobias had been training in his absence as instructed, and was keen to play a bigger role in his service and Em, he smiled broadly as he walked, Em! His personal life had never been better. On the minus side, Matthew Spence could turn out to be a viper, Ravenswood was untouchable and profiting, presumably still with Drake in his pocket; Cornelius had disappeared and he had no proof that he had recovered from his ordeal on the *Leonora*; and Kizhe was presumably still on the loose menacing the seven seas. Optimistic by nature, he decided that the pluses had it, as the minus points only concerned work, whereas the plus points included work and his personal life, which is what really mattered. But then he thought again of Cornelius Lee, and there was nothing he could do for him but wait.

Squaring his shoulders against the rising wind, he held on to his hat and pushed on along the Paragon towards the York House. The manager was in the hall after greeting a coach full of important visitors from London and welcomed Nathaniel warmly, recognising him from his wedding celebrations, which he was eager to point out, had been his very great pleasure to provide for such a distinguished family and their highly esteemed connections. Such was the esteem, that there was no problem consulting the hotel register at leisure, ostensibly checking for the whereabouts of friends. Nathaniel turned the pages back to his wedding day, and there was Sir Giles Mortimer-Buckley, along with Drake and his wife, in two of the most expensive rooms. And there, the following week was Buckley again, taking his leave on Wednesday the 30th January. Nathaniel and Caradoc made their way to the stables and after some well paid conversations located the footman who had taken the message to the Saracen's Head on the night in question. He remembered the incident well, especially as he had heard that the old man died that very night. And much more interestingly, the resident had not given the note to him personally, but sent a stranger; a man from Bristol had handed it to him, and paid him handsomely to look lively.

The walk down Broad Street to the Saracen's Head was a short but also a thirsty one. Nathaniel settled himself at the bar with beer for himself and Caradoc and bided his time until the barman was ready to talk. His luck was in. Not only did the barman remember the night because of the excitement of the murder, but also as he had trotted out the details to the watch, the coroner and by the sound of it, also in response to the earnest questioning of one Tobias Caudle.

"I do recollect the man who died, as I have said a few times before," he said, pausing mid-way through polishing a glass. "Poor old devil, burned all down the side," he rubbed his own cheek in sympathy. "Waterloo veteran he was. He'd been here pretty regular over the previous weeks, since he moved into digs up Walcot. Sometimes he was with Matthew Spence and a blonde lad, and I've told him what I remember already," he sighed theatrically and then resumed. "Anyway, on that night the man in question was moping, as he had notice from the York that whoever he was waiting for wasn't coming. Then a stranger from Bristol way talked to him and bought him drinks. Like I told the others," another sigh. "They yarned about Spain then the stranger drank up and went. Mr Prestwick was left on his own, then he drank up and went, and it was the last we saw of him. The last anybody saw of him!" finished the barman, triumphantly.

"What about the others here that night?" probed Nathaniel. "Which local men did you recognise?"

Usual crowd," he said, "but a bit sparse, for it was a cold night. There was one pair we don't see much of, but they're locals, Jabez and Billy. They work for Joshua Shadwell."

It was all Nathaniel needed to know. He slid a sovereign to the barman and leaned over confidentially. "It has been suggested that Ben Prestwick was murdered. If you hear anything else at all let me know. There is more where this came from."

The barman shed his boredom on the instant, dropping it like an ill-fitting coat. "Yes, sir," he said, almost at attention. "Right you are, sir."

Three o'clock in the afternoon: 14th March, 1833.
The Peterson Residence, Marlborough Buildings, Bath.

Emma had arrived in plenty of time to meet her mother, but Lydia Peterson was far from ready. An afternoon visit to Tilly Vere's home in Lansdown Crescent was an occasion, but when the party included Mrs Vere's mother, Dr Parry's wife and also the fashionable and elusive Mrs Ravenswood, it was an event which required meticulous preparation. As hats were still being chosen and discarded, Emma had made her way to the schoolroom on the top floor and whiled away half an hour with Madame Junot who was supervising the twins as they laboured through a French grammar test. Emma's facility for French had made her a favourite with Madame. Smarter than her clodhopping elder sister and the young, giggling twins, Madame had singled her out for special attention and still fed her with reading to stoke the fire. Emma left the schoolroom with a slim volume under her arm and went to find her father. Captain Oliver Peterson proved to be in his study in order to avoid the possibility of being involved in the selection process for his wife's outfit, but he was pleased to welcome Emma.

"Come in, come in! Sit down. How beautiful you look, my dear!"

"Thank you, Papa," said Emma, brushing his ruddy cheek with a kiss and moving a chair close to his at the desk.

"What have you there?" he asked, reaching for the book, his eyes crinkled with good humour.

"Madame Junot has had it sent from Paris. See," she said holding it up for inspection. "It is called *Indiana* and though it says it is by George Sand it is written by a woman called Aurore Dupin, and Madame says it sheds much light on the human condition, in particular the female one." Emma leaned forward, excitedly. "Madame Dupin has written for *Le Figaro* in Paris and has published other books with a gentleman, Monsieur Sandeau, and she uses part of his name for her pseudonym. I'm not sure about the George part, Madame had nothing to say on it. Anyway, I can't wait to start it. Would you like to read it after me, Papa?"

"Perhaps," said Oliver, doubtfully, as vague memories surfaced of the scandalous career of the individual known as George Sand. Adultery came to mind, and a life occupied with writing whilst racketing around Paris in company with highly suspect intellectuals and smoking cigars whilst dressed as a man. He decided not to disturb any more vague memories; he had enough to be going on with. It had occurred to him before that Madame Junot was less conventional than her appearance suggested. He'd always thought her a dashed handsome woman. Not that he had ever felt inclined to get to know her better, he reassured himself. But she was his daughters' governess. There was a duty of care.

Madame Junot had come to the Peterson household, a very young, impecunious and grateful widow, towards the end of the wars with France, and she came by a most unlikely route: sponsored by her famous namesake and distant relative, General Jean Junot, Governor General of Portugal and Duke d'Abrantès. In the summer of 1808, after the British under Wellington had beaten the daylights out of the French at Vimeiro, the Duke had had the unenviable task of surrendering Portugal *in toto* to the British forces. Thanks to the bungling deal signed at his Palace of Queluz Sintra, he had been conveyed, bag, baggage and army intact, to the safety of his own shores by the British fleet. Captain Peterson had sailed with the flagship and had found himself in company with the Duke during the strange limbo period before the evacuation. Addresses had been exchanged, goodwill had been extended. He had thought little about it until after the war, when he was prevailed upon at short notice to take on Junot's distant relative, who apparently, whilst being entirely suitable as a governess, was no longer welcome or happy at home in France. Some family squabble had come to a head and

177

the family was unwilling to support her. Junot had volunteered to place her far away where she could no longer drain family coffers or irritate her nearest and dearest. Shortly after this, Junot, erratic and volatile since sustaining a head wound, appeared to have committed suicide, leaving his estranged wife widowed and thrown back on her own devices in Paris, deaf to all enquiries as to the likelihood of a distant relative being returned to France. He resolved to sound out Madame Junot's taste a little more searchingly, but for now it was enough to change the subject.

"I gather that Nathaniel's visit to London went well, my dear?"

"Moderately well I think, Papa. But not exceedingly well if you know what I mean. He has gone to Mrs Spence's to see what he can do for her. Has anything else come up about her poor tenant's death?"

Oliver could well guess that any meeting which included John Drake was unlikely to have been a resounding success. He had recognised the streak of self-seeking in the man on first sight and from fifty paces. Something was not right in the cut of the jib. But he would do all he could, he still had a little influence, a little weight, which might steady the ship for his son-in-law. He smiled at his favourite daughter.

"I rather think that nothing at all will come up unless Nathaniel digs it out, my dear."

Eventually her mother was prevailed upon to leave. Their *Berlin* had been brought round from the livery stables and after only two false starts, with the footman being sent back for the forgotten reticule, then the forgotten card case, she climbed in and the door was slammed shut for the trip up the hill and their invitation to tea with Mrs Tilly Vere. It was to the footman's credit that he managed to stand to attention on the pavement and smile, even as he cursed his employer to hell and back. The minute the *Berlin* turned the corner and passed out of view he bolted for the kitchen, just in time to catch the last wisps of

178

steam rising from his own brew of tea and slap away the thieving paw of the boot boy as he reached for the very last jam tart.

Daintier fare was on offer in the gilded drawing room of Tilly's Lansdown mansion, and a great deal of it. Her ambitious mother, the corpulent Mrs Danby, had overseen the preparation of the menu and had proceeded to outstrip all comers in the speed with which she devoured the offerings as they were served. This was useful in so far as that it occupied her fairly comprehensively and prevented her from dominating the afternoon, as she had dominated most conversations since her arrival. Tilly was looking forward to her mother's return to the family home in Beckington, as her extended visit had become trying in the extreme. She had been supposed to go the previous day, but to Tilly's horror had insisted on staying for the tea party.

It was now well over a year since Tilly's husband had disappeared and her dalliance with the wealthy Howard Dill was going splendidly. Thus far she had managed to fend off her mother's visits and enquiries as to her plans, as she had a bevy of sisters who had all occupied her mother with their children and their various ploys, but nemesis was nigh. Her mother had taken to bewailing the fate of, "Poor, poor Tilly, left high and dry by the tragic disappearance of her dear husband", to all who would listen. Tilly objected to the infliction of martyr status and, free from her elderly, philandering and criminal husband, was happier than she had been for years. To lighten the afternoon Tilly contrived to saddle Mrs Peterson and the senior Mrs Parry with her mother. They were more of an age and once her mother was unleashed on the delights of Beckington and the magnificence of Howard Dill's holdings throughout rural Somerset, Tilly could focus more agreeably on Amanda Ravenswood and Mrs Parry junior who had chanced on the subject of Coco's impending trip to France.

"I remember you said you had been to Paris, Mrs Ravenswood," said Emma, who noticed that the chilly Amanda seemed more strained and preoccupied than before.

"Yes," she said snappily. "And we spent our honeymoon there. I would like to go again. Mr Ravenswood is much occupied in London at present and opportunities for travel are rather limited."

Amanda glared moodily at the assembled covey of women. Why on earth had she consented to come? As much as she now loathed Lottie Drake for poaching her husband, this provincial little crowd and their mealy-mouthed conversation was desperately dull. She tapped her foot angrily, and looked at the clock on the mantle shelf. Could she go in half an hour? Yes. But what would she do at home? She felt a rush of fury at the straits he had forced her into. She had never felt so rudderless and alone. And when Edwin came home she was often afraid. With a sinking heart she acknowledged that she was there because she needed some friends. She needed to be away from the oppressive grandeur of Arno's Tower and to be with some people who wished her no harm.

"Do you read French, Mrs Ravenswood?" persisted Emma. "I have been trying to improve my grasp of it. Today I collected a novel from home. Our governess, Madame Junot, recommended I read the work of George Sand. Do you know her? She is very popular in Paris."

"Junot you say," said Amanda, taking the chance to lift her spirits by showing off her contacts. "When we were in Paris we attended the *salon* of the Duchesse d'Abrantès, who is Madame Junot, widow of Napoleon's general."

"Well, what a coincidence," said Emma. "Our governess is a distant relative of that same Junot family who my father befriended during the war!"

Little by little, Amanda Ravenswood softened. Remembering the pity she had felt for her after the dinner, Emma worked hard and let Amanda shine. Tilly helped doing what she did best, which involved sitting close, stroking her shoulder periodically, offering her delicacies and trailing mounds of corkscrew curls over Amanda's arm, like an over-friendly dog. They were pretty, they were kind, and in her disordered and

180

miserable state, Amanda realised that they gave her strength. It was as if she had withdrawn to a cave to lick her wounds. She could do without Lottie Drake, and maybe she could do without Edwin as well. She listened with half an ear to Tilly's contribution to the conversation about France, an excited and rambling description of the latest Parisian designs for summer, brought round only yesterday by her dressmaker. And as Emma tried more energetically to interest her in literature and tried out a few political ideas, Amanda smiled, parting her red lips and displaying her little pointed teeth.

The Parry Residence, Saint James's Square, Bath.

Nathaniel had returned home with Caradoc whilst Emma was still out visiting. He had promoted Tobias from boot cleaning duties, told him to cast off his apron, collect his walking cane, hat and muffler and be at the garden gate directly. For his part, he ran upstairs for his additional clothes and his swordstick, got half way down and ran back again for one of his pistols, which he shoved in his belt, hurriedly checking his appearance in the mirror. He buttoned his frock coat over the pistol handle, took the stairs again, two at a time, and left through the back door, whistling up Caradoc as he did so. Tobias was waiting, and the three of them headed through the park to the Bristol road dropping down from the highway to the path which ran along the side of the river towards the quays.

"Where are we going, Mr Parry?" asked Tobias, slashing his cane at the bushes by the path as he went.

"Joshua Shadwell's place, Green Park," said Nathaniel. "I know his boys, Jabez and Billy, were in the Saracen's Head the night Ben died and I am going to try a little leverage. It is daytime Tobias, you are in the capacity of a footman and there should be no trouble, but be on your guard. I have had a run in with the two of them in the past and they might just remember me. Pull your hat low and wrap your muffler round your face."

"You can trust me not to let you down, sir!" said Tobias fervently, winding his scarf up to his nose and ramming his hat down hard.

"I do," said Nathaniel. "Remember, your training is for a purpose. You will not be the boot boy for ever." He looked Tobias over as they walked. The boy was shaping up, still slender, but developing strength, and growing tall. "I know you are friendly with Frances," he added, watching the boy colour up, shrug and avoid his eye. "I don't need to know what she has told you about her early life but it could well have included mention of the man we will see today. Remember, we had an agreement between us when I brought her and the others from Bristol, to leave some things unsaid. But now you and she are friends and it is natural that she will talk in confidence to you."

"I don't mind you knowing, sir," said Tobias earnestly. "I know Fran and Abi, the girl she came with, were tricked into going to Bristol by this man in Green Park. I know Abi worked for him, and Fran was made to go by her mother. And I know the name of the man who owned the ship."

"Do you now," said Nathaniel. "Well keep all those cards tight to your chest, along with our own names. We'll make this an anonymous call if we can."

They walked along the path in company with a few other pedestrians and horsemen. The traffic on the river was leisurely, the odd narrow boat hauled by a horse, one small steam barge chugging in from Bristol. As they tramped along Nathaniel became aware that Tobias was excited, but also increasingly on edge.

"Is something wrong, Tobias?" asked Nathaniel, for the boy had stopped in his tracks as the Abbey bells rang six.

"No, nothing," he lied, regretted it, and explained. "It's just that I was listening for the time. I promised to see Robert Turner in the George tonight sir. It's a meeting to read the papers."

"What time?"

"Eight o'clock."

182

"Shouldn't be a problem," said Nathaniel, intrigued. "I'm pleased to see you are taking the state of the nation seriously."

"Oh that I am, sir," said Tobias in a rush of enthusiasm, and suddenly he seemed to be inhabited by a different creature; he frowned with the effort and spoke the words of Robert Turner and the men of the George. "The working men have been abandoned by the middle classes. They got their votes in '32 with the help of millions of us ordinary folk. We were the ones who made the lords give in. But now, instead of spreading the vote to decent working men, even Earl Grey says: "Stay, enough!" And Lord John Russell who was a champion for reform now says what was done in '32 was final. The last word! It can't be right sir."

"So what now, Tobias?" asked Nathaniel, suppressing a smile.

"Mr Hetherington and Mr Owen's papers say we must build up the unions into mighty forces, but they must be peaceful, show the lords that we have power and we can use it well. They say there's laws ready to go through to stop slavery and to stop the owners working children too long. Change is still happening after '32!"

"I'm sure it is, Tobias, but do not expect too much from the law. There will always be bad men finding new ways to make mischief. Speaking of which, keep your wits about you, here's Green Park."

They turned off the river path and passed through a gate in the iron railings to a well-paved road, smooth greensward and elegant row of Georgian houses. As they had come within sight of the dens of Avon Street, the stench of the river had grown worse, but Green Park felt a world away from those once fashionable terraces, which now housed cheap lodgings, brothels and pubs, their crumbling facades masking stinking alleys, courts and pig sties. Green Park provided an oasis of calm down-river from that notorious slum, but all was not as it seemed. They walked the length of the terrace and passed the front of Shadwell's brothel, which nestled shamelessly amongst the respectable homes, then cut around the corner to the mews behind.

"Shadwell's office is in the stables," said Nathaniel as they approached the rear entrance. "Look, there's a light burning in the upper room."

In the falling dark, Joshua Shadwell could be seen by the window illuminated by his reading lamp, spectacles on his nose, peering at a folded copy of the *Bath Chronicle.* Nathaniel tried the gate, which did not budge. He checked swiftly, up and down, to ensure that the mews was free from watchers, then leapt at the wall, grabbed the coping stone and pulled himself up to snatch a view over it. "It's bolted halfway down Tobias, but the garden's empty. Shin over and open it."

He looked down at the terrier, who was busy nosing round a pile of wood.

"On guard, Caradoc," he whispered. The dog cocked one ear and continued in his work whilst Tobias put his foot in Nathaniel's hands and was hoisted over the wall. He landed silently and slid back the iron bolt. Within a minute they were both in the garden and padding over to the stable block. Nathaniel turned the handle and pushed open the door to reveal a flight of steps rising to Shadwell's office above, and also, in the corner of the entrance room, a small deal table, at which sat two men, frozen in the act of playing a hand of cards.

"What in damnation are ye a-doin' of 'ere?" demanded one, a bull-necked, swarthy individual, rising to his feet, whilst the other flung down his cards and drew a knife from his belt.

"I have come to see Mr Shadwell," said Nathaniel smoothly, as Tobias raised his stick and clenched it firmly in both hands. "He will be very interested to hear what I have to say."

"He said nought about a visitor," said the second man, who on closer inspection resembled a weasel who had done too many rounds with a fox. He made a sudden move towards them, brandishing the knife so it flashed in the light.

It was exactly the kind of split-second when training takes over. Without consciously deciding to do so, Tobias made a lightning short-circle swing with his stick, smashing it down hard on the knife arm. The weapon dropped, bouncing away on the flagged floor as the weasel-faced attacker yelped in pain and cowered on his knees, nursing his injured arm. Tobias raised his stick for a second blow, but held it high to one side of his head: "Stay still!" he commanded.

Simultaneously, Nathaniel had drawn his swordstick blade in a scorching forward thrust, stopping the tip two inches from bull-neck's throat.

"Not one move more," he hissed.

And into the shocked silence which followed broke the unmistakeable and menacing growl of an angry dog from behind the wall.

"I'm not alone, this time," said Nathaniel.

Jabez watched the eyes above the muffler warm in amusement. It was a treat for Nathaniel to see the progression in the shifty face before him. The righteous rage of the bodyguard was first baffled by incomprehension at the speed of the moves, and then swamped by a slowly dawning and horrid realisation.

"No, it cannot be," said Jabez, his eyes wild, fear clutching the pit of his guts, which had never fully recovered after his first brush with the man who now threatened to stick him with a sword. "You're Jack Drake, the same bastard who stabbed me in the vitals and smashed up old Billy 'ere, the bastard with the eyeglasses and the limp!"

"The very same," said Nathaniel, "but in better health. Now listen, I'm going up to see your master. I want some facts and it has to do with the death of an old man here in the city early this year. I want you two as well, so, Billy, get yourself off the floor. Both of you go ahead of me."

Motioning to Tobias to wait, Nathaniel sheathed the sword and drew his pistol to encourage Jabez and the snivelling Billy to climb the stairs.

Joshua Shadwell expected visitors. He had heard the footsteps on the garden path and the voices, low and guttural from his men, then more cultivated tones. He had heard the

185

bedlam break out, blows, cries, growls, and then be stilled, to be followed by the expected tap on his door. Disappointingly, his men shuffled in first, Billy cradling his right arm, Jabez whole, but with a snarling fear etched on his face. Behind them came a stranger with a face partly muffled against the cold, prodding Jabez into the room at pistol point. Shadwell eyed the tall man uneasily. He was handy-looking, and apart from the pistol, had a stick in his other hand that was probably a blade. He had bright blue eyes emitting a steady glare, and looked ready for business.

Shadwell was usually confident in a situation like this, knowing his own pistols to be lying in wait in his desk drawer, primed and ready, and with Billy and Jabez, making a healthy three against one. But somehow the odds had become hopelessly skewed.

"You seem to have convinced my men that you mean no harm, so what business do you want with me?"

Nathaniel looked hard at the well-built figure before him, immaculate in a steel-grey coat, silk waistcoat and garnet pin in the gleaming white stock. His clothes did not proclaim his loathsome trade, a man who would deal in women, would sell children and probably even his own grandmother for profit, but this man would. The clothes spoke of a man of taste and discernment but his eyes betrayed him. Cruel and calculating, they raked over Nathaniel, assessing his threat and the scale of reprisals he might deserve. Nathaniel glanced quickly at Shadwell's hands: they were bunched into fists so he moved quickly onto the offensive.

"As I told your men here, I want to know more about the death of a man called Benjamin Prestwick. He died here in Bath on the 30th January this year, and he wasn't just any old soldier. He had information that some very powerful friends of mine need."

As Shadwell opened his mouth to discharge a stream of lies and abuse, Nathaniel raised his hand to silence him. "Save it. First understand that I know a great deal about you. The only reason that you and your men were not arrested for the villainy on the *Mathilda* and the *Blue Dragon* was your link with their owner. The link stands. That man has friends in high places at present and his business will continue unmolested. I am not after you or your business."

"I've killed nobody," said Shadwell, struggling to control his voice as his stomach knotted in horror.

"I'm pretty sure you haven't," said Nathaniel. "But I know that these men, Billy and Jabez here, were in the Saracen's Head on the night in question. It was the last place Prestwick was seen. They know I haven't the patience to hear a pack of lies, so all of you, listen carefully. A stranger was there that night with Prestwick, a Bristol stranger, and I need to know his name."

Shadwell shot his visitor a look of pure malice and considered his position. He could not give Trevellis's name. Any linkage of the murder to Ravenswood was more than his life was worth. And closer to home, he had never told Rosie he had let Trevellis use the boys for the caper and the royalty payment had gone straight into his pocket. Who could blame him? It had never been the same since his injury at the hands of Abigail, the murderous drab! Rosie had run the business for months on her own whilst he recovered, and the bloody woman had a taste for power. The thought of her outrage made his scarred leg ache. Damn Ravenswood! He was safely away in Bristol, or London, or wherever he was spending his time these days, insulated from the sharp end of business. His wife would never dare challenge him. How would he manage if he had to share a bed with Rosie! But even as he let the comparison take shape in his mind, he had to acknowledge that Amanda Ravenswood obeyed her husband not so much for love but for the sake of her health. He had never knocked Rosie about, with her guaranteeing his living and running the girls it had never seemed worth it, and he could not let her even suspect he had lent the boys to Trevellis. Before he had to wrestle further with this particular difficulty, it was taken out of his gift.

"Cove never gave no proper name," blurted out Billy. "We were in the Saracen's that night, weren't us, Jabez? And we saw

187

an old soldier talkin' to a man. We did talk to 'im ourselves now I recall. Man was called Eli. That's it," he finished defiantly, attempted to fix Nathaniel with a stare but gave it up and looked down at his boots instead.

That was all it needed to be, for the time being. Nathaniel knew that one of Ravenswood's most trusted henchmen was Eli Trevellis, Captain of the *Blue Dragon*, and that he could expect nothing further.

"Well, thank you for your help, gentlemen," said Nathaniel, backing out of the door and disappearing into the dark of the stairwell.

"Don't cross me again," growled Jabez, staying prudently out of reach as he shouted from the top of the flight.

Nathaniel emerged from the coach house just in time to see Tobias bid goodnight to a buxom young woman with a cloud of wild dark hair and her body wrapped in a shawl, who was making her way up the path to the house. They wasted no time in quitting the mews, whistling up Caradoc and heading straight up the hill to Queen Square then sharp left to the Circus, to blend in with the more salubrious crowds making their way to the Assembly Rooms. As Nathaniel turned towards Brock Street, Tobias stopped short.

"I'll go off to the George then, sir."

"Right then. And well done tonight, Tobias. We made progress and you played a good part."

"Thank you, sir!" said Tobias; still basking in the glow of his success. "Oh, I almost forgot. That woman in Shadwell's garden. You remember. She spoke to me when she was going back to the house from the privy. She's going to call on you at home on Wednesday morning next week."

"What for? And how the devil did she know who I was?" He stopped short, surprised. "So we managed to fox Shadwell and his clowns but not the whore! And Tobias didn't you mention I hadn't asked for any professional services? It wasn't that kind of business call."

"She knows that, sir. It was Clari, Clarissa Marchant" said Tobias, "she's the most popular of Shadwell's girls. Everybody knows of her round the quays. Anyway, she said she had listened to the row we had with Shadwell's men and she's got something to tell. Something you said must have given you away. She knew of you right enough."

Nathaniel watched the slight figure scud over the road and head towards Lansdown. How the devil had she known? He shrugged his shoulders. As long as he could reconcile his wife and housekeeper to the arrival of one of Bath's most notorious prostitutes on the doorstep, this could be very good news indeed. Putting that thought aside, he looked about him for Caradoc, convinced the terrier to abandon the innards of a dead bird, and set off for home.

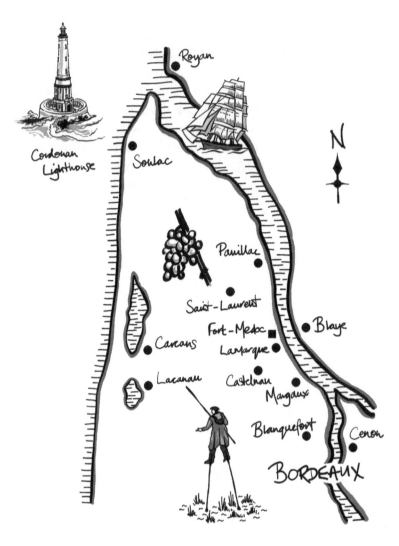

The Medoc: South-West France

Chapter 6

Dawn: 19th March, 1833. Off the west coast of France, approaching the Gironde Estuary.

"Can you make it out? It flashes then disappears. There it goes!" exclaimed Dairmuid triumphantly, gripping Coco even tighter and leaning further out over the rail of the clipper. His finger stabbed excitedly towards the faint twinkle which intermittently pierced the murk of first light. "It is herself sure enough! *Le Versailles de la Mer! Le Phare de Cordouan!* We're getting close to landfall in *la belle France!* What a beauty. Look at her would you now! The finest lighthouse in the world so she is, complete with all the trimmings. She's got royal chambers, and a chapel, in case himself comes a-visitin'. Damn fine!" He grinned, vastly enjoying the opportunity to show off his local knowledge, though truth to tell he could barely remember his last visit. He was sure he knew more than she did, and that was enough.

As bidden, Coco looked.

It was her first sighting of the lighthouse, but it seemed very familiar as she had listened many times to Émile's descriptions of it and the extravagant trips he had taken as a youth, up the estuary and south to Spain. She smiled tolerantly at Dairmuid, allowing him his moment. He took her arm and pulled her closer. Their sails were full and the ship was skimming over the last choppy stretch of the Bay of Biscay before they entered the placid, muddy shallows of the Gironde. Once there they would hook up with a pilot to steer them through the sand banks to the safe haven of Pauillac. She inspected the lighthouse as it neared. The ghostly tower emerging from the mist was, as billed, a beauty. The lower floors rose in pillared tiers like a palace, the slender tower was studded with stone windows, each tricked out with a jutting pediment, and the whole was crowned by a revolving light, searching and brilliant as the pole star.

She had never made the sea journey before, though she had once visited her brother Jules by road after he had moved into the ruined *château* north of Saint Laurent. It had been a lengthy, uncomfortable haul from Paris; over a fortnight cooped up in a succession of stinking, oily carriages, every one of the stages packed and flea ridden, with only a makeshift bivouac for all of them at the end of it, hugger-mugger by the fire in the *château's* one habitable room. Now she was scudding over the water in one of the fastest sailing ships ever built with the graceful pinnacle of the lighthouse shining out a welcome. Its honey-coloured limestone was clear now in the daybreak: light and fair, like Bath stone, a good omen.

It was four days since they had left Bristol on the steam packet for Dublin where, courtesy of his old friends from Tipperary, Dairmuid had arranged their onward passage to

France. This had turned out to be in conveniently adjoining cabins on a smart new clipper bound for the Medoc. It was only when they were boarding that she realised just how useful Dairmuid's connections were, for his friends were the Bartons, who not only owned the vessel but were also one half of the greatest wine growing and shipping partnership in Bordeaux: Barton & Guestier. She smiled to herself at the thought of Jules, mighty impressed, rolling his eyes, giving his long, slow whistle.

As they were on a working ship, Coco and Dairmuid were spared the annoyance of other passengers, with their attendant stench of vomit and the caterwauling of their seasick infants, both prime factors in the notorious discomfort of sea travel. The clipper was carrying an inert cargo of Irish wool, to be traded for claret and cognac, the weather had been tolerable, and they were both good sailors. Fine, cold days had allowed them to spend much of their time on deck and the nights had been whiled away pleasantly enough in the cabin, as Dairmuid was a familiar and congenial lover. Coco had been pleased when he had offered to arrange her trip to visit Jules, and even more so when he offered to finance it. Travel was much easier with an escort, and though she could have paid, she was pleased not to have had to. Also, she was glad he still needed her, as he was less keen on her company than he had been. His position as an MP, though his seat was in Ireland and far away from Bath, had made him more aware of his public image. He had ambition and was less disposed for sport, but he needed a partner for this trip and more particularly, a French speaker. His French was patchy at best, though he made the most of what he had. She smiled at him.

"As you say, the lighthouse is fine, *mon cher*. And this is altogether a wonderful trip. Thank you." She kissed him lightly, her gold-flecked lambent eyes burning directly into his: a warm fire in the cold morning.

"Oh, Coco," he breathed, wrapping his arms around her, reaching inside her cloak and pulling her close for a deeper kiss. "It's going to be a famous stay, so it is."

Invigorated, he pulled back, suddenly business-like, and held

193

her round the waist at arms' length.

"Contacts, contacts, contacts! Make 'em and keep 'em!" he declared. "The party on Saturday week is the t'ing. Your mission is to stun 'em! You know General Palmer. He'll be hosting alone as the missis is sulking in London. He's lost a king's ransom on the vines already and she's pig-sick of it all, but she's no loss, he'll be a grand host and his place in Bordeaux will be worth a view. I'll be staying at the Château Langoa with mi'dear man Hugh Barton, like I told you. Remember now, we'll collect you in his carriage before noon on the day. He is a force to be reckoned with in Bordeaux, and so is his business partner, we'll meet him too and he'll probably have more of his kin in tow. And, Mademoiselle Coco, he's Baron Guestier, by the by!"

Coco raised an eyebrow, amused. "So when will you admit that you're not investing, Dairmuid?"

"Tscha!" Dairmuid waved a lordly hand. "The Bartons and their pals are the main targets. I'm there as a little touch of the blarney mi'darlin' to lighten the mood. I told you I had connections in Tipperary. Well I know young Barton, Hugh's son, Nat, that is. Like brothers we are. And I know the Phelans too from the old country, and Bernard Phelan himself will be there with his missis."

"And Mr Phelan is?"

"Another mighty Irish vineyard owner haling from Tipperary!" said Dairmuid laughing. "I know young Marie, his girl, and her man. I'm well on the inside track."

"Impressively so," she said, looking up at him, her eyes sparkling. "So am I there to make sure you make no promises?"

"Only partly. You're also there to tempt, to tantalise and, note this well, to translate when I need it: verbatim and discreet! I want nothing getting by me on the night. The men's talk after dinner will be in English in honour of the host, but earlier on there'll be French whispers a-plenty." Suddenly serious and more confidential, he continued, "The General is a good man in the Commons, Coco. He's a reformer and he's paved the way for me a few times. This will make sure he does so again. If I can help him keep his French adventure alive it's all to the good, for he's on his uppers at the minute. He's not just running the mansion and vines at Cenon, where we'll visit, he also has a packet of other places and the greatest of them all is just down the coast here," he gestured vaguely into the mist which was clinging to the left bank, "down there somewhere, bordering Château Margeaux. That was his first investment." He winked conspiratorially. "Bought on a whim from a lady on his journey home from the wars. Proper lady's man is the General."

"Had he any knowledge of the trade?"

"Not a jot. He first started losing money with wholesale replanting schemes. He was trying to suit his wine to the taste of old King George, fat jaded slug as he was and addicted to cherry brandy. You can guess what that had done to his palate! The General had been his *aide-de-camp* so the connection was there, and I suppose once he started experimenting he couldn't stop. More land, new vines, new methods, and all directed from London with no sound men here to keep it in check. Disastrous! He'll have to throw his hand in, and Palmer's famous claret will be no more. He needs cash and pretty damned quick."

Coco wrapped her cloak tighter round her neck, feeling for the familiar metal rim of her brooch. In her mind's eye she saw not the flash of the Cordouan light, but dazzling diamonds, emeralds and sapphires set in interlocking golden "Ms". The Wheel of Fortune was turning and Château Palmer was going down. With any luck at all, the house of Montrachet might be on the rise.

Morning: 20th March, 1833.
Chateau Pèlerin, the Medoc, France.

Birdsong woke Coco; though the shutters and the heavy, patterned bed curtains conspired to keep her room as black as pitch. She slipped out of bed, pulled her cloak around her, pushed her feet into her slippers and made for the window. The stone tiled floor made the room cold as a crypt and as she fumbled the casement catch, the chill struck up like a knife into the soles of her feet. Cursing as she wrenched the metal clip free, she folded the windows back to the wall, leaned forward and pushed open the creaking worm-eaten *volets*. No more Queen Square with its mannered terraces: no hackney carriages, sauntering crowds or crossing boys. The *volets* swung out and thudded to rest against the outside walls, letting in a flood of pale golden light. She looked out on regimented lines of grapevines below, striping the fields as far as she could see, rank after rank, low, brown and skeletal, up and over the rise, off to the distant tree line. Shuddering suddenly in the cold, she closed the window and went back to bed, wrapping herself in the eiderdown and pulling her knees up under her chin. She felt victorious; the room was clean but otherwise as she had left it after her first visit when she had staked her claim. A watercolour of a lakeside scene still hung askew on the wall opposite her bed, the iron hooks remained behind the door: a chair, a washstand, a chest of drawers and an *armoire,* all in place. It was to be hers, forever, but she had expected to find it re-arranged by her sister-in-law, the dolorous and matronly Claudette, small and subtle changes made as markers to remind her that she was not the lady of the house. There was just one addition; a small wooden crucifix had been attached to the wall by the bed.

Claudette had not turned out to be a soul mate for Coco. If the *château* had run to a chapel Claudette would have been at Mass daily, and left to her own devices would probably have scuttled into a nunnery, taking the veil before she was twenty and staying there. But her father, M. Delgarde, had ambitions for her, both carnal and dynastic. Jules had figured prominently in M. Delgarde's dreams and was promoted from right hand man to son-in-law on the understanding that he took Claudette's name, coupling Delgarde with Montrachet in perpetuity. Rumours of Jules's activities amongst the local girls and disputed paternity suits had been a recommendation rather than otherwise, and Claudette's delivery of a son had cemented the bargain. Delgarde senior had been a well-fixed Bordeaux wine trader and the gift of the derelict *château* had been the bait to draw Jules into the family. He was expected to revive its fortunes without further help, but the pump needed to be primed. In exchange for permanent tenancy, Coco had promised Jules she would pay for the upkeep of one suite of rooms, including their rickety roof. But secretly, and if funds ever allowed it, she planned to pay for the renovation of the whole wing which contained them. Her rooms were located in an out-riding spur of the building on the side furthest from the farmyard and nearest to the road: the part least useful to Jules and his family. She saw the project as the creation of a sanctuary, a precious one in her haphazard life which was even more rackety than the *château*. The unfortunate circumstances of the Delgarde family had allowed her scheme to take root. The early death of Claudette's mother and the reluctance of M. Delgarde to remarry had limited the family to two. The second daughter, younger but barren, was married to a lawyer who had been energetically contesting his father-in-law's will for the last year. Claudette was deemed to have had more than her share already so the chances of inheriting enough to fund the entire refurbishment of Château Pèlerin were slim. For this reason alone, Claudette tolerated her sister-in-law's presence and financial contributions, which as she rightly guessed, were earned by methods entirely disreputable.

Coco had looked forward to her first sighting of Jules as she had waited in the foyer of the Pauillac hotel. She had had time to count, and it was fully six years since her previous visit. At twenty-three years, Jules had still had something of the young man about him, and his child was a mewling baby boy, clutched tightly to Claudette's bosom. Apparently there was another infant now to join him, and Jules had prospered. Her bags waited ready on the floor at her feet, and she had rehearsed careful plans with Dairmuid, who had been collected hours earlier by his friends' servants and rattled off in their coach to the *château* in Saint-Julien. She had sat uncomfortably on a hard settle, the air heavy with the lingering smell of lunch and sweat, time crawling by, ships docking and leaving, the hotel dogs already settled down to sleep off the afternoon. The sun was low and the room in deep shadow before he had arrived, roaring a welcome, his arms wide, filling the doorway and letting in a great gust of fresh air.

"Coco, *ma petite!*"

Stocky and powerful as a Pyrenean mastiff, bigger than before and becoming grizzled, he had shaken his great head in delight and kissed her soundly, crushing her close and squeezing her face between his calloused hands until she squeaked. Coco had pulled back to get a better look of him, holding his hands tightly in hers and a tide of faded memories had flooded through her, ambushing and embarrassing her: Jules as a boy; their dead brother, young and reckless; her parents' faces; their first home. Tears had pricked her eyes whilst her mouth worked, struggling for control. Wordless, she had occupied herself showing him the bags, allowing him to hurry her out onto the quay, listening, managing to smile, but by the end of the drive she had revived and was herself again, engaging and flirty, touching on nothing serious, preparing the ground work for what had to come.

Later, the meal with Claudette and the two children had been pleasant enough and the servants were clearly competent, taking the edge off Claudette's martyrdom. There had been some levity during the meal and much more after Claudette bustled off with the small fry; the nephew, Marc, named in memory of their late brother Jean-Marc, and the little niece, Simone, who had turned out to be bold. Coco had been pleasantly surprised by the child and *Tante* Colette in her turn, had been favoured by the girl.

"*Maman* has a new brooch!" Simone had cried, safe on Coco's lap and keen to entertain. "She doesn't like jewels but she likes brooches when they are shells. Look! There on the wall with the old one. She has polished it and will wear it to church."

On the wall above the fireplace, at the feet of the crucifix, were hung two scallop shell lapel pins. One Coco had seen before. It had given rise to the re-christening of the mansion as Château Pèlerin. The road by the fields was part of the old pilgrim route through France to Saint James's Spanish shrine at

Santiago de Compostella and a battered metal badge, relic of some long forgotten journey, had been dug up by Claudette when they first began to work the vines. She had seen it as a sign.

"Papa was digging out the well and found the second one last week. It is treasure. Silver treasure!"

Claudette had given a rare smile. "It is indeed treasure, Simone. We treasure the pilgrim's badge of honour in our hearts. And it will come to the church with us on Sunday. As will *Tante* Colette I am sure."

"I look forward to it," Coco had replied sweetly, with a modest smile, avoiding even half a glance towards her brother.

After breakfast, which she had alone as the rest of the family had scattered to their daily tasks long before, Coco returned to her room and swapped her dress for a pair of men's trousers and a jerkin, the discarded set of riding clothes she had left mouldering in a bottom drawer. It was necessary to bide her time, make an impression, and not a pretty one, before presenting her scheme to Jules and she had gathered that mid-morning would usually find him in the barn. She crossed the farmyard to the side of the *château*, shooing a belligerent covey of hens before her as she picked her way through the mire and made for the vast out-building bordering the yard on its north side. Lofty as a church but derelict as the house had been, its tiled roof was in the final stages of drunken collapse. The high doors, wide enough to swallow a coach or a haywain, were sagging open, allowing the sounds of muffled thuds and sharp slaps to float out into the yard. As she had hoped, Jules was training, but he was not alone. She slipped in quietly, keeping to the dark walls, treading softly and using the cobbles as stepping-stones. Her brother was practicing kicks and punches with another man, similar in height, but even bigger in build, both well-muscled, stripped to the waist and glistening with sweat despite the cold. They traded blows, light taps, and then harder, focusing an inch into the flesh, then away, back again, now

199

punching to the side and into the bag, full power. Punch bags hung from a beam on ropes, swinging out of synchrony, recalling long gone days with Jules and Jean-Marc. She had toddled in between them to join in with their efforts to perfect their French boxing, the *savate* of the streets, and they had howled with laughter, tripping her up, tapping her head. But as she grew older, she had become a pet and they had wanted her to succeed.

She approached the men silently as they continued with their routine, aware of her presence, but not distracted by it. A front right kick from Jules was followed by a step forward and scorching left kick, skimming his opponent's head close as a coat of paint, a right punch followed up. She watched them, her fingers and feet tingling to join in. She padded closer, stretched her legs, her arms, her back, and warmed her limbs. Leaning forward to the ground she lifted her body onto her hands, walked a dozen steps upside-down, and then sprang back to her feet with a bounce. A quick glance exchanged with Jules and she had leave to join them.

A little demonstration was needed for the benefit of the other man, who was a stranger to her. She needed to lay down her own marker for the future. Facing the bag, she started to land front kicks lightly, feeling the hardness of the compacted straw, then harder. It had been a few years since she had practiced and it was not easy to make the bag swing, a useful reminder. Making moves in the air alone in her room had some value, but she needed to do more. The men stopped to watch her. Right kicks, then left, spinning kicks, front punches, blows from the elbow: warmer now, she felt her skills waking up and she showed them off. She would pay for it in aches and pains, but later and alone.

"Bravo, Coco!" said Jules. "May I present Pierre Valdez, the best labourer and bare-knuckle fighter in town: apart from me!" His sparring partner's face told the same story. A regular fighter's broad and crooked nose was crudely set in a battered chestnut-brown face; deeply seamed by a life lived outdoors. Grey streaked his dark shock of wiry hair, though he could not have been forty.

Coco took the outstretched hand which closed round hers like a bear's paw. "Pleased to meet you, Monsieur," she said, sidling up to him. "I'd go a long way to see you fight. When's your next bout?"

"You'll be the first to hear after I do!" said Pierre, looking her over appreciatively. "Unless your brother tells you first. He's the new manager of our little local entertainments. Meet the impresario of Saint-Laurent."

"Since when?" said Coco.

"Since very recently," said Jules, very pleased with himself. "I have a new friend, the Commander of Fort Medoc. We have a few shared interests."

"I need to go now," Pierre broke in, reaching for his shirt. "The men are waiting by the canal and we need to start if we are to finish digging the new drain this morning. Pleased to meet you, Mademoiselle."

Pierre marched out into the yard, struggling into his coat as he went. Jules turned to Coco, amused. "You have a new admirer. He could barely take his eyes off you. Perhaps I could lend you another shirt. With a more seemly fit!"

As Coco glanced down to check her buttons, Jules whooped with laughter, caught her round the waist and flung her over his shoulder into the hay bales.

It became their own morning routine, first sparring with Pierre, and sometimes half a dozen others from the gang of vineyard labourers. Then, Coco and Jules re-forged their own bonds. After the first few days she had improved enough to catch him with a kick to his stomach and he had collapsed on the floor in a pantomime faint.

"You still kick like a mule! Lucky it wasn't my balls," he laughed, stretching back and groaning in the hay.

"The luck was yours, the judgement mine," she said.

Jules knew little for sure about her judgement or lack of it: nothing about the brief jail term, little about her patrons and clients, or the additional tricks up her sleeve, her use of poisons, her guns and her knives. It was all for her to know, and others to find out. But the bonds between them were re-made and she judged the time to be right. She flung herself down and snaked her arms around him to whisper into his ear.

"I suppose your little smuggling enterprise into Devon continues to run smoothly."

"It may well do," he said, amused. "What made you think about that?"

"No problems all these years?"

"No problems. Why? Are you here to offer a warning, Coco?"

"No, not a warning: a proposition."

And there it was, though the chatelaine of Arno's Tower did not know it, that plans were first laid to prise apart Amanda Ravenswood's grip on her emeralds. No stranger to a spot of larceny and game for the chance of redeeming his family's treasures, Jules was willing to enlist in Coco's scheme to give the Wheel of Fortune a helpful push.

Mid-morning: 20th March, 1833.
The Parry Residence, Saint James's Square, Bath.

As Coco was slipping into the Medoc barn to watch the men sparring, Nathaniel and Emma had returned to their bedroom in Saint James's Square. Emma was talking about paint and wallpaper, whilst Nathaniel was pulling out his father's strongbox from behind a camouflaging baffle of blankets that lay in a disorderly pile at the back of the wardrobe.

Over a mile away, in Green Park, Clari Marchant was closing the back door of Shadwell's brothel. She had put on her best boots and gloves, buttoned her coat up to the neck against the cold and was turning to make her way to the garden gate, when a voice bawled out above her.

"'Ere Clari, moiy love, don't forget mi'red laces for mi'busted stays! Oiy 'll be wantin' 'em for tonight."

Letty, or at least her grinning face under an untidy pile of bright auburn hair, was leaning down above her from a second-floor window.

"What did yer first servant die of, yer lazy baggage?" shouted Clari, but immediately regretted it.

A sharp tattoo of rapping on the windowpane by her ear was followed by the sash rocketing up and a furious Madam Shadwell sticking her head out.

"Trollop!" she hissed at Clari, eyes glinting behind her tiny gold spectacles as she twisted her head round, hoping to catch Letty before she dodged out of view. "And you, hussy!" she hollered above the noise of the window slamming shut above their heads. "What have I told the two of you about shouting in the open air? And now look what you've made me do!"

"Sorry, Madam," said Clari, shamefacedly.

"Manners maketh money. You'll be demoted to Avon Street if you can't behave."

Clari grinned. She liked Madam and felt sorry for her. Joshua might have recovered in a bodily sense, bar a slight limp, but he was still drained, enfeebled, and could barely keep a check on the men, who in their turn were not as effective as they should have been in running the riverside stews. Rosie Shadwell looked like she had the world on her shoulders.

"Will yer be a-needin' anythin' from town, Madam?" she asked.

"No Clari, but thank you. On you go," said Rosie, pausing with her arms raised to lower the sash. She still cut a graceful figure and had a harsh beauty, but the early sun caught a network of fine lines round her eyes and her mouth was tautly drawn.

Clari turned away from her, knowing that she would be watched until she closed the gate, and hurried off down the lane behind the Green Park terrace towards Kingsmead Square. Once there and sure she was unobserved, she veered away from the town centre and headed for Queen Square, then made the steeper climb to the Circus and the Crescent, on her way to the select residential enclave of Saint James's Square.

"Are you sure we need to keep the sapphires in the bank?"

Emma was sat on the bed with the jewels spread over her knee, idly tracing the golden links with her finger. She had up-ended the strongbox they were kept in and a pile of other necklets and bracelets had slithered to rest next to her in a haphazard mound, winking and flashing their charms.

"I think so," said Nathaniel, reaching for the box and inspecting its lock. "And whatever else you couldn't bear to lose must go too. Father never kept the best pieces at home. Anyway, this box is too much of a target if thieves ever come to call. It might as well have instructions carved on the front: Loot – Open Here."

He picked idly at the worn silk lining.

"I'd never get rid of it of course, being Father's."

Suddenly he stopped.

"Em, look here!"

As he had run his fingers along the back of the base, the silk had split.

"It's false: the bottom of the box is loose!"

She was over in a moment, excited, and watched him lift out the wooden square to expose a shallow void. Within it was a small, leather-bound pocket book.

Nathaniel picked it up and leafed carefully through the fragile pages. "It's Father's! Look, he's signed the first page."

He felt his heart beat faster, for it was more than a list of appointments. It was a journal: dates; people and places; thoughts and sketches; specimens of dusty herbs and grasses, some crumbling onto his lap as the pages turned, releasing a final breath of musky scent into the air. The sight of the familiar writing wrenched his heart and he ran his fingers over the script tentatively, feeling the irregularities in the ink.

But his exploration was cut short by a jangling pull on the doorbell, sounding up from the hall below. Emma ran onto the landing and leaned over the banister.

"Frances has let in a woman who is asking for you, Nathaniel," she said, pulling a face. "She is no lady. I'll put the diary back, shall I?"

Nathaniel had sent Frances off to bring coffee, shown Clari to the small front parlour and settled her into a chair.

"Tobias told me you were coming to speak to me on an urgent matter, Miss Marchant."

"That Oiy am, sir," said Clari, eyeing Nathaniel with professional appreciation. She particularly liked the look of his thick black hair, which was shoulder length and had a raffish look about it. He had an endearing habit of putting his hand to his forehead and pushing his hair back as he thought of what to say. He had done it twice, once as he spoke to her in the hall, and now as they were about to talk. She had noticed both times, and she would have liked to see a great deal more of Mr Parry, but men like him did not pay for company. He was tall and strong-looking with clean hands and sparkling linen, no tobacco marks or smell of spirits. His eyes were a curious bright blue and she looked into them directly, took a deep breath and started to tell him what he needed to know.

"This is confidential, sir. The people Oiy work with are 'andy with their fists, and Oiy need mi'looks, so this can go no further." She paused, checking his reaction, and went on.

"Oiy knew who you was straight off when Oiy saw you 'avin' the row at Shadwell's the other night and they called you Mr Drake. Oiy'd already found you out through Letty's brother Fred. She works with me and 'e's guard on the mail coach to Gloucester."

There was no need to say more.

"Then," said Nathaniel, "I would guess he has made the acquaintance of a servant at the Pelican by the name of Abigail and her story has now made its way via the brother to Letty and now to you. Remember Miss Marchant, the fewer who know of Abigail's history and her whereabouts, the better for her health."

"Oiy'd never tell on 'er, Mr Parry, sir! And neither will Letty, nor 'er Fred. Oiy knew Abi was in trouble in Bristol and you saved 'er life, prob'ly twice, as Joshua Shadwell would wring 'er neck if 'e caught 'old of 'er now and that's the truth. She told Letty's brother you called yerself Mr Drake, and Oiy 'eard you talkin' to Billy and Jabez 'bout the old soldier dyin'. Prestwick wasn't 'e? Oiy want you to know Oiy think one of moiy customers 'ad something to do with the poor old sod. Moiy customer was a gent called Mortimer-Buckley. 'E came for Oiy the night the old man died. Goin' at it hammer and tongs 'e was."

She took Nathaniel by surprise by abruptly throwing her head back and letting out a peal of laughter at the memory, slapping her knees and stamping her little boots. And he saw why she was a favourite. She had undone her coat as she had started her tale, revealing most of her large pair of white breasts, which were falling out of a plunging neckline and shaking with her delight at the memory of Buckley and his fancies.

"All sorts of ideas, has that gent," she said, wiping tears from her eyes. "Had me wearin' a flounced milk maid's cap of all things!"

A tap on the door was followed by Frances and the coffee. Frances, agog with gawping curiosity, could not take her eyes from Clari as she placed the tray on a side table.

"Shall I pour, Mr Parry?" she asked, but knew what the answer would be.

Nathaniel saw her off as quickly as he could, but it reminded him that the visit would have caused a stir below stairs. Explanations loomed. He shrugged off the thought and carried on.

"What's your evidence he has anything to do with it, Clari?"

"Well 'e was that done in afterwards," she said, with a measure of pride, "that 'e fell straight asleep. Done that before 'e 'ad and 'e dreams and talks in 'is sleep. That night 'e called out 'Prestwick! Prestwick!' quite a few times, no mistaking that, then 'e was mumblin' rubbish about jewels and Napoleon, all sorts of jumble. 'E seemed to be talkin' away to someone else, frightened loike. Then 'e started to roll and thrash 'is arms, sweatin' the while, and shouted somethin' foreign *"las tres*

206

hermanas!" whatever the 'ell that is. But 'e knew about the old man roight enough. Oiy made that out clear and Oiy thought you should know, sir. I want you to know us girls are still grateful you 'elped Abi: one of our own. Not many would 'ave given 'er the time of day."

Emma had put the pocket book and jewellery away and allowed him ten minutes before she made her way downstairs. She lingered only briefly at the parlour door, as the voices were too subdued to repay eavesdropping, then continued down the next flight to the kitchen. She walked in to find the staff immobilised in a hostile stand-off. Tobias had paused mid-way through brushing a boot and was glaring daggers at Mrs Rollinson, who in her turn, was quivering with fury, floury arms folded and biceps on the bulge, squaring up to Frances. Harriet was likewise transfixed, but crouched over the table, her eyes rolled up fearfully to view Mrs Rollinson, knife in mid-slice over a turnip. Only Caradoc, hunched by the fire and locked in a growling battle with a bloodied leg bone, soldiered on with his task, oblivious.

"Now everyone," said Emma briskly. "What's amiss?"

"Do you know who's in the parlour, Madam," exploded Mrs Rollinson, glaring at Frances and Tobias in turn. "These two know who she is all right. I caught them talking of her and Master Caudle here gave me a mouth full of cheek, I might add, when I challenged him. She is a common bawd and they know more about her than is decent! She has no place in a respectable house and Master's on his own with her! It's not right."

Tobias stood up, ignoring Mrs Rollinson and dealing directly with Emma. "Madam, the woman has information Mr Parry needs. Mrs Rollinson was making to call you but the woman won't talk if anyone goes in."

It was a chance Emma knew she had to take. Though at first things had gone tolerably well between them, recently Mrs Rollinson had made it clear in many ways, small but unmistakeable, that she thought little of her. The tight lips and the shake of the head after they discussed the weekly menu had moved onto the substitution of Emma's choice of dishes for a favourite of her own. She had become bold enough to interfere with every domestic decision Emma made, almost on principle; and meanest of all was her continuing petty cruelty to the miserable Harriet in the name of "training", despite Emma's mild attempts to shield the girl.

"Thank you, Tobias," said Emma, with all the regal chill she could muster. "I see you all have work to do. Please return to it. And Mrs Rollinson, yours does not include remarking on Mr Parry's visitors."

As Emma strode back into the lobby and made her way to the stairs, she could not suppress a silent huzza of triumph. Though with her mouth open to give it full vent, she did not cut quite the figure she had hoped as she met with Nathaniel and his visitor in the hall.

Evening: 30th March, 1833.
General Palmer's Château, Cenon, Bordeaux, France.

Coco stood by the bedroom window in General Palmer's mansion, looking out over the park and the ranks of vines lining the steep decline to the river. The Garonne shone like steel in the distance under the white moonlight, and up-river on the far bank she could pick out buildings on the outskirts of the old city of Bordeaux. By daylight it was a ravishing view and her room for the night was luxurious, impeccably appointed in the latest style, and in view of his dire financial situation, provided another example of the General's profligate extravagance. Charles Palmer had proved to be a charming host: generous and ill-advised, both faults making him the best of company. And the rest of the evening had provided far more of interest than it might have done. She had accepted the invitation to do Dairmuid a good turn, a *quid pro quo* for helping her visit Jules, but it had blossomed into much more, and might even dose the Wheel of Fortune with a little more oil and encourage it to turn in her favour.

Dairmuid's hosts, the Bartons, despite being extremely elderly had proved to be excellent company. During the long journey in their coach to Cenon, which included embarking the whole equipage on the ferry at Lamarque, Mrs Barton had proved to be a raconteur.

"It was in 1794, before the two of you were born," she had declared fiercely to Dairmuid and Coco, her head on one side, peeking out from under a lace cap as big as a bucket, "when this land was a hell on earth. There we were, Mr Barton and myself, all in the flower of our youth, imprisoned and like to have our heads sundered from our shoulders by the scoundrel rogues of the Revolution. All foreigners were doomed!" She fixed them all with a scything glare and delivered a lengthy tale honed to perfection. "And don't talk to me of the Emperor Napoleon!" she had ended triumphantly. "A lamb he was in comparison with the devils in the Reign of Terror but I thwarted their evil purpose! I disguised himself here in a woman's petticoats and wrap, and we were out through the gates in quick sticks, onto the ship and sailing back to Ireland!"

"It was exactly so, Mrs Barton," agreed her husband fondly. "You were ever a woman of remarkable resource." Squeezing her hand affectionately, he transferred his twinkling smile to Dairmuid and Coco, "And you young folk will shortly be meeting another man who kept his head as well as keeping our business afloat during all that terrible time."

But Hugh's business partner, Baron Guestier, had failed to put in an appearance at the dinner, which in the event did not surprise, for at almost eighty he was even older than the Bartons. However, his debonair and imperious son Pierre, and his wife, had been at the table, along with Pierre's sister Eliza, and her husband, the same Bernard Phelan whom Coco remembered from Dairmuid's stories. It was a heady company of Bordeaux's wine Czars. General Palmer could not have hoped for more and Dairmuid's work in arranging the evening would presumably not go unrewarded.

To her delight, matters of more immediate interest to herself had been touched upon towards the end of the evening when the talk had veered towards construction. The Bartons did not spend much of their year at the *château* in Saint-Estèphe and were more regularly to be found in Ireland. Hugh Barton enlarged on the details of a palatial spread he planned to build in County Kildare and Eliza Phelan had not missed the opportunity.

"Mr Phelan and I might well build in the Medoc. Mightn't we, Bernard?"

"Indeed, indeed," said Bernard Phelan, smiling expansively. "I wouldn't give up the Bordeaux house, but a *château* by one of my vineyards is a likely possibility as you say, my dear, probably Ségur de Cabanac."

"You will not regret it!" Pierre Guestier had declared. "I have had Beychevelle for over seven years now. Depend upon it, on my watch it will be the Versailles of the Medoc again! And I hear that the Marquis de la Blanquefort has some interesting plans. He's back with a wife and is making moves to resume his residence here in the Medoc. He's started on some landscaping at a site he has acquired on the outskirts of Blanquefort. Not the old white fort itself but a better situation altogether, the ruins of the mansion at Fort du Lac."

"So lovely to see the Marquis happily settled at last," said Madame Guestier generally, then as an aside to her sister-in-law Phelan. "She is extremely wealthy: older than him," she raised an eyebrow and then added generously, "but altogether delightful. *Très élégante.*"

"So the Marquis has returned," said Eliza Phelan. "And in transports of delight by the sound of it."

The tide of talk had moved on, but not for Coco. In her mind's eye she was back to Paris and remembered his careless warmth, his slow mocking smile. So, the Marquis had surfaced, and married to a rich woman, an older woman.

"Has he now," Coco thought to herself, and not for the first time, as she watched the moon glide behind a bank of smoky cloud. "Has he by God. Well perhaps his life could be even more

delightful if he renewed his acquaintance with one of his dearest
old friends."

Late morning: 2nd April, 1833.
Mayfair, London.

Nathaniel had left his rooms in Lambeth, crossed
Westminster Bridge and concluded some swift business at the
Home Office in Downing Street. Drake had been loitering by
Melbourne's door and they had made arrangements to dine
together that evening at the Travellers' Club in Pall Mall. After a
brief word with Percy, Nathaniel scooped up his mail and made
for Birdcage Walk; skirted Saint James's Park and then headed
straight over Green Park to Mayfair. He hoped to catch Sir Giles
Mortimer-Buckley and confront him at home before he left for
the House, or to his club for luncheon. Nathaniel was alone as he
had planned only a brief visit to London, and decided to leave
Caradoc in Bath. The dog had seemed more than happy with the
arrangement. With age, Caradoc was proving to be increasingly
pragmatic and independent. Ever since Mary Spence had
befriended him he had shamelessly exploited the females of
Bath. Tilly Vere had been an early convert, as were all the
Peterson women and he was a favourite with Em, obviously. At
home, Harriet and Frances also competed in plying him with
extravagant attention, and most surprisingly, Caradoc's recent
ratting exploits in the larder had won over the hard heart of Mrs
Rollinson. He had laid down the bloody corpses of his kills at
her feet as tribute, and now had a guaranteed lounging space in
front of every fire in the house, not excepting the kitchen range.

But Nathaniel had not had spare time on his hands to dwell
on Caradoc's absence. He had brought his father's journal with
him and been occupied in reading through all the entries for the
winter of 1808/9. They included confirmation of Buckley's
participation in the raid on Napoleon's baggage train, which he
had denied, as well as the unexplained disappearance of some of
the loot, which had not been reported publically at the time.
Likewise, it corroborated the fact that Buckley knew Philip

211

Spence and Ben Prestwick from the mission. Furthermore, his father's distrust of Buckley was made plain. Owen had concluded that he was a rogue, and in his dealings with women, a cad. The entries made on his father's return to Britain made more mention of the missing pieces of jewellery and included a brief report of what he had learned about the shambolic retreat to Corunna: the crippling cold and disease, the atrocities inflicted on the Spanish villages and the sorry toll of executions which followed. But his father's sketches were of even greater interest. As well as a set of drawings of the jewels from the loot, which were architectural in their accuracy, there were others, done impromptu and out of doors, which brought the beating heart of the Montes Vascos to Nathaniel's cosy digs in Lambeth. Wild cats and wolves, leaping chamois, vultures and ravens decorated the margins of the notes and there were portraits. Two he noted most particularly: the faces were mesmerising, proud and hawkish. Below it said 'Izar and Amaia': *Las dos hermanas.* Again, the mention of Spanish sisters, but this time just two, not three. At the sight of those words he had a vision of Clari Marchant struggling to get her tongue round them. It seemed that Buckley was familiar with an additional Spanish *señorita.*

On his arrival at the Park Street mansion, the butler showed Nathaniel into the hall, and reappeared almost immediately to hurry him into the front parlour. He entered to find Giles Mortimer-Buckley looking as if he had just sprung guiltily to his feet, his pre-luncheon drink still quivering in his hand and his eyes bulging in alarm.

"Mr Parry!" he exclaimed, over heartily. "Welcome! Lady Leonora is lunching with our daughter, so do join me, take a seat. Will you have a drink?"

Nathaniel accepted, judging it to be a quick route to relaxing his prey.

"Bristol Milk! Hope sherry is to your taste," said Buckley nervously. "Appropriate, as we last met in Bristol if I remember correctly. How may I be of service?"

Nathaniel placed his drink down silently and looked straight into Buckley's eyes and down to the depths of his lost soul.

"Sir Giles, although you sought to hide it from me I have received confirmation that you knew my father and were recruited by him to join a mission in northern Spain during the French Wars. You and the other members of the group profited from the success of the mission and one of the men, Ben Prestwick, reacquainted himself with you the week before he met his death. On the night he died, rather than keep an appointment to meet him, you attended Shadwell's establishment in Green Park and then left Bath." Nathaniel ignored the rising tide of bluster that was almost choking Buckley and pressed on. "Edwin Ravenswood's employee, Trevellis, was connected with Prestwick's death and I put it to you that, at the very least, you were well aware that Prestwick was in danger."

The room swam before Buckley as if he had been struck by a pole-axe. He had not slept soundly for weeks, since that cursed rat Prestwick had turned up in Bath to haunt him. And Prestwick was not the only ghoul to terrorise his nights. No, no! He must not think of them! He focused hard on the man sitting opposite him, on his pale face and piercing eyes, his right hand resting lightly on a silver-handled stick. Undoubtedly a weapon and the bastard could no doubt put it to deadly use.

"Think, Giles, think!" hissed the voice.

He managed to gulp down a shuddering breath and tried to compose himself. He drank his sherry in one swallow and slammed the glass down hard on the side table.

"Yes, Mr Parry, I misled you. The mission was secret you see, long time back, but old loyalties die hard." He smiled warily, treading like a man on a tightrope. "The drunken old fool had a loose tongue. I admit, I asked for help to frighten him off. I wanted him away from Bath, away from me. He was a man of no discretion and it was clear that he needed money. All manner of unpleasantness might have arisen."

"So you asked Ravenswood for help?"

Buckley nodded violently.

See, he said to the voice, so far, so good, no mention of gold or jewels; of the burning village and the girl or of blasted Maisie Trickett.

He dared to hope. "Yes, but I'm sure he did nothing rash. I had no idea that Prestwick would come to any harm and surely Ravenswood would do him no mischief. Damn it the man's a Justice of the Peace! Though I cannot speak for his servant. Trevellis, you say? Contacts might be dangerous, what!" he said, daring to relax and warm to his theme. He risked an olive branch. "And speaking of which, be warned Mr Parry, I know he is your colleague, but John Drake means you no good. He warned Ravenswood that you intended to investigate his new ship, the *Leonora*. Named for my wife, you know. Now if that is all, will you stay for luncheon?"

"I could not impose, Sir Giles," said Nathaniel, preparing to take his leave. "And I sense we will make no further progress today."

Buckley stood at the window as the front door closed behind his visitor, his lips working as if deep in conversation, his eyes staring bleakly at Nathaniel's retreating back. Another drink was already in his hand and his knuckles showed white as he steadied his hand on the ledge.

Early evening: The Travellers' Club, Pall Mall, London.

It was Nathaniel's first visit to the new incarnation of the Travellers' Club and he was pleasantly surprised to find that his membership still stood; financed by some labyrinthine means on an old account of his father's. Owen Parry had been a founder member of the original Club, which had been set up after the war, and had taken Nathaniel there countless times, but the current new and splendid building had only been finished the previous year. It was the natural habitat of diplomats and their distinguished foreign visitors, a facility supported from the start by Lord Castlereagh, the legendary Foreign Secretary during the French Wars, and by Lord Palmerston himself. Drake's ambition to join Brooks's had been side-lined of late as he had found membership of the Travellers both congenial, and more importantly, extremely useful in terms of the advancement of his career. This being the case, Nathaniel was surprised by Drake's appearance as he caught sight of him crouched in an armchair by the fire and staring moodily into the flames. He was clearly in low water, glum-faced and absently rubbing his old neck wound, a sure sign of anxiety, his brow furrowed and back bowed. Nathaniel had noticed that Drake had been preoccupied and strained when he had spoken with him briefly that morning at the Office but had put it down to the discomfort of having to wait upon the pleasure of Lord Melbourne, a notoriously lengthy business.

Drake looked up, eyes hollow and dull. "Hello, Parry. Have some port?"

Nathaniel caught the slight slur in his voice, noted the careless pouring of the drink and exaggeratedly careful replacement of the decanter on the table. Drake had been there some time. Nathaniel nodded and settled down quietly, letting Drake take up the slack when he felt equal to it.

"Any progress with the death of the old soldier?" said Drake finally, draining his glass and reaching again for the port. "Any more progress, what!"

"Oh yes," said Nathaniel. "I know that Sir Giles Mortimer-Buckley was involved with the consignment of treasure from France, that he knew the soldier by the name of Prestwick, who introduced himself and seemed ready either for a spot of blackmail or to divulge details of the mission. I also know that Sir Giles sought help from Edwin Ravenswood to remove Prestwick from Bath."

At the mention of Ravenswood, Drake's brow furrowed even deeper and he slammed down his glass, leaning over the table towards Nathaniel. "Ravenswood!" He spat out the name in a rasping whisper. "Ravenswood has much to answer for Parry. You do not know the half! He is an evil man."

"I am aware of that, Drake," said Nathaniel carefully. "As you know, I am also aware that you were obliged to work closely with him by our superiors. I know that you had to keep his trust by informing him of my interest in the *Leonora.*"

Drake's eyes glinted, still sharp enough to recognise dangerous ground, he struggled to steer the conversation to safety.

"I'd no choice; you know that Parry, had to work closely with him for the Office. With Pam's ambitions for the opium trade, I'd no choice. The independent merchants will be running the show by next year." he paused, overwhelmed by other memories. "But the business with the trade in girls, that bad business...." His voice trailed off.

Nathaniel smiled. "I know. You did what you had to do."

Nathaniel was certain that Drake remained ignorant of his connection with Cornelius Lee and that Cornelius had informed him of Ravenswood's affairs. For Drake, if he thought of him at all, Cornelius was just another treacherous member of Kizhe's staff, an operative who had unaccountably abandoned last year's voyage at his first chance after landfall in China, risking the wrath, not only of Kizhe, but also of Ravenswood himself. Drake was still unsure as to whether Ravenswood had informed Nathaniel of the details of the illicit trade in girls and Drake's readiness to take a cut. There seemed nothing further Drake wanted to discuss about last year's cargo or its fate. But there was clearly some other issue bearing heavily on him. Nathaniel refilled Drake's glass and waited.

"Thanks, Parry," said Drake, and with Nathaniel's words of reassurance still sounding in his ears, and with that final port slackening the last bonds of distrust, the light of caution died in his eyes and Nathaniel Parry seemed suddenly to be a friend. "I suppose you know that Ravenswood is conducting an affair with my wife," he blurted out, adding bitterly, "I am sure all London knows. I don't like it, Parry! Didn't think she meant that much to me, damn it. Of course I knew the value of her family. Thought that was enough. Seems it isn't. Feeling damned sorry for myself to tell the truth. And for Mrs Ravenswood, Amanda, pretty woman that. I can tell you she has been dashed open in her comments to me. The man's a monster."

Nathaniel's mind had wandered back to the docks and his last sighting of Cornelius. Amongst the pile of correspondence waiting for him at the Office had been the long-awaited note from his friend. Cornelius would be waiting for him at the same riverside pub they had used before, the Prospect of Whitby. He would be there each Friday night in April, waiting. Perhaps he could take something worth hearing to repay Cornelius's patience.

"Yes indeed, Drake," said Nathaniel easily. "Mrs Ravenswood does not deserve such neglect. I am sure you can be a great comfort to her. A problem shared lightens the load."

"Quite," said Drake, confidentially, seeing the possibility of a nobler role for himself: not the cuckold, but the rock, the manly shoulder for her tears. His head rose, he sat straighter in the chair.

"In fact, your conversations with Mrs Ravenswood could be of great use," said Nathaniel. "She will be less loyal to her husband in view of his treachery and I would like to know more of the whereabouts of the man you dealt with in connection with Ravenswood's more disreputable trading interests. A Mr Kizhe if I remember correctly." Nathaniel took a gamble; it was extremely unlikely that Drake was still ignorant of the extent of his role in foiling the shipment of girls last autumn. He could have read Captain Peterson's reports to Melbourne, which would undoubtedly have spelled out the details. Also, the presence of Frances in his house, and his connections with another victim, her friend Abi in Gloucester, were becoming more widely known. He needed Drake to feel he was being taken into his confidence. "As you will know, I was involved in frustrating Kizhe's dealings in a minor way. He will not have been impressed by my work and I like to know where my enemies are."

"Leave that to me," said Drake, suddenly lordly. "If Mrs Ravenswood has any knowledge of his movements, I am well placed to find out."

Evening: 5th April, 1833.
The Prospect of Whitby, Wapping Wall, London.

It was Friday night and Nathaniel had packed his bag with the few clothes he had brought and his swordstick, to be ready to catch the mail coach for Bath at dawn. Before that, he had business to attend and had dressed for it in black, and shabbily. As on his last visit, he chose to take the makila, which did not mark him out as a gentleman, checked the hidden blade and practised a few swings before he left. Almost out of the door, he had returned for a pistol and loaded it, before tying a muffler round his face and catching the river ferry to Wapping. He found the pub easily as the Prospect could be heard before it was seen and was heaving with customers. He worked his way through them to take a seat by the wall, kept his eye on the door, ordered a jug of porter from the potboy and settled down to wait for Cornelius.

The crowd in the bar was rough and as the night wore on the volume of the banter rose to a thunder, the air was hot as a furnace and thick with the stench of bodies, tobacco and spilt ale. Most customers were English and Irish sailors keen to spend their money, but there were a few lascars in a knot by the door, some African deck hands playing dice and half a dozen whores scattered round the tables, squawking like Matthew's parrot and chaffing the men. Nathaniel was busy catching the eye of the barmaid when Cornelius materialised silently from the crowd and slid into the seat by him.

"More porter, if you please," ordered Nathaniel, as a barmaid bustled by, her hands full of empty glasses.

They sat in silence until the drink stood before them, the barmaid had moved off and the crowds had surged back, a solid mass, isolating their corner and shielding them from view.

"It is good to see you," said Nathaniel, "but I was pleased to find you gone from the *Leonora* when I got back with the police." Nathaniel smiled, remembering the weary state of some of Ravenswood's men, "You seem to have made an impression on the crew before you left."

Cornelius bowed his head briefly in acknowledgement. "I have to say they made themselves known to me also. I needed a while to recover and luckily I had some assistance on the night. Two of my men, Fong and Chen, had been sent to join the *Leonora* when the *Blue Dragon* returned for refit to Bristol. They are still here with me in London and they are the reason I was delayed. We were instructed to stay here longer so they resolved to make themselves some money on the local boxing circuit. I just stood as Fong's second. There is a competition going on in the yard at the side of the pub and Chen's turn is in about half an hour. It earns them a living, which they prefer, rather than being reliant on me, or depending on government pay. They also get sparring practice. Such as it is."

"Won't Ravenswood's crew recognise them, or maybe Kizhe's men?"

Cornelius laughed. "Englishmen are easily confused by Chinese sailors of average height. Different clothes, longer hair, moustaches and beards: the slightest change and we are unlikely to be recognised. Even you can confuse your countrymen without too much trouble, Nathaniel! And they do not have to try too hard as Kizhe and his men planned to sail with the *Leonora*. The crew who knew Fong and Chen well are on their way to Africa. So, unfortunately for me," he continued, suddenly grave, "Kizhe is out of reach."

"I might be able to help you find him," said Nathaniel. "It seems that Drake has taken against Ravenswood for having an affair with his wife and that he and Amanda Ravenswood have struck up a friendship. As revenge, she might be persuaded to tell Drake of her husband's business affairs that are of interest to us. Drake owes me some favours and has promised to find out all he can about Kizhe's whereabouts."

"Good," said Cornelius. "We have a start." Though, he reflected to himself, he had not mistaken Amanda Ravenswood's looks in his own direction. She might have warmed to Drake as to a fellow sufferer, but her signals to him were not of suffering.

219

He resolved to renew his acquaintance with Mrs Ravenswood and investigate her new thirst for vengeance more closely.

"Have you ever wanted to get married, Cornelius?" asked Nathaniel, relaxing back against the wooden panelling and sinking more porter. "Ever wanted someone to go home to?"

Cornelius looked up, intrigued. Nathaniel was not usually given to asking personal questions. "There are places I think of as homes," he said. "There are people there, but no wife. My life's work excludes a personal dimension: for now. I am different people in different places. The still centre of my world is within me."

Nathaniel fell quiet. Perhaps he also was two different people, at least two, and each with an entirely different life. He loved Em but had thought of her only fleetingly over the last few days. He had been consumed by his London life and had slipped into it as into an alternate reality.

"Emma is a woman of beauty and awareness, of unusual emotional depth," continued Cornelius.

Nathaniel looked at him, surprised. "I was just thinking of her."

"Of course, you mentioned marriage; she must be in your mind. Emma is unlike most English women I have met. Time spent with her will never be wasted. I could be happy to go home to a woman like her. "

Nathaniel felt no jealousy, no petty annoyance at the suggestion and noted that Cornelius had known how he would take such a remark before he made it.

Cornelius glanced at his pocket watch.

"Time for Chen's bout," he said, and they made their way out into the yard and the bawling scrimmage of men under the swinging lamps.

They pushed their way round to where Fong and Chen stood waiting by the river wall for Chen's turn. Both men were watching the contest animatedly, and as Nathaniel turned to look at the make-shift ring, he realised why. Half naked, oily with sweat and mud, panting for breath and locked in a grappling hold were two fearsomely powerful women. Roughly-muscled and liberally insulated by rolls of fat, they careered round the ring, struggling for a throw, until one lost her footing and they both collapsed in a shouting ball of filthy petticoats and flailing arms and legs. The mood of the crowd was generous and uproarious; the two fighting prostitutes had given light relief, a spicy novelty turn before the serious bout; time to laugh, size up the slatternly charms on show and take the chance to empty their bursting bladders against the yard wall. Some had chanced a bet, but most were already turning their attention to Chen, who had stepped forward to face a brutish local fighter, twice his size, thick-necked, sponge-eared and gap-toothed.

"It is good training for Chen as your male fighters are not allowed to use their feet," said Cornelius. "He would win too quickly otherwise and attract too much notice."

The umpire had started the match when Nathaniel looked back at the ring, marked only by the thick sawdust coating the cobbles of the yard to give some grip and soak up spilt blood. Chen was in the centre, his pivoted fists up, but still and watchful whilst his adversary bobbed and weaved in front of him. Big as a haystack, the man jeered and cursed him for a coward until he lost patience and flung a swingeing punch. Chen dropped into a low stance and with one blow took the wind out of him. He let him recover and then surgically landed a blow, then another, but not too hard as the bout must not end too soon and disappoint the crowd. He allowed his man to catch him once, then again in the ribs. Chen automatically raised his knee to prepare for a retaliatory kick but managed to lower it again in a second.

"Well done," breathed Nathaniel, whilst Cornelius observed it without comment, and no one else seemed to have noticed at all. The betting took its normal course; the crowd hollered encouragement and chose their champion. But at an upper window, the curtain twitched.

Nathaniel reckoned that Chen would let the bout run for at least five minutes more and took the opportunity to glance round the crowd. In the shadows away from the competition one of the

221

prostitutes was slumped on a chair, winded but bloodily triumphant and cradling her prizes for the night, a wool coat and a bottle of gin. An old woman in a filthy cap was busy pouring brandy over a jagged claw mark on her neck whilst the other fighter was squinting in the smoky light of a lamp, threading a needle with twine and preparing to draw the wound together. Otherwise, the crowd was largely male and very mixed. High beaver hats bobbed above the caps, voices of privilege carried above the tumult and fine wool coats rubbed shoulders with fustian jackets. Some men had barrel-shaped fighting dogs with spiked collars, growling and snarling on their short leads. A thought of home: it was good to know that Caradoc was probably spread-eagled by the fire in Saint James's Square. It occurred to Nathaniel that he enjoyed his two lives: the comfort of the one and the knife-edge of the other; it was right to keep them separate.

The crowded scene in the yard burned like a watch fire, the bundled scrum of humanity enjoying the frantic blaze of life and light corralled by the makeshift screen of low walls and tumbledown buildings. Above was the vast black night with its wheeling stars and, below the wall, the dark river flowed fast and treacherous. Standing out up river at low water mark, now deep in the tide and skeletal in the moonlight, was the abandoned gibbet of Execution Dock, wreathed round with swirling rags of mist, silent and by most, unheeded. But for those alive to such things, it emanated an unmistakable warning that hissed, sibilant over the water, and crept with the mist over every inch of exposed skin. The warning was of the wolves which prowled still, circling the flickering warmth. Cornelius raised his head, looked and listened.

Isolated from the dark and deep in the boisterous crowd, Nathaniel was attracted by a change in mood round the bookmaker's table, voices were raised and betting slips were waving high in the air. He caught sight of Cornelius motioning to Chen, who promptly knocked out his man, raised his arms in triumph and backed out of the ring. Fong was ready with his coat

222

and the three of them went to collect Chen's winnings. The timing was tight, as the shouts by the table had been succeeded by bellows and a couple of blows had triggered a brawl. Nathaniel raised his makila as a quarter-staff and cleared a way for himself through the high hats who were rushing for the gate in panic. He worked his way round to join Cornelius and his men who had cut through the crowd, done their business swiftly and were making for the exit. As Nathaniel moved in behind them as rearguard, a burly seaman broke from the pack and was almost upon him, a couple of followers on his heels. Nathaniel floored him with a stunning head blow from the makila, stepped in and swung the stick in a wide arc. As the followers paused, uncertain, he drew his pistol, persuading them to give him the space he needed to back out smartly from the yard. Once out on Wapping Wall he kept close to Cornelius and his men and they allowed themselves to be swept away on the tide of the crowd towards the ferry.

As they neared the mooring, Cornelius leaned closer and spoke urgently above the gabble around them and the drumming of feet. "We were watched from an upper window. Beware. We will separate now and I will contact you in Bath before the end of next month."

Nathaniel nodded and made for the boat without looking back. The pavement had become more spacious as the crowd thinned out. Between him and the ferry there were just half a dozen men and a gang of small children with famished faces, hovering mudlarks waiting to jostle passers-by and frisk their pockets. Nathaniel smiled to himself, tightened his grip on the makila and strode purposefully past them to climb aboard.

As the boat pulled away up river, a figure in a heavy cloak detached itself from the shadows of the buildings, watched the progress of the ferry for a moment, and then turned to plunge back into the dark.

Chapter 7

Noon: 10th May, 1833.
The harbour, Hope Cove, Devon.

The two Frenchmen stood on the sandy foreshore, muffled up to their eyes in scarves to keep out the blustery wind. The cold air was searching, shot through with the scents of iodine, brine and fish. Clouds scudded across the grey sky and the air rang with the noise of the gulls. Some were wheeling high above their heads whilst others stalked over the beach picking at worm casts. Half a dozen were fighting over mackerel heads on the slipway.

"It's cold as charity here, *mon frère,*" grumbled Pierre, thrusting his hands deep into his pockets. "We've waited over a week already. Are you certain she's coming?"

Jules was climbing onto a rock, placing his feet with care to avoid the slick greening of the sea and the brown swag of seaweed that crowned it and clung to its sides. He was watching the progress of a three-masted lugger which was tacking into the cove between the headland he now knew to call Bolt Tail, and the Shippen Rock. The vessel was heaving in the heavy swell, struggling against a contrary wind to make a safe landfall and join the knot of boats already at anchor. The sheltered harbour was busy with fishermen working on their catches between piles of crab and lobster pots and pyramids of coiled nets. From the main street, women's voices carried over the beach from where they stood at their front doors, some gossiping, one calling her man home to eat, and a dozen children scurried amongst the tide wrack, circling and squawking like another flock of birds.

The boat was coming in bravely enough but Jules knew enough of the coast, and this cove in particular, to know it had teeth. Dodging the wrecks was as much a skill as skirting the rocks. He glanced over to Bolt Tail and caught sight of a wiry figure standing out black against the horizon. Antoine had been a good choice for the trip, young and adventurous, an expert seaman and strong as whip cord; but a man who said little and followed orders. The fewer involved in Coco's little caper the better, but he had needed at least a three-man crew to handle his boat, *La Coquille Saint-Jacques,* and bring her safe into this harbour. The trip needed more discretion than the usual smuggling run, which normally involved a deal in Roscoff and a sea anchorage off the Devon shore where the sealed kegs were lowered overboard in the night, marked with buoys and left to bob innocently on the tide, waiting for collection.

Jules had never had cause to land at Hope Cove before, but he had known the welcome would be warm. He had left the arrangements to his usual contact, a mop-headed fisherman called Pascoe, superficially affable and slow of speech but cunning as a monkey. He had proved his worth a dozen times over the years and for this visit had arranged for a room to be made ready for them with his brother-in-law Jarvis, the landlord of the Hope and Anchor. Jules had brought a case of claret for Pascoe and one for Jarvis, with a collar of *Alençon* lace for Esther his wife: these considerations had made the room very ready indeed.

Jarvis, though not yet thirty years of age, was garrulous and expansive. Each night in the bar he had entertained them with tales, some of which might even have been true. Last night it was the legend of the "galleon timbers" which framed his fireplace.

"Salvaged from the *San Pedro el Mayor* they were," he had declared, rolling his eyes upwards. "As God's my witness she was the only Armada ship wrecked on an English coast in that terrible autumn of 1588, after Captain Drake and the weather had done for the rest of 'em. Stripped bare she was, down to every last spar."

Jules had inspected the fireplace, running his hands over it, admiring it. It was a good story. The wooden lintels looked like ship's timbers and they were of great age. Altogether the tale fitted well with what he knew of the men of Devon who were notorious wreckers, scavengers and smugglers, and now, especially the last of these. Devon and Cornwall were united in their hatred of customs men. It was common knowledge that no local jury would convict a smuggler as anyone risking their liberty to thwart the Revenue was a hero. He had heard of men in gangs of up to a hundred strong unloading a cargo by moonlight despite the gathering strength of the King's officers, the preventive boats, the watchtowers planted on the headlands and coastguards prowling round every coast and creek. They well knew that smuggling, like privateering, which was common and profitable in times of war, was illegal and the penalties, if a man were to be convicted, could be fearsome. Despite this, here they persisted in the old ways; their women provided cover and aid, helping run teams of donkeys and Dartmoor ponies up the steep cliffs with the children as look-outs. Wine, brandy and French lace, at reasonable prices and tax free, were seen as the birthright of Englishmen. Any French man conniving to supply them was welcomed with open arms.

"She will be here one day, Pierre," said Jules absent-mindedly, still keeping track of the little boat as it zigzagged home. "We have a month to spare. *Tu es en vacances*! Once she's here there will be more then enough to do."

226

It had been a good time to indulge Coco as there had been little to keep them at Château Pèlerin. Though some called it summer and it was easier to sail, the work on the vines had not yet really begun. The buds were out and the frosts were over, though they rarely amounted to much in the sheltered Medoc, insulated from the gales of Biscay and far from the bitter cold of the Pyrenees. There was little new growth needing to be tied, and the men left behind could deal well enough with what there was. The flowers had yet to bloom and it would be June before the fruit started. He was even at a lull between his boxing competitions at the Fort. It could not have been a more suitable time for a little foreign enterprise and he was enjoying it. It was the chance to enter a different life for a few weeks, a rest from Claudette, though she had become dear to him, and the children, though he had surprised himself by being a doting father. Jules rarely made the sea trip with the contraband these days but let his men deal with it whilst he played *le grand seigneur* at home. The trip was a novelty and he felt suddenly younger, invigorated.

"Mornin' to ye."

Jules turned to see a short, squat figure standing by him, eyes crinkled and gazing out to sea.

"Hello Pascoe, *mon vieux*! How long do you think that ship will tarry in the bay?"

"Not long," said Pascoe, slowly. "No, she will not tarry long. She be the *Lively,* skippered by Shadrach Hollis who do know every tide and every rock in the bay." Pascoe then sucked in his breath, short and sharp for emphasis, just in case the foreigner had missed the point. "Every last rock 'ee do know."

"Has the Salcombe mail cart come in yet?" asked Pierre.

"Full an hour ago," said Pascoe with relish. "There were no passengers on 'im." He paused, allowing them time to accept that fact before adding, "But there do be a beautiful young wench asking after the two of ye. Came in a carriage she did. Jarvis and Esther settled 'er into a room d'reckly. Though she may 'ave taken off for a saunter to stretch 'er legs by now."

227

"Why didn't you tell us?" said Jules, as he took off from the boulder, landed hard in the gravely sand and set off at a trot.

"Yer didn't ask!" called Pascoe, smiling broadly at his retreating back. "I be a-tellin' ye now."

Jules and Pierre strode up the shore and turned left into the high street, striking out for the thatched cob cottages that clustered round the Hope and Anchor. Coco was waiting for them in the dark of the front bar. It took their eyes a moment to adjust to the gloom before they saw her in a quiet corner, lit by the filmy rays of light slanting through the mottled bull's eye glass of the windowpanes. Pleased with herself, and smiling, her honey-brown eyes glinted gold as she stood up to greet them, turned out like a lady in shimmering oyster silk, as if the dust and fatigue of the road had never been.

"Coco, *ma chérie!* It does my eyes good to see you," said Jules, kissing her soundly.

"We thought you'd never come," said Pierre, taking her hand and kissing it, holding on too long.

She squeezed his hand then pushed it away, laughing and excited. "Well, here I am. I see you are favourites already and so am I. They welcomed me like a long lost cousin. I've eaten already and recommend the mutton pie. But for now, sit down and have a drink." Coco sat down and poured them each a glass of wine as the men took their seats, expectant, before her.

"I caught the mail coach to Exeter," she said, delighted to be able to tell her tale, "and then hired a *Berlin* and driver to bring me down here to the edge of civilisation! He is waiting with the team in the stables and will take us all back to Exeter tomorrow. Once there we will travel on to Bath separately, and then have a few days to finesse our arrangements quietly in my rooms. I live in the centre of town, it is easy to find and there are crowds of people there. Strangers are common in Bath and you will not be noticed. We will return here to Hope Cove after our business is done and I will drive us from Bath in a carriage I have on a long lease. It's a four in hand I am keeping in a private stable, so we can use the horses for our business trip, then ride back to Bath, pick up the carriage, and as I said, I will drive you back here. The job itself will be done on Friday 24th May and theoretically I will be in London from the previous Wednesday until the following Monday. I have a busy friend who will be taking me to the races but will sadly have to let me occupy myself with sightseeing for a few of my days with him. No one will know that I am back in Bath."

Both men, stunned to silence, took deep drafts of their wine.

"We will hear the rest on a full stomach," said Jules, walking over to the bar. "Esther! Two mutton pies, *s'il vous plaît*!"

Coco had laid her plans well. This spring had been chosen for the burglary, as the Ravenswoods had embarked on a lengthy building project at Arno's Tower that would continue until the autumn. Two more gothic towers were to be added to the wings and on the back of the building at ground level a palm house was to be constructed, a glass conservatory heated by stoves to exhibit not only exotic plants but also the immense wealth of Edwin Ravenswood. Heedless of both glass and window taxes, he was creating an object of awe, and focus of envy, for friends, enemies and competitors alike. Builders arrived in a cart on a daily basis and it was to be their misfortune that they were excellent time-keepers. Interception of the builders and their cart would not be difficult. Friday 24th May was the day that the Ravenswoods were to attend an exclusive luncheon party in the City of Bristol at the new Mansion House in Great George Street and Amanda had unwisely advertised that fact widely to her circle of lady friends in Bath. The new mayor, His Worship Mr Charles Walker, was to entertain a prestigious gathering of Councillors and Aldermen, Justices of the Peace, Members of the Society of Merchant Venturers, the Dock Company and the West India Association. The Ravenswoods would drag themselves from their death-beds to attend. The event would be lavish and well victualled, but it would be a serious gathering. The main topic of conversation was likely to be the impending abolition of slavery and the urgent necessity for the slave owners to extract maximum compensation from the government for their loss. It would be a hot topic, as many of Bristol's finest examples of that class would be present and Ravenswood was one of them.

It was too good an opportunity to miss. Amanda would not be wearing her emeralds, as it was a luncheon party and not dinner. The house was in disarray and infested by strangers in the shape of the builder's labourers, who were ubiquitous and anonymous. As an added bonus, most of the indoor staff had been given the afternoon off. The Ravenswoods had a pack of guests arriving within a few days and all leave for domestics would therefore be temporarily cancelled. The Friday off in *lieu* could not have been better timed.

Somehow, when Coco talked, it sounded an easy business. Disguised as builders, with Coco in men's clothing and passable as a youth, they would feign attention to the building of the palm house, but Coco and Jules would steal indoors to remove the jewels and any other items which took their eye. Antoine would watch the horses nearby and they would be off to Bath before the alarm was raised.

Jules poured himself another drink. "How many men do the family employ at the house?"

"They would have taken the coachman and two footmen to Bristol so, ignoring the rest of the indoor staff, who will be unlikely to be at home, that would leave six of Ravenswood's guards. There are four of us Jules. They are no match."

"Three if we leave Antoine with the builders and the horses. Are they armed?" asked Pierre.

"Yes."

"Dogs?"

"Two. But I can provide you with something tasty for them if they appear," said Coco. "I assume you have brought handguns and rifles?"

"I was not planning on murder," said Jules.

"Neither am I," said Coco. "But have you brought your weapons?"

"Of course."

"And I see you have not left your hands and feet at home so all should be well."

Coco raised her glass. "*À votre santé*! And as the English enjoy saying: Confusion to our enemies."

Morning: 24th May, 1833.
The outskirts of the City of Bristol.

Cornelius had spent a useful week based at the Crown, the coaching inn on the main road running through the town of Keynsham. He, together with Fong and Chen, had quit London as they had had no more sightings of the man who shadowed them at the boxing match and Kizhe's trail was cold. They had made for the West Country so he could renew ties with Amanda Ravenswood. Once there, Cornelius had assumed the role of a merchant with time to kill, travelling at leisure with his servants whilst his vessel was taking on supplies in Bristol. He had stationed his men in a tavern by Redcliffe Back where they could sound out the crews and dock workers whilst he spent his first few days watching the Ravenswoods and reconnoitring the fields and woods of Arno's Vale. Edwin Ravenswood's daily routine was not difficult to predict. He spent most days and some nights at his townhouse on Redcliffe Parade, overseeing work on his vessels, terrorising his men, and using it as a base from which to attend court and discharge his duties as Justice of the Peace. Cornelius was in no doubt that the sentences handed out in his court would be as savage as the law could possibly permit. He watched Ravenswood's guards from the safety of the woods and recognised most of them from his weeks spent at the Tower as Ravenswood's guest. They tended to double as gamekeepers and carried shotguns, but when the master was out the patrols were cursory and usually ended with lengthy stops in the lodge house where two of them lived: feet were put up on the fender and drink was taken.

He had also taken the opportunity to visit the lady of the house one morning when her husband was out. Amanda had

231

been more than pleased to see him; within minutes he had been seated in the drawing room, welcoming drink in hand. At liberty to observe, he had been struck by the change in her. Though sharp featured and too spiteful for his taste, she had previously had an astringent elegance, a minx-like cleverness and self-possession which could be admired. Those attributes were all but gone. She was as if blunted by anxiety and desperation. Nathaniel's story of her husband's philandering could be read on every strained new line on her face. She had willingly given up her freedom to become the possession of a ruthless man in exchange for a life of luxury and the thrill of living dangerously, but the awful realisation seemed to have dawned upon her that there was more to pay.

Cornelius had dallied away the morning with her, accepted sherry, flattered and listened. Within the hour he had extracted all he needed to know about the imminent return of Kizhe, who was apparently not continuing with the *Leonora* but would spend time in Holland and then return to England. Next he had learned of her loneliness, of Ravenswood spending increasing amounts of time in Bristol and London, and of her distrust of many of her house staff, which had grown since the Bristol Riots and the burning of their vessel in the harbour. Apart from incompetence, she also sensed their contempt and disloyalty. Every one of them had been appointed according to their suitability to serve her husband and any she formed attachments to were dismissed. Chivalrously, as he took his leave, Cornelius had expressed a hope that he may be of service to her, stressed how much he looked forward to seeing her again and, of course, meeting with her husband. He had expanded on how much he also looked forward to seeing Mr Kizhe and taking the opportunity to explain exactly why he had not travelled north through China as planned after the *Blue Dragon* had docked there the previous year.

Within days of his visit, Amanda had persuaded Ravenswood to entertain Cornelius at dinner and he had received a letter at the Crown inviting him to Arno's Tower the following week. No doubt Ravenswood was keen to question him closely about his absence, but Cornelius also knew that his old master had a high opinion of him and his skills, and had valued his presence at the Tower. As in his favourite game of strategy, the encircling art of Wei Ch'i, Cornelius felt his first stones were placed wisely on the board. Now was the time to consolidate, to reflect on the significance of what he had done and wait for his adversary to make his move.

That morning, mindful that the Ravenswoods were going out for a lengthy lunch, he had decided to run to his old training ground by the ruins at Saint Anne's Well and spend a few hours practising before having another close look at the Tower. An hour before dawn he crossed the Bristol Road and struck out over the fields towards the woods. After a brisk few miles, and without seeing another soul, he recognised the abandoned workshop buildings, and near them in the clearing, the stony rim of the well-head which was all that remained of the old shrine. He bowed briefly in respect, then knelt, silent and still, to be at one with the wood and its music, to feel the gentle lift of the tree branches in answer to the low west wind, and once, to be aware of a dry rustle of paws in the undergrowth.

Then, flowing slow and faint, a familiar stream of echoes ran through his consciousness, an awareness of the place that had been before: shuffling lines of penitents with their tributes, sheaves of grain and flowers, prancing horses' hooves raising dust before the grand entourage of a king. Then all were prostrate before the altar and the image of Saint Anne, her circling arms cradling the Holy Mother and the Christ Child. Above her hung a golden crucifix encrusted in gems and, all around, he heard the shrouded choirs of holy sisters. Cornelius let the vision wash over him, the alien strangeness of the chanted Latin prayers for the dead, the flash of medieval glitter. It was there for a space, then before his gaze it disappeared, dissolved in fire, wails and cries, to be replaced by men with carts and spades, the dry scratch of pens on parchment. He let it go and his own world emerged. The spirits of the place rose up again to fill his soul: the earth, the trees and the wind, the first rays of the sun.

On these things he meditated, gave thanks, and his mind cleared. Rising to his feet he began his training regime. Slowly warming every limb he worked through the first dozen of his patterns of movement: each move designed to destroy his imaginary enemy, each move a battle with himself for perfection. By six o'clock he felt ready to move on. Already he had heard working men making their way along the path behind the wood, their feet and carrying voices breaking into the quiet. He bowed a farewell to Saint Anne, ran four short steps, dropped his hands down into a stand, somersaulted once, twice, glanced round once more, then slipped away into the woods. He kept to the dark ways, avoiding the road, and built up his speed to an easy loping run.

Within half an hour he was trespassing on Ravenswood land, jogging along behind the hedge that shielded the long drive to the house, when he heard the grinding wheels of the builder's cart bringing the labourers to work on the new palm house. The driver was keeping up a shouted conversation with a man and a boy sitting behind him on a sack of sand and Cornelius paused to listen as they passed. The voices grew in volume as the cart approached, spoke of mortar and mixes, then faded, overtaken in volume by the turning of wheels and the steady clop of the horse's hooves. He was poised to move on when all those noises came to a rude halt in a confusion of blows, strangled cries and crashes. He sprinted forward and knelt by a low gap in the hedge. Three powerful looking men and a youth had bundled the builders out of the cart, knocked them all but senseless, and were making short work of tying and blindfolding them, stripping them of their jackets, waistcoats, hats and neckerchiefs, and man-handling them through the opposite hedge to the shelter of a copse. From the sound of it, Cornelius guessed that the gang had lashed the builders to the trees and covered them. He heard a rapid exchange in French and one voice amongst the four was different, lighter and higher. Soon three figures emerged from the hedge, took charge of the cart and drove on to the Tower.

Curious, Cornelius shadowed them as they trundled round to the building site at the rear where they commenced, slowly and deliberately, to unload the sand and a collection of building tools. He circled the park, found a convenient tree with a dense cloak of foliage and climbed up until he had a full view of the back of the house and an opportunity to watch the morning unfold. The little charade was of interest as the gang would probably make a move as soon as the family left for the luncheon, and that move, undoubtedly criminal, could very likely do him some good. If Ravenswood's current cohort of guards proved unequal to the challenge he could become a valuable addition to the staff, so he resolved to smooth the way for the enterprising French and spent the next few hours monitoring the movements of Ravenswood's men.

Coco's heart was banging in her chest as she sidled round to the stables to check if the carriage had really gone. The morning had progressed as planned but the suspense was almost choking her. It had been essential for the plotters to catch the builders early, just as they were arriving for work, so they could ride up to the house on the usual cart. Antoine would watch over them in the copse as they lay blindfolded, gagged and bound under a tarpaulin. His knife was sharp so any attempt to move or cry out would be discouraged easily. She was not worried on that score, but still, the hours had crawled by. As planned, most of the indoor staff had disappeared early for their rare day off and the builders had been left to muddle on unmolested. Just before eleven o'clock she had crept round to the front of the main house and heard a brief and bitter exchange between the Ravenswoods by the entrance before they left. Fortunately, it was not serious enough for the trip to be called off and she had lingered to hear carriage wheels on the drive. A glance round the stables assured her that the only family carriage had disappeared and she doubled back to Jules and Pierre.

235

"They've gone. Are you ready, Jules? We must go in now," she said, her eyes feverishly bright.

"I am ready. Take care, *ma petite*," said Jules. "Check your weapons."

"It's done."

She and Jules stole into the house whilst Pierre set up a busy tapping on a cornice stone to provide some extra cover. Coco's instructions had been precise. Jules made straight for the dining room, slipping his knife into his hand as he went. Closing the door behind him, he scoured the paintings she had described to him. One was certainly familiar. If it was not his grandmother's landscape it was close enough. He pierced the canvas and slid his knife round the frame, excised the oil in seconds, rolled it and dropped it into his sack. His eyes roamed the room at the ranks of art works lining the walls. No time to choose. He took another, then another, then headed for the oak buffet where he swept up silver caviar dishes, epergnes, extravagantly worked silver bowls, one with crouched lions as handles, and most stunning of all, a solid gold Renaissance salt cellar, a full foot high, in the shape of a ship in full sail, nestling delicately on the curved back of a miniature golden mermaid. Shouldering his sack, he retraced his steps through the hall and made a silent escape to the terrace unobserved.

Meanwhile, racing up the stairs two at a time, Coco had been inside Amanda's bedroom within the minute, rifling through the drawers. Top, middle, bottom: nightgowns, petticoats, stays, stockings, letters, diary, no jewel boxes. Her hand shook slightly as she moved to the tall drawers. Top drawer, yes! Pearls, diamonds, semi-precious: no emeralds. She took two handfuls at random and shoved them into her pockets, then froze as she heard a light step on the stair. The bed was made up, no fire was set, maybe a maid seeking out mending to occupy herself? Coco dropped like a stone and rolled behind the bed. The steps receded, a door opened, a pause, it closed again, steps trotted downstairs. She tried to breathe, struggling as her chest constricted. Perhaps there was a strongbox? Rattled now, she checked behind the paintings for hidden cupboards, behind mirrors: nothing, no panelling, no bookshelves. Her eyes raked round the room and rested on the mahogany nightstand by the bed. She knelt before it and pulled on the handle of the pot cupboard. Locked: a good sign. She took out her pocket knife and broke in, the door swung wide and there it was, not a chamber pot but a strongbox, small and perfectly formed. She pulled it out, closed the cupboard, and as she stood to leave, arms tight around her prize, the door opened to admit not a maid but a manservant, levelling his handgun at her head.

In the same second that the door swung wide she flung the safe at her assailant, and herself after it, rolling over the floor towards him as his deafening yell of surprise and cracking retort from his gun rocked the house and sounded out, muffled but unmistakeable, to the back terrace and beyond. Her hand was in her pocket by the time she jumped to her feet before him, her pipe was out and she blew a stinging spray of burning pepper into his eyes. Blinded and staggering, she floored him with a blow, seized the safe, tore the key from the lock and was on the landing, locking him in before he lifted his dazed head. As she fled down the stairs with her heart pounding, thanking God for the extra training she had done with Jules, she heard raised voices and running feet in the direction of the passage leading to the back terrace. Her fastest exit was blocked. She skidded to a halt and then bolted down the west wing corridor towards Ravenswood's private suite.

Outside on the terrace Jules and Pierre's eyes met in despair at the sound of the commotion above. Earlier, Pierre had seen four of the outdoor staff making their rounds in the distance, armed and watchful with the gun dogs frisking alongside them, taking the odd potshot at game for their dinner at the lodge. They had not re-emerged from the woods but two others rounded the corner of the house, guns cocked, looking up as the yells redoubled from the bedrooms above and Coco ricocheted out behind them through the west wing door, her jacket bulging, a metal box under one arm. As Jules and Pierre dropped low, drew their handguns and fired at the legs of the guards, she flung herself flat to the wall. Guns discharging wildly, they were both brought down and she sprang at them, smashing the strongbox down hard on the nearest head, Jules and Pierre were already by her side, crouched over the second man, and in one bloodied minute both had been silenced and bound tightly.

"Drive the cart over," ordered Jules to Coco. *"Vite! Vite!"*

He staggered slightly, unbalanced by the weight of his sack whilst Pierre, pausing only to gather up the guards' guns, flew on ahead. Chests bursting, they flung themselves in the cart and rattled off down the drive, the old horse lashed to full gallop and the empty cart careening left and right behind them. Once round the bend they pulled up, set the horse loose and scrambled through the hedge to where Antoine waited, having readied their own horses at the sound of the racing cart. Astonishingly, with no sounds of pursuit, they were free to mount, secure their haul and ride off at a trot towards the Bath road.

But in the woods behind Arno's Tower, four bodies lay insensible. Two dead birds had been delivered to them by the dogs, who lay panting in the grass, tongues lolling, whilst half a mile away a figure dressed in black flitted through the trees, silent as a shadow, setting his course for Keynsham.

Late-morning: 26th May, 1833.
Abbey Churchyard, by the Great West Door, Bath.

The Petersons were out first, but were soon joined by Nathaniel and Emma, closely followed by Dr and Mrs Charles Parry, Tilly Vere, Howard Dill and Mrs Danby. Lydia Peterson had been grossly inconvenienced as she had failed to corner the party before the service to apprise them of all the grisly details of last Friday's outrage at Arno's Tower.

"Have you heard?" she demanded, cutting into Mrs Danby's continuing monologue to Howard about her recent martyrdom at the hands of her portrait painter. He raised his head eagerly, never to his knowledge having been so very keen to hear from

238

Mrs Peterson.

"Heard what, Madam?"

"About poor Mr and Mrs Ravenswood!" she obliged him, pausing briefly, eyelids fluttering, hand lightly placed on her bosom to still her racing heart. "I was so shocked to hear! They have been burgled in broad daylight. All her jewellery gone, the silver, paintings, his Oriental Salon turned up-side down, his builders kidnapped and his servants shot! Beaten senseless!"

Nathaniel had sensed that the Captain had news, but he and Emma had been on the last minute for the service and had been seated too far away for a word. "Is anyone dead?" he asked quickly. "Are the builders still missing?"

Lydia shot him a suspicious glance. "No. They were found tied up in a field by the drive and no one was killed. Thank God!" She added quickly and piously. In the shadow of the Abbey she could not even admit to herself that reporting bloody murder would have been even more delicious than audacious robbery. But what she had was meat enough.

"Mrs Ravenswood was to pay me a call yesterday but instead up rode Mr Ravenswood himself, explaining all. She is too distraught to leave home. Poor Amanda! And Mr Ravenswood so exercised by all this unpleasantness."

Nathaniel exchanged glances with Captain Peterson and the two stepped back from the circle as the clamour rose. The manly chorus of, "By Gad!", "Scoundrels!" and "Dashed impertinence!" competed with Tilly's wails of commiseration for Amanda and Mrs Danby's demands to be told exactly which paintings had gone and how much the jewellery had been worth. Mrs Charles Parry stood by, watchful and amused, noticing how the Peterson twins took advantage of the noise to renew a heated personal squabble behind the backs of their parents and Emma contrived to move towards her father and Nathaniel to hear exactly what was being said.

"Ravenswood's in a cold fury," said Captain Peterson, lips pursed at the memory, bushy eyebrows drawn up tightly to meet each other. "Came round demanding I rouse every watch in the

239

city! No stone unturned, what! He's already got the Bristol constables scouring the countryside." He shook his head at the memory. "He'll have the perpetrators flayed alive if he ever gets his hands on them. And I wouldn't have liked to be in the shoes of his ground staff. They are all laid up and not fit enough to make themselves scarce, two shot in the legs and the others nursing broken bones and sore heads."

"So no one was killed," said Nathaniel thoughtfully. "It sounds like a professional job to me. How many does he think were in the gang?"

"There were three impersonating the builders, but four of his men were attacked in the park. They don't seem to know what hit them."

"Do you mean by the woods at the far side of the lawn behind the house?" said Emma suddenly. "Because that is where I saw a figure running in the dark when we went to the Ravenswood's for dinner after our wedding." She looked quickly to Nathaniel. "Do you remember?"

He did, and he remembered an evening round the fire in Anglesey with Emma and Cornelius. He smiled to himself. "Well enough," he replied.

That afternoon Nathaniel decided to walk over to see the Spence family. Matthew's continuing employment with Declan O'Dowd could have brought him into contact with some of Ravenswood's men or O'Dowd himself might have spread some inside information about the burglary. He was sorry that his last visit to Martha Spence had not been a happier one. He had been able to support her theory that Ben Prestwick had been murdered but was still unable to bring her the good news that the perpetrators were in custody, or better still, were already paying the price for their crime. She was a stoic and had accepted that powerful men were involved and it would take considerable time to bring them to book. He whistled up Caradoc, leaving Emma to prepare next week's menus and her plan of campaign for imposing them on Mrs Rollinson. He kissed her on the head, jammed on his top hat and strode off in the direction of the Crescent.

As they neared Walcot, Caradoc's hackles rose at the prospect of his continuing trial of strength with Matthew's bird, the infuriating and despicable Jimmy Congo. It had been a while since his last visit but he had smelled the creature on his master once or twice, a vexatious reminder of unsettled scores. He could almost taste the feathers and vowed to make them fly. They had crossed Lansdown at Guinea Lane and made their way to Walcot Street, but just as they neared the house and he was fully prepared, growling to himself, rehearsing his opening barrage, they crossed again. He stopped bewildered.

"No lagging, sir!" shouted Nathaniel. "Come on! They've moved."

He trotted on behind as his master turned left into Chatham Row and stopped before a different terrace of houses, taller and more commodious than the Spence family had occupied before. Regular rents from both tenants, coupled with Matthew's wages and the maturing of the larger of Martha's investments had combined to elevate them in the world.

"Stay," said Nathaniel. "You're on guard, Caradoc, 'til you and the bird are on cordial terms."

A disappointment.

Caradoc cocked his leg on the railing, turned his back and spread-eagled himself on the pavement.

"I won't be long," said Nathaniel, as the door closed behind him.

"Good to see you, Mr Parry," said Matthew Spence, looking fuller in the face and more content than Nathaniel remembered. "Mother's in the dining room with our guests if you need to see her. They are still yarning after their meal."

"It is you I want to see," said Nathaniel. "Could I have a word?"

"Yes, indeed. Come into the front parlour," said Matthew. "But will you say hello to Mother first?"

241

"With pleasure."

Nathaniel put his head round the dining room door and interrupted a jovial party in the final stages of a Sunday dinner, collars loose and chairs pushed back. Martha was on her feet, red in the face and directing Frances and Mary's removal of the dessert plates. At the sight of Nathaniel, old Mr Spence set up a cackling cry of welcome whilst the Johnty continued to flail around on his lap, jumping up to lean precipitously over his shoulder and feed seeds to Jimmy Congo perched behind him on his stand. Tobias, earnest and animated, was caught in the middle of a tale and two men seated by the wall were hanging on to his every word. These last he was not familiar with but was introduced to them as Martha's new lodgers, the bargees Mr Declan O'Dowd and Mr Finn O'Malley, who looked shifty but declared themselves delighted to make his acquaintance and were at his service. Tobias sank lower in his seat and coloured up at the sight of his employer.

"Good day, everyone," said Nathaniel with a bow. "I am sorry if I have interrupted your meal." He smiled easily at Tobias and Frances. "I am glad to see you have been fortunate enough to have such a kind invitation on your day off."

"No interruption at all, Mr Parry," said Martha. "I wish we saw more of you, though it is a tonic to see these two young ones thriving."

Tobias, puce with discomfort, managed a sheepish grin.

"Thank you, Mrs Spence. Good day, Mr Parry," said Frances, bobbing a curtsey.

"Mr Parry wants a word with me, Mother," said Matthew. "We will go into the parlour."

"You will want tea," said Mary.

Nathaniel and Matthew stationed themselves in the front room, which was chilly despite the season, and exchanged pleasantries until the tea was brought and the door closed.

"I hear that the Ravenswoods were burgled," said Nathaniel, watching Matthew closely.

Matthew's eyes blinked wide at the memory and stood out from his head like the hat pegs at Martha's chapel. "Burgled! That they were, sir! Last Friday, and in the morning if you please! All the men were knocked about and the blackguards got clean away. Though how anyone dared do that to Mr Ravenswood beggars belief," he muttered, running a nervous hand over his face before rushing on: "Declan, Finn and me have been asked to work up at the house while the men get back on their feet, but I doubt he'll keep them much longer when they do." He grinned suddenly. "We are pretty well placed there Mr Parry. We've been doing a few bits for Mrs Ravenswood, and after the thieving she's determined to see off all the outdoor men. Says she can't sleep easy in her bed with such as them keeping watch. And she's been kind to us, showing us favour. Extra pay all round and a brace of game birds last week for Mother." He paused, watching Nathaniel's reactions, sensing he was not convinced of the virtue of the new situation.

"Mr Parry, Mother was grateful you came round to tell her she was right about Ben Prestwick's death being no accident. She went to his grave, just to let him know, and she's confident you will get to the truth if anybody can."

"As I told your mother," said Nathaniel. "It might take some time before the law lays hands on the guilty parties. But she knows her Bible well. If she asks again, tell her to remember that the mills of God grind slow but exceeding small. We are not finished yet."

Matthew smiled. "Right-ho, Mr Parry. The mills of God. She will like that."

Nathaniel glanced at his pocket watch, preparing to go. "Is there anything else you can tell me about the burglary, Matthew? Have any strangers called recently or any odd events occurred?"

"Yes," said Matthew. "Though it seems an age ago with all the fuss at the end of the week. Your acquaintance, that man I met in Bristol when I came back from overseas, the man from China, he came to call on Mrs Ravenswood. He's at the Crown at Keynsham and he's to dine at the Tower with both of them."

Nathaniel looked down at his watch again. "Is he now?" he said with a smile.

"And what of Captain Trevellis and the *Blue Dragon*?"

"Still at sea," said Matthew. "And do you know, Mr Parry, no one ever talks of Captain Trevellis, no one at all."

Nathaniel took his leave of the Spence family quickly, though leaving Chatham Row was not quite so swift. Caradoc had obviously ceased to sulk and made off on a mission of his own.

"Caradoc! Show yourself, sir! Caradoc!"

Nathaniel strode off down the road towards the river, checking the railed off deep-set areas of the houses, a favourite haunt of Caradoc's as they gave access to the subterranean kitchens. The dozen plots of Chatham Row ran down a gentle incline to the River Avon, so Nathaniel followed his nose and made for that. Before he reached the water he was rewarded by a sighting of Caradoc clearing the boundary wall and racing towards him with a dead rat clenched between his teeth.

"Well done," he said. "Is that for me?"

Normally it might have been, but even those most highly esteemed must bear some disappointments in life. Caradoc gave him a look, at once mournful and resolute, and passed his master by to deliver the corpse to the doorstep of the family Spence. A double-edged sword, it was not only tribute to his friends but also a warning to the evil bird whose day of reckoning was yet to come.

Jobs done, they sauntered down Walcot Street, crossed the bridge and made their way to the livery stables of Moses Pickwick at the White Hart where Nathaniel had kept his horses and carriages since Tasker's had closed. He had decided to drive over to Keynsham and seek out Cornelius without delay so he had his two-wheeler made ready, a new green and gold gig, took his fastest horse, and within half an hour they were bowling through town for the Bristol Road.

Cornelius was easily found in his room at the Crown.

"Matthew Spence told me you were back," said Nathaniel, settling into a window seat opposite his friend, whilst Caradoc leapt up beside Cornelius.

"He hasn't seen you for a while but he doesn't forget."

Cornelius smiled. "We three are not the forgetting types. Your information about Mrs Ravenswood turning against her husband was very interesting and I decided to pre-empt Drake's efforts on our part to extract information from her. My moves so far have paid off. I intended to contact you when I had firmer news of Kizhe's return but it is good that you have sought me out. I assume that you know about the break-in at Arno's Tower?"

"It is the talk of the town."

"I was fortunate enough to observe the events at first hand and ensure that the outcome was satisfactory."

"For the burglars?"

Cornelius bowed his head briefly. "Of course," then continued: "It was a bold plan, imaginative, and unduly optimistic. The group of four, who spoke together in French, were taking a risk as they were so few in number. That said, they moved well and disabled the builders effectively, but they were all very soft targets. I took it upon myself to reduce the odds in favour of the French against the more effective opposition, with the effect that the Ravenswoods are very interested in improving their security. Ravenswood knows my skills and soon it will suit him to re-instate me in the house. Doubtless he will take the opportunity to try to extract details from me of my movements after the *Blue Dragon* docked in China in '31. Mrs Ravenswood seems disposed to make overtures of a different kind."

"And how will you respond to them?"

"As effectively as seems necessary."

Nathaniel laughed. "Is there anything else that struck you about the burglars, Cornelius?"

"Oh yes," he said. "One of the two who entered the house was smaller and younger than the others, and undoubtedly a

245

woman."

Nathaniel's eyes clouded. "I rather feared that might be the case."

Afternoon: 31st May, 1833. The Ravenswood Residence, Arno's Tower, Arno's Vale, near Bristol.

In the wake of the events of the previous week, a grand house party that the Ravenswoods had planned was called off and only one couple had been encouraged to make the journey to the Tower. At the insistence of Edwin Ravenswood, John and Lottie Drake had arrived for the weekend, wisely leaving their daughter with her nanny in London. Drake had not had high hopes for the weekend and even those had not been met. The conversation thus far had been limited to a detailed post mortem of the daring and successful robbery, the intricacies of Ravenswood's plans for the detection of the culprits, the subsequent exacting of revenge upon them, and how Drake could make himself useful to those ends. It was fortunate for the burglars that execution for theft was rarely sanctioned in these enlightened times, but Drake had no doubt that transportation for life to the most unattractive of Australia's prisons would be guaranteed for anyone that Ravenswood managed to lay hands on. They had been even luckier that a clumsy blow had not accidentally killed one of the staff, or it would have been the noose for at least one of them.

Ravenswood's handsome face, always on the edge of sinister, had developed a new quality of menace and the only one of the party keen to look him in the eye was Lottie.

"I shall examine the lists of all criminals I have dealt with since taking office as magistrate. Every one shall be tracked down, as will each and every visitor to this house since the building project began," continued Ravenswood relentlessly. "Alert all your London contacts, Drake. If the wretches intend to sell, some of the gems will need to be fenced on the London market to realise their value, unless of course," he added bitterly, "they are out of the country already. With that in mind I have sent notification to my contacts in Amsterdam to watch for the pieces and they will contact their men in the Paris markets. As for some of my personal treasures, the net needs to be cast even further afield than Europe. I will soon meet again with my Far Eastern partner and he will do what he can to track down any attempts to sell my property."

The partner in question had to be Kizhe. Drake blenched at the thought of him, remembering the massive bulk of the man, the reptilian eyes, his preference for carrying a brutal short sword, his "helmet breaker".

"They invaded my Oriental Salon," Ravenswood added, almost to himself. "My collection of *tanto* daggers alone is priceless. Most unusual early medieval examples, small, neat, so perfectly formed. They stole one, threw the rest on the floor, then snatched up the objects easiest to hide," he paused, still barely able to contemplate the enormity of the crime. "They forced the door of one of the seventeenth-century cabinets. The cost of repairing the inlays will be almost as great as the value of some of the curiosities they stole. What in God's name was it all about? A handful of coins, some Egyptian beads?" For a moment words failed him. "Some items I can understand," he said at length. "The greatest value was in the gold and silver ware from the dining room, and one of the paintings they took was particularly valuable. Of course, my wife's jewels were also of considerable importance. But, thank God, they had no time to plunder my collection further."

During the silences between Ravenswood's outbursts Drake had allowed his mind to wander. He was picturing one of Ravenswood's cabinets of curiosities, a vast piece of furniture in black walnut with gold decorations, which housed sets of drawers and cupboards for the more miscellaneous, bizarre and macabre pieces in his collection. Mummified bats, finger bones of saint and sinners, preserved organs, a pitch-black obsidian mirror which Drake fantasised could reflect back into the black pits of his eyes the evil spirit in Ravenswood's soul.

247

"Remember, Drake," said Ravenswood, whose eyes were now no longer dead pools, but glinted dangerously. "If you have any luck in tracking down the criminals, they must be handed over to me. I will have every last shred of evidence extracted from them, the time taken will be no object."

Amanda stirred uneasily and made herself busy pouring tea. The last few days had been a living nightmare with the extent of Edwin's rages, truly terrifying. She had suffered only a few bruises during his conversation with her about the losses from her room but she doubted that some of the injured men would be better before autumn after their interrogation at his hands, and if it suited his purposes, they might not survive. Not that she cared less about them or her loss. Her stolen pieces of jewellery were the least of her worries, though once she had taken pride in their grandeur and worn them with pleasure. Every single piece had been his choice; all were symbolic of her servitude and could have easily been shackles for all they meant to her now. Keeping them in the box had been by way of a silent protest. But she had resented, deeply resented, the intrusion into her room. She felt no pity for the burglars despite the baroque excesses of her husband's wrath. Unmoved, she could watch them dangle at a rope's end. In fact, she thought to herself, she would like that very much. A vision from the aftermath of the 1831 riots flitted through her memory: bodies twitching their last above the door of Bristol's New Gaol. No, she would not mind that at all.

She forced herself back to the business of serving tea and ensured her smile was still in place: it was.

"For you, Lottie, my dear," she said, placing a cup just out of the Honourable Charlotte's reach and returning to her own thoughts.

On the positive side she had continued her campaign for freedom in other small ways, making sure that the most objectionable amongst the servants took most blame for the burglary. She had started to nurture the careers of others and best of all, had ensured that Cornelius Lee was welcome in the house. He had come to dinner and it had gone well. Soon, when Edwin was next away from home, she would suggest he came back into the house to improve security, perhaps with a few of his hand-picked men. And it was not all he might be good for. She looked up to see Lottie watching Edwin, her lips parted in excitement at his rage. Then over to Drake who looked horribly discomfited, looking anywhere but at his host, their eyes met. Perhaps, thought Amanda, though not a first choice, maybe a second. Perhaps the mysterious Mr Lee might not be her only possibility.

"Your cup, Mr Drake."

Afternoon: 1st June, 1833.
The Parry Residence, Saint James's Square, Bath.

Encouraged by their host to explore the countryside before dinner whilst he attended to some shipping business in Bristol, the Drakes had borrowed a coach and pair and gone for a drive to Bath. Drake wanted to get out of the house and make contact with Nathaniel, whilst Lottie was disinclined to spend the afternoon in Amanda's company. The previous night she had managed her usual illicit session with Edwin, and really, the liaison was still quite thrilling, definitely in the category *dangereux*: the anticipation, having to make the delicious choice from the array of silk nightgowns she had brought, the silent tip-toeing down stairs in the dark to meet him by the fire. John had not drunk as much as usual at dinner and been tiresome before he went to sleep, but she did not really begrudge him his rights. It was not that she had completely tired of their marital arrangements, but they were readily available and they were simply not enough. Occasional bouts with Edwin were breath-takingly exciting, though, she had to admit, they were becoming increasingly violent. There might come a time when she had to move into quieter waters. As it was, he had used her so roughly on the previous night that she had been obliged to cover the bite marks on her neck and shoulders. She had not yet had the courage to inspect her aching limbs but already she could feel the bruises blooming under her skin. It was some consolation that he would not have escaped unmarked.

249

John and Nathaniel had disappeared into the study whilst she had been ushered into the drawing room to find a ladies' tea afternoon in full swing.

"How lovely to see you, Mrs Drake," said Emma, rising to greet her and show her to a seat. "You will remember Mrs Vere and Miss Montrachet? Ladies, the Honourable Mrs Drake."

"Oh, how absolutely wonderful to see you again!" gushed Tilly, leaning over to pat Lottie on the arm. "We heard you were at Arno's Tower but we never thought we would have a sighting of you this weekend. You have come just in time to hear that our little circle is to be reduced! Coco is returning to France: permanently! Aren't you, darling!"

Coco managed a sad little smile, a sigh, and a resigned shrug.

"I have enjoyed my few years here," she said wistfully, "but my family and friends in France are demanding my return. So, my belongings are packed and I leave on Monday." Caradoc was draped over her feet, a few stray crumbs in his beard providing evidence of a successful afternoon. She stroked his head affectionately as she spoke. "As I said, I shall go first to Paris."

"It is all too exciting!" squeaked Tilly. "Can we write to you there? What will be your address?"

"I will let you know where I am, depend upon it, once I am able to receive mail," said Coco evasively.

"You will keep up with dear Mr Casey, won't you?" said Tilly. "He knows where your family live in the Medoc doesn't he?"

Coco's face hardened. "I will be nowhere near the address he knows, but I'm sure we will keep in touch. Though not through his Bath address," another regretful smile. "Mr Casey is giving up his rooms in Queen Square as he is too busy in London to make it worth his while to continue maintaining a base in Bath."

"Especially with you gone," said Tilly.

"Quite."

Emma made herself busy during this exchange, serving tea and observing Lottie Drake who looked tired and abstracted. Emma made a move to include her in the conversation.

"Mrs Drake, it must be a rather traumatic time for the Ravenswoods after that frightful burglary. How is Mrs Ravenswood? We have heard that she is distraught."

"Really? I would not say so. She is well enough, considering," said Lottie, though at the same time reflecting that, in her brazen refusal to show guilt, she had taken almost no notice of Amanda. In retrospect, her hostess had behaved oddly, perhaps she was in shock? There had been some indignation, but no anger, no tears, no real regret at her loss. "She is resigned to the reality of the situation," said Lottie blandly, "whereas Mr Ravenswood, as you would expect, has a more robust view. My husband and he have discussed the matter and John will do all in his power once we return to London. Some of the gems were quite remarkable and the villains might seek to dispose of them in the larger markets there."

"Excellent idea," said Coco. "I remember that Mrs Ravenswood had an interesting collection. London would definitely be the place to start a search."

"I must confess it has made us even more determined to take my few pieces to the bank," said Emma thoughtfully. "We have talked of it before, but never made time to arrange it."

"Emma," said Coco suddenly, "has Mrs Drake seen the wonderful new curtains you showed us? My dear, your taste is absolutely *impeccable*! I am so pleased I saw your changes to the house before I leave tomorrow."

Shortly after Lottie's guided tour of the new soft furnishings and Tilly and Coco's final giggles and declarations of undying regard, the men emerged from the study and the party broke up. Frances waited by the hallstand ready to help Tilly into her outdoor coat and Coco into her cloak. As she waited, she put out her hand tentatively to stroke the velvet collar of the cloak. It was sumptuous and silky to the touch; she crushed it lightly between her fingers, rolling it against the grain, then on an instant let go as a searing jab pierced her thumb. Suppressing a squawk of pain she inspected the damage and saw a trail of oozing blood. Sucking it clean she looked at the back of the collar more closely and found the culprit, a brooch pin sticking proud, and holding a delicately painted miniature firmly in place. The image was of a woman; white-faced and white-wigged, dressed in a ball gown. Frances was entranced by the beauty of it and held it closer for a better view. The gown was oyster silk and sprinkled with tiny gemlike flowers, the neckline was edged with gauzy net, fine as a butterfly wing, and round the lady's neck was a rope of diamonds, intricately cut and held on a heavy gold chain of interlocking letter "Ms".

Evening: 4th June, 1833.
The Guildhall, High Street, Bath.

Captain Peterson, Emma and Nathaniel had secured good seats for the debate on social reform. The Guildhall was full and they were just two rows back from the dais where the speakers were taking their places.

"So," said Emma, "enjoy Mr Casey's speech because he will rarely be here in the future." She looked up to the platform and caught his eye. He needed no more of an invitation, bounded down the stairs, wrung the men's hands and lavished kisses on Emma's kid gloves.

"Well now, Mr Casey," said the Captain, "I gather we shall lose you in the near future. Our provincial meetings will be the poorer!"

Dairmuid bowed. "Grand of you to say so, Captain! But I'm preaching to the converted here sure enough. The keeping of slaves throughout the British Empire will soon become an evil consigned to the past! And before this summer is out we'll get the majority in both Houses on a short-time bill for our own factory children, at least for those in the cotton trade to reduce their working day, and very likely we will secure a consideration to promote their learning."

"I will look you up in the House when I'm next in London," said Nathaniel.

"And don't you dare be forgetting, sir!" said Dairmuid.

"Please explain, Mr Casey," said Emma, reluctant to let him go. "Government money for the schooling of cotton labourers? Are you sure?"

"Almost, my dear Mrs Parry," said Dairmuid indulgently. "The nine to thirteen year olds are likely to have short-time and specified hours for learning in the day. Money is likely to go to the Anglican and Nonconformist education societies to help provide more places."

"What about the Catholics?" said Emma.

Dairmuid raised his eyebrows. "How could they be helped, dear lady? There might be Catholics in Parliament but there aren't enough to make a play for that."

"And will the children pay for the schooling?"

"It will be taken out of their wages if the factory owners are involved in provision, but otherwise they'll pay their school pence," said Dairmuid, sad to see Emma's frown deepening, and her father's warning hand on her arm.

Nathaniel had also noticed. "Well then, Mr Casey," he said. "I look forward to hearing your speech and seeing you again, perhaps in London?" He glanced over to the dais. "We should take our seats. I see General Palmer is preparing to open proceedings."

As they settled down and looked up expectantly at the Honourable Member for Bath, across the city in Saint James's Square a slim figure dressed in dark trousers and buttoned jerkin climbed over the wall of one of the houses backing onto the park. Dropping to its knees, the figure patted a black and tan terrier which had rushed over, growling and belligerent from its hiding place behind a tool shed. After a few pats and explanations, its tail commenced to wag and when a handful of meat was offered it was wolfed down. For a few moments they stayed together, the figure bent over the dog, whispering and stroking, until the creature's legs suddenly gave way and it collapsed to the ground. Just one last caress of the dog's head, then the figure crept soundlessly up path, leapt up onto the wall and started a careful ascent of the climbing shrub which wound around the drainpipe and reached up to the bedrooms. The climbing ceased at the second floor, a knife flashed in the moonlight, silently, a window sash was pushed up and the figure disappeared inside the house.

Downstairs in the kitchen, Mrs Rollinson and Harriet were mending before the fire.

"Sounds like the wind's getting up," said Mrs Rollinson, pausing to re-thread her needle. "And I thought I heard Caradoc a few minutes back. Hunting again!"

She nodded sagely to herself. "He is a champion amongst dogs, and with a better temperament than most humans." She stuck the needle back into the linen with renewed ferocity. "And speaking of temperament, that Tobias Caudle had no business taking young Frances into town for that meeting."

"No, Missis. That he had not," said Harriet, her head down and her bottom lip thrust out as she mechanically repaired a stocking.

"Did he ask you to go?" demanded Mrs Rollinson.

"No, he did not," said Harriet out loud, then mouthed a soundless, "More's the pity."

By the time the Guildhall speeches were over, the applause had died away and Captain Peterson and the Parrys were sauntering up Milsom Street, a bedroom in Saint James's Square bore traces of a thorough and successful search. Drawers and cupboards had been opened, their contents ruffled, then closed. Nightstands had been minutely investigated, and lastly the great wardrobe had been opened, the blankets moved aside and the strongbox taken to the bed.

Relieved by the sight of it, the burglar decided to risk a light. From a pocket came a pair of pliers and a small glass capsule. A sharp crack and the Promethean match hissed into life,

254

illuminating the contents of the box. A hand darted in and drew out a string of faultless sapphires, the gold links winking in the dying flare of the match. Just one gasp of delight, then the prize was tucked into the breast of her jerkin. Totally unmoved by the possible consequences of the night's work; Coco Montrachet allowed herself a satisfied grin of triumph, replaced the box and stole out the way she had come. Down the pipe she went, across the garden, past the slumped figure of Caradoc and away across the park to her stable, where her carriage was waiting. For the second time within the month, she led out the team, checked the reins and then whipped up her four in hand towards the Exeter road.

Chapter 8

Early evening: 21st June, 1833.
The Saint-Laurent to Pauillac road.

Nathaniel's head was pounding and his eyes burned. He had not quite shaken off the low fever he had caught on the boat from London, though he had already been obliged to waste two days recuperating at General Palmer's mansion at Cenon. His genial host was in London with no immediate plans to leave, but had been pleased to equip Nathaniel with a letter of introduction and put the *château* at his disposal on learning of the plan to visit Bordeaux. The generous offer had been made in the Travellers' Club at three in the morning during one of Dairmuid's "famous nights".

"Feel free, dear boy!" Palmer had said, scribbling a note to his housekeeper in erratic French whilst Dairmuid, with super-human effort, successfully waved over a club servant.

"Just one more," he had managed to say, very deliberately. "Just one more. One more bottle of your excellent brandy, my very good man."

"National business, what!" General Palmer had continued, signing off with a flourish. "Pleased to be of service. Least I can do for a member of Lord Melbourne's staff and my constituent, by God! Privilege! Dashed coincidence meeting you here, my dear boy!"

Over the night, as well as agreeing with them on all questions of reform, denouncing their opponents, pulling the world by the ears and setting it to rights and, by way of a finale, encouraging Dairmuid to croon his way through a selection of Irish ballads, Nathaniel had managed to extract from them what he needed. He knew the details of their Irish contacts in the Medoc, had a full report of Dairmuid's last visit to the Bartons and had ascertained the exact whereabouts of Château Pèlerin, which turned out to be situated just outside a town by the name of Saint-Laurent. He had learned that it was the estate of that relatively new owner, Monsieur Jules Delgarde-Montrachet. He had also investigated Coco's alibi for the thefts at Arno's Tower and learned just how little time Dairmuid had had for Coco when she was supposedly visiting him in London and attending the Epsom races at the time of the attack on Ravenswood's property.

After his talks with John Drake, Matthew Spence and Cornelius Lee, Nathaniel had been in no real doubt about the identity of the burglars at Arno's Tower, but the break-in at his home in Saint James's Square was less clear-cut. Supposedly, Coco had left Bath before the event, but the work had her hallmarks all over it. That she might be a sneak thief was no surprise and Frances had made an interesting connection, which could provide her with a possible motive. The maid had come up to their bedroom in some distress, not to attend to Emma, but to report that Tobias had just found Caradoc laid out in the garden. Frances had arrived moments after they had discovered that the sapphires were missing, as it was that very morning that Nathaniel had planned to go to the bank and deposit the best pieces of jewellery. When he had opened the strongbox, he had realised that he was too late. A cursory inspection of the windows overlooking the garden had provided all the evidence he needed of the burglar's progress.

"It's really strange," Frances had said. "Madam's necklace was so unusual, but last week I saw one that might have been its sister. I seen Miss Montrachet's brooch when she visited. Under her cloak collar it was: a miniature of a woman in a ball gown with a string of brilliants round her neck, mounted on a heavy chain just like Madam's. I never did see such a setting before." Frances had hesitated, biting her lip. "Such a coincidence, isn't it Madam, Miss Montrachet calling so often, and she has been in this room. Once she was left on her own whilst you called out for me. Do you recall, Madam?"

Emma had recalled and sent Frances away.

It had surprised him that Emma was not more enraged by the theft. The violation of their privacy had seemed to move her more than the material loss and after Frances had gone she had even tried to rationalise why Coco might have committed the crime. "Even people we think we know have secrets from us, Nathaniel," she had said. "We know nothing of her real circumstances. She cannot live on fresh air and her sources of income," she paused delicately. "Well, they might have run out. The gems are French and so is she." She shrugged resignedly. "And she's gone back for good, or so she said."

But Nathaniel was not reconciled to the loss of his mother's necklace, and the poisoning of Caradoc rankled. He had to admit that it had been better to find him out cold than with his throat cut, but the terrier had been in a poor way afterwards, vomiting steadily for days and was still dragging himself round, whining. So, it was for various reasons, not all of which he admitted even to himself, that Nathaniel resolved to leave for London, ascertain a few facts and try to pick up Coco's trail.

After the successful evening at the Travellers' he had taken a travel bag from Carlisle Lane and boarded the steam packet for Calais. It had proved to be a pleasant trip. The steam engines always reduced the incidence of sea-sickness and in the benign midsummer weather they also made excellent time. Within fourteen hours he had landed and was on the fast coach to Paris. On arrival he transferred to a hackney cab and made straight for the Quai de l' École and the *atelier* of Maison Bapst to see if he could nail the provenance of the sapphires.

258

Though the court jewellers had travelled a dark road during the 1790s, when it was a capital crime even to sympathise with aristocrats, never mind be one, it had re-emerged, formed a new partnership with the Ménière family and was thriving. Nathaniel was in luck as his outfit for the day and Parisian accent marked him out as a potential customer, the shop was not busy and the assistant had time to kill. He was taken to the workroom and introduced to an ancient man, bent and crabbed over his work, but he was also talkative, and remembered the old days very well. A glass of wine shared during his break, a perusal of Owen's sketches in the battered journal, and stories of the great collections began to flow. Yes, he remembered the interlocking "Ms" of the chain links favoured by the Montrachet family, and their bespoke suite of gems, from the hours he spent in a corner studying the pattern books as a boy. There had been necklaces, and much more, tiaras, ear-rings, bracelet cuffs and the brooches, what he could not tell of them! And there was silver plate. There was no time for that, but he had said enough.

Nathaniel had travelled through the night to the coast and boarded a merchant ship leaving for Bordeaux. The journey could not match the Channel crossing on the steam packet for smoothness, and proved to be exhausting. Not one fellow traveller was sorry when they reached the smooth waters of the Gironde Estuary and made their way to the Bordeaux quays. On arrival he had left the city centre behind and travelled to Cenon where he found the mansion of General Palmer, built on a commanding ridge above the river valley. Though much of the house was closed up, there was a handful of permanent staff and the housekeeper had helped him weather the worst of the fever that had tightened its grip on him even before he left the ship. He had also needed the time to tune his ear to the local dialect. His Parisian French had been fluent since childhood, but in most of the provinces he might just as well have broken out in Greek. He had learned passable Gascon, Basque and Spanish from his father and, combined, they gave him the tools to cope with the assortment of Bordelaise servants: the housekeeper, maids and outdoor staff.

As soon as he was able, he made ready to track Coco down. The odds on retrieving any of the stolen goods were low and he was no longer feeling particularly lucky, but he did feel driven to reach some sort of conclusion, some closure, and perhaps it was not all to do with what was lost. He felt too ill to delve into his motives more deeply. He had risen before dawn, been pleased to find himself steadier on his feet, dressed as a gentleman, complete with swordstick, borrowed General Palmer's new *Stanhope* from the stables and driven down to the river to take the ferry to Lamarque. Though the gig had handled well, the General's stallion had not proved to be a good sailor and despite the break at the port, he was skittish and the journey had been heavier work than it needed to be. Once they had passed through Saint-Laurent, Nathaniel pulled on the reins and brought the gig to a halt. Despite the scorching heat of the last few days, the drainage ditch by the roadside was still brimming with water so he loosened the harness, led the horse down the bank to drink and sat down beside him on the grass verge.

The lines of grape vines, decked with blossom and alive with bees, stretched out on either side of the deserted road, their symmetry relieved only by occasional clumps of trees and on the horizon, a low stone tower. On its dome perched a bird, a smudge of black behind the heat haze. Sweating in the heat but with a shaking hand, he fumbled in his pocket for his flask and drank some of the wine, tepid now and souring; not a good choice. Too late he realised that he should have brought some laudanum but he had left his stock behind in his travel bag at Cenon. He shook his head to clear it but the world swam around him. Slowly, he brought himself to his knees and after a moment's pause, was back on his feet. He harnessed the horse and pulled himself up into the driver's seat.

Within the quarter hour he had come upon a newly painted sign announcing the boundary of the estate of Château Pèlerin, passed its fields of vines and was approaching the high stone wall surrounding the mansion, which basked serenely in the sunshine beyond the open gate, surrounded by dusty trees. A flight of steps led up to the balustraded terrace that ran across the front of a single-storied building. Two slate-roofed wings rose at either end, both dilapidated and one half-smothered in ivy. Away to the right was a farmyard, an abandoned cart standing at its entrance. Nathaniel pulled up the horse and became aware that he was observed. A young woman dressed in black with two small children at her skirt, was standing behind the balustrade watching him. He managed to climb down from the carriage and make his way unsteadily to within hailing distance of her, but it was as far as he got. His legs buckled beneath him, the house and sky slewed round above his head and the ground rushed up.

The Parry Residence, Saint James's Square, Bath.

It was early that morning when they had first missed Tobias. Mrs Rollinson had started by stamping around the kitchen as she prepared breakfast, periodically shouting for him to come to the table and taking out his non-appearance on the porridge pot which she had commenced to stir with the brutal energy of a steam engine.

"Though," she said, above the drumming of the spoon and at a theatrical volume in order to annoy Frances, "I suppose he's no better than he should be, seeing as what he is. He should never be going out and taking drink on a Thursday night. I wouldn't have allowed it if I'd been Madam. Slack, that's what it is. There's a duty to the young and foolish," she continued relentlessly, casting a meaningful and venomous glance to the door leading to his room, which remained stubbornly closed. "If they are not taught the error of their ways they will soon be doing the devil's work! Mark my words."

By half-past six, with all other staff breakfasts eaten and cleared away, it had been Harriet's task to beat on his door. She got no response and when she finally summoned enough courage to push it open, she discovered a bed as smooth as a flat iron and the day's clean linen, folded and ready on his bedside chair.

261

Emma first heard of his disappearance as she pulled herself up in bed to greet Frances but instead of chirruping round the room, opening the curtains and laying out her clothes, the girl had remained at the door, wide-eyed and tear stained.

"Oh, Madam!" she blurted out, choking down a sob. "Tobias has disappeared and Mrs Rollinson's fit to murder him when she catches hold of him!"

Oddly, and she was ashamed to realise the truth of it, the shock of the news brought some relief to Emma and energised her. It was something new to think about. Since Nathaniel had left for France she had felt oppressed, as if a band had tightened around her heart. She had thought that her old jealousy of Coco was dead and buried, but it had just been sleeping. Now it was awake, tightening its coils and preparing to crush the life out of her. The new friendship between them, which she had foolishly encouraged, she now saw as a sham, and it seemed more plausible for that.

At first, the bizarre possibility that Coco had been involved in the burglary then migrated to France for good had been of some comfort. It stood to reason that anyone using Caradoc cruelly, then violating their home and stealing precious memories of his mother, should be unforgivable in Nathaniel's eyes. Let it have been her! Emma could put that misdemeanour to great use in her campaign to neutralise the threat from Coco. But later, after he left, and of course returning ten-fold in the darkness of the night, she had realized the danger. Though she had never visited the Medoc or the city of Bordeaux, she could read and she could imagine. And in that dream of heat, of wine and soft air, of lapping waters and sandy lakes, what spell could not be cast by a woman like Coco?

Why had she ever allowed him to go without her?

How often had she resolved to be with him whenever she could?

But she did know, deep down she knew. She had not wanted to see their eyes meet, had not wanted to see their reconciliation and endure the forgiveness. And now he was far away, pursuing the beautiful, the dazzling Colette Montrachet. Oh, she could imagine the lakes, the lazy rivers and roaring seas. She could drown in them.

So, fired with new purpose, she had dressed quickly and swept down to the kitchen with Frances in tow to check the facts and make a plan. But her moment of sublime control was short lived, for even as Mrs Rollinson was denouncing Tobias for the feckless young scoundrel that he was, simultaneously reducing Harriet to a cowering jelly by the fire and Frances to wringing her hands ever tighter in misery, events had overtaken them. Police officers had arrived, officious, grim faced and in possession of a search warrant.

The rest of the morning had been both miserable and disturbing. Tobias's room was searched because he had been followed whilst hawking unstamped papers around the town the previous night, and he had been arrested outside the George and Dragon. They were not burdened by the officers of the law for long as it took less than ten minutes for brown paper packages to be discovered beneath his mattress. They had proved to contain not only copies of Hetherington's *Poor Man's Guardian* and *The Destructive*, which brazenly advertised that it was published *"contrary to the law of the land"* but also, beneath those copies, a stock of the notorious Richard Carlile's republican rag: *The Gauntlet*. The victorious search party took itself off to Grove Street police station, complete with the incriminating evidence, leaving Emma free to send word to her father. Captain Peterson had acted swiftly, first taking both Emma and Frances to Grove Street to visit Tobias, then insisting that Emma come home to luncheon.

"Obviously you must dismiss the boy," said Lydia Peterson, opening the conversation disapprovingly as soon as desserts had been finished and the twins had been banished to their music practice. "Really, Emma, I do not know why Nathaniel was so generous to him in the first place. There are respectable young

263

people seeking domestic employment, one does not need to resort to urchins like Tobias Caudle. And, I might add, as he has now shown himself to be dishonest, I hope you are considering the possibility that he might have been the thief who took your jewellery?"

Emma made sure she paused before answering, folded her hands and reined in her temper. To lose control was to lose the bout, but her mother was no ordinary opponent. She had made it a career choice to be uniquely infuriating and was an expert in the field.

"I will not be dismissing him." Emma managed to reply calmly, holding steady eye contact. "And there is no question of him having been involved in the theft. Please do not suggest that again, Mama. Nathaniel has spent considerable time training Tobias and he is fond of him, as am I. If you remember the poor boy was sleeping at the back of the stable at the White Hart when Nathaniel first employed him. He was an illiterate orphan with no one in the world to care for him. He has positively blossomed over the last few months and ..."

"And this is how he repays his master!" cut in Lydia triumphantly. "Breaking the law, deceiving you and using his new talents to acquaint himself with treason! Anyone reading such publications should be ashamed of themselves. And not satisfied with corrupting himself he was seeking to spread the contagion to others!"

First blood: Lydia one, Emma nil.

"He is young and he has offended us by breaking the law," replied Emma, regretting making the emotional appeal, which had clearly been a poor move. "But I cannot see that helping poor people to read the news is so very bad if it helps them to understand how their country is run and how they can help themselves, through their unions and on their own. They can become better subjects by reading. In my view spreading information can be seen as a noble cause."

"But surely," said Lydia, as sweetly as she could, as she had seen the warning signs. The umpire was becoming restive. Her husband's bushy brows had drawn together, preparing to call time. He was unlikely to leave her uninterrupted for long. "Surely, my dear, you see that the material he was trying to sell is seditious. *The Destructive* if you please! Also, a publication rejoicing in the title: *The Gauntlet!* I have read of it in my newspaper. It is against the King, it is republican! Its very title is a crude challenge and a call to arms. It is seeking revolution and Richard Carlile is an evil man. Isn't he otherwise known as 'The Devil's Chaplain'?" she said with a shudder.

"I really have no idea, Mama!" said Emma, successfully hiding the fact that she had a very clear idea indeed after nipping into Madame Junot's schoolroom before luncheon and exchanging a few hurried words. And she hoped to be even better informed after reading the dog-eared journal edited by Carlile's notorious mistress Eliza Sharples, which the French governess had slipped inside a poetry book and pressed into her hands.

"I have not researched Mr Carlile, or his ideas."

And she had not, at least not yet.

"And I do not think Tobias has either. He was trying to sell *The Poor Man's Guardian* and he did not know that *The Gauntlet* was included in the batch. It was crucial for the working men to know the latest about the new law for short time working in the cotton mills. He was doing it as a favour to his friends. They were being watched, and they were family men. They could not risk prison."

"And neither should he have," said Lydia bitterly. "The shame of it! Having one of your own staff in the hands of the law!"

"It is unlikely that he will be imprisoned on a first offence if his fine is paid," said her husband, trying his best to fix his two volatile women with a masterful glare. It really played gip with his digestion to have dispute at the table, though at least they had had the grace to wait until he had cleared his plate. "Hundreds have been imprisoned in London it is true, but I have some influence here and I will ensure he avoids gaol."

Emma flashed a grateful smile to him. She felt flustered and had lost count of the score but felt certain that Lydia had been pulled back to a draw.

"I gather that a man called Mr Lovett has set up a Victim Fund in London, Father," said Emma. "Five shillings a week is provided for the prisoner and his family during his sentence. Though I think most of those selling are boys like Tobias, or young men in their twenties with no families to care for. They are like soldiers in their way. It is called a war, a war of the unstamped press! Are there others arrested here like poor Tobias? We could do with a fund in Bath."

"Fund! Fiddlesticks!" exploded Lydia. "The publishers should pay their stamp duty as their respectable colleagues do. That is the law."

"My dear," said Oliver Peterson, putting a restraining hand on her arm in an effort to distract her. "If they did, no poor person could afford to buy the papers. If they are more than a penny they are out of reach, which was the intention of the government when they raised the tax in the first place. And I must say that public opinion seems to be moving in favour of a repeal of the duty. I don't think the Whigs will be long before they support a change in the law."

"Do I sense that you are applauding the movement, Oliver," said Lydia, twitching her arm away. "As a magistrate you must uphold the law."

"I have every intention of doing so, my dear," said Oliver firmly.

"You know what it says on *The Poor Man's Guardian* Mama?" said Emma. "Knowledge is power. And a symbol the reformers use is the beehive to represent the workers. Poor men and women should understand the world they labour in."

"They labour," said Lydia tartly, stung by Emma's attempt to instruct her, "on the instructions and in the establishments of their betters. Look to France, young lady. Can you see the destruction that comes from letting the masses rise? Well, can you?"

"One day, when the poor are educated and wiser they should be allowed to vote. Mama, you must have looked at the papers this week! The new Factory Act states that child workers in the cotton factories will have compulsory instruction each day."

"They will be able to follow instructions more easily, my dear," said Oliver. "That will enable them to keep pace with the demands of working with the new machines. They will hardly be equipped to vote."

Lydia had tired of the discussion. Her husband's interest in politics was understandable, especially now that he was a magistrate, but her daughter's enthusiasm was simply bewildering, as well as being unedifying in the extreme.

"Perhaps it is better to wait until Nathaniel returns before making a decision about the boy," she said. "No doubt he will know absolutely the right thing to do. When is he returning home?"

Emma looked hard at her mother. She and Nathaniel had agreed that no one would know about his journey to France, not even her father, until he was back with some answers.

"No date as yet, Mama."

At least Nathaniel's line of work closed down idle enquiries. Lydia had to leave it at that, sensing a defeat on points but lacking the resolve to slug it out to another round.

"Well," she said, as she rose, exasperated, from the table. "At least take our footman for the afternoon, he can help in Saint James's Square whilst you are operating with a reduced staff." She raised her head, conscious of the nobility of her generous offer, and as a final touch to reinforce her image as martyr added. "I shall now listen to Maddy and Ginette's scales." With an acidic parting smile for her daughter, she swept out and Emma was left with her father.

"Come into my study, my dear," he said, kindly, as he led her out. "I'll have some coffee brought in for us."

Once safe in his den with the door closed, Emma relaxed.

"Do you think Tobias will be released on bail, Papa?"

"He could be. But it might be wise to leave the young rip to stew for a few days: for his own good, you understand. Nathaniel can pay the inevitable fine, since he is so attached to him. But be prepared for young Caudle to have to endure a few hours in the stocks."

"Must he, Papa?"

"I'm afraid so. The borough justices will take a dim view of him supplying Carlile's blasphemous scribbling. They won't want to be seen as lax in their duties, my dear."

Emma's face clouded with concern, she had seen the victims often enough, exposed for all to abuse in Orange Grove, humiliated and showered with missiles, rotten vegetables and dead cats if they were lucky, stones if they were not. At least the pillory was not used as freely as in the past, but she had seen men stripped to the waist and flogged until they were bloody, and once when she was a small child, a woman too, screaming, cursing and terrified.

"Papa, Tobias looked so afraid and so alone. I want to see him again, take him something."

"Take him some food, and a change of clothes. But do not stay long. He needs to be left alone. It will concentrate the mind," said Oliver. "Let him learn a lesson early, Emma. It is right for young men to be passionate and reckless, but they must learn to temper their recklessness or they will become men without judgement who are dangerous to everyone about them."

She heard and she understood, but as she sat quietly she was nurturing the beginnings of a plan.

"I agree with you. May I take up Mama's offer of the loan of your footman? He can escort me to Grove Street."

Morning: 22nd June, 1833.
Château Pèlerin, Saint-Laurent, France.

Nathaniel had been aware that he had been lifted, his head raised from the white dust of the drive and his body carried by at least three men, up steps, through a dark doorway and into the *château*. Deciding it was a wise move, he had allowed his

268

removal to take its course, kept his eyes virtually closed and his body relaxed. He had achieved an entry to the house and attracted a degree of sympathy, or so it appeared. It was more than he had expected.

"Take him to the drawing room. Put him on the *chaise longue.*"

A man's voice: rough edges, but a proprietorial one, probably the brother.

"Bring a basin of water and a cloth."

A woman, a lady: perhaps the one watching his arrival from the balustrade.

"And bring some wine," she commanded. "Go now! Hurry!"

Pattering steps receded.

His memories of the evening were sketchy. He had managed to produce his card and offer some garbled apologies for the imposition of his presence. As he had gained strength and sat up in the chair, drinking his wine, he had put in place a barricade of contacts which could prevent the brother from murdering him in his sleep. Heavy names were dropped: General Palmer, friend and host, whose staff, even now, were aware of his destination and anticipating his return to Cenon; Monsieur Barton and his partner, Baron Guestier, and closer still, their mutual friend Dairmuid Casey, Member of Parliament and close confident of Mademoiselle Colette Montrachet, to whom Nathaniel wished most earnestly to pay his respects, which was the sole purpose of his unannounced visit. It had been enough. He had been helped to a bedroom, where, once assured that his horse and gig were stabled, he allowed himself to fall into a deep sleep.

On waking he found himself in a plain white room, the darkness pierced only by dazzling needles of white light shafting through the fixings of the shutters. Heavy mahogany furniture roosted anonymously in the shadowy corners, but on the wall facing him, a metallic shimmer flashed off a brass crucifix which rose up, starkly erect, above a wooden *prie-dieu.* He dressed quickly, checking his pockets: money, watch, some personal

269

papers, all there, even his hat and swordstick were on a chair by the door. So far, apart from the fever, it could not have gone better, but he was under no illusions. If Coco, her brother and some of his men had risked their lives and reputations for the attack on Ravenswood's home, then he was by no means in safe hands. He slipped out onto the corridor to search for his hosts, but it was Coco he found. Rounding the corner, she came to an abrupt halt at the sight of him, stock-still and radiant in a pale blue gown, her lips parted in surprise, her body framed in a glowing nimbus of gold by the morning light streaming in behind her.

"Nathaniel," she said, a catch in her breath, running lightly to him, arms wide. "Have you recovered? What a wonderful surprise to find you here last night!"

In a moment she was pressed against him, kissing him a welcome, smiling into his eyes. He could not help but smile back. Blame it on the fever, the heat or her beguiling smile, he took her in his arms and kissed her again, and not in welcome.

"Coco, we need to talk," he said, pulling away.

"I am so much looking forward to it," she said, too quickly. "I could not believe it when I came home to hear that you were laid-up in the guest room. How extraordinary of you to turn up here like this! But come now to meet my brother and his family. Have breakfast then he can show you the vineyard. He is very proud of it."

The hot day slipped through his hands like sand. First breakfast, where he got nothing out of the massive and taciturn Jules, engaged in polite conversation with Claudette, managed to make her smile and successfully amused the pair of chattering children. For the rest of the morning he was marched round the estate by Jules who had moved on to a transparent assessment of his level of threat, which after Nathaniel's sustained charm offensive he seemed to rate as low. The heat and brilliant sunlight had lifted his mood, but as he felt physically better he felt even more frustrated in his purpose. Jules introduced him to

270

a gang of labourers, the leader of which was a man called Pierre who was built on similar lines to Jules, powerful and heavily muscled as a carthorse, but with a touch of melancholy about him which made him even less amenable to small talk. According to both of them, they had never been to Britain and knew nothing of Bath. Their words told him about the vines, the wine and the *terroir* whilst their battered faces and Pierre's cauliflower ears spoke of other enthusiasms. At the lengthy luncheon Coco managed to be evasive, express proper regret concerning the Ravenswood's misfortunes and act out a pretty show of surprise and sorrow when she heard of the burglary at Saint James's Square. Luncheon was followed by a *siesta* which engulfed the afternoon, but on the plus side, after swallowing a draft of Claudette's own narcotic remedy, Nathaniel slept off much of the remains of the fever. This was even more fortunate than it might have been, as the early evening required him to accompany Jules and Pierre to their next fight at Fort Medoc.

The three of them climbed into the farm wagon and set off down the dirt track to the old fort, Jules and Pierre in the front, Nathaniel behind and able to keep an eye on them, which he preferred. Lit by the moon and stars, and to their left, the distant glimmer of the Gironde, they rode through the velvet midsummer night. If the occasion had been different Nathaniel would have been enjoying himself. The perfumed air was alive with the soft burr of the cicadas and the swooping flutter of bats' wings. Once or twice a pair of bright, feral eyes burned out at them from the undergrowth of a copse in answer to their swinging lamp.

"Pierre is our champion tonight," said Jules over his shoulder as he flicked the whip over the horse's head. "We have a team and we are fighting men from over the river, from Blaye, but there's room for strangers as well. You might like to join in." Nathaniel could sense his crafty smile; saw the wink exchanged with Pierre as the words were left to lie.

"Do you think so, Monsieur?" he said.

"I am sure of it," replied Jules.

They crossed the shallow moat and entered the fort through a great triumphal arch.

"What is this place?" asked Nathaniel, looking up at the stone face of the sun below the pediment, its carved white rays of greeting picked out by the moonlight.

"It was one of Louis XIV's forts," said Jules. "This is *le porte royale* just in case the Sun King ever paid a visit, but of course, he never did."

They passed through the tunnel of the entrance below the guard-house and emerged into a vast square surrounded by low buildings, some derelict and few with lights burning. Ahead, in the dark and fronting on the river, Nathaniel could make out the back of the cannon emplacements. Closer to the gate there was a makeshift ring marked out in the centre of the parade ground and a small crowd milled around it: otherwise the place was echoing and deserted.

"How many soldiers are based here?"

"Just a couple of dozen now," said Jules. "Marshal Vaubon built it to guard the estuary and the route to Bordeaux but the cannon have never been fired in anger. After the defeat of the Emperor the place was more or less given up. The men have nothing to do except survive their posting, do a bit of training and scratch their arses. I rent out some storage space in some of the empty buildings, sell them wine, on reasonable terms of course, and organise our little sessions of *savate.*"

It was then that Nathaniel realised what he was in for. It was not to be sticks, swords or a bout of prize fighting with men's rules, but a free for all. *Savate*, the street fighting of Marseilles, was more suited to Cornelius's fighting style than his own. It had the makings of a difficult night.

Their wagon was taken to the stables and they joined the crowd of soldiers and local men by the roped-off ring. A lean, swarthy man advanced on them, his lined face pock-marked, his jacket off and shirt sweat-stained, but with his sword buckled by his side and an aura of authority.

"Ici le Chef!" announced Jules delightedly. "Monsieur Parry, here is the Commander-in-chief, Colonel Lesparre, who so graciously provides us with a venue for our little shows."

Introductions made, they pushed their way to the front and the fighting began almost immediately, giving Nathaniel some thinking time. Jules obviously had a nice little deal going on with the Colonel. Assuming he was involved in smuggling, as virtually all sailors and fishermen he had ever known were, he would have a convenient storehouse here, well away from his own property with no questions asked. From the state of the soldiers and the barracks he guessed that Paris would have only the vaguest notion that this place existed and left the skeleton staff to its own devices. This was a place you could easily die in and leave not one trace behind.

The first bout was innocent enough, a lengthy brawl between two youths, farm boys with their forearms scarred from the crops, short lads, but rock hard and sinewy. What they lacked in finesse they made up for in speed and audacity, raining down indiscriminate punches and kicks on each other with their horn-hard hands and rough-booted feet until one caught a blow full in the face and was dragged out of the ring insensible. Betting was proceeding freely at a trestle table, and next to it sat Colonel Lesparre, enthroned on an armchair, worm-eaten, but high-backed and elaborately carved. Jules was on a seat by him and it was clear they were fast friends, sharing jokes at the expense of the fighters and the platoon. Nathaniel stayed on his feet, weighing his options. Generally the mood was good and as the night progressed some of the soldiers brought out fiddles and others sang to while away the pauses between bouts. Nathaniel moved over to stand by Jules and the Colonel.

"A pleasant spot, Colonel," he said. "Did you live here before you took this post?"

"I'm from the Pyrenees, born and bred. But this billet could be worse," said the Colonel suspiciously. "Jules tells me that you have travelled from England and are visiting his sister. Beautiful woman, beguiling, no? *Très belle!* I also hear you have other interests; maybe you would like to try your luck against one of the men here. You think you are their equal perhaps, maybe their superior, Englishman?"

"I am not English, Colonel," said Nathaniel quietly, changing to Euskara, the language of the Basques. He was pleased to see a change in the Colonel's face, a dawning of greater respect. "I am Welsh, perhaps you, who are from *Euskal Herria* know the importance of such a difference?"

The Colonel bowed his head briefly, his eyes never leaving Nathaniel's.

"And I would not presume to spar with an expert *tireur*," continued Nathaniel. "I have not the skill. It would be an insult."

Quiet had descended on the crowd as they heard the pure Basque replace the faultless French. The stranger was of interest and they gathered for the spectacle.

"Perhaps you would like to test your weapons skill?" suggested Colonel Lesparre, his eyes now gleaming with malice. "*Canne de combat* perhaps?"

He spotted a soldier loafing by the storehouse at the back of the crowd. "Bring a stick for the visitor!" he shouted and then turned to Nathaniel. "Are you a swordsman, Monsieur? Jules told me you had served in the military, so you could regard a bout with the sticks as a little light sabre training."

Nathaniel bowed and took hold of the wooden stick. It was heavy, but with good balance and a basket hilt. He swung it round in his right hand and whistled it through the air. This was safer ground, as he was no stranger to practising with sticks. His father had encouraged him to train with a makila when the stick was taller than he was and if all else failed he could take it in both hands and use it as a quarter-staff. Nathaniel threw two gold napoleons on the table.

"I accept with pleasure. My own stake, winner takes all," he said.

After a hurried huddling of the men, shuffling of feet and searching of pockets, a lieutenant stepped forward into the ring, his hands cupping a mound of silver which he threw down on the table.

"A match for you, stranger."

The man's upper body was bare except for his braces, greasy with sweat and smeared in dust, as were his raw-boned calloused hands, and his chin, blue-grey with dirt and two days' growth.

"Shirt off," commanded the Colonel. "It will be easier to count the hits if you run to a draw."

Nathaniel unbuttoned his shirt and hung it on the back of Jules's chair. He was ready, one slight knee flex, then totally still, waiting, watching. He needed to finish it quickly but with maximum spectacle, as he was still weak from the fever and lacked stamina. His opponent had the best part of a bottle of brandy inside him and expected to bludgeon him to his knees, first blood within two minutes and then back to the unfinished bottle.

He allowed the man first swing and side-stepped, no point losing his strength too early. Then the second, another and another, Nathaniel danced round him lightly, driving him to fury. The man let out a bellow and hewed forward again. Nathaniel side-stepped again, then parried with all his strength. The man stumbled, almost toppling over, but recovered and hacked forward. Nathaniel countered five blows and on the sixth deftly turned his weapon, flicking the lieutenant's stick out of his hands to bounce away over the dirt to the feet of the audience. In two strides he was on his man, the stick across his throat and the crowd in a roar.

Nathaniel stepped back to bow but as he did so the lieutenant rushed forward, his face flushed and working in fury.

"Come on," he yelled, out of control. "Let's see what else you are made of, Welshman!"

Jules and Pierre exchanged glances. The heavy names the stranger had dropped still rang in Jules's ears. He half stood, nudging the Colonel and whispering in his ear, when to his surprise Nathaniel caught the soldier's blow even as it cannoned towards him, wrenching the arm back and flooring the man in a tearing arm lock. Nathaniel released him, but the fight was still

275

just about in him. The man lunged again and Nathaniel stopped him with a right hook, landing it square on the man's cheek and followed through with a left-handed undercut to the jaw, scouring his throat on the way. Fighting for breath and spitting blood, the man doubled-over and sank to the ground. His friends rushed out, took him by the underarms and dragged him away.

Nathaniel looked round the ring, holding the men's eyes. "I look forward to the rest of the bouts. My stake and his go towards the rest of tonight's brandy."

The acclaim echoed round the barrack square, a chair was brought and as Pierre took to the ring, Nathaniel took his seat by Jules and Colonel Lesparre. He had survived the test, but as yet, with the prospect of, at most, one more day before he had to leave, that might be the sum of his achievement.

Late afternoon: 23rd June, 1833, the Eve of the Feast of Saint John. The road to Carcan, the Medoc, France.

"Coco, I need to leave tomorrow."

"I know."

Nathaniel rode alongside her as they made their way to the lake through the marshes and sheep pasture that lay between the vineyards of the estuary and the ocean dunes. The burning heat of the day had slackened and was now languorous and heavy with the scents of summer. Wild ponies grazed undisturbed, giddy midges hung in clouds by the small clumps of trees and, on the horizon, he had caught sight of a shepherd, raised high on his stilts above the plain, resting, triangulated on his crook, like a painter raised on his easel.

Today he had stayed, and she had insisted that it was necessary to ride out to the water.

"We shall be *en fête,* Nathaniel," she had smiled. "The fires have to be lit, and the best place is by a lake."

"The fires?" he had enquired. He had lived in cities for too long.

"It is the Eve of the Feast of Saint John! What were you thinking of in church when you should have been listening to the priest?" she had laughed. "We must light the fires of purification!"

She had stood before him in men's breeches and boots, with an open-necked white shirt like a farm boy's, her skin golden-brown, her hair plaited down her back. Before leaving, she had slung a bag over the pommel of her saddle.

"We've got bread, some cheese, a flagon of wine and a cake, and I have the herbs and flowers. It's what we have to do," she had said.

That morning, under a sky of cerulean blue and past the ranks of flower-decked vines, he had driven into town with the family to attend Mass, retracing his journey along the Saint-Laurent to Pauillac road until they reached the crumbling church of Saint Laurentus, which squatted uncertainly in the centre of town. Claudette said it had stood there since the twelfth century and it crossed Nathaniel's mind that the stones thought it was long enough. They looked ready to subside back into the earth from whence they came, though the carved gargoyles still clung gamely to the walls, to watch and to warn.

Crossing from the white glare of the town square into the shadowy nave, they had passed through the arched doorway under the eyes of a line of stone heads. Nathaniel had returned their gaze as he walked beneath them, and realised he was looking into the eyes of the seven deadly sins personified; each capital vice was featured above the door; each vice a corruption of a natural passion. He sat in the pew, sunk in thought. What was life but a search for balance, a walk along a tight rope between vice and virtue? Each reflected the other, was its alter ego, so knowledge of each must be equally necessary. The seven provided an allegory of the human heart. Take self-hood and ambition, both so necessary for survival, they exist also in corrupted forms as hubris and selfishness. Our bodily needs, our appetites, also necessary for life and bringing such pleasure, when indulged to excess brought degenerate addiction. He had

277

continued to think idly of such things during the priest's address, most of which he had managed to filter out, including, so it seemed, all the pious recollections of the saintly John and his works. His mind had wandered to thoughts of Cornelius and his Taoism, of balance and harmony, of the rich duality of life, the inter-connectedness of good and evil, of God and of Lucifer, his fallen angel.

And he had looked at Coco. He remembered his first sighting of her in Bath, two years back or so, once in the Pump Room, on Dairmuid's arm, with her knowing smile, her brown eyes shining gold, her skin like almond milk. Then he revived an image of her mourning her murdered lover in the Abbey; her customer, the lost ticket to a life of ease. She had been a friend, a reliable one, and he remembered too that once, for a few hours, she had been something more. There was pride in her for certain, but never wrath or sloth. And the sins of desire and appetite? Lust, envy, greed and gluttony? He watched her breast rise as she breathed, the white fichou softening her neckline, auburn curls escaping her bonnet and glinting in the coloured lights of the stained-glass windows. Her whoring was a means to an end, a practical solution to social and financial needs, but there was still a joy in her for lovemaking. If she was his thief, he could not believe it was just for naked greed. There would have been another reason. There was a feral and reckless love of life in Coco, like the wild eyes that burned from the thicket in last night's twilight.

All this Nathaniel recalled as they rode together through the golden afternoon and his heart was heavy. Oddly depressed by the necessity for him to break the spell of the day and speak of thieving, deceit and betrayal, he had put off the inevitable, but it could be evaded no longer. He brought his mind back into focus and listened again to Coco's chatter.

"Jules said there is often a gathering tonight by the Hospitallers' Commanderie at Benon. The villagers light their fire by the stream and dance through the night. But we are going

278

to the lake. There is said to be stronger magic there, and the odd prowling wolf," she said, her eyes alive with mischief. "We shall have our own celebration, we two."

Nathaniel made no answer, so she continued. "You must have Saint John's fires in England. Though I must say I never heard of them in Bath."

"No," he answered abruptly. "You wouldn't see them in the towns. In the villages they have the fires still. The people jump over them for luck and some roll flaming cartwheels downhill to the streams. The longer the flames last, the longer the luck and the better the fruit." He shrugged his shoulders and then turned to her, his eyes searching her face. "So Coco, have we had enough of this? Have we exhausted our reasons for the ride? I need some answers about burglaries before I return to England."

She looked over to him but barely heard his words. The preliminaries were over, he had tired of the sport and moved to the end game, but it did not seem to matter any more. She felt a sudden rush of longing, more ambushed by desire than anything he had said. She turned her gold-flecked eyes on him hungrily. Nathaniel rode as he walked, with an easy elegance and dishevelled glamour. His shoulder-length black hair, blue-black as a raven, was pushed back from his eyes by a broad-brimmed hat he had borrowed from Jules. Unusually, a light tan lit his pale skin, which further accentuated the brilliant blue of his eyes, watchful and more grave than usual, but looking as always into her soul. Her breath came faster and she felt her heart pound.

"I have made some enquiries about a certain set of family jewels, made by Maison Bapst before the Revolution. They were unmistakable; the gems were set in heavy gold with the family initial repeated in the double chains. The makers' mark tallied exactly with the string of sapphires I knew as the property of my mother, a gift to her from my father when I was a small boy. They came as prize money from a cache of jewels and he gave them as a symbol of their love and his safe return from the wars. In their present life they are a gift from me to my wife, to Emma, your friend."

He paused, watching her. She rode by his side, silent and expressionless, but now she was listening.

"My father's prize also included gold coins. The jewels and the money were all taken from the Emperor's stores towards the end of the war. Now, I think you know that the jewels were not the only losses suffered by the family who had commissioned their making. Their property was confiscated during the early stages of the Revolution and the senior members of the family were executed. Very unjust wasn't it, Coco? Very sad for the Montrachet family. You share their name, don't you? You might even think you should share more than that."

She looked him full in the face, defiant, and achingly beautiful.

"Officially, I admit nothing, Nathaniel, and explain nothing. I am no fool. But yes, together as we are now, whilst we are on the road and alone, we can speak of injustices; they suffered the same fate as many other great families. Only a few scraps are left to mark the passing of my grandparents. Yes, my own grandparents, I share more than a name. There is no doubt. I remember my father and my mother, and all their stories. We were close, Nathaniel."

Just for a moment, she lowered her eyes, hesitated, then ploughed on. It was the time for confidences.

"All I had left was a brooch. It is a miniature of my *grandmere*."

She felt, without looking, for the familiar metal rim beneath her collar and turned it to him.

"When I was last in Paris, in 1828, I was with Émile, the Marquis de la Blanquefort at the Palais Royale. We were dining at Le Grand Véfour in the company of a Duchess, Madame Junot. It was an important night, politicians were there, and foreign diplomats. That night she helped me find the start of the trail which eventually led to my discovery. Later, I found it was the Ravenswoods who owned the Montrachet emeralds. Whether they were stolen or purchased was irrelevant to me. Do you understand at all, Nathaniel? I wanted to retrieve something of my life which had been lost. It became an obsession or a pilgrimage perhaps." At this she had the grace to laugh at herself.

"I left Paris, followed them first to Ireland and then to the south-west of England, but the trail went cold. I settled in Bath until I could track them down. It was later that I found out about your sapphires."

The intelligence he had travelled to discover now seemed of little worth. His eyes had lit up as he was transported back to Paris. He saw before him the crowded restaurant, and his father.

"Coco, I was there! I met the Marquis de la Blanquefort. I was at the table with the ministers, and then I stayed on with the *literati*. I knew Hugo from an earlier visit."

He took off his hat, rubbed his eyes and ran his hand through his hair, a despairing gesture.

"It was the week my father died."

He was unable to say more and she was unwilling to disturb him, so for a further mile, they let their horses find their own way along the path, hooves padding softly in the sandy earth. They passed a small farm, wooden and white-washed with its sheep-fold thatched and its hen-houses built tall enough to escape the attentions of nimble foxes. Before one wooded corner, the tinkling of sheep bells warned them of an approaching flock, which poured onto the path before them, driven by a boy and his dog. They let the woolly flood surge round them and then ambled on.

"I have no interest in fighting Edwin Ravenswood's battles for him," said Nathaniel when they were alone once again on the track. "And I do not want to take from you anything which is rightfully yours. But you might be able to help me. The jewels and the gold were not the only things taken from Napoleon's carts the night my father led the raid. There was also a stock of treasures looted from Egypt. One item is a matter of some importance, a necklace of gems bearing a representation of the falcon headed god, Horus. You wouldn't know anything about that, would you?"

Coco pursed her lips. "Unfortunately not. It sounds like a trinket I would enjoy owning. I did go into Ravenswood's private suite but I was in a rush and only had chance to look in one cupboard. I took one handful of bits and pieces, a dagger and a few coins, gold napoleons. *C'est tout.*"

"I have some too," said Nathaniel, "my father's."

They rode on, the silence now easy and companionable; she stole a glance at him.

"How is Emma?" she asked. "I do like her and I see why you do. She is unusual."

"So are you."

She put her head to one side, and smiled, half to herself.

"I love her, Coco. I have married her." He looked at her and paused as if seeking affirmation. "She is my *Bright Star.*"

"You are a Romantic, Nathaniel," said Coco with a laugh. "But never mind Keats, what about Shelley? Have you heard his views on having only one love, one mistress or one friend? He could not understand why it should be necessary to forsake all others to "*commend to cold oblivion*" someone you care for. The cruelty of it! How can love be only for one? There are many loves. You must know what Shelley said: "*to divide is not to take away*". And speaking of loves, I have met Émile again, Nathaniel. He has started to build a new house at Blanquefort. He has such plans. The landscaping will be a fantasy of grottoes and fountains. He too is such a romantic, though not in a literary sense! And his wife is a nice old thing, we get on famously."

They looked at each other and Nathaniel laughed out loud.

"Coco, I wish you well, though you did abuse my friendship. Your little charade with Emma was despicable and, I might add, Caradoc has not yet recovered."

"Sorry for that, *mon cher.* Needs must. Tell Emma I love her and I am sorry, and tell Caradoc too. I mean it, Nathaniel. I love them both, and I love you."

They skirted the small village of Carcan, once a small fishing port, now miles from the sea, distanced by the rolling dunes and marsh, just one in the dotted string of coastal settlements now sheltered from the bay, becalmed behind the lakes. They dismounted and took a sheep path through the bushes and stunted trees, heading for the small sandy beach by the glittering water. They tied up their horses in the brown shallows, tiny fish teeming about their feet. A solitary heron stood on a fallen trunk by the water's edge, white and graceful, but otherwise they thought themselves unobserved. He set about collecting brushwood and lighting the fire whilst she took from her bag a wreath of soft leaves, crushed from the journey, exuding the headiest perfume: Saint John's wort, rue, rosemary, lemon verbena and fennel, bound crown-wise around the circled stems of three white lilies. She placed the circlet on her head, peeled off her breeches and let them fall. Her shirt followed so she could stand naked, feeling the soft evening breeze caress her body.

Then she turned to Nathaniel. "Come with me," she said.

He shrugged off his jacket and shirt, watched her walk into the water, then, with decision, he shed the rest and followed her.

By twilight, a striding shepherd, high on his stilts behind the tangle of gorse bushes and marsh grass, heard the soft whinnying from their horses as they grazed by the trees, saw the discarded clothes of the lovers by the fire and passed on his way to his cabin by the stream. They did not see him, though Nathaniel heard his rapid stride as he passed and looked up from where they lay by the water.

"We need to go back," he said. "Tomorrow morning I will return to Cenon and I will not visit again, Coco. It will be goodbye. I wish you good luck with your Marquis."

She rolled over towards him, laughing. "We have lit the fire of purification so we will have at least one whole year of luck. It is a good night for saying farewell."

And she kissed him again, a kiss of melting sweetness, and he pulled her to him for one last time by the dying flames and dallied there until the fire went out.

283

They rode back, mostly in silence, and after stabling the horses went to their rooms. Nathaniel sat on his bed and set to winding his watch by the light of the candle. The sight and feel of the exquisite Breguet timepiece always brought pleasure, and that night it also conjured up a vision of Cornelius Lee. As his mind roamed back to a dark, cold Anglesey night and the ties of friendship, the door opened and there she was, holding two glasses of brandy.

"A nightcap? The last one?"

He shrugged in agreement, for friendship's sake.

They took a deep draught each and exchanged a last kiss, but before the glasses were drained a tide of weariness coursed through him. She pushed him back, carefully, onto his bed, and drawing a pair of scissors from her pocket, cut off a lock of his hair and wound it round her finger. She unfastened her brooch; pulled open the golden back plate, curled her prize round in the small empty space behind the miniature and snapped the case shut. She covered his sleeping body, ran her hands over him for one last time and pressed her lips to his.

In the morning, after a dreamless sleep, Nathaniel woke late and had breakfast in the dining room alone. The maid told him that Coco had left before dawn, Claudette had taken the children to town and the men were in the fields. When he returned to his room he opened his bag to pack for the drive to Cenon, and there on top was a small leather pouch. Inside were six perfect sapphires, smaller than the great central drop and lower gems of the necklace, three stones had been taken from each side near to the fastening, each clipped away from its housing on the golden Montrachet chain: a peace offering and a farewell.

Morning: 24th June, 1833.
Hyde Park, London.

The Honourable Lottie Drake and her daughter Lizzie had left the house in Mayfair with two footmen trailing behind at a respectful distance. They made their way along Park Lane and entered Hyde Park by the Stanhope Gate. Lottie walked quickly towards the Serpentine, hiding her face behind her lace parasol and avoiding the crowds, especially a bevy of a dozen young women whom she knew. Apart from the captive Lizzie, whose presence gave her a reason for being out, she did not want company. Quite the reverse, as she had had rather too much of it of late and her main ambition was to be rid of it. She chose an empty bench under a shady tree and arranged herself to cover as much of it as possible, spreading her wrap and reticule around her like a barricade and dispatching Lizzie to the waterline with a substantial bag of crumbs for the ducks.

It was essential that her affair with Edwin be concluded, which was annoying as it had been extremely good sport until very recently. It was after the burglary at his home in Bristol that he had changed and become past tolerating, which was odd, as she had never thought that such a trivial matter would have bothered him in the slightest. Of course there might be other problems with his mercantile pursuits, business affairs of unspeakable tedium and vulgarity. She sighed, but wished she had not as she jarred her jaw as she did so. He had actually struck her, in anger. The affair was no longer amusing and when she told him she would never see him again he had laughed, rather horribly, and said that she would do exactly as she was told. Her stomach turned over merely at the memory of his cold anger and her throat constricted in fear.

It had all seemed so exciting at first. Edwin was so broodingly handsome and undoubtedly dangerous, all rather thrilling. But the sport had become increasingly rough. Fortunately John had not noticed her bruises; she had always changed alone in her dressing room, or in the dark. Not that he could have prevented her from doing as she wished. He had warned her off Edwin which had made her all the keener, and to have him know she had made such a dire mistake would have been unbearable.

She had also lost Amanda, who had been a friend of sorts, an excellent sparring partner, in a verbal sense of course. It had

285

been rather fun at first to think that Amanda was afraid of her husband, but now she was not so sure. She had also been visiting Sir Giles and Lady Leonora more frequently of late. They continued in low water, with the nanny issue unresolved, although she had been replaced. Sir Giles seemed almost to cringe at the mention of Edwin's name, all of which was most odd. Lottie shivered despite the growing warmth of the day. Edwin's grip on her was debilitating, and becoming terrifying. As she gazed, unseeing, at the murky water of the Serpentine, she became aware that Lizzie was busily watching. She was enthralled by a small boy baiting a fish-hook with a worm. He skewered it and cast it adrift on the water. All three of them watched as the line floated over the surface, but they had not long to ponder its fate. Within a minute there was a convulsive jerk and the worm disappeared beneath the surface.

The Prospect of Whitby, Wapping Wall.

Whilst Lottie shifted uncomfortably on the bench, tormented by how she might make her last encounter with Edwin Ravenswood the final one, the man himself was sitting in the back room of a tavern by the docks. He was in the company of a sparely-built local man in a dark cloak and two formidable Asiatics whose frames occupied the whole of the wooden settle. One of the foreigners was finely dressed and appeared to be a gentleman, though his eyes flickered with forensic precision over Edwin Ravenswood, appraising him like a hunter whose skinning knife was already drawn.

"My men have not been idle whilst I was in Holland," said the foreigner. "After the unfortunate episode before the *Leonora* sailed I left them with instructions to seek out the Chinese man who so much enjoyed his little charade, which he played out at our expense, and also to find the gentleman who pursued him so self-righteously and boarded the ship with the marine police. It is plain now that they were accomplices. The two sailors, Fong and Chen, whom we mistakenly believed to have been drowned, are also in the pay of the Chinese man, whom I believe to be none other than Cornelius Lee. All four have been seen together, in the yard of this tavern, by this man." He waved his massive paw of a hand to the man in the cloak. "He acts as my shadow and knows every by-way of the docks. He sees a great deal, and reports to my associate, whom you may call Mr Qiang."

The man on the settle bowed to Ravenswood.

"His name means: The Strongman. You will find it is so!"

"I will take your word for that, Mr Kizhe," said Ravenswood smoothly, noting only that Qiang seemed to have been cut from the same cloth as his master. No one in their right mind would knowingly cross either of them without a brace of guns to hand, primed and loaded.

"The gentleman," said Ravenswood. "Would he be black-haired with eyes of bright blue? Tall, strong, about six and twenty in years?"

"He was," said the man in the cloak, the leering smile of recognition on his ratty face baring a full set of yellow teeth.

Ravenswood sat very still and then nodded, his mind made up.

"Gentlemen, accompany me to Somerset. It is time for the brightness of those eyes to be extinguished. And I think, Mr Kizhe, that we both have questions that Mr Lee needs to answer."

Edwin Ravenswood was not one to dwell on reverses but preferred to right them. The task of neutralising Parry would not be a simple one, but he had effective help. Lee he hoped to utilise in other ways and had postponed a decision on his fate. The man had delivered the payment from China reliably enough, but probably had other secrets that he needed to be persuaded to disclose. The Honourable Lottie's usefulness was almost over. There were places she could go, many fates might await. She may yet look back at her nights with him as the mildest of diversions, veritable walks in the park. And at that thought he flashed his cold smile round the table and raised his glass.

"To Somerset then," said Kizhe. "Mr Qiang and I are at your service."

287

Chapter 9

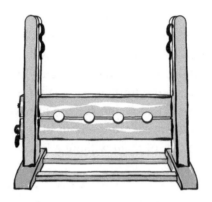

Morning: 28th June, 1833.
The Police Station, Grove Street, Bath.

The metal cover on the spy-hole in the cell door snapped open and a beady eye peered through.

"Tobias Caudle?"

"You know very well who I am, Silas Monkton."

The eye swivelled round the cell, creasing in delight as it settled on the slight figure standing by the window.

"Time to show yourself to your public!"

Tobias straightened his back, tried to take a deep breath to steady his racing heart, and made for the door. He had two things to do and he hoped he could do them both that day. He would try not to think any further than the doing of them and getting through to the night without disgracing himself. But even as he resolved that it would be so, his stomach betrayed him and turned over at the prospect of what might come. He swallowed down a rush of bile and forced his mind onto the well-trodden and narrow path that he had made for his thoughts during the miserable days and nights since his arrest. First, he would do his time in the stocks without flinching: no matter what. He would not call out for mercy, God help him. He had seen the town drunks wailing for help like babes after the crowd tired of pelting them with rotten fruit and moved on to more imaginative missiles which usually included bleeding gobbets of offal from the nearby butchers' stalls. He vowed he would never sink to their level, but despite the heat of the day a clammy shiver ran through him as Monkton snapped a cuff on his outstretched arm, dragged him down the dark passage, past the desk sergeant and out through the studded front door onto the street. Tobias struggled to ignore the creeping fears that clawed at his belly and focused on the second thing he had to do.

Two things: he could only permit himself to think of two things.

The second one was harder than the first as he had to face Mr Parry and hear the verdict on his future and all his dreams, which were probably now doomed and rattling off to hell in a handcart. His decision to sell the papers might have lost him the best job he had ever had, and the trust of Master and Madam, and the daily sight of Frances. At the very thought of such a fate his stomach threatened to turn over again, so he dragged his mind back to his second task. He had to see Mr Parry and apologise to him, but he also had to act the man, like Mr Parry had told him, over and over again. Madam had been to see him and had been very kind, but she was not Master. Not that he knew when Mr Parry would be home. He just prayed to God it would be today so he could get everything over at once. Only then would he allow himself to think of other things, of what to do with what was left of his life if he found himself back on the street.

The officer strode ahead of Tobias, his long legs eating up the distance as he hauled his shackled prisoner behind him at a trot. They rounded the corner of Grove Street, crossed Pulteney Bridge and made their way to Orange Grove and the stocks. As the Grove came into view Monkton gave an additional yank on the cuffs.

"No laggin' Caudle. Regular criminal like you shouldn't be affrighted by yer just desserts!"

289

If only it had not been him.

Tobias had known Monkton from his days as a boot boy at the York House Hotel, but Monkton had not been an officer of the law then, far from it. He had been a stable lad, a brawny, rough customer, with a broad streak of cruelty to match, and as idle and shifty as he could manage without getting the sack. A speciality of his had been to terrorise the younger boys and, like the rest, Tobias had kept out of his way as much as he could. It had been a relief for all the small fry when Monkton had tired of life in the stables and taken a job as a police officer. Sadly for Tobias, a few crumbs of authority had done nothing to improve Silas Monkton. He remained brutal, small-minded and peevish, and worse than all of these, he had a vague memory of Tobias and singled him out for special treatment. He recalled a destitute child employed as a Christian duty by a pious housekeeper, a popular boy, whip-thin and eager to please. In the York House days, Monkton had despised Tobias, but now he resented him for his fine clothes, for his visits from Madam and Frances, and he resented the gifts, the tid-bits the women brought for Tobias at every visit. Always a greedy hog, Monkton had been quick to pilfer the food as soon as the visitors turned their backs, but before they did, it had amused him to make himself agreeable to them, chatting about the weather and bringing chairs so they could sit.

"Oh thank you, sir," Frances had said to him. "So kind of you, sir."

That hateful memory had a use: it made his blood boil and you don't feel afraid if you're itching to strangle somebody.

He stumbled as they rounded the corner to the green and for the thousandth time wondered how he had come to this. It had all seemed so right at the time. Just sell a couple of parcels of papers to help the cause, just once or twice until the new boys were ready to take over. And the cause was a grand one. There was no doubt about that. No doubt at all. What had Mr Jamieson and Mr Turner said? Unstamped papers were - now what was it? - "an instrument of civilisation", that is what they were, bringing knowledge to working men which would bring happiness to all! He was a hero, they had told him that, and there were hundreds like him, the numbers growing every day. They were heroes like those who smuggled the papers from London, like Mr Hetherington himself and Mr Carlile, the great publishers, both still locked away in London gaols. Not that they cared! Mr Hetherington had said if he had twenty thousand lives he would sacrifice them all for the cause!

Tobias held himself straighter as they approached the crude wooden stand near the stone obelisk. No one was going to kill him today. He had committed no hanging offence and he would not even go to gaol, Madam had told him that, and she had said she would pay his fine. He could think on that. It would help with jobs one and two.

Officer Monkton unlocked the cuff from his own wrist, transferred it and Tobias to the wooden upright and shoved him roughly towards the bench behind the stocks. Tobias sat down, stretched out his legs through two holes of the wooden yoke and glanced round the Grove. It was almost deserted: a good start. A hackney carriage picked up a fare at the stand, moved off the line and rolled by. Two couples were sauntering along taking the morning air, the odd working woman scurried past and two men in silk top hats marched on a mission to the Guildhall, looking neither left nor right. Perhaps the first task would pass easier than he had feared.

Feeling bold, he shouted out: "The red stamp is the mark of the beast, a blood mark of might against right! No tax on knowledge!"

Almost before he finished the back of Monkton's hand split his lip and bounced his head off the wooden upright.

"Shut yer mouth, Caudle. Save yer breath."

The advice was good as far as it went. He lifted his head to offer one more challenge to Monkton and the Grove, deciding it would probably have to be the last, as the blow had been a hard one and he did not want much more of the same, but it was too

291

late. Tobias's heart sank and the brave words died on his lips, for round the corner of High Street pranced a trio of urchins he knew of old. They used to be some of his boys, his neighbours, fellow guttersnipes and thieves from Little Corn Street, but he had left them behind and bettered himself. After the first few months of working for Mr Parry he had given them nothing, not even his friendship. There had been neither a wink nor a nod about the best houses to rob in Saint James's Square; he had not made them one visit, nor shared one drink with them. Some would barely have noticed he had gone; some would have wished him luck, but not these three. They would not have forgiven his neglect.

Attracted by Tobias's shouts, the boys recognised him and set up an answering cry of their own. Obscenities streamed through their bared teeth, their eyes turned hard in their sallow faces, pinched by drink and putrid food, their fingers pointed accusations and crude gestures to shame him. Two doubled back to the market for ammunition; one picked up stones, stole a bucket and filled it from the steaming pile behind a horse at the carriage stand. Tobias steeled himself, head down for the onslaught.

"Caudle!" yelled one.

He looked up. Should he try talking to them?

From every hand the missiles rained down. He tucked his head into his breast, squeezed his eyes tight shut and prayed.

"Been a bad boy, Caudle!"

"Breakin' the law don't pay, Caudle!"

Dollops of stinking manure hit his defenceless head, along with decayed fish heads, fly-blown fruit and mildewed vegetables from under the market carts. Before he could catch his breath they were sharply followed up by stones. Two hit him square in the face and he spat out blood as it coursed from his nose into his mouth and from behind his closed lids, watery rivers of shock and pain flowed to follow it.

"Stop it!" he yelled. "Stop it, you cowards!"

But it did not stop. Hyena laughs rose to a demented crescendo around him, his head was buffeted left and right, blow followed blow until he felt he was slipping away, the noise closing in on him.

"You don't look so good now, Caudle!"

"Nor smell so good neither!"

The torment continued as the morning dragged by. At times his persecutors disappeared, only to return with more ammunition and fresh taunts, or, tiring of the sport, they sat by the stocks and were content simply to watch him suffer. At length, when the onslaught resumed after just such a pause, Tobias felt he could take no more. In a despairing gesture he lifted his head for one final time, dragging his burning eyelids back from his eyes, and was rewarded with the best sight in the world. It was his salvation, in the shape of a black and tan tornado with a head like a brick, flying at his gaggle of tormenters like a thunder ball and scattering them in a furious maelstrom of barking, growling, teeth and claws.

"Caradoc!" he cried with relief. "Oh Caradoc, you beauty!"

And behind the terrier came Madam, and Frances. His head fell forward, but he heard a lady's voice raised to Monkton.

"Were you planning to let those louts kill Mr Caudle?"

"No, Madam," blustered Monkton. "Just letting him have a taste or two of chastisement before I sent them on their way."

"The purpose of the punishment was not to have this young man murdered! Your superiors will hear of this."

Tobias lifted his head again and heard himself trying to splutter out words of thanks. Frances was on her knees by him.

"Don't try to talk, Toby, you idiot."

She wiped his face and made him wince.

"Sorry! Oh Tobias Caudle, what a state you are in! Now don't worry. You have to stay a while longer, but Madam says we shall be back to collect you in the carriage when it's done and there will be no more a-showering of you with filth. Look there!"

As his eyes struggled to follow her instructions, he managed his first grin of the day, albeit lopsided and giving him as much pain as pleasure. There, rounding the corner of the High Street was not another gang of louts, but a smiling crowd led by Arthur Jamieson. Most of the men were printers, with some from other trades, and all from the radical reading group of the George and Dragon. He even caught sight of some women, two he knew as working wives he had seen in the bar, but one was dearer and the sight of her warmed his heart. There was Martha Spence, and alongside of her was Robert Turner, pushing a chair with four wheels cunningly attached to better convey the oldest man in Walcot Street, Mr Thomas Spence

"Sit steady, young'un!" called out Arthur. "We're all here to see you through your 'ardship. We shall be as a shield wall with umbrellas at the ready and woe betide any rascal who tries to assail ye!"

Nine o'clock in the evening:
The Parry Residence, Saint James's Square.

After bringing Tobias home and seeing to his injuries, Emma had insisted that there would be no more discussion of the incident that day and no work for him until tomorrow. He had been anxious that Nathaniel had not yet returned home, and she was with him on that, but had swept aside his concerns, seen him fed and watered and told him to go to his room and rest. He had hesitated, unwilling to give in, his conscience heavy with thoughts of the work left undone during his wasted days in Grove Street, until Caradoc forced his hand. The terrier had sat by Tobias all the way home in the carriage and stayed by his side during the lengthy cleansing session in the kitchen. When Emma ordered Tobias to his room, Caradoc jumped up to accompany him and when he made no move, bolted down the corridor to the boy's room, dived onto the bed and set up a persistent bark. It was a rare mark of favour for him to quit the comforts of the kitchen when Nathaniel was away and he meant everyone to know it.

"Well go on then!" Frances had ordered. "Before we are all deafened."

Exhausted by the day and keen to have some time to herself, Emma chose to retire early, which also released Frances from duty. Once she was alone in her room, she wrapped herself in Nathaniel's Damascus dressing gown, held its folds to her face to breathe in the scent of him, then propped herself up in bed on a mound of feather pillows, preparing to read unobserved.

In a drawer of her nightstand, discreetly hidden from view, she kept the journals which Madame Junot had lent to her. The French governess was now much more to Emma than her parents' employee: she was Céline, a friend and *confidente*. Emma still saw Tilly Vere occasionally, and more rarely still, the haughty Amanda Ravenswood. Anna, her old friend from Portsmouth, was less of a pleasure to meet than she had been, as she was now obsessed by talk of babies to the exclusion of all else. She was not close to any of them, any more than she was to Lottie Drake who deigned to drop in occasionally on an infrequent visit from London. Céline was different, as her conversation fed Emma's soul. Her political awakening had taken place at reform meetings with her father and she still accompanied him when she could. It was part of their relationship; part of their conspiracy. Her mother never came to the meetings, and neither had her elder brother or sister when they lived at home. It had given her an outlet for her thwarted ambition, allowed her to have her father all to herself and, miraculously, the rest of the family seemed to understand and let them be. But her new friendship with Céline had brought her face to face with a more extreme world than that inhabited by her father.

She took out the well-thumbed copy of the *Isis*. It would soon be a collectors' item, no doubt of it. Céline had ten issues in her collection and had been pleased to inform her that the magazine was created not by a man but by an *editress* by the name of Eliza Sharples, and had been published by her imprisoned partner, Richard Carlile.

The copies were precious as the magazine had only run briefly in 1832, collapsing before the year's end. Carlile had moved on to other publications like *The Gauntlet,* which she had seen in Tobias's bundle, but his relationship with Eliza was far from over. According to Céline, his wife had left him to set up her own radical bookshop and Eliza had given birth to his child. This, along with the notorious scope of his republican views and his abuse of the church, was the scandal that her mother had vaguely heard of, though mercifully she was ignorant of the details. If she had known more, and also of the extent of Céline's admiration for Eliza Sharples, the Peterson residence would have been short of a French governess in quick time.

Emma turned to the page where she had left Eliza's philosophising. She smiled to see Céline's jottings in the margin and the fierce underlining of the passages she particularly wanted to be read. Amongst other matters the piece dwelled on the injustice of the newspaper tax, which Emma now understood on a personal level, and the undue submission of women, which had never been anything other than personal. Eliza said women should have equal rights in law with men. She believed that the cause of the child worker and the cause of the slave were both worthy but were well rehearsed and supported by all liberals, whilst the repression and servitude of one half of the population, the female half, was one which had few supporters. Her voice seemed to be the only female one raised on a public stage to plead the case.

Céline's attachment to Miss Sharples had started in early 1832 on one of her regular trips to London and she had entertained Emma with a breathless account of attending one of Eliza's famous lectures at the Blackfriars Rotunda. A handsome and striking woman at any time, Eliza had appeared on the stage in a sumptuous evening gown against a theatrical backcloth of Egyptian and Greek symbols and over a floor strewn with laurel and whitethorn. She was at once posing as Isis, the Egyptian goddess of health, marriage and wisdom, friend of the down-trodden and mother of Horus the falcon headed, and also conjuring up the image of Hypatia the Greek philosopher. Eliza was a latter day "Pythoness of the Temple" and at the same time another Eve, daring to pluck the fruit from the tree of knowledge. It was heady stuff. In another age Miss Eliza Sharples could have been burned at the stake, but after careful cross-questioning of Céline, Emma found that her current fate seemed to be bankruptcy and ridicule.

Despite the failure of Eliza's public career, Emma drank down the strange words like nectar. Some were too sweet for her taste, but all stimulated her senses. Perhaps a woman had to play the showgirl to attract attention and had to work under the cloak of a male protector to capture even a few months of attention from the world before she disappeared again from public sight, back to acceptable obscurity. Perhaps that was the way the world was always going to be, but just for today, Emma felt that even she had not been obscure. She was proud of Tobias and his war wounds, his misguided attempt to help his friends. On the ride home he had been touchingly anxious to share his beliefs and justify what he had done. It was now clear to her that she had misjudged him to a degree. Not all his nights out had been spent at the George, as after a full day's work the boy had often taken to attending lectures at the Mechanics' Institute in Chandos Buildings. Yes, there were reasons enough to take pride in him. She was also pleased with herself. Using her parents' footman as chaperone she had been able to make the house call she needed without attracting attention. She had sought out Matthew Spence in Chatham Row and he had made himself useful at the George and Dragon, getting the men in the reading group to rally round and give up their break to protect Tobias.

She smiled to herself. It had been a good day, though little was settled and there was much to do. She had exchanged a few words with the demonstrators from the George about their campaigns and learned that the general feeling on reform of the press was combative and optimistic, they seemed sure that the government would relax the newspaper taxes before too long. But other campaigns, once thought won, had turned out to be hollow victories. The new Factory Act might be of as little use to the working child as last year's Reform Act was to the working man. Though the middle class men in towns had gained votes, the few poor men who had votes had lost them, and the rules for child labour, though protecting workers of less than nine years of age, applied only to those in cotton factories, whilst the rest could slave round the clock, unregulated and unobserved. The elusive ten hour day for all, long desired and long sought, was as far away as ever. The men had joined in a chant before she had left them.

"We will, we will, we'll have the Ten Hour Bill!" But it was a token performance with no real fire in it.

Those thoughts were sad, but thinking of the wider world had helped her today and would help her tomorrow. It preoccupied her and stopped her haunting the hall, waiting for every morning and afternoon post, it clouded her longing for Nathaniel to come home and her dread of hearing the news that he had found Coco. The thought of their meeting and possible reconciliation was too painful to be borne. Like Tobias, she had also given herself just two things to do that day. First task accomplished; Tobias had been rescued and now she was going to finish reading the article she had started the previous night. Pushing aside all other thoughts, she reached over and turned up the lamp.

Three o'clock in the morning: 29th June, 1833.
The Shadwell Residence, Green Park Buildings West.

"Oiy thought Oiy saw a light!" said Letty, roguishly, sticking her head round the kitchen door and beaming at the back view of a young woman seated at the table clad only in a petticoat and fringed shawl, her thick brown hair loose and tumbling down over her bare shoulders. Letty bustled in, wrapped her arms round the woman's neck, popped a smacking kiss on her head and thudded down into the chair next to her.

"I guessed it was you! Not seen you all the day, Clari. What've you been doing moiy girl?"

Clari giggled and waved her arms over the random collection of left-over food she had assembled. "Oiy've taken too much

298

brandy and Oiy'm moppin' it up with some supper. Want some?"

She took up the kitchen knife and set about slicing into the remaining half of a high-raised mutton pie.

"Make it a fair size. Oiy be starvin'," said Letty. "And while you're at it, Oiy'll brew some tea." She jumped up to poke her nose into the kettle, find the poker and rattle up a blaze amongst the dying embers of the fire. "Shouldn't be long it's still warmish. 'Ow's business?"

"At it since nine, moiy love," said Clari as she hewed off another piece of pie and shovelled the fall of crumbs into her mouth with her fingers. "Mmm, is this the best pie in Bath? Well yes, Oiy do believe it is!" As the fresh assault of dry pastry coincided with this declaration her chest convulsed. "Damn," she spluttered. "Cold drink, Letty, moiy love. Quick! Oiy'm gettin' the hiccups!"

Letty slopped a draught of small beer into a glass from the jug on the shelf.

"Get it down, Clari."

"Thanks, better. Now what were we sayin'? Business you said? Well, moiy last customer wouldn't go without buyin' a bottle and draining it dry. Oiy 'ad to 'elp the daft old sod with it, specially as Madam's started chargin' over double the rate on brandy and 'e wanted to see it off. We need 'im to come back! And you?"

"Good enough. Better'n last week," said Letty, moving to the window and pushing up the sash. She leaned out to breathe in the night air. "God, it's that 'ot! Who would 'ave thought it at this time of a mornin'. It's like livin' in the tropics!"

She checked the kettle again. "It'll do," she said doubtfully. "Now where's that caddy to?" She searched the cupboards, found the tea, scattered a few leaves into two cups and filled them with the lukewarm water.

"Come and sit!" commanded Clari. "Oiy didn't tell you who Oiy seen this mornin'!"

"'Oo's that then?"

"Well," said Clari, in a carrying voice, designed to be confidential but suffering from a lack of judgement brought on by the half bottle of brandy, the numerous beers and the bottle of wine she had taken over the evening. "Oiy was in town this mornin' and who do Oiy see clamped in the stocks but that lad who was 'ere with, well, shall we call 'im Mr Drake!"

Guffaws of laughter rang out from the two of them at the table and carried well, out through the window, into the dark and down the garden path .

"What 'ad 'e done, Clari?"

"Sellin' papers with no stamp."

"Don't 'e work for that gent now? That "Mr Drake" moiy Fred found out about in Gloucester?"

"Course 'e do. Tobias Caudle, the lad is called, 'e 's training up as Mr Drake's valet, Mr Parry that is. Does all sorts in the 'ouse and follows 'im round as a manservant."

"What's 'e like that Mr Parry, when 'e 's not actin' as someone else that is!"

Clari rolled her eyes. "Letty, up close 'e 's as 'andsome as ever Oiy seen! And strong too. As ye know, Oiy seen 'im myself 'ere with young Tobias gettin' the better of Joshua and the men out the back. Remember like Oiy said before, 'e was the one who sorted Billy and Jabez out good and proper a couple of years back!"

"You're roight," said Letty, hacking off another piece of pie. "And Abi said 'e was a marvel gettin' her out of that toil in Bristol docks when poor Babs died. God rest 'er!"

Behind their backs, as they paused respectfully and took another mouthful of tea, the kitchen door swung back on its hinges.

"Having a little recreation, ladies?" The tall figure of Joshua Shadwell, black against the hall light, stepped into the kitchen. He drew back his thin lips in a cheerless smile. "Don't tire yourselves out."

They exchanged terrified glances, plastering on smiles as they desperately tried to remember what they had said, and when.

"Join us for some tea, Mr Shadwell?"

"Not tonight, Clari," he said. "I had enough of your talk as I walked up the garden. And yours," he said, with a venomous glare at Letty.

He limped over to the table and struck Clari a blow across the face, leaning over to her as she froze in her seat.

"Your information about the enterprising Mr Parry was interesting and I am disappointed you kept it from me for so long. You're drunk, you're careless and you are too stupid to keep secrets from me so don't try it again."

He straightened up and served Letty the same, the flat of his hand leaving her face burning red.

"And you. Don't you ever deceive me again." He glowered at the two of them, his harsh voice rising to fill the kitchen and batter their ears. "Anything to do with this house, or any girl in this house, is my business. You speak to me first or I'll make you wish you'd never been born!"

Without another word he turned abruptly and left them transfixed in misery. The door slammed behind him and they sat listening to his retreating steps, uneven and dragging on his injured side, as he made his way upstairs.

"Oh Letty," whispered Clari. "What 'ave we done! Oiy wish to God Abi 'ad made a better job of stickin' that knife in 'im!"

The Parry Residence, Saint James's Square, Bath.

Later that morning, the bell jangled in the Parry's front hall and Frances trotted down the stairs from Madam's bedroom to answer it.

"There is no point waiting for Mrs Rollinson to go," Madam had said with a smile. "From what you said she's at a crucial stage with the seed cakes so she won't have much patience with visitors."

Frances was humming to herself, preoccupied with her own happiness. Tobias was on his feet despite his bruises and his swollen face, the sun was up and she was looking forward to an exchange in the fresh air, probably with one of Madam's lady friends, or maybe the post boy. She opened the door with a flourish, smiling a welcome, only to sustain a shock cruel enough to knock the breath out of her. Horrified, she stepped back gasping, her hand flying to her mouth, as she stared into a face that was terrifyingly familiar. The man before her was foreign, an Asiatic, tall and powerful looking, with thick black hair and expressionless eyes. He was also a spectre from the darkest hours of her short life, from a foetid cell in the Redcliffe caves where he had visited with other men, and worst of all with the terrible dark man who owned the ship that was to have taken her away.

"You must be Frances," said the man quietly whilst watching her intently, holding her still in his gaze. "I know you saw me once in unpleasant circumstances and you are alarmed, but think carefully, you must also remember the other Chinese men who helped you on the night you escaped. They had been sent by me. They are my friends and I am a friend of Mr Parry. He is the reason I am here. I need to speak with him urgently, Frances."

"He's away, sir," said Frances uncertainly, but feeling calmer as she looked back at him more closely, listened to him speak and ran over her memory of him again. He had not been the one who had frightened her, or made her stand before him like a beast at an auction. He had not touched her, or even approached her, but had remained like a statue at the door, then left without a word. She realised she had bunched her hands into fists, took a breath, and allowed them to uncurl.

"But he will be back any day now, sir. Madam expected him before now."

The man reached into his pocket, brought out a silver case, heavily engraved and with a miniscule silver pencil attached. He set about writing a note on the back of a visiting card.

"Frances, this is important. Take this and ensure that Mr Parry receives it the moment he returns." He made a slight bow: "Please convey my respects to Mrs Parry."

He left her staring after him on the doorstep, untied his horse from the railing and mounted up.

Half-dressed, Emma had walked out on the landing to lean over the banister and see if she could catch more of the conversation below. As she heard Frances closing the door, she shot back to her bedroom and lifted the curtain. Her heart gave a thump as she recognised him: there, riding a chestnut mare down the hill towards the Bristol Road, was Cornelius Lee. Hearing Frances running upstairs she moved away from the window, embarrassed, and took up a position by her dressing table.

"Madam," said Frances breathlessly, holding out an embossed visiting card in ivory white. "There's a message for Mr Parry on this, but I thought I should bring it to you straight away. The visitor was a foreigner, Madam, and I think he's part of Mr Parry's business. I didn't want to leave it on the hall table."

She did not need to say more. Open messages on public display were fair game for domestic staff. Emma smiled at her, for Frances would know all about that. She was without doubt the canniest servant Emma had ever known. Even after being acquainted with her for nearly two years and having some sketchy details of the trauma of her early life, Emma sensed she had little idea of who Frances really was, or who she had been, other than that she was a born survivor. Luckily for Emma, the life of an unwanted child in Avon Street, who had been sold on by her mother to the first offer, was as alien as the life of the poor in Timbuktu. Her mind wheeled back to Cornelius and the tales he had told them of the sad wretches in his own land. Round the fire that night on Anglesey he had urged Nathaniel, and not for the first time it seemed, to realise the scale of the menace of opium addiction in the coastal towns of China, fuelled by smugglers from British India and abetted by native criminals who defied the Emperor's laws. Degradation and squalor: always just a step away from gentility. Alien worlds, but some souls moved between the two and become wise enough to have lived twice over.

"You did right, Frances," she said. "Now, I may have other callers, so bring the cream gown with the sprigged flowers. We need to hurry."

As Frances helped her into the day dress Emma tried to recall Nathaniel's exact words about Cornelius before he left. He had mentioned that his friend had returned to Bristol and that they had met, but the robbery and Tobias's problems had driven the details from her mind. Then she remembered. Cornelius planned to take up residence again in Arno's Tower. Looking down at the card in her hand it was plain that he was not at the Tower today. The note announced that he was returning to the Crown at Keynsham throughout the next week, every afternoon, at five o'clock. She had a vivid memory of him and his striking looks, but more than that, the magnetism of the man, his prescient understanding which was so piercing it was almost a second sight. And she remembered his gift to her, the bolt of embroidered blue silk. Today at least, he would not wait alone.

Later that afternoon Emma had Frances prepare her for a drive. She was feeling expansive, and if she had admitted it, on the border-line of reckless. On an impulse she had summoned Tobias from his labours on a neglected pile of boots and Caradoc from guard duty by his side. He had seen her order as a mark of favour, which made her all the more glad for having thought of it. She knew he was still anxious about Nathaniel's return and found it touching to see him strive to impress her.

"Right away, Madam," he had said, rushing to wash his hands in the bowl before doubling back to his room to brush his hair, and even more important for the boy, to collect his stick. Every spare minute since returning home he had spent perfecting the techniques that Mr Parry had taught him and he was keen to play the bodyguard. It was another step down the road to redemption. As it was another fine day she had walked with them to Pickwick's Livery at the White Hart to pick up Nathaniel's post chaise and both of his horses.

"Thank you," she said, as the hired driver handed her up to the seat and Caradoc bounded up beside her. "And I have a request. I would like my boy here to sit up in front with you. It is time he learned to drive."

The two half-crowns she slipped into his hand made him a patient teacher, and for the trainee, there could not have been a better gift. Tobias, blushing under his bruises, his clear eye shining with excitement, climbed up eagerly and as they left Bath, was transported not just out of the town but also, for a while, out of himself and his worries.

They bowled along the toll road, over the New Bridge on the outskirts of Bath and on through the village of Saltford, all in the brilliant golden blue of a mid-summer afternoon. The fields swooned in the heat and not a breeze ruffled the bulrushes in the water meadows by the river. She let her eyes flow along the scene as they passed at a brisk trot and had a moment's view of a heron rising lazily from the river's margin, flapping his great white wings and trailing spindly legs in the water as he gained height and lit out over the sparkling Avon. A sudden thought intruded: a thought of other rivers and warm lakes. She looked away.

"Well done, Tobias!" she called, seeing the boy had taken the reins on the easy straight. "Have you ever ridden a horse?"

"No, Madam," he called back, not daring to take his eyes from the road.

"Well you shall today. Driver, put him on one of the horses as we slow down in the Keynsham traffic."

The Crown Inn, Bristol Road, Keynsham.

Within the hour and close to five o'clock, they arrived at the Crown and drove round to the stables. Emma, with Caradoc at her heels, had Tobias and the driver escort her inside and was relieved to spot Cornelius by the window as soon as she entered the front parlour. Whilst the dog made a bee-line for him and settled at his feet, she pressed a florin into Tobias's hand and sent him and the driver into the tap room to wait with the other

305

servants and coachmen. She struggled to ignore the fact that for the first time in her life she was entirely un-chaperoned, and furthermore she had chosen to arrive unannounced to meet a man in a public house. Confronted by the extent of her indiscretion, the remnants of her euphoria evaporated and she felt excruciatingly exposed. To give her courage she thought of Eliza Sharples standing proudly on the stage as Isis, mother of Horus, posing as a new Hypatia, another Eve.

"Mrs Parry," said Cornelius, standing to greet her, noting the blush of discomfort rising up her cheeks. "Thank you for making the journey to meet me. I gather by your presence that Nathaniel is not yet home. And by the presence of his fellow," he said, ruffling Caradoc's head, "I assume he is away on business."

Immaculate as usual, and in black with a severe white stock at his neck and gold stitching on his waistcoat to relieve it, Cornelius cut an exotic figure. She could feel the eyes of the other customers turning to them.

"May I order some refreshment for you?" he was asking. "There is a coffee room here, and it is quiet."

They quit the busy parlour, Caradoc pausing only to lift a chop bone from a discarded plate, and she followed Cornelius to take a seat in a shaded room away from the road. As they waited for the waitress to finish unloading their order from her tray and sneaking curious glances at Cornelius, he took the chance to observe Emma. She was as beautiful as when he had first seen her in the cold of the Welsh winter, highly strung and ready to run like a roe deer, her fine skin glowing, and tendrils of red-gold hair framing her face. On his second sighting of her, she remained an unusual woman. Her lavender gown and pelisse were cut close to her body, restrained and in the classical style, still resisting the swags and flounces of the fashion plates with their bizarre sleeves billowing ever larger like hot air balloons. But her eyes were troubled now. Whatever her motive had been in coming to him, he needed to make time to listen.

"I thought it would be helpful if I came to see you," she started hesitantly, "to let you know of some problems we have had. You see, after the robbery at Arno's Tower," she paused, feeling horribly awkward, and then began again. "I think you know that there was an incident, you spoke with my husband shortly afterwards, I believe? Well, before long we were also visited by a thief. The sapphires were taken, those we showed you which Nathaniel's father brought from Spain."

He noticed she did not lay claim to them, she did not call them: "My sapphires".

"Nathaniel has travelled to France."

How much to say? How much to leave unsaid?

Cornelius resolved her dilemma.

"Following the woman? It was I who told him that the robbers were French and I know there was a French woman in Bath who knew of the wealth of the Ravenswoods. I know also that the sapphires were in an identical setting to a piece owned by Mrs Ravenswood. There was a clear link, especially as you mention no other loss from your collection. A long shot perhaps, but it is natural he should seek to recover the property."

"Yes," said Emma carefully. "It is natural."

"Mrs Parry," he began.

"My name is Emma. Please feel free to use it as you did at our last meeting. I hope you regard both Nathaniel and me as friends."

"Yes I do, Emma." He watched her closely, gauging how much he should disclose to make her able to unburden herself of whatever troubled her. "I called on you this morning as I need Nathaniel to know that events are moving to a possible conclusion in my pursuit of the man known as Kizhe. It is a priority for me to track him down, and Nathaniel also has an interest in this. I now know that he is in Bristol with at least two others and he has a ship, fully crewed, docking there from London. For now he is staying at the Ravenswood town house in Redcliffe Parade. The reason I left Arnos' Tower this morning was that I heard this news and furthermore I learned that he is accompanied by Edwin Ravenswood himself, a man with whom Nathaniel and I also have unfinished business. It is imperative that Nathaniel speaks with me before he has any further dealings with any of these men. Certain matters came to light in London which compromised our position."

He watched her deal with the threat. She would be prudent in her use of the information and she would be efficient, of these things he was sure. It was unnecessary to burden her further with the fact that Ravenswood, Kizhe, and his henchmen, were looking to eliminate Nathaniel and make his own life as difficult as possible. She was not informed that Fong had accompanied him to Bath and had stayed there for her protection, watching the house in Saint James's Square until Nathaniel returned. He also kept to himself the details of Amanda Ravenswood's desperate flight from Redcliffe that morning. She had attended a dinner there last night and heard all she needed to know about the aims of her husband and his conspirators. To compound the news, Shadwell had arrived early that morning with information that hammered the final nail in the coffin for Nathaniel, proof of his involvement in the release of the girls who Ravenswood had been hoping to sell in the autumn of 1831 and therefore also in the burning of Ravenswood's ship, the *Mathilda*. And Amanda had become another counter on the board. He had allowed her to come closer to him, to become involved, and so now she cared, clutching at straws of comfort from him, a stranger and potentially a very dangerous one. The relations had paid off, as now she feared for his life and had warned him. He had been able to leave the Tower without a confrontation and well before Ravenswood returned.

"Nathaniel must know of these developments immediately upon his return," he said, closing the subject. "But I sense there is more to your visit, Emma. What troubles you?"

Again, as it had happened the night in Anglesey when she first met him, almost involuntarily she spoke to him frankly, with no blush or embarrassment, though not this time of dreams and ghosts.

"I am afraid of the consequences if Nathaniel finds the French woman, Colette Montrachet. They were friends before he loved me, probably more than that, and perhaps they are again."

Cornelius's eyes searched her face.

"Emma, be surer of yourself and take strength. You are a lady, and a beautiful one, if I may say so. You love Nathaniel and he is deeply attached to you. From what I gather she is a fortune hunter ready to go with any man who suits her purpose. Who is he likely to prefer? And think on this, would it not be strange if such a successful man, such a man of talent, had no other friends or had not had other lovers?"

"Yes, of course. But I fear he will be tempted away and our love will be ruined. The life I have would be lost, Cornelius. I do not think I would recover easily."

Tears slowly welled up in her eyes. "I am sorry," she said, looking away in confusion. "I should not have spoken. I should go, and I will make sure Nathaniel has your message as soon as he returns."

"It was not wrong to come to me with this Emma, but be sure, none of what you fear will come to pass," said Cornelius gently, taking her hand. "There is something between them for certain, as there was before, and probably always will be. But it is not what he has with you."

"Should he not forsake all others? We are married Cornelius we have made promises."

Cornelius shook his head dismissively. "In my country the rules and the promises are different from here, but neither code is superior and in the end neither is designed to cater for the strangeness of each individual life. Our Emperor makes promises to his Empress, but he also has responsibilities to his Noble Consort." He smiled at her surprise. "And the ordinary Consorts, and of course the Concubines, and the Noble Ladies, and of less importance, the ordinary ranks of female attendants. Emma, they number in thousands. Such rules are not limited to the Emperor; successful men have their concubines too. It is simply a matter of scale."

"And of course," said Emma. "It goes without saying that noble women will not have the same rights!"

"There is a saying in my homeland. One teapot is usually accompanied by at least four cups, but one cup does not need four teapots."

She nodded. "Women as receptacles: it's a familiar image."

"It is, but what is familiar is not necessarily wise or harmonious. Emma, irrespective of social conventions we have to make our own path in this world and the next; we must all find our own way of being. Say little when Nathaniel returns. His journey will be at an end and he will be back with you, which is as it should be. If he met with her and wishes to speak of it, then listen, otherwise, do not pursue it. There are many kinds of love, Emma, deep and abiding love for a lifetime is just one of them. You seem to have found it, though I suspect I never will. Physical love can be many things; it can be a welcome and a farewell. It can be a convenience, or used to cloak another purpose, but even then it is not always without pleasure. Life is cruelly short; we should always consider that before passing judgement on another."

"Do I ask too much?"

"You fear too much."

Emma sat in silence for a moment, feeling the warm pressure of his hand on hers and strangely, an overwhelming sense of peace.

"It is a relief to discuss such things, though I am unused to it, and certainly not with a man who is not my husband. Thank you, Cornelius."

He took her hand and pressed it to his lips.

"Know that Nathaniel loves you and that he will return to you. Others are like the moon to your sun. Be strong, believe in yourself."

She stood to leave.

"Will I see you again?"

"I am sure of it," said Cornelius.

The Parry Residence, Saint James's Square, Bath.

Emma was quiet on the journey back, tightly wrapped in her own thoughts, but no one noticed, as the driving instruction continued from where it had left off on the outward journey. She had them take her home to Saint James's Square leaving Tobias with the driver to enjoy a final ride through town before walking back from the livery stable with Caradoc. She took dinner alone and retired to her room as the sun was setting. The room seemed the same, but things had changed, she still felt at peace and could still feel the warmth of Cornelius's hand on hers. She had been mistaken to think of her marriage as a sacred relic, to be kept in aspic as it was on the day they exchanged vows. They were living and breathing creatures, with patchwork emotions from the past, old friends, and for Nathaniel, old loves as well.

Perhaps concern for our relationship is rather like concern for our bodies, she thought, perhaps we should not fear challenges or disease and dread them coming to corrupt us, but rather see that what we fear is probably within us already. We live with it and through it, and we must gain strength with every new experience. She found she could think of Coco without dread or resentment and admit that, despite her suspicions and jealousy, she had enjoyed her conversations with the vivacious French woman. She also found room in her heart for gratitude. Coco had once been of great service to Nathaniel, sheltering Frances's wayward friend and taking the trouble to place her in employment, out of harm's way. Emma took off her wedding ring and held it to the lamp light to read the engraving. On that freezing January day when they married she had been his "*Bright Star*".

She walked over to the curtains and opened them wide. Looking up, above the sinuous curve of the Royal Crescent, she saw the limitless bowl of the heavens scattered with thousands of stars, millions of pin-pricks of light, some indistinct, woven in the swirling translucent skein of the milky way, some placed precisely in their ancient patterns, studding the impenetrable

311

darkness as they always had and always would do: but brighter than the rest was the pole star, brighter than them all. Let them all guide him home. She slipped the ring back on, climbed into bed and took Eliza's journal from the drawer.

Caradoc heard him first. Spread-eagled on the floor by Tobias's bed, he raised his head and just one ear. There it was again, an unmistakeable voice sounding low in conversation outside on the road, a carriage door slammed and a trunk dropped heavily onto the pavement. The terrier jumped up and scratched his way out of the door, ran through the kitchen, his claws skittering on the flags, up the stairs, into the hall and in one flying bound leapt straight into the arms of his master.

"Good to see you too," laughed Nathaniel, dodging the barrage of yapping and the wettest of the welcoming licks. "Quiet, sir! You'll rouse the house."

"I should think he has already."

She stood for a moment at the top of the stairs, pausing to tie his Damascus gown more securely around her, then with a laugh ran down to them.

"Em, darling!" said Nathaniel, struggling to plant Caradoc on the floor. "Down, you hooligan!"

She flung herself into his arms and kissed him, burying her face in his neck with Caradoc capering around them in a frenzy of excitement.

"My love, how I have missed you," she whispered. "How did you fare?"

She pulled back to look at him. He was tanned, but thinner than when he left; his cheeks gaunt, his eyes smudged with dark shadows.

"Are you well?"

"Yes," he said. "Don't worry. All's well. We will talk of it later." He reached into his pocket and drew out a small pouch. "For you," he said. "To have strung as you wish."

She emptied the pouch into her hand and six perfect blue stones tumbled out.

"So these are to be mine," she said with a wry smile. "I take it that the excess has been discarded?"

Evening: 30th June, 1833.
The Crown Inn, Bristol Road, Keynsham.

Cornelius had not risked signing in as a resident at the Crown, so had taken Nathaniel and Caradoc to a back room where they could dine well away from the front parlour and its regular influx of coaching trade.

"I hear Emma visited you yesterday," said Nathaniel.

"She did. She was lonely and she missed you."

"Was that all?"

"No. She feared you would leave her for the French woman."

Nathaniel nodded. "I see. But there was no need to consider that a possibility."

"So I told her."

They sat in silence by the empty fireplace as an evening breeze crept through the open window and stole round them, relieving the torpor of the summer night.

"Did you recover the jewels?"

"It turns out they should have been hers in the first place. They had belonged to her family, so I felt there was no call to recover them, but she made me a present of some of the sapphires. Emma can have them made up as she sees fit."

"And did you recover your French friend?"

"I bade her farewell," said Nathaniel.

"And Emma, was she in good spirits on your return?" asked Cornelius, observing his friend closely, noting the exhaustion and the familiar gesture, the hand raking through his long hair, pushing it back from his face as he gathered his thoughts. He noted also the absence of anxiety, and of guilt: the reunion must have been satisfactory for both parties.

Nathaniel smiled. "She certainly was. She seems to have been well occupied whilst I was away. One of our servants had a brush with the law and she saw him through it. His recent

passion for reform had prompted him to sell unstamped papers."
Nathaniel shrugged. "I was pleased to see him cope with the
experience, and learn from it. It is what youth is for."

"This boy is a protégé of yours? You have plans for him?"

"Yes, I do," said Nathaniel. "And he shows promise."

"In life we only truly know ourselves, and understand our
potential, when we are faced with a severe threat," said
Cornelius half to himself, and then paused, lost in thought,
before continuing. "Our Masters only know if we are capable of
facing such challenges and profiting by them if we are put to the
test. I remember a time in my youth when I too was imprisoned.
You know that I lived in a temple as a child where I trained in
the fighting arts. In my country, such training is usually done in
secret, outside the law, as our Manchu overlords are few in
number and fear rebellion. I had been on an errand for my
Master, taking a message to a village a day's journey away, but I
walked into a trap. I was arrested and held prisoner in an animal
shed for five days. They beat me to try to make me reveal the
name and whereabouts of the sender of the message I carried. I
tell you, I suffered more from the shame of capture than the
treatment, which I was trained to withstand. I should not have
walked into the house like a lamb to the slaughter but as I had
done so, I tormented myself with the thought that it might have
been better to fight back. But as the days passed, I came to
realise that my first reaction was the better one. Fighting would
have revealed my skills, and as my life was not in danger I could
not let that happen but had to endure the test. So I continued to
play the frightened farmer's boy, but all the time fearing what
my Master would say. I kept to my story that a man on the road
had asked me to deliver the message to his sick family, but my
captors were not convinced and would not let me go."

"So how did you escape?" asked Nathaniel.

"I drew on my training and started to watch the pattern of the
guards' movements. The room was dark, lit only by a crack of
light from the window. Every morning two soldiers would
unlock the door and come in to me, one carrying a jug of water,

the other a lamp. They would walk directly to the corner where I slept. Every other day the job was done by a man and a youth of about my build. I targeted them. One day the jug was held out as usual, but only to a bundle of my clothes stuffed with straw, whilst I lay motionless and half naked behind the door, covered in the filth from the floor. As the other guard raised his lantern to inspect my rags, I struck. In the temple we learn the ways of many creatures. Some are mythical like the dragon, some real and ferocious like the tiger and the leopard, but some are more humble, like the crane and the snake. Did you know that this is the year of the black water snake? It is a good time for this story, and in the darkness of the shed it was also a time for the snake. I rolled over the floor, keeping low and fluid, swept the legs from under them and struck them both as they hit the ground. The village was surrounded by a forest and I knew I would be safe there once I escaped from the hut, so I took the clothes from the smaller guard and slipped away through the trees."

"You were lucky that neither of them saw you by the door."

"The eyes often see what they expect to see and my disguise worked. As you know, it is important to blend in with your surroundings."

"If possible," laughed Nathaniel. "Especially when you are in a net on Wapping Wharf!"

Cornelius grinned. "The blend there was not so good: but there was a lesson to be had. A sacrifice was needed in order to get on board the ship and it turned out to be me."

They laughed together, feeling their renewed bond of friendship.

"What did your Master say when you returned?" asked Nathaniel curiously.

"I tried to explain what had happened, but I sensed he already knew. He did not ask me to explain my delay but just said that lessons are learned in various ways, experience is gained on which we can build. The next day he moved me on to a different type of training. At the time, I thought it was some

315

form of punishment, but later I realized that I had progressed to the next level."

Nathaniel nodded, he felt that he too had progressed in the process of understanding his friend, but there was a long way to go.

Cornelius glanced round the room. The nearest customers were still a good way off and out of earshot, a group of three men, commercial travellers locked in their own buzz of conversation. "To business, our enemies have gathered at Redcliffe Parade," he said quietly. "Kizhe's war junk, the *Zhen Tian Lei,* arrived yesterday and the *Blue Dragon* is also in port."

"*Zhen Tian Lei!*" exclaimed Nathaniel. "Does that mean something about thunder shaking the heavens?"

"Yes, as in thunder crash bombs. Kizhe doesn't like mixed messages."

"You were very fortunate to be given warning," said Nathaniel. "Emma passed on your message and I have written to Drake in London. He has a personal interest in Ravenswood's career so I told him to come if he wants to help make it less profitable. I have advised him to bring Home Office authorisation to call out a platoon of troops. We might need them and I don't want to involve the Yeomanry. We need regulars if we are to attempt to arrest Kizhe when he has the backing of an entire crew and I want Captain Trevellis for the murder of Ben Prestwick. We will have the crew of the *Dragon* to deal with when we go after him."

"Amanda Ravenswood travelled from Redcliffe alone to warn me," said Cornelius.

"She is now your ally then?"

"We have an understanding. Her suffering as Ravenswood's wife has been extreme and it has grown to hatred because of his affair with Drake's wife. She turned to me for consolation, and has returned the favour. Unfortunately she has also found other means to lift her pain."

"Other men?"

"No, laudanum, and it has made her reckless. Not to say she is without other friends. The new men employed at the Tower are more hers than Ravenswood's. In particular, the two Irish, and Matthew Spence, the man who used to sail in Ravenswood's crew, all three are loyal to her. She favours them and keeps them close to the house. I know she has gained access to duplicate keys and has searched Ravenswood's study. She has plans of her own, but tonight my friend, we must finalise ours. We have a small window of opportunity to settle some old scores."

Chapter 10

Evening: 5th July, 1833. The Ravenswood Residence, Arno's Tower, Arno's Vale, near Bristol.

It had become habitual for Edwin Ravenswood to choose to sit at the opposite end of the dining table from his wife and so far this had proved to be a night like any other. He surveyed her bleakly across the long run of cloth, cluttered at each end by the remains of the last course, each set of glasses, plates and cutlery corralled round its diner like a barrier of circled wagons. He could barely remember the last time they had dined close enough to touch each other during a meal, for his hand to hold hers, or brush her back; for her feet to twine themselves round his. Not much of a loss, but it irked him that she appeared unmoved by the change.

His jaw tightened in annoyance. After spending a relaxing hour in his Oriental Salon adjusting the face mask on his Japanese samurai armour, she had managed to irritate him within minutes of her arrival in the dining room. His temper was unusually short as he had had an intense week of negotiations with Kizhe and his officers at Redcliffe Parade. His visitor had been as demanding as he knew he could afford to be, testing Ravenswood's patience and pushing the boundaries to breaking point. As the right-hand man of the Count, the facilitator of the clandestine routes into China and grand master of the human trafficking which enhanced his income from the opium trade, he was an important cog in the wheel of the Ravenswood fortunes, one which must be well-oiled, feted and indulged. It had been a trying week. Apart from the drain on his personal time, there had been collateral losses, in particular the injuries suffered by a couple of the prostitutes sent to the visitor. They had been lent by a contact who expected them back and earning the next night but their experiences at Redcliffe Parade had made that impossible.

During their meetings Kizhe had outlined ambitious plans. His trips to Holland and regular meetings in London had not been part of his trafficking endeavours as Ravenswood had first thought, but a new and lucrative branch of the Count's business in the shipping of stolen art and jewels. His hand-picked forgers were at their creative work, making pieces to plant in the place of stolen goods and Kizhe had brought a trunk full of gems and very superior paste for Ravenswood to compare. It was not a trade of interest to Ravenswood and his dilemma had been to keep Kizhe committed to the existing side of the business without extracting a promise from him to contribute to the new schemes. This was his first night at the Tower since returning from London and he had expected it to be more congenial than it was proving to be.

He surveyed his wife with distaste. She had arrived late for dinner and distinguished herself only by drinking too much and keeping up a stream of inconsequential chatter; a pathetic attempt to stave off the questions she needed to answer when they found themselves alone. But answer she would.

"More wine," demanded Amanda, raising her empty glass to a footman, her eyes glassy and her cheeks flushed.

"I think, Madam, that you have had more than enough," said Ravenswood, waving the staff away. "Leave us. I will take brandy presently in the west wing."

She had been ordered to join them at Redcliffe Parade for the welcome dinner on his return with the guests from London. The

319

evening had passed well enough, but she had claimed to be unwell and returned to the Tower the next morning, shortly before he dispatched his men there to pick up Cornelius Lee. Ravenswood had been distracted by a visit from Joshua Shadwell whose news made the detention of Lee even more desirable. But far from supervising security at the Tower, Lee was nowhere to be found. His men interrogated the staff and checked in local inns but at every turn they drew a blank.

"Still no sign of our Chinese security guard I see," said Ravenswood, leaning back in his chair, dangerously quiet. "How very strange, was it not, that your return coincided with him disappearing into thin air? One might almost think that you rushed back to warn him to make himself scarce, which suggests he is a person of some interest to you."

Amanda's flush drained from her face and her eyes flashed with anger.

"A person of interest! My God, yes! How unusual it has been to have a man in the house who concerns himself with my needs! A cultivated man, a gentleman!"

And unsaid: also a thrillingly imaginative lover, capable of appearing unannounced in her room in the night and transporting her to a much better place. Attack was her only defence.

"And do not think Edwin, that I am unaware of your own extramural interests: in particular your liaison with Charlotte Drake. I am sure there are more, though once I thought you were immune to such temptations. Such a cold fish with such particular appetites! There must be plenty of women who enjoy the punishment you like to give, especially when they are paid to do so."

Ravenswood stood, furious, his hands gripping the edge of the table as if he prepared to launch it at his wife and slam them both to fragments against the wall. Her mention of Lottie infuriated him. It was a reminder of more unfinished business.

"So," he countered, "you dally with the hired help whilst I am negotiating the fortunes you would like to spend. Are you so different from the harlots in Shadwell's brothel, Madam?"

He surprised her by following up with a swift move towards her and she leapt to her feet.

"Damn you, Edwin! Damn you to hell where you belong!" she screamed, flinging her glass wildly at him, to fall just wide and smash like a shrapnel shell into the wall behind his head.

"Predictably unbalanced, as well as disappointingly barren, Amanda," said Ravenswood with distaste as she stood, head bowed and gulping down air, her body starting to shudder with raw, racking sobs. "Are you of any further use at all?"

He covered the remaining ground between them before she looked up, grabbed her by the arm and pulled her to him. She struggled to push him away but his grip on her left arm tightened whilst his other hand tore the gown from her shoulder and pushed up her skirts. Always aroused by fear, he pulled her to him, pinioning her arms and burying his face in her neck.

"No, no!" She struggled, twisting her body away from him and rolling her head out of reach, but he held her tighter still as he pushed her back onto the table.

Her body flat, but with her legs still free, she took a desperate chance and brought her knee up hard between his legs. She wriggled from under him as he gasped and doubled-over in pain, but his hold on her arm never faltered. He straightened up and struck her twice across the face. All the frustrations of the last week were in the blows and Amanda fell to the floor choking, her mouth full of hot blood and her arms circling her head in defence as she curled up in a ball on the floor.

"Get up," he said curtly. "There might just be a few more uses for you. Go upstairs and get ready, perhaps you can redeem yourself before morning."

She rolled onto her knees, cradling her jaw. "You've broken my back teeth, you bastard."

"You heard me. Go and clean yourself up. You are marking the carpet and it is worth considerably more than you are."

She heard her husband stride away, the sound of his footfalls retreating towards the west wing. Shaking, she rose unsteadily to her feet, wiped her eyes on the back of her hand and walked slowly out of the dining room and up the stairs. As she stood on the landing she looked up. The moon was out, its pale beams illuminating the dragon window in the roof. Despite her sad state, she smiled at the memory of standing below it in the arms of Cornelius Lee, bathed in the green and silver of its scales and the yellow fire of the flames which gushed from its mouth. He would not be far away, and from that thought she gained strength. She went to her dressing room, crouched on the stool before the mirror and rinsed out her swollen mouth. Wincing in pain, her hand automatically reached for the laudanum bottle and she took a deep draught, but then she paused and put it back on the shelf, looking instead at her reflection in the mirror. She sat up straighter and stared deeply into her own eyes. There could be someone new, a life force not dulled with drugs or the pain of rejection, and not her old self, sharp, catty and trivial, but someone different, someone capable of much more. It was within her power to conjure that person from the depths of her misery and she would do it.

Leaving no time to think any further she kicked off her shoes and ran quietly down the stairs. All the staff had gone to ground, wisely staying clear of the fracas in the dining room. It suited her. Edwin would be in the Oriental Salon with his brandy, and with any luck he would be standing at the window looking out on the completed palm house which overlooked the garden, illuminated now by gas jets for his evening pleasure. She slipped across the hall towards his territory, a walk which usually made her nervous: but not tonight. Tonight would be the last time and it would be different. As she stole by the disembodied sentries in the dark entrance corridor, the ghoulish empty suits of armour with their hollow heads and limbs, their metal hands and scabbards bristling with weapons, she stopped abruptly at the masked figure of the Japanese samurai. She had listened to Edwin's proud descriptions of his collection so many times that she could name each part and even conduct a tour herself. The warrior wore two swords, the long katana at his left hip and cross-wise in his belt, and to his right, a short wakasashi. She reached out to the smaller weapon, grasped the handle and pulled. It slid soundlessly from its shark-skin scabbard; she touched the blade and saw a fine line of blood start from her finger.

There was no going back. She gripped the handle tightly in her hand, held the wakasashi above her head and crept through the open door of the Salon. Ravenswood was standing, brandy glass in hand with his back to the door, looking out, as she had hoped, towards the side window of the palm house. Sensing her movement he whipped round as she closed in on him, but he was too late. The raised sword slashed down through the air at his neck as he dropped the glass, dodged away and clawed at her with both hands to deflect the weapon as the blade bit into his shoulder, cutting through his jacket to the flesh. She slashed again, catching his defending arm and hand.

"Stop it, you mad bitch," yelled Ravenswood in an agony of pain, as she screamed a volley of curses at him, then backed away, swivelling her head round, searching for an escape. Sobbing now with fear she bolted for the door to the garden and fled into the night, zigzagging over the green towards the dark line of trees.

Ravenswood paused only to grab a pistol from his desk drawer before chasing after her. Despite his wounds he picked up speed over the short dry turf, visibility was good and she was an easy target in the moonlight. As they neared the trees he was within ten feet of her but she reached cover just ahead of him and plunged into the undergrowth.

"Come out!" he shouted, ploughing in after her and coming to a stop as he emerged into a clearing, his pistol raised, his eyes raking the darkness. As the silence grew around him, he forced his voice to soften. "You are ill, darling. Come out and we'll have a drink together. No harm done."

As he raised the gun, his hand and body start to tremble. He glanced down and saw the dark bloodstain from his shoulder had spread, soaking his jacket. The glade was strangely quiet as he turned painfully, struggling to focus in the shadowy moonlight.

In the distance beyond the trees, the sundial and the sloping green, the house reared up black against the night sky, lit along the back by the flaring jets of the palm house. He turned again to a surge of cold air, and felt rather than saw the dark shade of a man rush by him, a heavy bag dragging at his shoulder, his breath painful and ragged. Confused he staggered after it and in the distance saw a light bobbing in the wood. He raised his pistol and fired wildly, but before the cloud of smoke cleared a searing pain scorched through his neck from behind. Amanda brought down the wakasashi and felled him to his knees. She struck again and again, without mercy, until he lay slumped on the grass, blood pooling around him.

"Madam, Madam! What in God's name is happening?"

She looked up, disorientated, the dripping blade in her two hands. Matthew Spence was standing on the edge of the clearing, holding a lamp high. "I was doing the rounds with Selwyn, the new man, and we heard voices. He's shot back there in the wood, Madam! He's not movin', either. Bit like Master."

Amanda dropped the blade as though it burned her. Her next move could dictate the rest of her life, and the length of it.

"Matthew," she said slowly. "Matthew, thank God it's you." She searched for words, her mind racing. "Mr Ravenswood heard noises in the trees and came out." Again, a pause: she gathered her wits. "I followed him and found that," she pointed to the wakasashi at her feet, its steel still wickedly bright, but streaked and livid with blood. Her eyes roamed around the clearing, seeking inspiration.

"Did you see a figure pass you?"

Matthew dragged his eyes from the body crumpled at their feet and looked into her eyes. There was no need to struggle further, there was an unspoken agreement. She was his employer and his benefactress: he put a protective arm around her.

"Can I help you to the house, Madam? There's been a lot of talk about folk seeing things just here in the wood. I reckon intruders get in. Thieves probably, like the last time. Come away.

324

I'll have these bodies taken to the house and send for the magistrate. There's nothing we can do for them. Master mistook Sel for the intruder." He looked at her; they both nodded in silent agreement and turned towards the house.

Matthew had never touched Mrs Ravenswood before. She was shivering despite the warmth of the night, like a sparrow he had once caught in his hands, its wings beating on his palms, its heart pounding fit to burst. He glanced down at her as they neared the lights of the house. Her dress was torn from her shoulder, the fabric lying limp over her breast, her feet were bare and scratched, the side of her face was swelling and it was smeared with blood. He was in little doubt about the identity of her attacker, or what deed she had done that night. But for now he would keep that knowledge close. He led her back through the open door to the Oriental Salon and closed the door on the night.

Late afternoon: 17th July, 1833.
The Church of Saint Mary Redcliffe, Bristol.

The widowed Mrs Amanda Ravenswood sat demurely in the front pew of Saint Mary Redcliffe Church. The heavy black veil draped over her hat and face fell in gauzy folds to her shoulders, obscuring every expression, and to the minds of the congregation every bitter tear, from the prying eyes of the public. The funeral of Mr Edwin Ravenswood had attracted many sight-seers and the nave was full. By Mrs Ravenswood sat a distinguished figure: Mr John Drake from the Foreign Office in London, proof of the national standing of the late Mr Ravenswood and close friend of the bereaved widow. There was also an array of important men of Bristol, the social elite and business magnates, resplendent in the front pews with their wives. The Mayor, Aldermen, Councillors and Members of the Bench were in attendance, also a group of foreign business men, Asiatics, seated away from the rest in the aisle, their dealings with the famous Mr Ravenswood cut tragically short.

No close relatives were left alive to attend and the few distant ones were occupied on the family plantations in the West

Indies. It was just as well, as there was nothing for them. Mrs Ravenswood had inherited all of her husband's possessions: the businesses, the houses and all their contents, as well as the distant sugar plantations with their complements of slaves. The loyalty of the staff had been established quickly, once they realised that their new pay-mistress guaranteed the security of each job and that compassionate leave, without pay, was available for all who might need it. Gratifyingly, none did, and Matthew Spence had been as good as his word when the time came for him to give evidence. The tragic events which led to the deaths of two men, one a pillar of society and invaluable magistrate, the other his loyal servant, were blamed on misadventure following the pursuit of a brutal intruder. Though Ravenswood's profile demanded continuing enquiries, the coroner agreed that the funeral could be arranged without delay. And there was one other who had been invaluable over the difficult days. She had sent a message in search of Cornelius on the morning after Edwin's death and he had been at Arno's Tower by nightfall.

As the funeral party made its way to the burial, a hectic, and for some a very satisfying scene was playing out on the wharf below Redcliffe Parade. A detachment of dragoons dominated the quay, mounted and with drawn sabres, their horses skittish and prancing. Huddled before them, rounded up and trapped between the troops, was the crew of the *Blue Dragon,* with Captain Eli Trevellis singled out and bound in chains before a magistrate.

"Eli Trevellis," snapped Captain Peterson. "I ordered your arrest in my capacity as Justice of the Peace concerning the death of Benjamin Prestwick in Bath on the 30th January of this year."

Trevellis scowled and struggled, making to pull himself free from the men who held him. "I never did 'im in. There's no true proof in the world could pin that on me."

"I have heard evidence linking you to the death, Trevellis," said Captain Peterson.

"Who the devil from?" snarled Trevellis.

"Evidence gathered at Joshua Shadwell's brothel ties you very tightly to the crime. You may not have landed the blows but it appears that you were the puppet master in the sorry affair. You won the poor man's friendship and delivered him to his killers. Take him away!"

As Trevellis was dragged towards the ramped walkway leading to Redcliffe Parade he caught sight of Nathaniel and Cornelius waiting by the troops.

"Lee!" gasped Trevellis. "I heard a rumour you'd surfaced but I didn't believe it. By rights your bones should be bleaching by the Pearl River after you jumped ship."

"Expect the unexpected," replied Cornelius drily.

"And this ship is impounded until further notice," declared Captain Peterson. "A word gentlemen!"

He motioned Nathaniel and Cornelius over, out of earshot of the troops.

"Mr Lee, you clearly know a considerable amount about Trevellis. If the charges do not succeed I may need to speak with you on this matter in the near future."

"I may be of even greater assistance," said Cornelius quietly. "I saw Trevellis assault Mr Raphael Vere of the New Bank in Bath. He intended to drown him on Ravenswood's orders."

"Good God!" exclaimed the Captain.

"But," cautioned Nathaniel, "that intelligence should only be used if Trevellis appears to be escaping conviction. It is in the national interest, as you know, for the Ravenswood businesses to continue for the present and a resurrection of the Vere enquiry might place them in jeopardy."

Captain Peterson puffed out his cheeks, thwarted. "Indeed. Thank you Mr Lee, your information stops with me for now."

As Cornelius bowed the Captain turned from him abruptly. "Well, Nathaniel, a successful caper so far. For my part I'm going aboard the *Blue Dragon*. It's a while since I've been on a deck and theoretically I own a share in her, so I have a mind to inspect my property!"

327

With a spring in his step, Oliver Peterson made for the gangway.

"Nathaniel," said Cornelius urgently. "I need to leave now and ride to the church before the burial is over. The *Zhen Tian Lei* has not only quit this wharf but is not in any of the boatyards for refit as some of the crew claimed. It has left Bristol and my men have reported that it is idling at anchor below Clifton Rocks. It will be waiting for the evening tide and I suspect that Kizhe and his party may not return to Redcliffe Parade for the funeral reception as planned, but go straight to the ship. I need to complete my mission with regard to this man and I need to do it alone."

"I can come with you," said Nathaniel.

"Cornelius shook his head. "Thank you, but it is better not to involve any British government official in this. Nathaniel, I assume that you and Drake will need to be in London to see your masters next week. Shall I see you there?"

"You will," said Nathaniel. "In London then: Carlisle Lane, Monday night." He held out his hand. "Good luck."

Cornelius bowed, clasped his hand and then made off through the ranks of dragoons to where his horse was tied by the locked doors to the red caves. Nathaniel watched as he swung himself up into the saddle, galloped up the steep path to Redcliffe Parade and was lost to view.

As the funeral party left the graveside, Amanda took Drake's arm and prepared to lead the procession for the short walk through the churchyard back to Redcliffe Parade. As they moved off she heard hurried footsteps behind her and turned to see a servant approaching from the group of Asian businessmen.

"Madam," he said with a bow. "Mr Kizhe sends his respects. As Mr Lee has not attended as he was told to expect, he is leaving now. He will contact you with regard to pressing business matters at a more suitable time in the near future."

"I see," said Amanda. "How unfortunate. I am sure that Mr Lee will be waiting at the house. Perhaps he was unable to attend church. Do tell Mr Kizhe that he is very welcome to join us."

"It is too late, Madam," said the servant, turning away and disappearing amongst the crowd.

"I see Kizhe's coach," said Drake. "Look there!"

Down the road and ready to head to Bristol Bridge, was the garish red coach Kizhe had hired in London.

"I see it. And he will be safely stowed in it already!" said Amanda, annoyed, but then she laughed. "But look who is behind them!"

Cornelius, astride Ravenswood's fastest chestnut mare, rode by the church railings from the Parade as the servant made it to the coach and climbed up to the driver's seat.

"He will not be the only one," said Drake, waving a signal to a horseman at the gate. "My man will shadow our foreign visitors."

And, he thought, but left unsaid, with luck will see them all off the premises. He took Amanda's black-gloved hand and looked down fondly on her pale face, shadowed and indistinct behind the folds of her veil. Their alliance forged in the worst days of Lottie's infidelity with Ravenswood had not lapsed with the cooling of the affair. "Don't rely too much on your new right-hand man, Amanda. He is not just an enterprising associate of the opium traders. I believe that Mr Lee may be quite a different person from what he has led us to believe."

"Yes, John," she said meekly, her expression conveniently masked behind the filmy net of her veil. "I think you may well be right."

Cornelius kept well back in the press of traffic approaching the bridge but never let the red coach out of his sight. Kizhe had planned his exit strategy well, baulked of his chance to settle with Cornelius he had packed his belongings at Redcliffe Parade and had his war junk waiting on the tide down-river from the city. Chen and Fong were already in position, hiding in the rocks overlooking the anchorage to make sure that Kizhe did not give him the slip again. He shadowed the coach through the city and out on the road towards the coast. The fashionable village of Clifton which clung to the rocks overlooking the river had been left behind and the road became lonely.

Cornelius unwrapped his bow and quiver from their carrying cloth, placed the bow across his back and the quiver by his side. He rode closer to the scrubby trees overhanging the road, crouching low on his horse, feeling the body and gait of the animal to move with her as one. Round the next bend in the river he saw the *Zhen Tian Lei* at anchor and the coach coming to a halt at the bank. His quarry leapt out and stood by the horses, a mountain of a man, rectangular, with his massive head rising from his shoulders, the hachiwari thrust in his belt. He heard a guttural order barked out: a heavy chest was carried from the interior of the coach by two servants whilst the driver and one other unloaded the trunks from the back.

Still a hundred yards from his target but with the two men holding the chest in plain view, Cornelius urged his horse forward to a gallop, drew his bow, and fired at one of them. Sliding from the horse and letting it run, he dropped into the bushes for cover, shot again and dropped the man left standing. At the sound of the approaching horse Kizhe had wheeled round, saw the slumped bodies on the road and rolled under the coach bellowing orders. The remaining two men struggling with the rest of the luggage instantly ditched the trunk they were carrying and drew their percussion pistols, scouring the road and the rocks above their heads as they backed closer to the coach. For a moment, silence, as Cornelius waited for a clear shot at Kizhe, then an ominous hiss as fused missiles flew down from high above them on the rock face. Four consecutive explosions rocked the coach and smoke filled the air. Fong and Chen scrambled down into the thick of the confusion and ran through the choking smoke towards Kizhe's guards. They opened fire, felling them both in a precise fusillade of arrows.

But the crewmen on the boat were already out on deck. Their enraged shouts floated over the water accompanied by the unmistakable sound of the launching of a jolly boat to bring a gang of them to assist on shore. Under cover of the explosions Cornelius knew that Kizhe would have taken the chance to slip away in the smoke and had run up to a terrace on the rocks to get a higher vantage point. As the smoke started to clear his adversary materialised on the terrace not ten feet in front of him, levelled his two pistols and opened fire with his right. Dropping to his knees Cornelius dodged the shot, drew an arrow from the quiver at his side as if it were a sword in a sheath and flung it at Kizhe's head, following in quick succession with another, and another. As his target dodged and deflected, Cornelius narrowed the distance between them, closed in on his foe and parted Kizhe from his remaining loaded pistol with a high sweeping kick.

As the two men squared up to each other in the clearing gloom Kizhe drew his hachiwari, the helmet breaker, and launched himself at Cornelius, the weapon scything round and down, aiming to bury itself in his head. The weapon missed its mark, but despite his size, Kizhe's body followed its circular path, flying towards the ground, rolling over on his free arm, and snapping back onto his feet like a monstrous mountain cat, weapon still in play. Cornelius remembered the move, had anticipated it, and waited for the next. Again, the scything blow came, but now as a feint, stopping short and pulling back, raking Cornelius's arm with the hook as a kick powered through to deliver a glancing blow to the side of his head.

A surprise. Cornelius shook his head clear. The last time they had fought, Kizhe he had never used his feet, and also this time, as the hook of the hachiwari had bitten into him, he had looked at it. There was a discrepancy, but only a split second to register it. Sounds of the oarsmen on the jolly boat drew nearer. He had only moments and used the first to clear his mind. He must respond to the attack and not to the individual. He exhaled, coordinating his body, mind and spirit. The advancing sounds from the water faded away and time slowed. He summoned his whole being and delivered a lightning left-fist thrust to his opponent's throat, followed up by a right-hand punch to the chest so fast that it had landed before the eye could catch it in flight and so deadly that it collapsed the lung and pushed a rib into the heart. He bent down swiftly and put his hand to his opponent's neck. It was finished. He glanced around, gave a shrilling double whistle of confirmation, heard the same in distant response from Fong and Chen, thrust the fallen hachiwari into his belt and pushed the body over the edge of the terrace to roll down to the road.

By the time he was half-way up the hill, working low through the overhanging trees, the boat had reached the river's edge and a dozen men poured over the side onto the path. Ragged cries floated up as the men swarmed over the scene, some checking the road fearfully, most helping up the injured and lifting the fallen, taking them on board to be ferried to the ship. He made more height and gave a low bird-call. An answer from even higher up by a small cave led him to the eyrie of Fong and Chen.

"Thank you, friends," said Cornelius and then looked down at a locked chest at their feet. "What is this?"

"We came down just after the explosion," said Fong, grinning. "We couldn't leave a strongbox lying on the road. There are too many thieves about!"

Cornelius did not answer, but he could not begrudge them their prize. He had more on his mind as he looked back to the abandoned coach and watched the distant figures rowing away from the shore. He thought instead of his adversary and the way he had moved, he glanced down at the helmet breaker, then looked up to watch the sails of Kizhe's ship billow out on the early evening breeze, catching the tide to the open sea.

Late morning: 22nd July, 1833.
Downing Street, London.

Drake and Nathaniel had first met in the Foreign Office and gone up to the junior clerks' attic to while away the time before Lord Palmerston condescended to join them for their meeting. The Foreign Office ranged over four rickety houses at the far end of Downing Street, on the left of the cul-de-sac as one entered from Whitehall. The accommodation for the juniors, though shabby, was informal, comfortable, and in their opinion had an excellent view, which was of Fludyer Street and its gin shops. A few youths were tinkling on a piano, trying out some new tunes and from the wall hung some moth-eaten boxing gloves. Neither activity was enticing. They settled on a hand of cards, swept aside an abandoned game of backgammon, and took over the table.

"You deal," said Nathaniel.

"Mi'noble Lord will not be pleased to hear the details of the loss of Ravenswood," said Drake, dashing out the cards.

"Never thought he would be," said Nathaniel, swiftly rearranging his hand.

"With no Company monopoly he would soon have been all legal and above board," said Drake opening the play.

"Apart from the slaving, murder and extortion," said Nathaniel, sweeping up the trick.

"Well, yes, obviously."

Drake's finger strayed to fiddle with his collar, that old nervous tic was so nearly extinguished, just like old "John Company", but it could still rear up in moments of stress. It did so now at the thought of his close shave with Ravenswood's business empire. He played his next card.

"No more "*sneer of cold command*" from that "*shatter'd visage*" what!"

"How's that?" asked Nathaniel.

"You know, Shelley's *Ozymandias*. Ravenswood fancied himself as a King of Kings: "*Look on my works, ye Mighty, and despair!*" Drake sniggered, well pleased with himself. "I had a man trailing Lee along the river road by Clifton. It looks like he saw off that devil Kizhe and I gather he is helping Mrs Ravenswood keep the business on an even keel."

Nathaniel watched Drake carefully. Cornelius was no longer seen by him as just another henchman, but it was important to keep Drake in ignorance with regard to the full scope of his friend's mission. To the same end, additional clever footwork

333

had been required to cool the Captain's enthusiasm for interviewing Cornelius about Vere's death.

"Yes," he said casually. "It is useful to leave Cornelius Lee in place for now. He might be helpful to us. My trick I think."

Drake stuck out his bottom teeth in frustration. "I suppose it is, and I suppose he will. I warned Amanda. I don't want her relying on his support for her business."

He paused before playing his next card.

"Damned relief for me that Ravenswood's gone though. And that scoundrel Trevellis!" He smiled. "Made my life a bit smoother at base camp I don't mind telling you. You must come up to town and stay with Lottie and me. Bring Emma. We could go to the theatre. London shows will knock your provincial offerings into a cocked hat." He looked down. "Damn it! Yours again!"

"I was pleased to collar Trevellis," said Nathaniel. "And I heard that his two henchmen from Shadwell's have disappeared. They caught wind of Trevellis's arrest and guessed he would give them up to save his own skin."

Nathaniel had been pleased to hear that the unwholesome presence of Jabez and Billy had disappeared from the streets of Bath. Tobias had reported the news after seeing Clari Marchant in Kingsmead Square. She had been in high good humour and was delighted to tell the tale of their replacement, Letty's amiable brother, Fred, who had abandoned coach driving and moved into Green Park West as Rosie Shadwell's right-hand man. Joshua would be spending more time than ever in his office at the bottom of the garden. He might have to move into it permanently.

"Mine! At last!" Drake smirked.

As he swept up the cards a servant entered.

"Mr Drake, sir, Mr Parry, sir, Lord Palmerston is detained at Brooks's and you are invited instead to report to Lord Melbourne's office. I'd be sharp if I were you," he added as an afterthought. "He's got Percy putting all the papers away and he just said he could eat a horse."

They descended from the clerks' "Nursery" and made their way from the Foreign Office quarters to the luxury of the Home Secretary's rooms to find that the servant was spot on. Melbourne was hovering by the window, shooting his cuffs and muttering to himself, clearly ready for the off.

"Excellent to see you both," he said. "Splendid, splendid. Don't sit down gentlemen. Just a word will do. Just a word. Ha! Ha! Now, the news! That blasted pirate in Bristol has had his come-uppance I gather as well as some foreign rascal! What!"

"Yes, mi'lord," said Drake levelly. "Edwin Ravenswood was killed in an incident with an intruder. Investigations are ongoing but no arrests as yet. His firm's business capability for engaging in the opium trade is unaffected so Lord Palmerston will be gratified. Other less acceptable activities are more likely to cease, especially as his Captain has been arrested on suspicion of conspiring to murder. Your contact, Captain Peterson, remains connected with the business as you will be aware and will exercise more influence as required. He is acquainted with the widow who has inherited the business in its entirety."

Melbourne nodded vigorously. "Good, good, case closed. That's the ticket. I must say it is also most edifying to see the spate of kidnapping in the city reduced. Perhaps the removal of Mr Ravenwood's unsavoury associate is not unconnected with that." He clapped his hands twice to emphasise his approval, lost his thread, and then resumed. "Oh yes! A bit of good news on that score. Remember the Honourable Member whose servant disappeared? Well, the woman's turned up! Most pleasing for the morale of the House. And the other business? Murder of the old soldier settled?"

"Yes, mi'lord."

"No Egyptian jewels I take it? No Napoleonic loot? Damned wild goose chase. Percy will be disappointed. Won't you, Percy?"

Richard Percy poked his head round the door. "Yes, mi'lord."

"Very taken by romance of the Nile weren't you, my boy!"

"Very, mi'lord."

Percy retreated to his desk and continued packing up the papers. It had been a short day and he was not complaining. He felt pleased to note the improvement in relations. Drake's attitude had mellowed and he seemed on positively cordial terms with Nathaniel Parry. He was grateful for the improved atmosphere as, apart from that, the year had been an unrelieved slog and it was only half done. It was common knowledge that Earl Grey was worn to a frazzle and the continued rise of Lord Melbourne's star was inevitable. The punishing legislative programme would not be letting up any time soon, the Whigs were on a roll whether they deserved the credit or not, and his lord and master was limbering up for the premiership.

The dulcet tones of Melbourne boomed through the open door. "So there we are. Done and dusted. Written reports on my desk before tomorrow morning, gentlemen. Then back to Bath with you, Parry. Keep your ears open for reactions to the new Factory Act in the clothing towns. Put yourself about in the Political Unions. The Act has no teeth whatsoever in terms of their adult workers so the owners should not be too vexed even if the operatives are. And the Slavery Bill should be through very soon to lighten the mood round Bristol. Compensation for owners will be fair, to be frank, more than fair."

Evening:
Nathaniel's Rooms, Carlisle Lane, Lambeth, London.

"What is it?" said Nathaniel, looking up from the table and his preoccupied labours over the Ulrich pistols which involved ramrods, assorted wire brushes, soap, boiling water and grease.

Caradoc had been stretched out on the floor by his feet, growling periodically in his dreams and deaf to the evening serenade of bird song which floated sweetly through the open window from the Bishop's gardens, but without warning his head had shot up, and just one ear. Even before the footfalls on the stairs announced the arrival of the housemaid and a guest, the

336

terrier was at the door barking a welcome to Cornelius Lee.

"It is tranquil here, for London," said Cornelius, pausing in the doorway as Nathaniel strode over and took his hand.

"It is," said Nathaniel. "Close enough to the centre, but as you say, tranquil. Come in, be seated. Brandy?"

They sat in the fading light and Caradoc contrived to spread himself equidistantly between the two of them. The heat of the night made it an unattractive prospect to sprawl on their feet or favour one of them with his head on their lap. He had given a decent welcome, drunk his bowl dry and now needed to focus on finding a pitch with the maximum draft.

"Cornelius, my friend, you rarely give much away, but your face shows not even a flicker of the conquering hero."

Cornelius smiled wryly. "No. The ambush of Kizhe's coach went according to plan. Fong and Chen played their parts. And they rewarded themselves." He took a string of brilliants from his pocket and threw them to Nathaniel. "A sample for you."

Nathaniel turned them over in his hands. "Beautiful," he said.

"Look closer."

Nathaniel went to his table, rooted out a magnifying glass from his cleaning kit and took the gems to the window.

"Astonishingly good paste!" he said.

"It looks as though Kizhe might be developing another side line."

Nathaniel looked up at him sharply. "Present tense?"

"The man I killed on the river road may have looked like Kizhe, but he did not move like him. I also took the hachiwari so I could inspect it later. Do you remember that he carried a helmet breaker like the ones some Japanese officers carry? They are heavy and blunt on the side with a pointed end and a hook to trap a sword thrust. I had seen Kizhe's weapon close up before, this one did not have the same detail on the lacquer. It was a replica, a replacement, as was the man. I have no doubt that my foe sailed with his vessel. I will return to China in the spring once I have put in place all the contacts I need in the Ravenswood business."

"So Amanda Ravenswood will continue with the trade?"

"With some aspects of it. The drug trade outside the East India Company monopoly will be legal within months, though it still contravenes Chinese law. My mission is incomplete."

"And are your dealings with Mrs Ravenswood concluded?"

"Not quite," said Cornelius. "I shall advise her on the trade to suit my ultimate purpose, and as that is diametrically opposed to the wishes of your government I had better keep that advice to myself."

"And your dealings which are not concerned with trade?"

"It is in our mutual interest for me to return briefly. I will help her gain strength. One of my duties," he said with a smile, "has been as her instructor. She has developed an interest in weapons training, in particular the use of the short sword."

"Has she become a formidable woman, Cornelius?"

"All people can have the capacity to be dangerous, Nathaniel, men and women alike. Take your French friend for instance. Training is an essential in life; it makes us aware of our weaknesses as well as our strengths. We need to know ourselves before we can ever know another."

For a while they sat together without speaking and listened to the last soft notes of the evening chorus, until at length just the voice of a lone nightingale remained to drift between them through the growing dark of the room.

"We trained together for years. But now I feel I know my father better than I did before," said Nathaniel. "This year has resurrected ghosts from his wars and most of them have been laid to rest with poor old Prestwick. I was glad to leave the fate of the jewels for Coco to decide. It seemed the right thing to do. She had more claim on them than I had. And the strangest thing happened, Cornelius! When I spoke with her in France, we discovered she had seen me before, when I visited Paris with my father, the year he died. She is taking up with a wealthy old lover of hers, a Marquis. I met him too that night. And so the world turns. She sees life like that: as a capricious turn of the wheel, a random spin from Lady Fortuna."

He poured another brandy for them both and lifted his glass, swirling the spirit round to cling to the sides and slowly recede like waves from a shore.

"Life isn't just linear, is it? It has a circularity about it. I found my father's journal of the Spanish campaign in one of his old strongboxes. He had the measure of Sir Giles when he was plain Captain Mortimer-Buckley. From what Lord Melbourne said today, his missing servant has returned and it also appears that he has escaped all blame for Prestwick's death. So his reckoning will have to wait, but I am sure his turn will come."

"Consider that life is not linear or circular my friend but an eternal present, an everlasting paired and balanced existence of the dark and the light, an inseparable whole."

Nathaniel stretched out his glass. "Here's to the delicate balance. Long may it hold!"

As the glasses clinked in agreement they fell silent, each lost in his own thoughts until Caradoc sensed a change and ambled over to his master for an explanation.

"Visit us in Bath before you leave," said Nathaniel, scratching the terrier's ear. "This fellow will not forgive you if you don't, and Emma will be pleased to see you. We both will. She is keen to entertain you and show off the gown she made with the silk you brought from China."

"I will not leave before making that visit," said Cornelius.

Evening: 1st August, 1833.
The Mortimer-Buckley Residence, Park Street, Mayfair.

Sir Giles Mortimer-Buckley had dared to believe that his life was starting to return to its customary ease. Ravenswood was dead. As far as he knew there was no record of his role in Prestwick's death, or the abduction of Maisie Trickett, and his lawyers were busy claiming back his investment in the Ravenswood businesses. With the little widow left in charge that could hardly prove to be a difficult manoeuvre. There was just Parry's knowledge of his connection with the raid in Spain, but he was a busy man with no proof. The future had indeed started to look bright. But one ring at the door had reduced that hope to ashes.

Last week, Maisie had returned like a bad penny. Stupid and venal she may be: she had also proved to be a survivor, slipping away from her captors in Holland and working her way home to London. There she had stood at the door, her pregnancy grossly advanced, the return of the lost lamb. Leonora and Prudence had welcomed her with open arms and installed her again in triumph. Everyone had been told of the brutal treatment she had received at the hands of her captors, the assaults and the obvious violation of her person, the subsequent mortification of a pregnancy. She would, of course, be cared for by the Mortimer-Buckley family in perpetuity as an old and valued retainer. Her position with Lulu would be restored and the unwanted child adopted. The nightmare had returned. Maisie seemed to be running with the explanation of her plight and had not yet linked her abduction to him but was starting to complain about the disappearance of her trunk, which she claimed she never did send for, as Sir Giles seemed to think. And so she paved the way for relentless extortion to come.

Buckley had taken to retreating to his dressing room for brandy after dinner, always French these days, never Spanish. It was August but it was an unaccountably cold day. He had demanded the fire be lit for warmth, and had taken himself off to be in the company of his own dark thoughts, and of that low, grating voice. It always had some ideas, some suggestions for his next move. He locked the door, pulled his chair close to the flames and soon dropped off into a troubled sleep, wrapped in his trailing dressing gown, his glass and bottle cradled slackly in his lap.

The nightmares were not slow to intrude upon his dreams. As always, the two sisters: both darkly beautiful, Izar with her whore's eyes and behind her the graceful Amaia, silent and so bizarrely named: The End. Their fair faces lasted only moments, eclipsed by a fiery chaos of murder, sundering timbers and the

340

crashes of collapsing buildings, a naked woman sprawled dead on a cabin floor, Prestwick's burned face lolled before him, growing ever larger, incongruously superimposed on the head of a hanged man dangling from a gibbet.

Sir Giles woke; howling in anguish, to find himself lurched forward towards the fire. His glass of brandy spilled over his lap as he looked directly into the smoke billowing gustily from the hearth, and there wreathed in its toils was the third sister with her empty eye sockets, her gash of a smile, reaching out with skeletal arms.

"Get away from me, witch!" he screamed. "Damn you! Damn you all!"

"Now! Throw it!" The voice, no longer low, rose to a wild shriek. "Blow her back to hell where she belongs!"

And he flung the bottle into the fire.

The sound of shattering glass and a muffled explosion, thudding crashes and cries of pain sounded out above the drawing room where the women sipped their coffee, and reverberated down the stairs to the servants' quarters. None of them could have run any faster, the footmen clearing the steps two at a time, the women pattering and puffing behind.

"Giles! Giles! Lord preserve us, I smell smoke! Look, look through the door. Fire! Fire!"

"Sir! Open the door! Sir!"

But it was all too late; the roaring flames fuelled by the exploding spirit had him in a death grip, consuming him as he writhed, screaming by the toppled chair, pains locking his chest in a grip of iron, his fingers clawing his neck for air, tearing his silver chain asunder and sending his lucky medal spinning away across the floor, rolling away from him and the blazing hearth, to a place of safety.

Epilogue

Early evening: 7th December, 1833.
The Grand-Théâtre, Bordeaux.

As the claret-coloured carriage came to a skidding halt outside the theatre, the horses champing and blowing hard in the glittering dark, two liveried footmen sprang down to open the doors for their employers. Pierre and Anna Guestier, and their guests, Bernard and Eliza Phelan, were bundled out with some difficulty, encumbered by winter layers topped by fur-lined cloaks, their fingers clumsy in padded gloves. As Pierre issued orders to the driver, Anna stamped her feet in a vain attempt to accelerate the circulation and beat down the numb cold rising from her toes. She looked longingly up the steps to the light and warmth streaming out from the theatre doors, then rolled her eyes in barely concealed impatience until they lighted on a couple who had not been seen in the city since the summer, but who had been the target of malicious gossip at every day call and evening *soirée* since.

"Eliza!" she gasped, grabbing her sister-in-law's arm and inclining her head vehemently in their direction. "Look who's coming! It's the Marquis de la Blanquefort and he's with that woman he went away with directly after his poor wife passed away. You know who I mean! She came to dinner at General Palmer's with the Irish politician, that friend of the Bartons." She pursed her lips and raised her eyebrows. "He does not appear to be in mourning."

"My dear," said Eliza Phelan authoritatively. "Why should he be? The Marquis was never one for convention and he has married the hussy already. You can see why!"

Coco held her Marquis's arm as she picked her way daintily over the slippery pavement. She did not seem to suffer from the cold and allowed her cloak to blow wide, revealing a sparkling necklace of emeralds set in heavy gold above a green velvet gown with white fur trim. The dress was not cut as tight as fashion demanded, so as to allow accommodation for her swelling breasts and the rising mound of her unborn child.

"Well, I never!" exclaimed Anna.

"Bernard, look who it is!" exclaimed Pierre, orders now issued and the carriage rattling off down the road. "The Marquis is back! I need to catch him."

"Pierre," squeaked Anna. "Don't bring him over! He is with that woman, that Jezebel!"

"Be that as it may, darling," he said over his shoulder as he strode towards the pair. "They are married, therefore she is also a Marquise, and I have business with her husband."

So, despite Madame Guestier's orders, they all climbed the steps together and gathered briefly before stepping into the warmth and going their separate ways. For the Marquis there were rushed commiserations for his loss, congratulations for his gains, and rendezvous were agreed, for both gentlemen and ladies, for the very near future.

As they passed through the doors Pierre added, "Monsieur le Marquis, I rode by your landscaping at Blanquefort last week, it is progressing magnificently. The grottoes by the lake are quite magical."

"Spellbinding!" said Eliza.

"Yes, indeed," added Anna, looking hard at the new Marquise, "Utterly bewitching."

343

Coco smiled, inclining her head in a graceful bow to her new neighbours, her hand holding the edge of her cloak collar to her face. Out of sight, she rubbed her thumb along the hard metal surface of her hidden brooch, a talisman strong enough to re-kindle the midsummer fires of Saint John on a cold December night.

The Adelphi Theatre, The Strand, London.

Five hundred miles away, in another city, another quartet prepared to enjoy an evening's entertainment. John Drake and the Honourable Charlotte, with their guests, Nathaniel and Emma Parry, were settling into their box at the Adelphi.

"I haven't been here since September when the place was entirely refurbished," said Charlotte, excited. "I love the gold on the boxes; the blue silk was tired out."

"I have never been here before," smiled Emma. "And it all looks wonderful to me. This is such a treat, Lottie. Thank you!"

"Our pleasure."

Quite a different Lottie Drake, thought Emma, from the one I first met at Arno's Tower. It seemed a lifetime ago. The frisson between Lottie and Mr Ravenswood had been obvious for anyone with eyes to see, though by all accounts it had withered even before his ghastly murder that summer. John looked happier too, more relaxed. Apparently they had made something of a new start, sold in Mayfair and re-invested in one of the new squares in Belgravia.

Emma had been concerned when she had heard they were to see John Buckstone's new burletta: *The Rake and his Pupil; or Folly, Love, and Marriage.* She had feared it was rather near the bone, for everybody involved, given Lottie's indiscretions and major roles in the play being that of a Marquis, a Marquise and a certain Madame de Lignolle. This last, a flighty French minx played for all she was worth by the celebrated Mrs Laura Honey. But the play's fame had spread, it had been playing to full houses for a fortnight and the men swore they would not miss it. They had all come a long way.

As Lottie caught sight of friends in the stalls and started to tell Emma their life stories Drake shared a quiet word with Nathaniel.

"I entertained Lottie's brother at my club last week. He bought her share of the Mayfair house just down the road from Sir Giles's place. The widow has sold up apparently and gone to Gloucestershire to their country pile. Don't blame her in the slightest. Terrible way to go for Sir Giles."

Nathaniel nodded. "Indeed," he said, but thought instead of the inter-connectedness of life, of circularity and of reckonings. He looked at Drake, leaning over to watch the arrival of the orchestra in the pit. The man was quite boyish tonight and at one with himself. In some ways he could even be seen as a friend: though one to be kept at arm's length. Nathaniel had decided not to disabuse Drake of his belief that Kizhe had died on the river road, but to let him enjoy the cheerful prospect of closure on that particular problem, at least for the time being.

As the lights dimmed he looked over to the ladies and his eyes met Emma's. She looked radiant, three sapphires sparkling in the jewelled *aigrette* fixed in her hair, three mounted on a pendant hanging from a fine chain around her neck. The gems sat lightly on her now that she wore them on her own terms, fashioned to her design and freed from the heavy Montrachet settings. As Lottie continued to talk, Emma exchanged a smile with him. The autumn months had passed fruitfully for her in many ways. She had the house running like a well-oiled machine and had spent more time in the company of Céline Junot, who was now a regular visitor, as were other new friends. He often returned from London to find the drawing room full of ladies, a hand-picked collection of Bath's blue stockings, debating anything from religion to reform and putting the world to rights. He felt a pride in her. There she sat, her auburn hair shimmering in curls over her shoulders and the collar of her new loose gown of midnight blue, and lying in her lap, a reticule, a silk one, the fabric exotic and glowing, exquisitely embroidered in pink and russet blooms.

Morning: 9th December, 1833.
Saint Mary's Burial Ground, Bathwick, Bath.

Matthew, Mary and the Johnty accompanied Martha to old Saint Mary's burial ground whenever Matthew was home on a Sunday. Since Ben's death it had been an occasional custom for her to visit his grave and share a few words with him, but after the court case and the transportation of Trevellis it had become a weekly observance. She had gloried in the retribution meted out to that sinner, though she would have liked someone to have swung at a rope's end for the deed. That could yet come to pass.

"The mills of God," she had said, repeatedly and triumphantly. "They grind slow but exceeding small. Praise the Lord!"

The old lady also said that talking to Ben was the closest she got to having a word with her late husband. But there was no resting place for Father, Matthew had thought, but left unsaid. Philip Spence's bones were far away and likely scattered, left to rot on the road to Corunna. He folded his arms and clamped his hands in his armpits. He was growing to dislike the cold more passionately with every year. The hand with the missing fingers throbbed and the stab of pain transported him back to his years aboard the *Blue Dragon* and Ravenswood's other vessels.

Was a broken hand and recurring fever all he had got from working for that cursed slave driver? He smiled to himself. Not by a long shot. Without the years before the mast he would never have had his present job and Mrs Ravenswood's favour: a couple of days a week at the Tower, a fair wage to keep Mary and the boy and help pay Mother back for the years of his absence. He stood higher with Mrs Ravenswood than the other new men; he knew that, especially after the night he had found her in the wood. Nothing would ever change that. Though he did not stand the highest, that was certain.

He would also never have had Jimmy Congo.

Matthew looked over to the far side of the cemetery at the sound of sustained barking and a shriek of laughter from the

346

Johnty. Caradoc had come with Tobias and Frances, who walked out together on a Sunday when the Parrys were not at home. If he was left behind they usually brought Caradoc with them, who always took it upon himself to secure the perimeter of the cemetery and rid it of the two resident cats. With the Johnty as rearguard he seemed to be succeeding in his mission, which was more than could be said for his vendetta with Jimmy Congo, whose whistles and barks still drove the dog to the edge of insanity. His most successful move against his enemy was always a well-timed leap at the perch, up-ending both perch and parrot, but a recent use of this manoeuvre had caused him, once again, to be temporarily barred from the kitchen. Matthew's grandfather and the parrot were inseparable. As well as the baiting of Caradoc, Old Tom encouraged Jimmy Congo to maintain his extensive vocabulary of oaths, to squawk on demand "Napoley's Gold" as taught by Benjamin Prestwick (God rest his soul!) and extend his repertoire to broadest Somerset. The two of them comprehensively tormented everyone unwise enough to tangle with them in the kitchen, which was their stronghold. Not that they were always there these days. On occasions they came with Martha to the cemetery, Tom in the chair and Jimmy on his shoulder, but today the cold air had kept them indoors.

"Time to go, Mother," said Matthew. "Mary, I'll get the Johnty before him and Caradoc get us barred from the graveyard with their racket!"

He made his way round the mortuary chapel but did not have to search further. Tobias, looking taller and broader than ever, was walking towards him, arm in arm with Frances who had the Johnty hoisted on her hip. All were following on behind a swaggering Caradoc, crowned with the whitened stalks of dead bindweed and leading them out under the baleful glare of the two defeated cats, who now balanced, in the interest of self-preservation, on the extreme end of the boundary wall.

Morning: 10th December. 1833
The Pump Room, Abbey Churchyard, Bath.

The pumper applied himself with his usual energy, and also as usual, the rush of the waters surging into the glasses could barely be heard above the cacophonous tide of gossip generated by the morning crowds of Bath society, the visiting travellers and the prowling packs of fortune hunters.

Dr and Mrs Parry, Captain and Mrs Peterson, plus the two Miss Petersons were corralled in a tight group by the window overlooking the King's Bath, which mitigated Mrs Parry's claustrophobia to some degree. As the men had launched into a deep and exclusive discussion on shipping she was obliged to listen to Lydia Peterson's family news unrelieved by support or distraction. The continuing joy of Emma's pregnancy had been covered satisfactorily as had the immense importance of her son-in-law, who was at present, and even as they spoke, about business in the national interest in the capital city. Mrs Parry had been under the impression that the younger Parrys had gone up to town to see a play, a rather fast one, but let that go. Lydia had already moved on to the prospect of the two Miss Petersons continuing their education in Paris.

"Madame Junot will be chaperoning the girls," declared Lydia triumphantly, drawing an unusually subdued Maddy and Ginette into the circle from where they had been attempting to skulk behind her. "Marvellous opportunity. Though it took considerable effort to persuade the Captain to agree! One cannot imagine why. Paris is as calm as Bath these days."

She stopped suddenly as a trio approached.

"Oh, how lovely! Look, my dear! Look, Oliver! Dr Parry! Mrs Vere's party cometh!"

Captain Peterson's jovial face fell. How much he would have liked to give the beautiful Tilly Vere even a hint of comfort about the mysterious case of her disappearing husband! On Nathaniel's advice he had not pursued the startling evidence offered by Mr Lee about Raphael Vere's likely fate, and in the event Trevellis had been shipped off to Australia months ago on the strength of Nathaniel's evidence alone. Oliver Peterson blew out his cheeks in frustration, but made a mental note to keep a weather eye on the informative Mr Lee.

For her part, the elder Mrs Parry was even more delighted than Lydia to see the new arrivals and set about a fulsome greeting of Tilly Vere, Howard Dill and Mrs Danby, skilfully manoeuvring herself between her husband and Mr Dill to gain maximum relief from Lydia's relentless news.

"Hello, hello, hello!" sang Howard.

"How do, old boy!" boomed Dr Parry. "Haven't seen you for an age, Dill, but I gather we shall meet again before the end of the week. I take it you have had notice of the meeting scheduled at Redcliffe Parade?"

"Certainly have," said Howard, his eyes twinkling. "Splendid job Mrs Ravenswood's making of affairs, wouldn't you say?"

"Indubitably!"

"Poor lady!" exclaimed Mrs Danby suddenly. "Such a terrible blow to lose her husband so early. I know only too well myself of the miseries of widowhood!"

Tilly observed her mother glumly.

"At least she has the satisfaction of knowing where he lies, Mother," she said. "And I am sure Father rests easy in Beckington."

The spectre of Tilly's missing husband rose once again to sour the day for more than Captain Peterson. A brief, respectful hush fell on the party as Tilly's pretty mouth turned down in self-pity and annoyance.

What she would give to have news of his vile body resurfacing! Her marriage to Howard could take place without delay, babies of her own would surely follow, and of more immediate importance, she could pack her mother off to her own home in Beckington on the next coach. Mrs Danby's visits to Lansdown Crescent were frequent and protracted. There seemed barely a week's respite between one and the next and she did not know how much more she could stand. Her mother's portrait, undertaken by her distant relative, the acclaimed Francis Danby, had finally been finished to her satisfaction and was the current focus of her mother's attention. To Tilly's horror she realised that it was to be discussed yet again as her mother re-launched the conversation.

"Yes, yes, my dear. We all know how you suffer and you deserve to have a little gift!" She treated the company to a self-satisfied smile. "My portrait you know. Dear Francis has finished it at last and we have been vexed to decide where the best possible place would be for such a work to be hanged! But I have a solution: at Lansdown Crescent in the hall! I think I have convinced you of the wisdom of that thought, haven't I dear? I could keep you company and welcome you home every time you open the door."

"Mrs Danby," said Howard. "The idea is a capital one. It's as good a place to be hanged as any."

The Ravenswood Townhouse, Redcliffe Parade, Floating Harbour, Bristol.

Matthew, Declan and Finn were shown into the first floor room overlooking the wharf for the morning briefing. It looked very much as it had done in the days of the master, with the grand table in the centre, the fine wood cabinets by the walls, the shelves of leather-bound books, his jewelled paper knife lying on the desk. Mrs Ravenswood had made it her habit to speak to the men here in small groups every Monday morning to give the orders for the week and sometimes to announce changes.

The African and Far Eastern clipper trade continued to run, including the unofficial smuggling of Indian opium, but there had been no extra passengers. No more women had been shipped out since the day Madam took over. There had been extra wages for all, with promises of much more, as the compensation for the loss of the Ravenswood slaves on the West Indian plantations was to be considerable and Madam was one for sharing the joy. As she began to talk, Matthew looked at her closely.

350

Controversially, she had abandoned her widow's black weeks ago and was wearing a red silk dress, extravagantly beribboned, with tight cuffs, and sleeves blossoming out about the upper arms. Round her shoulders she had a fur wrap, as she liked to sit by the window, despite the cold drafts, keeping an eye on the dock. Her face was pale, but her eyes sparkled and she was amused, her lips drawn back in a foxy smile to reveal her tiny pointed eyeteeth.

As he watched her re-arranging the wrap, loosening it round her neck, his eyes strayed down to her throat where a new piece of jewellery caught his eye, an intricate gold piece of many coloured stones, blue, red and green with a large bird in the centre, a full six inches across. Looking more closely still he saw it was a bird of prey holding rings in its talons and above each claw, looped crosses. A distant memory: he had seen such a bird before, tattooed on dark brown arms on the North African run. Another image came to him: the black-rimmed eye, the eye of Horus. He looked again. Yes, there it was: the falcon's eye.

With a start he felt other eyes on him and looked up directly into the penetrating gaze of Mr Lee, dressed as always in sombre black and now, as usual, close by her side. In confusion, Matthew looked away, over Madam's shoulder and out of the window to the wharf below. It was alive with men working on two ships. One, the *Leonora*, had recently arrived from London and a new vessel was in the final stage of its commissioning. He could see the sign writer painting the name on the bow: she was to be called the *Amanda.*

Authors' Notes

The first book in the trilogy is called *Riot and Retribution*. The main plot is set in the autumn of 1831, and the epilogue in the autumn of 1832. In *Napoleon's Gold* Nathaniel Parry continues to collaborate in secret with Cornelius Lee, and the themes and characters develop in this second book, which is set mainly in 1833. *Napoleon's Gold: The Wages of Sin* can be read without prior knowledge of the first book.

In the second book, as in the first, real locations, some of which still exist today, are used in the plot. The Old Bull's Head Inn and the Castle in Beaumaris on the Isle of Anglesey, the Prospect of Whitby in Wapping, the Hope and Anchor at Hope Cove in Devon, the medieval church of Saint-Laurent with its stone carvings of the seven deadly sins, Fort Medoc on the Gironde estuary, the Paris restaurant Le Grand Véfour in the Palais Royal and the Grand-Théâtre de Bordeaux all remain. General Palmer's mansion at Cenon can still be seen, though it now serves as a community centre. The prestigious Château Palmer in Margaux, on the left bank of the Gironde, was built after the General had descended into bankruptcy and sold all of his vineyards.

Current Bath locations are also used. Saint James's Square and Marlborough Buildings remain as fashionable residential areas. The Spence's home in Chatham Row also still stands, though much gentrified over recent years. The burial ground of Old Saint Mary's Church can be visited, beautifully tended by volunteers. The Ravenswood townhouse is placed in Redcliffe Parade, Bristol, a terrace where many powerful Bristol merchants lived in the nineteenth century. The Bristol-Bordeaux link has been a close one since the medieval period and the port cities remain twinned today.

Edwin Ravenswood's mansion in Arno's Vale is fictional, though the Neo-Gothic design is typical of the period. Similarly, Château Pelèrin is an invention, though its location is based on an existing vineyard to the north of Saint-Laurent and its appearance is inspired by Château Beychevelle, located in Saint-Julien, the Medoc, which was originally constructed in 1565 and rebuilt in 1757. In 1825 it was bought by Pierre Guestier, who appears as a character in the book and was also Mayor of Saint-Julien. The Marquis's new mansion at Blanquefort was inspired by Chateau Dulamon, built in 1865, and the landscaped park and gardens of Majolan, which still exist in the town of Blanquefort. The entrancing network of waterways, paths, caves and grottoes were constructed in 1870 and reflect the earlier eighteenth century passion for the construction of follies.

Whilst most major characters and their adventures are fictional, some figures of national and local significance appear in the story for example, Lords Melbourne and Palmerston, the Home and Foreign Secretaries, Caroline "Naughty" Norton and Laure Duchesse d'Abrantès, who play parts which have been created to reflect their characters. Also, General Charles Palmer, the Bath MP at the time, was a reforming politician who invested heavily and ultimately ruinously in Medoc vineyards. His ill-luck stemmed in part because of the criticism his wine received from the Prince of Wales. General Palmer had been part of the Prince's high society set, until they fell out over a military dispute. Seeking to suit his wine, the famous "Palmer's Claret", to the Prince's palate, he undertook continual costly changes in the vineyards, which proved to be uneconomic. The details on his holdings, as well as the careers and characters of the Irish owners are based on research. Barton and Guestier joined in a partnership in 1802. Their company continues to trade and is the oldest wine merchant in Bordeaux. Bernard Phelan left Ireland at the end of the eighteenth century and married into the Guestier family. The family *château* was built by their son in the later nineteenth century.

In terms of the political background, the efforts to reform labour laws and abolish slavery were dominant issues of the time. The Factory Act of 1833 was a disappointment to campaigners, but as it included the appointment of inspectors it was the first of its kind to achieve even a modicum of success. The abolition of slavery in the British Empire in 1833 was a landmark act and reinforced the image of Britain as a pioneer of the abolition movement. No action was taken to prevent the exploitation of women at this time. Married women were unable to own property in their own right until 1870, but in 1839, after intense lobbying, Caroline Norton secured improved access to their children for divorced mothers. The age of consent varied between 10 and 12 years of age before 1875 and child abduction was only tackled more effectively after the 1880s.

The "War of the Unstamped" was an important issue in the early 1830s and took the form of a ceaseless campaign to repeal the newspaper tax. Real characters from that struggle, for example Henry Hetherington and Richard Carlile, feature in the novel. In 1836 they won a partial victory when the Whig government reduced the stamp duty from 4d to 1d (d was the symbol for penny before decimalisation and was worth 2.4 new pence), though penalties increased in severity for evasion of the duty. It was finally abolished in 1855, which stimulated the founding of the first penny paper, *The Daily Telegraph*, and in 1861 the remaining duty on paper was repealed. Punishment by humiliation remained and although the use of the pillory was banned by the late 1830s, the stocks remained in use until mid-century. In Bath, punishment in the stocks was last ordered in 1840. Transportation to a penal colony in Australia was favoured above imprisonment if detention was required, and by the 1830s execution was limited to crimes of murder, attempted murder, treason, piracy and arson in a royal dockyard. The Prospect of Whitby has a model gallows on its balcony overlooking the Thames to serve as a reminder that the Execution Dock was located close by. This was used for the hanging of pirates convicted in the Admiralty courts and stood below the line of low tide where the Admiralty jurisdiction began.

Smuggling also continued until mid-century despite the increase in numbers of revenue officials. It was a life style choice for those living in the coastal settlements of the south-west until Britain became the free trade centre of the world and the incentive to avoid duties was drastically reduced. After 1840 the British government began systematically to shed duties on foreign goods and the first international free trade agreement, the Cobden-Chevalier Treaty between Britain and France, was signed in 1860. The early 1830s saw an escalation in the illegal smuggling of opium into China by the British. Though other nationals were involved on a small scale, the British dominated and until 1833 the East India Company monopolised the China trade with Britain. After this time, the merchants who had worked for them, as well as others, were openly trading despite the banning of such trade by the Emperor. The situation continued to deteriorate and culminated in the First Opium War which broke out in 1839.

The references to Egyptian treasure reflect an obsession of the period. The birth of Egyptology in France and a craze for all things Egyptian in Europe followed Napoleon's Egyptian campaign of 1798-1801. Though the Emperor himself left Egypt in 1799, he had set up a headquarters in Cairo and 167 savants, scientists and scholars occupied themselves with local research. In 1802 the British confiscated looted antiquities from the French, for example the Rosetta Stone, and they were all taken to the British Museum. During the mid-1820s, British travellers brought back more antiquities and added to the collection.

Detail concerning the weapons is also accurate. Nathaniel's swordstick with spring loaded quillons forming a hand-guard was based on nineteenth-century examples, though his version has a special Japanese blade. The makila, a Basque walking stick, is still manufactured. In the nineteenth century it was common for one variety of makila to have a short concealed blade. The hachiwari referred to in the story is believed to be the forerunner of the jutte weapon and was used for law enforcement in Tokyo. Expertise in savate, French kick-boxing, was current in the early 1830s. This allowed Coco and her brother Jules to have experience of this style of fighting. The male and female bare knuckle fighting described in the novel is also based on examples from the time. The fighting skills demonstrated by Cornelius reflect the well-respected Chinese martial styles, known as Wu Shu, which were often taught in secret. During the reign of the Manchu Qing Dynasty (1644-1911) the indigenous Chinese (Han people) were officially forbidden to practise the fighting arts. In the west, these skills are usually known under the generic heading of Kung Fu and can occasionally be seen in traditional form on stage, for example in "The Wheel of Life" performed by Shaolin monks from China. These fighting methods underpinned and influenced further developments of martial arts and weaponry on what is now known as the island of Okinawa.

Acknowledgements

The details concerning the locations, the political situation, the characters of the politicians, the Bristol Riots and the disturbances in Bath were written as accurately as possible based on research conducted by Alex over many years. The staff of Bath and Bristol Reference Libraries and Colin Johnston and his staff at Bath Record Office were extremely helpful, as was Graham Snell, who worked as Secretary of Brooks's Club in London and was most kind in sharing his expert knowledge of the history of the Club. We extend our grateful thanks to them all. We would also like to take the opportunity to thank James and Claire Kolaczkowski, Chris and Sue Simpson, Sarah Sawyer, Diane Chorley, Alan Mather and Marina de Rementeria for their time spent in reading the draft chapters, for their comments and their encouragement.

We would also like to thank: Ana María Espiñeira Luksić for the original preparation of the background art on the cover and cameo image; Stan Kolaczkowski for his advice on martial arts and his contribution to the plots, as well as for the preparation of the outline sketches in the chapters and maps, and finally, Hilary Strickland for using her artistic skills to turn these sketches and the cover lay-out into high quality images.

We are now preparing Book Three, the final volume in the trilogy: *Deceitful Designs*.

Bath, October 2017
Dr Alex Kolaczkowski
Professor Robert Hayes

The Authors

The nominal author of the book, Alex E. Robertson, is a pen name, incorporating the names of the creators of the work. The text was written by Alex Kolaczkowski, based on an overarching plot from Robert Hayes, who also collaborates on research and contributes to the evolving story-line.

Dr Alex Kolaczkowski has taught history at schools in Bath and Bristol, as well as in Wiltshire, Oxfordshire and Surrey. Her B.Ed degree was awarded by the University of Bristol and her Ph.D by the University of Bath. A dedicated teacher, passionate about all aspects of her subject, she took her pupils on frequent field trips, making ancient, medieval, early modern and modern topics alike come vividly to life. Bath and Bristol are cities very well known to her having lived, studied and worked in both of them. Her expertise in Bath history stemmed from her years spent researching the city as a case-study for her doctoral topic on the development of municipal socialism and the civic ideal in the nineteenth century. By invitation from the Dictionary of National Biography she provided the entry for Sir Jerom Murch who was Mayor of Bath on seven occasions, and wrote a paper on aspects of Bath Non-Conformism in the Unitarian Journal. These research activities helped to provide her specialist background knowledge of the period and places in which the novel is set.

Professor Robert Hayes is a full-time academic at the University of Alberta in Canada. Apart from his distinguished research and teaching in chemical engineering, he is a calculating thinker with an interest in mystery and intrigue within a historical context. As a Ph.D student at the University of Bath in the early 1980s, he developed an interest in the game of Go (which originated as Wei Ch'i in China), often travelling to Bristol to play at the Go Club in Hotwells, and later was a founder member of the Bath Go Club at the Crown Inn,

Bathwick Street. During the 1990s he was a frequent visitor to Bath and Bristol. In addition to his passion for historical mysteries, he is a lover of fine wines, single malt whisky, and of course whiskey.

Brief introduction to the use of local dialect

To convey the atmosphere of the region, in some sections of the story conversations with people native to the area are expressed in a phonetic version of a south-west English accent. There are many different varieties of this gentle rural accent, and the version used in this novel is typical of the accent which could frequently be heard in Bath well into the twentieth century.

You will notice, as with many regional accents, the south-west style of speech tends to exclude letters at the beginning and ends of words, to shorten words, and alter grammar. Some speakers also lengthen vowels. In the nineteenth century it was normal for the lower classes in all areas to exclude the "h" at the start of words, and if they wished to sound very polite to include an "h" at the beginning of words where there was no such letter. Below we have provided the equivalent in standard English for a few examples of the accent as it features in the story. This has been included to help foreign readers and those unfamiliar with the south-west of England to identify and appreciate the local accent, which can still be heard occasionally today.

	Phonetic version	**Meaning**
Chap. 1	'Ee do be a caution	He is one who needs to be watched
	terrible toimes	terrible times
	Moiy	my
	Oiy	I
Chap. 6	'E come for Oiy	He came for (I) me
	Done that before 'e 'ad	He had done that before
Chap. 9	Where's that caddy to?	Where is the tea caddy?
	'E's as 'andsome as ever Oiy seen	He is the handsomest (man) I have ever seen